ALIEN 2
HORRORS 2

ALIEN HORRORS 2

TIM CURRAN

WEIRD
HOUSE

ISBN: 978-1-937128-35-7

Text © 2025 by Tim Curran

Cover Artwork © 2025 by K. L. Turner

Interior and cover design by César Puch

Editor and Publisher, Joe Morey

Weird House Press
Central Point, OR 97502
www.weirdhousepress.com

TABLE OF CONTENTS

Hunting Grounds	1
Mausoleum	34
The Skree	58
The Soft Ones	76
Mice	93
Lifeform	131
Slithid	156
Hellscape	174
Tentaculoid	197
When Yiggrath Comes	229
Sandtrap	246
Tomb on a Dead Moon	275
Host	294
Death Camp	303
About the Author	361
About the Artist	363

And out beyond the darkness,
There are voices in the stars
—Felice Holman

HUNTING GROUNDS
ᴸᴶ√ᴼ√⌐ √⌐ᴼ√øᴌ

1

In the rotting green world of Xenos, the acid rains came every few hours. Not just falling, but whipping in blinding sheets, hacking and tearing through the thick jungle, drilling through purple-veined fan leaves and punching holes in quivering corpse-white toadstools that stood high as a man. The rains were relentless, shearing, and glassy. If it hadn't been for the Tyrex e-suits that Fish's team wore, the rain would have burned right through them, dissolved them into clods of melting clay.

But that was Xenos: perfectly alien and perfectly deadly.

The planet was a hideous green world of perpetual rain, growth, and stinking rot populated by clouds of giant insects, fanged arachnids, predatory plants, and huge, voracious tiger worms. Some of which had grown so large in the rancid, flooded undergrowth they could bite a man in half and swallow him with a few tearing gulps of their spiked and serrated teeth.

On Xenos, life—all life—was cheap.

2

The hunters had been on the ground two hours and Fish was leading them—Tierney, Brickmyer, Kirth, and Bekele—through yet another bog of steaming gray mud, eyes peeled for danger because on that hell planet there was always something either trying to kill you or eat you, usually both. The bog was rank with decomposing matter, and they could smell its pervasive gaseous stench through the filters of their masks. The slopping, foul water came up to their chests, and they held their killing hardware high above it: pulser rifles and scatter guns, particle cannons and thermal grenade launchers. Next to the high-tech fighting suits they wore, their weapons were of the utmost importance. Without one or the other you'd last bare minutes on Xenos.

It was that kind of planet.

Then, again, Fish's team were that kind of men: mercenaries and hunters by trade, predators by inclination. They were all veterans of the Imperian Wars, blooded killers and survivors. All except Fish himself, who was an exobiologist, and Bekele, the tech jock who monitored the flying drones, Moba-1 and Moba-2.

"Cunting world," Kirth said over the comm as a swarm of needle flies buzzed around his faceplate, knowing there was food inside but not sure how to get to it. "Dirty cunting world."

Tierney laughed. "What's the matter, sweetheart? Xenos offending your delicate sensibilities?"

"Aye, it is. Violating them, in fact. The way I violated your whore of a mother every chance I got."

"You leave his mother alone," Brickmyer said. "He only got off her tit last week."

They kept at it, getting filthier and nastier, until Fish told them to shut the hell up.

Bekele bristled in his suit. They were on the planet to illegally take a Xenoid for a very rich collector of exotic lifeforms, the sort of guy who could buy worlds. He had some kind of museum of alien lifeforms and all he lacked was a stuffed Xenoid. And Fish, happily bought and paid for, was running the show, every bit as mercenary as the hard men in his employ.

Bekele didn't like him or the others, and he sure as hell didn't like this terrible, primeval planet. But the money was big, more than he could earn in a lifetime. Of course, Xenos was a forbidden world. No one was allowed there. They'd had to slip past the string of security satellites in full cloak. If the Agency found out about any of it, the lot of them would be spending decades in some hellhole penal colony for their troubles.

They moved on, pushing through the mud and water. To either side of the bog were huge spiky trees, green as frogs. Their boles were fuzzy, hundreds of strangling vines hanging from them. If you bumped one of them, they made high-pitched whining noises like cicadas.

Whole damn planet is insane, Bekele thought.

"All right," Fish said after about twenty minutes of wading in the sucking muck. "Dry land."

That was debatable. The ground was higher, yes, and they weren't in the water, but the jungle floor was soft as a three-week old corpse. With each step, their boots sank two or three inches, corrosive slime bubbling from the soil.

Fish took readings with his scanner, his magic box, moving in an arc. Poisonous clouds of mist blew past them. The green and purple undergrowth was thick and congested, alive with venomous insects, acid-spitting amphibians, and saw-toothed centipedes longer than a man's arm.

Fish had already warned them about the local wildlife, telling them in particular to keep their eyes open for tiger worms and bright yellow masses of predatory fungus which could shoot out barbed tendrils that would bore right through their suits.

"Take it you been here more than once," Kirth said.

"I have. This is my third trip hunting a Xenoid," he announced with more than a little pride. "No easy bit, that. But I got out okay, and you will, too, if you do what I say."

"What happened to your other teams?"

Fish laughed. "Oh, they're still here. Their bones are, anyway."

"Well, ain't you a fucking saint?" Kirth said.

Satisfied with his readings, Fish led them into the jungle. He hacked his way forward using a laser cutter, opening a path. The vegetation was not only dense and clinging, it was wet and dripping, sticky with sap that Fish said could peel the flesh from exposed skin in seconds. Gigantic hornets buzzed overhead, and titan leeches hung from tree branches like pulsating leather bags.

"Bekele, I want the drones to do a sweep around us for a good three kilometers in each direction," Fish said. "I want them to find a life form with a cooler body temp than the surrounding forest."

Bekele nodded, making adjustments to the peripheral strapped to the forearm of his suit. "Beginning … now."

He hoped they'd find the Xenoid by body temp so they could drop it, net it, and get it back to the ship. Then they could get off this terrible world. But he knew that was wishful thinking; nothing came easy on Xenos. They were hunting the planet's apex predator: one of the deadliest lifeforms in the galaxy.

They might not find it, but it surely would find them.

3

They pushed on and on, sweating inside their suits. Yellow miasmic mists rose from black sinkholes, acidic green vapors enveloping them in sheets. As the drones searched and scanned in the distance, Fish led them around the bubbling edges of swamps and bottomless mires. He moved carefully, expertly, over the spongy forest floor, avoiding roots and mud holes, ducking beneath the knotted vines of triple-canopied snake trees and avoiding the gigantic silver webs of colonial spiders, a single strand of which was as sharp as a razor.

The others tried to emulate his lithe movements with varying success. The mercs were getting the hang of it, if slowly, but Bekele, who was basically a techie, kept tripping and falling.

As they passed through a thick yellow fog of sulfur dioxide, he paused. "Wait," he said over the comm, studying the peripheral on his arm. "Moba-

Two has picked up a signature ... body temp seventy-seven degrees. Fits the profile of the Xenoid."

"How far?" Fish asked.

"Two kilometers and closing on our position."

"Targeting?"

Bekele shook his head. "No. Signature is moving through the trees and heavy undergrowth, staying away from any cuts or openings."

"Smart bastard," Brickmyer said.

"Definitely moving in our direction."

"Then let's make ready for it," Fish said.

He found a clearing. It wasn't much but an opening in the foliage maybe thirty-feet across, but it was a workable kill zone. Bekele settled in with the others, pulser in his hand. It felt like his guts were tied in square knots, his belly filled with white ice.

"One kilometer, closing fast," he said in a dry voice.

Fish cleared his throat. "Everyone hold their position. No firing without my order."

They waited, green globs of sap falling from the spreading tree limbs overhead and running down their faceplates like tears. The mists seethed and roiled, the jungle alive with animals shrieking and whirring with volume. Against that wall of noise, the Xenoid could easily sneak right up on them. But the scanners and drones would track it; it couldn't hide from them. The drones were what Fish was counting on. They were armed with Cyclacine darts with three-inch, armor-piercing needles. One dart would drop an elephant in its tracks and would easily disable even a monster like a Xenoid. Just in case, he carried a dart gun with him. Once they bagged their quarry, the drones would net it.

Now the jungle went quiet.

It was absolutely still save for things dripping and creaking. The animals sensed the Xenoid's approach the way gazelles could sense a lion stalking them. The silence was eerie and tense. Shadows knifed through the mist.

"Well?" Kirth asked. "How close is it?"

"Gone," Bekele said. "Moba-Two lost it half a klick from our position."

Tierney and Brickmyer grumbled.

"It knows it's being tracked," Fish said. "It's gone to ground."

He explained that Xenoids were not only chameleonic and masters of their environment, they were cunning as all hell. They used the bogs, mires, and acid lakes as camouflage if they thought they were being targeted, sinking beneath the toxic waters and steaming mud, slowly homing in on their prey.

"Now we wait," Fish said. "Let it come to us. It knows we're here and it won't stop until it gets us."

"I don't like the waiting," Brickmyer said.

Though Bekele wouldn't admit it to the animals on the team, he had never been so scared in his life. He had the most awful feeling that even though they couldn't see the Xenoid, it was watching them, scrutinizing them, waiting to spring. It was out there now, circling them as a tiger circles a campfire, patiently waiting for one of them to stray from the others.

He was nearly certain he saw it more than once—a shadow moving among the shadows, bunching, crawling, sliding through the black depths of the jungle. The world of Xenos was still deadly silent, and that meant it was close, very close.

Then, without warning, the noises started again and everyone relaxed a bit. The chittering and chattering of wildlife carried on as before.

"It's gone," Fish said, sounding disappointed. "So close, too."

Bekele licked the sweat off his lips, something like a fist unclenching in his chest. His instinct was not convinced the creature was gone, but if Fish said it was, he'd have to believe him.

You really want to take the word of a guy who lost two teams hunting that horror? he asked himself, but he knew he really had no choice.

Fish said, "Kierney, you and Brickmyer make a sweep through the jungle, quick-like, see if you can spot any more clearings."

"Let the drones do it," Kierney said.

But the drones were off searching again. Bekele's fingers paused over his peripheral to see if Fish wanted him to call them back in. But in his helmet, Fish shook his head.

"It's safe. Now get out there; you're not being paid to hide behind my skirts. Watch yourselves."

They moved off, entering the jungle, and Bekele was certain he could psychically smell the fear coming off them—it was bitter and metallic, like dirty copper.

Kirth laughed with a low evil sound. "You think that was a good idea, boss?"

"I do," Fish said. "You boys are being paid big money to risk your lives. You knew that when you signed on."

Kirth said nothing to that. It was obvious from the look on his face that he hated Fish. But he would do what he was told because he loved his money. They'd all been paid half up front to entice them to risk their necks. The remainder would be paid when they got back. Added incentive.

While they waited, Fish told them a horror story about how a Xenoid was brought back to the colonies once, purely by accident. And what it had done to the men, women, and children there.

"It's a real devil all right. It got seventy of them. It took their heads and skins as trophies," he explained. "Xenoids live to kill. There's nothing else for them—all their technology has been developed to further that end. They don't give a damn about exploration or world-building, literature or music or art. Everything they do is to further the art of slaughter."

"And our employer wants one of these demons from hell?" Kirth asked.

"Oh yes."

"Why?"

"Because it's unique and because he can afford it."

The conversation might have gone on, but out in the jungle there was a scream that came over the comm. A human scream.

They could hear Tierney shouting: "RIGHT IN FRONT OF US! IT'S GODDAMN RIGHT IN FRONT OF US!"

Fish vaulted off into the cloying forest and the others followed. They darted and ducked through the heavy growth until they came to a small clearing. Tierney was there, firing his scatter gun at a gigantic mass of vegetation that seemed to be walking.

"Slaggith," Fish said.

Bekele just stared, the weapon in his hand forgotten. The slaggith was easily twenty-feet in height, a mass of shaggy green and yellow leafage, tubers, and segmented stalks growing in wild profusion. It walked, propelling itself slowly forward on a brace of thick, snake-like roots that were a lustrous emerald. Whip-like tendrils sprouted from its apex, slashing the air busily. Huge, serrated leaves that were narrow and flexible held Brickmyer up like a doll, shearing him into pieces, squirting gouts of blood instantly absorbed by the mutant plant.

A red mist broke against the faceplates of the team.

Fish and the others fired and fired, blasting the slaggith into blazing fragments. Then it stopped moving. Its roots anchored it to the ground, and it was completely still, like any other tree. Brickmyer's bones dropped from its grasp and sank into the mud, his skull rolling across the ground.

Though the slaggith was blasted and broken, dripping red sap that looked like blood, it appeared to be whole.

"Nothing more to do," Fish told them. "It won't move for days now that it's eaten."

Tierney just stood there with the scatter gun in his shaking hands. "We gotta kill it, burn, blow it apart," he mumbled.

Fish shook his head in his helmet. "It won't do any good. Slaggiths are tough and fibrous. It would take us hours to completely destroy it."

Tierney glared at him.

"I told you to watch yourselves," Fish said.

Bekele followed him back into the jungle, doing everything he could not to drop to his knees and fill his helmet with vomit.

4

The river was a steaming slough of brown mud and slime, sluggish as jelly as it flowed into the primordial wastes of Xenos. Its waters would melt the e-suit right off a man, Fish said, so Bekele wisely kept his distance. Last thing he needed was the edge of the bank collapsing and submerging him in that goddamn acid bath.

As the others worked, arranging bait piles with special chemical attractants that would draw in a Xenoid, he uplinked with Moba-1 and Moba-2. They were currently back at the ship, charging their batteries. They would be airborne again in fifteen minutes.

The rains had stopped, and now the heat jacked back up, the 61 Cygni sun a hazy yellow platter trying to burn through the heavy cloud cover high above. Bekele's suit told him the temperature was hanging at a steady 120° F with 92% humidity, breeze negligible. Downriver he could see a freak electrical storm throwing out green bolts of lightning. Then the heavy mist off the river closed in again and visibility was down to twenty feet at best.

Xenos had no oceans, just the endless global forest like something out of Earth's Carboniferous: a hot green hell of primeval jungle pole to pole, broken only by swamps and bogs, rivers and poisonous lake systems, and all of it shrouded by heavy, wet fogs. Everything on the planet was in a continual cycle of death and decay that would spawn new lifeforms.

Through the filter of his mask, Bekele smelled something beyond the usual dank rottenness—a gagging, enormous stink that was sweet, musky, and repellent. It was as if he'd thrust his head into the decaying hollow of a beehive. The sweetness was sickening. And just beneath it there was a dark, vile smell that made the fine hairs at the back of his neck stand on end.

"What is that?" he said. "Can you smell that?"

But they ignored him.

Tierney was telling one of his stories and driving in whittled wooden stakes. Fish was attaching scent packs to them. An opaque mist crept in from the river. Kirth was near the tree line, gathering up his pack. You wouldn't have thought that they had just lost a man an hour before.

And when you die, just like Brickmyer they'll step over your remains and continue the mission, Bekele thought.

"What's that smell?" he asked again, knowing that neither Fish nor Tierney could smell it over the rotten-egg stink of the bait packs.

God, this place.

He wished he'd never come to Xenos, where the insects outnumbered men a hundred million to one at least. There were fleas crawling over his suit, and things like chiggers with dangling crab claws speckling his faceplate.

A striped six-legged lizard ran across the toe of his boot and he kicked it away. V-shaped birds or bats skimmed the surface of the river.

The smell was gone.

Funny.

Tierney went on with his wild tale of the enormous crystalline spiders on Metaluria that would swallow their prey (including humans) whole, only to vomit them back out in a snotty glob of digestive juices from their four stomachs, which would liquefy them to a soup of flesh, blood, and bone fragments that the spiders would then suck up with a funnel-shaped siphon.

Then the smell returned.

Bekele was about to comment on it yet again when he felt a surge of air rush over him. He sensed motion before him, behind him, to either side. It was as if some ethereal wraith was using the noisome mist as camouflage. The shape was there, then it was gone.

He pivoted in circles, but couldn't get a fix on it.

How could anything move like that?

After a few seconds, he told himself—unconvincingly—that it was some weird trick of the fog. Then he heard something.

What was that?

A rapid *swish-swish-swish* like someone was slashing the air with a sword at absolute hyperspeed. He saw Fish dive to the ground as if someone had thrown a grenade. Instinctively, he followed suit, face-planting himself in the sluicing black mud and tube-like marsh grass that broke apart into green slime like the blood of a grasshopper.

Tierney, in the split second since Bekele heard the manic swishing, was completely unaware of anything. The words were still coming out of his mouth when Fish and Bekele hit the ground. A second later, something like a triple-bladed boomerang came swishing out of the mist, neatly severing his head in an eruption of blood that seemed to gather in the air like a cloudburst before spraying in every direction.

Bekele brought his face out of the muck, wiping mud and ichor from his face bubble.

And Tierney was gone. Just … gone.

There was gore splattered in every direction, what might have been a pink strand of tissue hanging from the twig of a sapling. Blood dripped down Bekele's faceplate like red tears. Just before him, there was a huge three-toed print pressed into the mud.

"What the goddamned hell?" he heard Kirth say.

Then feet were pounding through the grass and Fish pulled Bekele to his feet. He saw Tierney's head, still in its helmet, floating out in the steaming river. And then that sweet, sickening stench came again. A black, blurring form seemed to move in the fog around them.

Then they were all running into the swamp and its thick foliage, away from the open hunting grounds of the river flats.

5

They stumbled through black, sucking bogs, tripping over limbs and snaking roots, gnarled branches scraping across their faceplates from the overhanging limbs of spiny trees. The water was warm and seething, like a primeval soup. They fought and swore and strained. Bekele found a submerged root with his ankle and pitched face-first into the muck.

Kirth grasped his arm and yanked him up. "Watch where you're going," he gasped, his wide piggish face inside his helmet beaded with sweat. Insects dotted his suit like acne, some of them swollen red and pulsing as if they were filled with blood. He slapped at them, catching one and smearing a red stain across his face bubble like war paint. A split second after his hand retreated, a dozen others descended.

"Just keep going, you silly nit! Keep going!" he snarled over the comm at Bekele.

Bekele was beside himself, trembling and quaking, his helmet slimed with Tierney's anatomy. *"I saw it!"* he cried, his eyes wet. "I saw it! I saw it take Tierney! I saw—"

Kirth cracked him in the back of the helmet with his fist. "Get a hold of yourself, you bloody fool! Tierney's dead! Keep going! That thing's right behind us!"

He shoved Bekele forward and Bekele fell again, pulling himself up, moaning. He dragged himself through the waist-deep swamp, navigating the waterlogged tree roots that arched from the water, mumbling to himself about Tierney, about the thing that had taken him.

He never saw what waited for him.

It looked like the hull of a submerged canoe plated with bony dorsal ridges as it moved through the brown, slopping water. It glided past Fish and zeroed in on Bekele. Maybe it knew a straggler when it saw one, a weak link in the chain.

Kirth saw its protruding blank-white eyes. When it was within four feet of Bekele, it vaulted from the water, jaws opening to reveal teeth sharp as steak knives.

Bekele screamed.

"TIGER WORM!" Fish shouted.

Kirth already had the beast sighted in with his particle cannon. When it made its lunge, he fired, a dozen blazing red bolts of energy ripping open the snout of the worm in a wash of bloody foam. He fired again and it rolled over, exposing its white underbelly and he blew it into fragments of meat and jelly that sank into the fetid waters.

"A twelve-footer," Fish said, intrigued by it.

"More coming," Kirth called over the comm, the waters around them alive with sluggish rolling forms. The blood always brought them.

Bekele just stood there, eyes glazed.

"Get moving," Kirth said.

"High ground ahead," Fish called back to them. "Not far."

The hot and stagnant air was suddenly thick with a flock of screeching and flapping arrow birds. They passed over the trees and shit white globs down on the men below. Kirth caught a gray smear across his bubble, another on his chest plate. Everywhere, the shit fell, raining into the water and tangled brush, sounding like gravel being dropped from above.

"You bastards!" Kirth cried out and brought up his particle cannon. He shouldered the heavy butt, and fired at the retreating flock, vaporizing at least a dozen. Their screeching cries thundered in the still, moist air. "Damn pissing birds!"

A luminous pink lantern tree came to life as hundreds of leathery black insects with the wingspans of gulls were frightened by the shooting. They began to squeak and chirp and stretch their wings. There were so many it seemed the tree was suddenly alive, a perpetual motion machine of claws and wings and suckering mouths.

"Shut up or I'll kill the lot of you!" Kirth shouted at them.

Up ahead in the oily water, Fish said, "Quit wasting shot for godsake! Stay with me!"

Kirth shouldered his weapon and followed.

Fish led them away from the tangled root systems of the snake trees, through thick floating mats of reed, and around sucking black holes that could swallow a man alive. He kept his eyes peeled for the slow, terrible motion and telltale snouts of big tiger worms waiting in the murky water. The one that had almost gotten Bekele was of average size. But there were some monsters out there, squirming nightmares that could reach twenty feet in length.

Fish got them to the verge of the jungle and its steaming, rank heat.

Kirth shoved Bekele up onto the bank and clawed his way out of the clotted marsh grass into the moist sand, panting and filthy. Blue fist-sized spiders sprang away through the growth. The ground was soggy and spongy, but it was ground. Sweet, solid ground. And on the ground a man had a chance.

They clustered there, the three of them, waiting, wondering, catching their breath. They listened to the jungle and Fish scanned for the Xenoid, but found nothing.

Meanwhile, Bekele uplinked with the drones. "They'll be overhead in five minutes," he said.

"Good," Fish said. "We need all the backup we can get."

Kirth grunted. "It was your Xenoid, I take it."

"Without a doubt."

"Two men the first day, boss. That's not so good." He watched the swamp on infrared, looking for a signature of what was hunting them. "How'd it get so close?"

"It used the river," Fish explained. "That's the only way it could have evaded the scanner. It moved underwater, homing right in on us."

"So it could be out in that swamp? Moving at us?"

Fish smiled. "That's what I'm counting on."

6

They waited with weapons in their hands, breathing the stuffy warm air of the suit rebreathers as night came to Xenos. The jungle was loud and alive with the sound of night birds and buzzing insects and unknown animals rooting through the clustered thickets. Out in the swamps they could hear tiger worms splashing from time to time, growling as they fought over meat.

Fish said, "Now tell me what you saw. Tell me the best you can, son."

But Bekele wasn't entirely sure; it all happened so damn fast. "It looked … it looked like a … I don't know. It was big and clawed and it had teeth … it killed Tierney."

Kirth sucked beef broth through his feeding tube. "Yeah, we figured that much, missy," he said.

Fish remained impassive. "Just relax now. Think back and describe exactly what you saw. This is very important."

"No point, mate," Kirth said to Fish. "Our boy here, he was too busy filling his pants."

Bekele was breathing hard in his helmet at the memory of what he had seen. The terror had not left him. "In the morning, we better make for the ship. We can't hope to fight something like this. It'll slaughter us."

"We're being paid very well to do a job, son. We can't back out now."

The dimmed lights inside their helmets painted their faces orange. Their eyes were huge and staring and filled with fear. But Bekele had to wonder if it *was* fear. Sure, fear in *his* eyes. Fear of dying in this macabre green world straight out of the Mesozoic. But in the eyes of Fish and Kirth? No, it was something else. Opportunity? Lust? Excitement? The two of them had found what they had come for and they weren't about to leave without it.

"We should never have left the ship," Bekele said.

Kirth laughed. "The Xenoid can gaff us back there as easily as out here."

"Now tell me," Fish said, "what you saw."

Bekele swallowed a few times. "The Xenoid. I saw a replica in a museum once. That's what it looked like—a goddamned monster," he said, expecting them to laugh at him. When they didn't, he elaborated. "It moved so fast. I only saw it for a second, then it was gone."

Fish and Kirth looked at each other, smiling thinly.

"Too bad about Tierney," Kirth said.

Fish nodded his head. "Indeed."

"We need to get out of here," Bekele said.

"You signed up for this, my friend. You wanted a tour of hell, and now you'll get it," Kirth told him.

Fish smiled. "To think, Tierney was killed by one of them," he mused. There was a savage, primitive gleam in his eye as if the idea excited him. "I saw something move back there, so damned fast. Amazing. What an animal! What a beautiful goddamned animal!"

"But don't you see? If there's one, there'll be others," Bekele pointed out.

Fish nodded. "Of course there will be. A population. There would have to be a viable breeding pool, or they would have gone extinct long ago."

"Thousands of them at the very least," Kirth said, tapping his particle cannon with one finger. "And we only want one of them. Just the one. That's not asking too much … or is it?"

"That's ridiculous," Bekele said. "Let's just get out of here. That thing … it's too fast. We're not equipped to hunt it."

No one objected to that, but he could see it in their eyes: they wanted the beast, and they planned on having it, one way or another. Money like this didn't come twice in a lifetime.

They were both insane. And, worse, they were obsessed.

Bekele sighed, looking around.

They were on a forested island stuck out in the middle of a steaming swamp bordering a tributary of that shit-brown river. To all sides were tiger worms and slaggiths and all manner of night hunters. Just a slick of land in a gaseous quagmire of black, sluicing mud. Mist was rising from the swamp now, heavy and shivering like jelly. It clung to the trees, floated in thick pockets and ribbons.

If something wanted to get them, it could do so easily. Particularly something that could camouflage itself like the Xenoid.

Sighing again, he interfaced with the drones. They were picking up nothing on the Xenoid. Countless other lifeforms, but no Xenoid.

Fish had a funny gleam in his eyes. "Hey, Kirth? How is it we draw animals to us?"

"We bait 'em."

Fish smiled. "Exactly."

7

"Anything?" Kirth asked.

"Drones aren't picking up a thing," Bekele told him.

They had decided to bait the thing, to draw it out … if it could be drawn out at all, that is. Fish was getting frustrated. He wanted a damn Xenoid. There was no damn way he was going back empty-handed.

Not with all that damned money waiting for me, he told himself. *This time I'm getting the beast and I don't care how many lives it costs me.*

Kirth slipped off into the bush and was gone maybe thirty minutes. They heard his particle cannon shrill once, but no more. He stumbled back into the clearing sometime later, dragging a large, stout mammal that looked like a wild pig with gigantic tusks. Fish and he hung it eight feet off the ground from a furry green palm and slit its belly open. The air was thick and reeking with the stink of fresh blood.

"If it's out there," Fish said. "This should bring it."

Bekele chuckled. "Don't you think you're underestimating its intelligence? It's not some dumb animal."

"Even the smart ones get hungry," Fish said.

"Should we set up the force cube?"

"No. Not yet. We're not wasting batteries until we have to."

The force cube was about the size of a hat box and could throw out a high-voltage force field. It was the ultimate in protection.

Now the jungle had gone quiet.

Bekele studied his peripheral. Moba One had a fix on the Xenoid— it was moving at them again. "Half a kilometer and closing. Making a straight line to us."

"Must have snuck up using the swamps," Fish said.

Bekele suddenly froze up. "It's close," he said. *"Thirty meters … twenty … moving fast … drones can't get a shot at it—"*

The smell fell over them like a tarp, that honeyed musky stench came through their filters and went down deep into the pits of their stomachs. No one had time to comment on it, because the Xenoid charged from the jungle just as they scattered and made for cover.

At least, Kirth and Bekele did.

Fish kept his head low, pulser rifle in his hands. There was a great gust of wind like that which a locomotive barreling through a tunnel would push before it. And a hot, fetid smell. Then a huge, streamlined shape rushed out of the marsh mist, shadows, and soft green jungle.

It was fast.

Incredibly fast.

It darted about in a hallucinogenic blur, its muscular rear legs pumping like pistons. It was a perpetual motion machine of spurred limbs, thrashing tentacles, scissoring teeth, and huge clawed forepaws like thrashing meat hooks.

It moved in and out of the jungle and fog with darting, jerky, bird-like motions. It never paused long enough so that they could get a look at it or draw a bead on it. Here, then gone; there, then gone. *Zip, zip, zip.*

Fish brought up his rifle, knowing he'd never hit it, but hoping he could get it to stay still for the few seconds the drone would need to punch a dart into it.

Kirth fired his particle cannon, the bolts coming dangerously close to Fish, vaporizing clods of dark humus and leaf matter.

"HOLD YOUR FIRE!" Fish called over the comm, his scanner beeping as the drone hovered high overhead.

All I got to do is wing you, he thought. *Incapacitate you for a few seconds—*

The Xenoid vanished, then it reappeared again like a ghost. It hit the hanging bait animal, cleaving it right in half with its scythe-like claws. The vine that held it was severed, the creature split and divided and then … gone.

Fish fired wildly, but didn't hit a thing. It was like trying to shoot lightning in sky. But he was not about to give up. He raced into the jungle after the creature, moving this way and that, tripping over rotting logs and sinking knee-deep in sucking black mud. Turning around, unsure, aiming this way and that, his heart pounding in his chest, his face streaked with sweat, he stopped.

It's here, he thought with a rising mania. *It's waiting for me.*

Yes, he could feel it in his guts and maybe even in his blood. He knew he was not alone; the Xenoid was with him. He could sense its nearness. The filter of his mask brought him a perfectly nauseating high, hot animal stink, a smell of blood, raw meat, and offal. The scent of a wild thing that rolled in its own kills and slept in a dirty warren of bones and scraps, a urine-stained nest.

Easy now ... easy.

With a trembling hand, he brought up his helmet spots, his heart nearly seizing in his chest. He played the light to the left and then to the right—

It was waiting there among the ferns.

Jesus.

It stood easily eight feet tall, serpentine and streamlined, its well-armored, spiked carapace going from a beaded green at its back to an indigo blue at its snout and a pale orange at its underbelly. Its head was elongate, lobed like a brain, at the end of a long, angled, skeletal neck, four gelid eyes yellow as urine studying him from beneath bony ridges. Grasping tentacles wriggled at its mouth alongside a pair of razored tusks that looked like they could split a man from stem to stern.

"Easy now," he said over his helmet's external speaker.

Hesitating beneath spreading tree limbs festooned with hanging moss, it studied him, cocking its head. Slime dangled from its mouth. Its chest expanded as it breathed, nares on its snout opening and closing.

Though its hot breath was foul and nauseating at such a close range, it was an absolutely marvelous animal. There was a row of triangular dorsal spikes that ran down its neck and back, its forepaws set with scythe-like claws as were its splayed triple-toed feet. Nature had designed it to one end—to kill, with speed, power, and precision.

Fish began to slowly bring up his rifle, struggling to grip it in one sweaty hand.

The beast flinched.

The beeping of the drone was louder as it closed in.

The Xenoid made a low growling sound in its throat.

Its body rippled with muscularity.

The jagged teeth jutting from its jaws gave the impression that it was sardonically grinning.

"Easy," Fish said again.

Then the drone swooped down, firing its dart and the Xenoid jumped clear of it with amazing speed. The dart with its three-inch needle tip impaled Fish, drilling right through his suit and emptying enough Cyclacine into him to kill him.

But he didn't die; he just went limp and numb.

The Xenoid leaped.

It hit him, knocking him to the soft, moist ground. He had no idea where his rifle was, because the hand that held it—and the arm itself—had been taken off at the shoulder joint. He was ripped open. He was gagging on the blood that bubbled up his throat and filled his mouth, splattering the inside of his helmet bubble. The beams of his helmet lights revealed the last thing he would ever see: the red-stained snout of the beast as it yanked out his intestines.

8

On Xenos, days lasted some thirty-six hours, nights nearly twenty-four. After the Xenoid got Fish—something they assumed from his screams, but weren't about to confirm by searching for him in the demon-haunted blackness of night—Kirth set up the force cube and put out a field of some twenty thousand volts to protect them during the long night. For well over sixteen hours, they listened to the local wildlife fry as they tried to breach the field.

Neither man slept.

Kirth, because he feared a Xenoid attack, and Bekele, because he feared Xenos in general and the Xenoid in particular, but mostly because he didn't dare close his eyes around Kirth, who was as much of a monster as anything on the planet.

20

But dawn finally came, and with it the hazy sun, 61 Cygni, made a showing. It did very little to burn away the ghosting sheets of night fog. The heavy forests, swamplands and tangled undergrowth were haunted by it, and it blew about in sodden rags and moth-eaten sheets, obscuring the wild landscape and creating legions of stalking shadows. Struggling beams of sunlight pierced the triple-canopy jungle, but couldn't touch the fog that was the hunting grounds of nameless shrieking, screeching, and roaring things that swam through it like sharks in a bloody sea.

After Kirth deactivated the force cube, Bekele and he viewed what was left of the various creatures that had died trying to get at them in the night: blackened carcasses of tusked mammals and three-eyed venomous toads the size of bulldogs, the leathery burnt remains of titan leeches that could suck a man dry and huge spidery arachnids big as footstools.

"Would have been a real ugly night without the cube," Kirth said.

After some nourishment from the feeding tubes and water drippers of their suits, they gathered their gear and began a grid search for Fish. They spent an hour at it, but never found him. But what they did find was a monstrous three-toed print in the mud like that of a gigantic rooster and a quantity of dried blood sprayed on the surrounding foliage.

"This is where it got old Fishy," Kirth said, flicking a bright yellow worm off his visor that had suckers on its underbelly like those of an octopus.

Bekele said nothing. He simply stared with wide, white eyes through his helmet bubble at the gore and the variety of multi-hued insects investigating it.

"Look there," Kirth said. "See that broken jungle? That's where the Xenoid dragged him off and that's where we're going."

Bekele shook his head. "Where we need to go is back to the ship so we can get out of this graveyard."

"No, no, no. We've got a job to do."

"I'm going back to the ship."

When he turned, Kirth had his particle cannon aimed at him. All three barrels were mere inches from his faceplate.

"You're out of your fucking mind!"

Kirth laughed. "Maybe. Maybe I am, you silly gob of shite. But you either join me in this merry hunt and put your drones to work, or I'll stake out your corpse for our friend. The choice being yours."

Bekele walked toward the cut in the jungle. There was no point now, he knew. The only thing left was to die. Ether the Xenoid got him or Kirth would. "C'mon already," he said.

Inside his helmet, Kirth grinned as he plotted his death.

9

Kirth kept a tight eye on Bekele because he didn't trust him. He was a weak man with a rubber spine and jelly for guts, but what he lacked in fortitude, he made up for in brains. And there was evil in that, in his way of thinking.

Can't trust that type, Kirth thought. *Probably scheming his way out right now. Well, try it, you fucking toad. Just try it and you'll see exactly how old Jackie Kirth operates.*

What made him nervous were the drones. Techie brain boys like Bekele had their ways. Cunning and treacherous is what they were. He could make those damn drones dance a jig or sit up and beg. That's why Kirth kept the cannon on him at all times as they marched through the hip-deep muck of the pale green marshes. Any funny business and he'd die first.

Fish's blood trail was hard to follow. They'd have lost it a dozen times without the scanners. The Xenoid seemed to know that, so it tore up the undergrowth so they would be able to follow it. It wanted them. They found Fish's left hand speared on a branch and sometime later, his pulser rifle (which Kirth took, of course).

The swamp was hemmed in by thick undergrowth. It was eerie and misting and cut by knife-edged shadows. Segmented reeds big around as broomsticks grew from the water, towering eight and ten feet over their heads. The Xenoid had crashed through them, leaving a path. The channels bubbled with black water and were edged by thorny brush like fans of bare, spear-like sticks. Steam rose from the sluice and mats of shaggy vegetation floated on its surface. Through their filters, they could smell it all—miasmic, hot and rotting.

"Keep going, you shat," Kirth said over the comm when Bekele paused.

"Look," he said.

Kirth did. In the lights of his helmet, he could see a strand of bloody tissue hanging from a spoking branch overhead. Attached to it was one of Fish's eyes hanging by its stalk.

"Do you still think we should keep going?" Bekele asked, tendrils of mist snaking past his helmet bubble.

"Yes."

Bekele laughed with a brittle sound. "Me, too. And why not? Neither of us will make it out of this alive. But if one does—" and here he laughed again "—they get all the money."

"It won't be you."

"Won't it?"

Overhead the drones whirred past and Kirth went cold inside. He didn't like smart men. He didn't like minds that were always in motion, plotting, scheming, weaving deception and evil subterfuge. He liked simple men with animal instincts. The predictable types. Push button A, they get pissy. Push button B, they take a swing at you. Simple, mindless idiots that were easy to read and easier to manipulate.

Bekele was too complex.

They pushed on through another dark channel, reeds bobbing and swaying around them. Things were moving in the underbrush around them, shrilling and piping. Great swarms of insects flew over their heads. The reeds seemed to be alive, rustling and scraping and making odd cracking noises.

"Wait," Bekele said. "Moba Two has a signature. The Xenoid. It's about twelve meters out."

Now they watched the reed swamp carefully. The Xenoid was out there, making ready for the kill. Kirth tried tracking it with his scanner. It was there, then gone. Suddenly somewhere else, then vanishing, only to reappear some distance away.

"Can the drones get a shot at it?" he asked.

"Negative. It's hiding in the reeds, then it submerges."

"It's baiting us."

Kirth was sure of it. Oh, make no mistake, it was going to kill them, but not until it got them where it wanted them: some kill zone it had already prepared.

The Xenoid was everywhere and nowhere in the misty reed swamp. They heard it splash off to the left and then tear its way through the swaying reeds directly in front of them. Kirth made ready to get a shot at it. Bekele just stood there, tracking it with the drones as it appeared, then vanished.

"Well?" Kirth finally said.

Before Bekele could answer there was a loud screeching noise in the distance like a dozen women screaming simultaneously. It echoed through the swamp, seemingly coming from every direction at once, a sonic weapon that made their skin crawl and their bodies shake in their suits. By that point, they were both blind with fear. The idea of going forward was suicide and the idea of retreating with that monster at their backs was terrifying.

So they did not move.

They waited.

Sweat ran down their faces.

Their guts stirred in their bellies.

Things swam around them, squirming over their suits. Clouds of insects speckled their helmets. The reeds were still in motion, the water splashing just ahead. Islands of vegetation and mats of weeds were rolling.

Kirth was grinning. He knew he had to force a confrontation with the Xenoid or it would toy with them for hours, tormenting them until they were both insane with it.

And there was only one way to do it.

10

"Now, chief, here's how this works," Kirth said over the comm, licking sweat from his lips. "Start walking. We need to draw it out."

Bekele stood there. The blood had drained out of his face. *"What?"*

"You heard me, chummy. Walk your pouty, girly ass out into the clearing. Just a bit."

Bekele, knowing it was pointless, did not argue.

He knew what this was about. Kirth wanted him as bait so he could draw the beast in. It mattered not to him that he would probably get killed. Human life, life of any sort, meant very little to a man like Kirth.

"It'll come for you, and I'll get it," Kirth said. "Don't worry, chief, I'll do my best not to hit you, so don't get your little twat in a bunch."

Bekele moved into the reeds, pushing them aside with his hands. After a few minutes, they parted and there was a wide black pool before him, its surface floating with patches of crawling red fungi. Gaseous fingers of steam rose from it, hanging in dense pockets. Things like huge gray ticks crawled over his suit.

He stepped out into pool, accepting the fact that he was now simply bait. There came a point when all men, he supposed, simply had to accept the inevitable. And the inevitable in the wilds of Xenos was that all things were prey and all men were just one sort of bait or another.

With such knowledge came peace.

In the thick, thorny vegetation on the other side he found the rest of Fish. He was like a scarecrow impaled on a stick, swaying back and forth. The blood that was splattered over him was black as ink. He was covered in feasting insects, his head cocked on a broken stub of neck, mouth locked in a final rending scream. In the hot, humid atmosphere of Xenos, he was already going soft with rot.

Moba-1 beeped. It had a fix on the Xenoid hiding in the undergrowth, but it wasn't telling Bekele anything he didn't already know. He could see the Xenoid watching him with bright yellow upturned eyes that seemed to flicker like those of a Halloween jack-o'-lantern. Through the filter of his helmet, he could smell it—sweet, horrid, sickening.

Then, like before, it was gone.

Kirth joined him.

They waited together, about as close to the epicenter of hell as they dared get. The reed swamp and its surrounding environs were the hunting grounds of the Xenoid. They couldn't hope to fight it here.

The bog water was oily and black, exuding a stench of organic decay and a sharp reek of escaping sulfur and methane gases. It made a near-constant bubbling sound like hot molasses boiling in a pot. A great witch's cauldron where toads and newts, the fat of infants and the entrails of dead men were kept at a low boil, a foul and pestiferous brew of noxious venom and corpse drainage.

Huddled together with drawn weapons, Kirth and Bekele were brothers in terror, twins conjoined by the creeping malevolence they could feel moving in from every quarter.

They sweated.

They trembled.

Their hearts raced and their limbs quivered from surging adrenaline. They watched the mist drifting through the tall reed stalks that were like crowded shafts of bone all around them. It moved in sheets like graveyard phantoms dragging their shrouds behind them at midnight.

As they sensed death drawing near in the form of the Xenoid, the apex killing machine of that forbidden world, they prayed to gods they didn't even believe in.

Him, let it be him! Kirth thought. *Kill Bekele! I'll give him to you in sacrifice! I'll lay him at your feet! Just say the fucking word!*

And yes, God, yes, he was willing to do that, to slit him open and offer his bleeding carcass like a suckling pig on a platter if it prolonged his own life.

Bekele's thoughts were no more pure or self-sacrificing. *I know you're out there ... I can feel you. Kirth is the one you want. Hang his head on your wall like a trophy, but let me live!*

Yes, they were fused together out of mortal terror, but there was no kinship between them. That awful place had turned them just as black inside as rotten teeth.

Now the Xenoid was moving again, sliding through the standing reeds like a viper through cane grass. Bekele had forgotten about the peripheral on his arm. He had been reduced to a superstitious savage and such technological marvels like hunting drones were beyond the scope of his simple thought processes.

The reeds were moving.

A sweet, sickening odor pervaded the air.

A grotesque shape seemed to move out in the reeds at the edge of the fog. Then there was a sound—*swish-swish-swish*. It grew louder as not just one but two blades sought them out. They went down in the murky water, sinking themselves until only the very tops of their helmet bubbles were above the slew.

The blades came out of the mist, decapitating at least a dozen swamp reeds. They circled above their helmets, seeking heads to lop off or limbs to sever. They came again and again burying the men in reeds.

Kirth fell apart. Something snapped in his mind with an audible (at least to him) splintering like a stick of green wood.

He vaulted from the muck, slicked and dripping with it, screaming his mind away. Inside his suit, his bladder let go and a single yeasty bubble of bile exploded from his mouth, spattering against the inside of his faceplate. He began firing the particle cannon indiscriminately, laying down a devastating barrage of burning red bolts of plasma, each one with the destructive power of a lightning strike.

The reed stalks were obliterated into glowing chaff. Floating islands of vegetation were vaporized. Trees fell. Bushes erupted into the air and fell in a storm of black ash. All in all, in some twenty seconds, he loosed nearly two hundred bolts until the cannon's battery was drained and it was smoking and smoldering in his hands.

It dropped into the water, sizzling as it sank and he shouted, "HE'S HERE! THE ONE YOU WANT AND MUST HAVE IS RIGHT HERE! TAKE HIM! I OFFER HIM TO YOU!"

By then, Bekele was out of the muck, trying to distance himself from the mad man who was offering him as sacrifice to the Xenoid, which was now his dark and malefic god.

"NO!" Kirth shouted. "YOU HAVE TO WAIT! HE'S COMING! YOU'VE BEEN OFFERED!"

And Bekele's answer to that was to fire his pulser at Kirth. The shots were wild, fired by a man in blind panic, still, they barely missed their target.

As Kirth screamed and ranted, Bekele stumbled away, splashing through the roiling water and floating heaps of stalks that came apart before him like dry corn husks.

Over the comm, Kirth, right out of his mind, called out to the Xenoid to accept the sacrifice he had promised it.

Bekele made it maybe twenty feet when something like a barbed arrowhead punched through his chest plate and suit, erupting out of his back with a spray of blood and meat. For one moment, he stood there in shock, then the agony set in and he screamed, blood jetting from his mouth and filling his helmet bubble like red, red wine.

He went limp, slowly sinking into the mire.

But he didn't fall. The arrowhead, or whatever it was that impaled him, was attached to a shining green cord that was drawn taut by something out in the mist. Suddenly, it was yanked with incredible force and Bekele was jerked off through the reeds at dizzying speed, cutting a path through them.

Then Kirth was alone.

The reed swamp was silent.

And in his helmet, he began to laugh with a low, evil chuckling as the darkness closed in on him.

11

As what remained of his mind blew around in his head, Kirth studied the wet jungle around him—the vines and creepers, tube grass and flat, dripping palms. And every bit of it crawling with mutant insects and nameless horrors.

Its belly is full now from Fish and Bekele, he thought. *It won't be so aggressive. It should be sluggish. This is my chance. The only chance I'll get.*

He was out of the reed swamp now on dry land. Mucky, soft land, but at least he was no longer in the water. That was something. Tracking the Xenoid was easy enough with the scanner. It had left a trail of Bekele's blood and he followed it like a hound.

This was doable.

This was survivable.

It was only a matter of finding Bekele's drone peripheral and bringing hell down on the Xenoid.

(go get 'em, Jackie)

(that's the boy)

(show that shit-eater what you're made of)

The voice made him giggle and he knew he was in a world of fucking hurt and you didn't giggle in situations like that; only crazy people did that … yet he couldn't help himself: the voice sounded so much like his mother. "I will. I came to bag a Xenoid and you can be goddamned sure that I will." Yes, he liked the feel of his confidence. It made him feel mighty. "I'm gonna be rich, Mom, rich! You wait and see, you rotten old cunt!"

His mother laughed at that because, *yes*, she *was* a rotten old cunt and that simmering evil that made her whip little Jackie with a belt and lock him in cupboards and burn him with cigarettes was the only part of her that survived death. It was with him now—plotting, scheming, cunning as a wolf.

(you been in tighter spots than this and you always came out smelling sweet, now didn't you, Jackie? You were a mean little shit, always a predator at heart, a real little monster, and I gave that to you! That was my gift!)

Grinning, Kirth moved forward through the heavy brush. He was going to get the Xenoid. Fate favored him and he was going to bag that sonofabitch.

But he had to be careful.

He needed to be cautious.

The trees around him were gnarled and fleshy, green as moss. Their spoking branches were draped with rusty orange plaits of parasitic fungi and dangling canopies of vines. Their leaves were wide and flat. Beneath them, among the crowded underbrush, were phallus-shaped toadstools larger than a man with cactus-like spines radiating out from them. An entire ecosystem of crawling, creeping, whirring, and buzzing things lived high above.

As he moved ever forward, following the blood trail, his boots sank into leafy, decomposing mulch that was six or seven inches deep. He placed them carefully so as not to make too much sound.

(*that's how it's done, Jackie*)

Like he needed the old cow to tell him that. He pushed through the jungle, breaking stems and green stalks that bled a viscous green sap. Then the vegetation parted and he stepped into a surreal netherworld the likes of which he had never guessed.

It was a valley of sorts with leafless black trees that grew up from the ground like the legs of spiders and towers of stone like leaning monoliths. Things were hanging from the trees, seemingly tangled in them, so that they dangled three and four feet off the ground: shining blue-black shells and narrow pipes, gears with spiky projections and saw-toothed staffs and metallic casings. More of it had fallen into piles on the ground. It was like a great collection of exotic, fantastic machine parts—

(*not machines at all, Jackie! Look! LOOK!*)

The old hag was right: these weren't machine parts; they were the cracked and desiccated remains of Xenoids: broken exoskeletons heaped and piled on the ground, hanging and suspended—carapaces and bony limbs; spurred forelegs and massive hollow, tusked death masks; ladders of alien vertebrae with projecting spikes; complete skeletons and jagged pipes and staffs. A gigantic ossuary that reached back through the ages. And all of it set off by those massive, double-lobed skulls with their side-to-side yawning mouths and serrated teeth.

And Kirth, lost among it all, thought: *Like that old myth from Earth about the elephant's graveyard ...*

Except this was a Xenoid graveyard. The place they all came to in the end. Either on their own or brought by others.

He walked through it, stumbled through it really, new skeletonized horrors coming out of the thin mist at every turn, jutting and dangling and rising up before him, remains crowding in from every side so he had to squeeze his way through.

Then he was out.

He got clear of it, his body drenched with cold sweat, the voice of his mother prattling on about the gutless little coward he was, afraid of the dead. Then a smell wafted from the jungle. Not the hot, decayed green smell of the primeval forest or the festering smell of the swamp. This was sweet and dark and ancient and Kirth recognized it for what it was.

(*this is your chance to be a man, Jackie*)

Fish's pulser rifle in his arms, he waited for the Xenoid as the smell got stronger and the jungle grew quieter and the scanner told him it was right on top of him.

"Come on," he whispered. "Come on...."

It dropped from the trees, a spidery, multi-limbed thing, its armor shining blue like steel, its four yellow eyes blazing with kill-frenzy. Claws came at Kirth, a brace of snake-like fangs—

He fired.

He hit the Xenoid and it shrieked in agony, tossed backward from the blast. It jumped again, slithering, twitching, a great section of its protective exoskeleton blasted and melted into a smoking cavity. Kirth fired again as one of its arms darted at him, a sheath of claws slashing at his helmet. The limb was burned into a blackened stump that oozed green blood with an overpowering stench of ammonia.

The Xenoid screamed in pain and mindless feral hatred, coiling and rolling, then springing up again for another attack. Kirth fired, missed, then fired again three times, punching holes through the beast from which flesh and blood boiled like hot wax.

Its claws lashed out yet again and this time, there was no avoiding them. They scratched against his helmet bubble and tore through his upraised left arm at the shoulder, instantly severing it. Kirth screamed and bile ran from his mouth, his stump gushing blood. He nearly went flat out cold.

As the suit sealed the tear and cauterized the stump of his arm, injecting him with pain killers that made him giddy, the Xenoid, grievously wounded, attacked yet again. But it was clumsy, damaged, trying to drag itself forward like a half-crushed spider. It shrilled and screeched, the clawed tentacles at its mouth writhing like the snakes of Medusa and its jaws snapping open and closed. And Kirth fired three more times, the Xenoid absorbing each shot, charred and bubbling and ripped open.

It fled into the jungle, loping, stumbling, dragging itself forward.

Kirth, full of the ecstasy of the hunt, his blood hot and his muscles hard and his brain boiling in the feverish pit of his skull, charged in after it. He pounded through the sluggish brown ankle-deep water, vaulting a maze of stumps and tree roots.

He would have it.

Now he would have it.

The jungle cleared again and the creature's blood was a trail of luminous green that was easily to follow. In a glade of churning mist, he saw a multitude of staffs jabbed into the ground. Speared atop them were the rotting heads of reptiles and mammals and bizarre chimeras, as well as the skulls of the men who had dared hunt Xenoids previously. Bekele's head was there, grinning at him.

And there was the creature itself, curled up and bleeding out, a withered and blackened thing. As he stood there, it died and he knew he had it. Maybe the carcass wasn't in great shape from the pulser bolts, but when he added some remains from the graveyard, it would be enough.

That's when he saw something else.

Just ahead, set in a steaming, cup-shaped crevice of rock, was a green ovoid about the size of an ostrich egg. Larger, maybe, like the petrified egg of an elephant bird. In fact, that's what it had to be: an egg.

Such a thing would be priceless.

Stoned on anesthetics, perfectly insane, the pulser rifle held limply in one hand, he approached it. The voice of his mother screamed in his head, but he ignored it.

The egg.

The beautiful egg.

But if there was an egg, it meant—

He took two stumbling steps back and a hazy, seemingly insubstantial shape came out of the roiling haze and cloistered gloom. It hit him with freight train force.

The female Xenoid nearly tore him in half, loops of moist bowel hanging from his sheared suit and belly as he pulled himself along the muddy ground.

It was the primordial mother of all Xenoids—a gigantic night-hunter with a mouth like a spiked mantrap set with skinning knives and a throat like a black sewer. It seized Kirth in its claws, tearing at him, its huge bifurcated head pushed in at his face bubble, mouth dripping copious amounts of slime.

He managed to scream as it seized him in its jaws, shaking him violently like a Rottweiler with a rat. His helmet shattered and its teeth speared deep into him, grinding and scraping over his skull. Blood bubbled out of his mouth and broke hot against his face. The nitrogen atmosphere asphyxiated him, but not before she sheared his face from the skull beneath in a bloody flap.

MAUSOLEUM

The rover pushed on through the rift valley, clouds of yellow sulfurous mist blowing about in loose, swirling pockets that completely enveloped it from time to time. And when it wasn't the mist, it was particle storms born from screeching winds that blew through the ragged canyons and dark chasms of Noctis Labyrinthus.

"How long until the habitat?" Perchant asked from the back seat, Linich snoring next to him. "Please tell me it's soon so I don't kill this guy."

At the wheel, Dr. Taiwo laughed. Perchant and Linich were her comic relief. Their constant good-natured arguing, fussing, and picking at one another made these long, demanding field excursions that much easier to bear.

"Not for another long hour," she told him.

He sighed. "God, I want a hot cup of coffee and something solid in my belly that I don't have to suck through a straw."

In the passenger seat, Van Huesen toyed about with his tablet. "Might be a rough ride. WeathSat says we can expect storms." He smiled and looked at Perchant. "Just trying to brighten your day."

"Thanks, pal."

The rover bumped along, skirting cup-shaped impact craters and cutting across ancient lake beds littered with small stones. Mesas and extinct volcanoes rose around them, craggy and prehistoric, throwing brown shadows over the red sand and orange boulders.

The wind shook the rover from time to time, Taiwo slowing down because as much as she wanted to reach the habitat, she didn't want to flip the rover in a sudden gust of wind. It had happened before and there was a ream of documentation that had to follow any accident. Such things were time-wasters and took away from the real reason they were on Mars: for the science.

Her legs were sore, her back aching from three days of hunting minerals and fossils among the broken, arid clay beds and deep-cut meteoric craters beyond Tharna Ridge with little to show for it but specimen bags of sulfate salts and hydrated silicas.

"Man, I'm so sick of that wind," Perchant said.

Due to attenuation, high-pitched sounds didn't carry on Mars, but low noises seemed that much lower. The wind droned constantly, howling and groaning. It had a lost, haunted sound that tended to get under your skin.

Creepy, Taiwo thought, feeling a slight chill run up her spine. *That's the only word for it. Like a million Martian ghosts moaning at the same time.*

"Hey, wait a minute, Doc," Van Huesen said. "Sat says you're taking a roundabout way back to the hab."

"Just a ten-minute diversion. There's a lava flow the drone picked up. I want to take a quick peek at it."

"Just when I thought the punishment was over, it begins again," Perchant said.

"Oh, be quiet. It'll just take a minute. A couple samples and we'll be on our way again."

"I've heard that before."

There was a beeping from the rover's comm system, Habitat #2 calling.

"Taiwo here, Benyon. Just about to check in."

"GPS is showing you off course, Doc."

"Ha!" Perchant said, vindicated.

"Just a quick little side trip. There's a flow I want to sample."

She could hear Benyon sigh. "Doc, you'll be the death of me." He sighed again. "Well, move it along, will you? That storm front is picking

35

up speed. Looks like it's building to Condition One. I want my kids back here and safe in their beds when it hits."

"Roger that, Mom."

"The things I put up with," Benyon said. "I've been way too permissive. You kids never think of my feelings."

Perchant laughed.

Habitat #2 cut out.

But despite the levity, what he said was worrisome: a Condition One sandstorm on Mars was nothing to tangle with. It could mean wind speeds up to sixty or seventy miles-per-hour, dust clouds towering as high as three-story buildings, a chaotic, electrically-charged maelstrom of flying sand, grit, and electrostatic dust that would stick to suits like packing peanuts and knock visibility down to a dozen feet or less. It would turn day to night, its electrical field dampening all communications.

Taiwo had seen them before and they looked very much like photographs of the black sand blizzards of the 1930s dust bowl she'd seen in school.

That lava flow can wait for another day, she thought. She had to consider the lives of her crew. They came first.

They drove on another fifteen minutes, the rover climbing one sand dune after another until the land flattened out. Finally, mercifully. Dust devils blew around them, sand scraping against the windshield. Then—

"Did you see that?" Van Huesen asked.

"I saw a flash or something," Perchant said.

Taiwo had brought the rover to a stop. "Silver," she said. "Something silver."

She backed up the rover and they saw it again. It was caused by the sun glancing off something in the craggy foothills. Whatever it was, they wouldn't get up there with the rover.

"Anybody feel like a hike?" she said.

It was quite a climb. The foothills were scattered with gigantic boulders and they had to take a maze-like path through them, climbing up irregular shelves of rock and crawling over flattened table stones, squeezing between rising spires like broken off pencils. They followed a dry ravine to more sand dunes, one after the other.

"I was sleeping peacefully," Linich said over the helmet comm. "You people realize that. When I volunteered for this mission, I was told I'd get my eight hours."

Perchant laughed. "Listen to this guy. Eight hours. You log ten a day if not twelve."

"I'm delicate. I need my rest."

Taiwo and Van Huesen ignored them; this kind of banter went on constantly.

She led them up a high, cresting dune of pink sand, the wind throwing spinning dust against her face shield. But from that vantage point, what they had come to see was easily visible.

"Jesus," Perchant said.

Taiwo brushed dust from her visor. "Tell me I'm not the only one seeing this."

"It's there, all right," Van Huesen said.

And it was.

Not fifty yards from them was a metallic dome partially buried in the sand. It looked like an overturned silver cereal bowl, but immense, maybe six hundred feet across. Sand blew and dust whirled about them. There was no doubt that they had found something absolutely extraordinary.

Van Huesen captured it on video as they moved toward it, slogging through the loose sand. Taiwo raised the habitat and reported what they had found, sending a quick video feed. The reception was bad with a building storm front beginning to sweep down over the Valles Marineris. Magnetic interference.

"I think we're about to make history," Van Huesen said.

They reached the dome, and Taiwo studied it in some detail. It was perfectly smooth, as if it had been forged from a single sheet of metal, if it was indeed metal. She couldn't get over it. They had found so many intriguing things on the planet that, upon closer examination, turned out to be nothing but geological features—cliff faces that looked like terraced buildings, cave mouths that resembled doorways, pyramidal outcroppings that were the spitting images of Egyptian tombs.

But this was the one.

The one everyone had been hoping for and dreaming of: proof of ancient, intelligent life on Mars. Proof that either there had really been a technological civilization on the Red Planet or that it had been visited by one.

"Wonder why the drone never picked this up," Linich said. "It mapped this entire area."

Van Huesen shook his head inside his helmet. "No mystery there. It probably wasn't visible until recently. That last storm two days ago blew through this area with maximum force. It probably peeled this thing from the sand."

"Where it's been hiding for millennia," Taiwo said.

Although she didn't know it was old, very old—hell, it could have been dumped there a week ago for all she knew—she felt it right down into her core: this thing was ancient, *primeval*, in fact. She could feel the age coming off it the same way she had felt the age coming off a Sumerian tomb in Iraq many years before on a tourist jaunt. It crept into her, filling her mind with dark and tangled memories that disturbed her on just about every level.

It is a tomb, just like in Iraq, she thought then. *I know it. It's filled with dead things ... only they're not dead enough.*

"Doc?" Van Huesen said over the comm. "Doc, you with us here?"

"Yes. Yes, of course."

"Sleeping Beauty found an entrance," Perchant said.

She followed them around the dome to the far side where Linich squatted in the dirt in his suit, staring into an oval passage. The sight of it made her skin crawl. She realized then as a vague fear gripped her that she'd been secretly hoping in the back of her mind that they wouldn't find a way in at all.

"It just opened," Linich said. He swallowed. "I just put my hand on it and the damn thing opened with a whoosh of air."

"Dark in there," Perchant said.

Taiwo nodded. Yes, it was quite dark. *Dark like a haunted house at midnight or dark like an open grave.* She swallowed, dismissing such absurd thoughts.

"Shall we?" Perchant said.

"Let's make this quick," Van Huesen told them. "We have to keep that storm in mind."

"Roger that," Perchant said.

Taiwo nodded, but first she tried to contact Benyon at Habitat #2 as per protocol. Whenever a field team involved themselves in anything even potentially risky, it had to be called in, logged and documented. Just in case.

Problem was, the background interference was even worse here closer to the dome. But was that because of the approaching storm or something to do with the dome itself?

Taiwo, as commander, led the way into the dome, even though it was the last thing in the world she wanted to do. They had to go in on their hands and knees because the passage was filled halfway with sand. The deeper she moved into it, the less sand there was. The walls of the tunnel were made of some black alloy speckled with nitrous deposits that sparkled in her helmet lights as if they were so old they were mineralizing.

She could feel the others bunching up behind her and she told them to take it slow, one at a time.

"Slow, yes," Van Huesen said over the comm, "but not too slow. Remember: that storm is coming. We can beat it, but we need to make this quick."

Realistically, Taiwo knew, she should have just logged the site and brought back a team at another time. That was protocol and would have allowed for a comfortable safety margin with the storm, because you definitely didn't want to tangle with a Martian sandstorm. But such a discovery … no, it had to be investigated. The others would have lynched her if she had called them off.

The passage began to widen and there was less and less sand. And as it did, that existential dread inside her began to rise until it felt like it filled her chest, compressing her lungs and making it hard to breathe. But that could have been the excitement, too. What they might find ahead could very well stretch the seams of human comprehension and imagination.

Yet down deep in her belly, she wanted no part of it.

$\updownarrow$

The chamber within the hollow of the dome was gigantic, the upward sloping walls made of that same black alloy, but they had a multifaceted, machined look to them as if they had been welded together out of gears and pipes, ribs and corrugated columns. Not an inch of it was without geometrical protrusions of some sort.

As Taiwo examined it all in her lights, she wondered if it was not simply mechanistic but artistic to its designers, representing some perfectly alien esthetic.

The four of them stood just inside, panning it with their lights. They could see very little of it, but what they saw took their breath away.

"What's the point of this place?" Van Huesen said. "It must have one."

The floor sloped downward at roughly a 45° angle and their lights could just pick out something like a depression or a pit at the bottom.

"I wonder what's down there?" Linich said over the comm.

Nobody bothered speculating.

It was easy going, the floor elaborately textured. They moved in single file—lights splaying about, beams filled with whirling disturbed dust—following the wall. The only sounds the external mics of their suits picked up was the thudding of their boots. It sounded oddly distant, as all sounds on Mars did.

Taiwo felt something clenching inside her. It was not only inexplicable but troubling, because she was not someone given to nerves. She wouldn't be where she was if she had been. The psychological screening for the Mars program was extremely rigid. She had been in her share of tight spots since arriving on the planet, but she'd never felt anything like this before—it was crushing, claustrophobic. Even when was she was trapped for twelve hours in a cave system below Tharsis Bulge, it had not gotten to her like this: the feeling that death was closing in on her.

The others weren't feeling it. At least, she didn't think so judging by their chatter over the suit intercom. They were excited; they could barely contain themselves.

But she just couldn't share their optimism.

That black dread was building inside her and she tried to tell herself it was the idea of the storm, but she knew better. This was fear of a completely different species: not fear of the known, but the *unknown.* Staring down at that dark pit at the bottom, the more she felt like a frightened child, the way she had as a kid waking from a terrifying nightmare at three in the morning: heart pounding in her throat, her breathing fast, cold sweat beading her skin.

She thought: *There's something down there and, God help me, but I don't want to know what it is.*

"Would you look at that!" Perchant said.

Now that they were farther in, they could see a great variety of things decorating the walls: *creatures.* An amazing profusion of alien animals fixed to the walls like trophies in a hunter's den. All of them, thankfully, long dead, prepared and embalmed like displays in a museum. Taiwo saw immense armored worms and things like washtub-sized multi-legged crabs, huge spider-like creatures that appeared to be as scaly as lizards and something terrible like a giant horseshoe crab with the stinger of scorpion and eyestalks like a snail. An amazing proliferation of life forms, all of them, she thought, simple invertebrates of one sort or another—arachnids and gastropods, mollusks and insects, as well as hybrid forms that defied classification.

Van Huesen walked down the rows of them, which were arranged in triple tiers by size. "These are ancient Martian organisms that were collected ages ago," he said, pointing at them. "And this place must be a museum of sorts. A huge biological collection."

"Or a mausoleum," Van Huesen said.

Taiwo had seen similar fossil forms to some of them and she knew they had been extinct tens of millions of years at the very least.

"This is the find of the ages!" Perchant said.

"I wonder what this stuff is worth?" Linich mused.

"Priceless," Van Huesen told him. He panned his light further on. "Hundreds and hundreds of animals."

Perchant nodded in his helmet. "Only question that remains is who was the taxidermist? It was no advanced Martian. We all know such a thing couldn't be. And that means it was someone else, aliens out collecting lifeforms like biologists collecting butterflies. Whoever it was, if they could get to Mars conceivably from another star system, chances are they visited Earth, too."

"But what happened?" Linich wondered. "Why would they leave all this here?"

"Maybe something happened. Maybe they died. Either way, it was a very long time ago," Perchant said. "I doubt if we'll find their remains." He looked over at Linich. "You said there was a rush of air or gas or something? This place must have been sealed for millions of years."

Van Huesen looked concerned. "It's kind of in good shape to be that old, isn't it?"

Though he didn't say it, they knew he was hinting at the idea that someone had been taking care of it, a caretaker of sorts. But through all the long ages? The idea was ridiculous.

"We need to go," Taiwo said. "That storm's coming."

Perchant slumped inside his suit. "But, Doc—"

"No buts. We leave. *Now*. This will still be here in a few days or next week for that matter."

She was right, and they knew it. Mars was an alien world, and safety was always the first protocol. There were no two ways about that.

Van Huesen put his hand on her arm. "Listen," he said. "Did you hear that?"

Taiwo felt a weakness under her heart. She listened. After a moment or two, her external mics indeed picked up something: a clicking sort of noise. It came and went very quickly, then it sounded again. *Click-click, click-click, click-click.* It echoed through the immensity of the chamber.

"It's coming from the pit," Perchant said, a tremor of fear under his words.

And it was.

⚲

Taiwo expected many varieties of unspeakable horror to reveal themselves, but the one thing she hadn't expected was a machine.

Making that ominous clicking sound, it came up out of the pit like a trapdoor spider emerging from its lair. It paused there, balancing on four blue-black legs made of spurred skeletal rods like the limbs of a sand crab.

"Shit," Perchant said over the comm with more surprise than anything else. "It's a drone."

It waited there as if it was unsure of the situation, making a low humming sound like the vibrating membrane of an insect. Sitting atop the pod of legs, it had an upright, wedge-shaped body with a single huge, perfectly spherical eye of green crystal.

Taiwo realized that it probably wasn't an eye exactly, but more of a generalized sensory mechanism. Regardless, it seemed to be looking right at them.

"Doc ..." Linich muttered. He was closest to it, maybe thirty-feet away.

"Nobody panic," she said, knowing she had to say something.

It was hard to know if the thing was hostile or not. Maybe it was simply a caretaker of sorts that saw to the displays. Then again, maybe it was a vicious junkyard dog programmed to aggressively protect its turf.

She didn't know one way or the other, of course, but her gut sense told her they were in a very dangerous situation.

"Let's just get out of here," she said. "Let's calmly go back the way we came."

"Sensible," Van Huesen said.

Perchant and Linich agreed silently.

They followed Van Huesen and Taiwo at a very gradual pace. No one wanted to startle the drone. Through the view plates of their helmets, their faces were strained and sweaty, eyes very wide and unblinking.

The green crystalline eye watched them, shimmering and hot like a glowing emerald coal.

The drone had two other appendages analogous to arms that protruded at right angles from either side of its wedge-shaped body. Like the legs, they were black as anthracite with that blue sheen to them, composed of narrow rods like twin femurs welded together, likewise jointed and flexible. One ended in a fierce-looking triple-pronged grasping claw, the other in sort of a hollow tube.

It still hadn't moved.

It waited there, vibrating.

Van Huesen was nearly at the passage mouth. A few more feet and they could scramble free of that damnable tomb of Martian mummies. The drone watched them as a snake watches a bird. As if waiting for the right moment to attack.

Van Huesen was at the passage. He hesitated just for a moment, and in that moment, the vibrations of the drone got louder and faster.

Linich gasped as a beam of green light from the drone's eye speared him, making him freeze up. Sparkling flecks like mica spun and whirled in it.

"Lin!" Perchant cried out.

He tried to get a glove on him to pull him free, but soon as his hand encountered the beam there was a brilliant flash and a crackling noise like static electricity. He flew back as if he had been kicked. In the low gravity, he bounced off the wall and would have spun down into the pit if the others hadn't grabbed hold of him. As it was, he was weak and loose-limbed, stunned by the apparent energy of the beam.

Linich was completely immobilized by it, held like an insect in amber. He actually hovered some three inches off the walkway.

Taiwo knew something had to be done ... but what? They couldn't touch him and they carried no weapons. There was no need for them on Mars; other than subterranean microbes and fungi, it was a dead world. There was nothing to arm yourself against.

"Doc, look," Van Huesen said.

But she had already seen it and was powerless to stop it: Linich, trapped in the beam, was floating toward the drone, drawn to it.

She instinctively made a grab for him and it was like getting struck by a battering ram. She went down, her body numb as if she'd been shot up with anesthetic.

Linich was pulled to the drone. When he was within range, it seized him in its claw, holding him up like a prized specimen. It stood nearly eight-feet in height, dwarfing him. From the tube protuberance of its other arm, a silver cylinder emerged, and from it, what looked like a ten-inch hypodermic needle that spun like a drill bit.

It jabbed Linich with it.

The needle went right through his suit as if it was made of cheesecloth. He let out a cry and jerked stiffly. That was it. He no longer moved. The needle retracted and was replaced by a sort of orb from which a pencil-thin beam of white light emitted, like the arc of a plasma cutter. It neatly, surgically, cut him from his suit. He didn't instantly asphyxiate, because he was already dead. The drone held his naked body up, then the arc was gone, replaced by a spout that sprayed him with a glistening, bubbling gel which Taiwo knew must have been some sort of preservative.

His body shiny and glossy as if it had been lacquered, the drone carried him away to the other side of the dome where there was an empty spot among the embalmed animals.

Thus, Linich was added to the collection.

⇕

Taiwo, still feeling somewhat loopy, was dragged by Van Huesen down the passage away from the horror of the mausoleum. By the time they pushed their way through the sand and climbed out into the world of Mars, she was feeling somewhat better.

At least, physically.

Mentally, she was a wreck: everything inside her was stark white and trembling from what she had just seen.

"Lin, oh Christ, Lin," Perchant said. "He was my friend … he was my fucking friend."

But there was no way and certainly no time to comfort him. Hell was behind them and ahead of them, it didn't look much better.

The wind was starting to blow, casting loose scree about that struck their suits like thrown gravel. The storm was coming. They were at its very outer edge, but it was definitely coming.

"Move!" she told them. "We need to get to the rover!"

There were no arguments on that.

Dust devils whirling about them, clouds of sand enveloping them like sea mist, they fought their way up and down dunes. There seemed to be no end to them—rising, falling, sloping, sharp-crested, rolling, eroding, multi-peaked, an endless desert of blowing, shifting sand. There was no way to navigate line-of-sight, so Taiwo followed the homing beacon sent out by the rover. If it hadn't been for that, they would have been lost in ten minutes.

Perchant and Van Huesen tagged along behind her, but regardless of the time they made and the high dunes they climbed and slid down the backsides of, it was never enough.

"Just keep moving," she told them. "We gotta reach that hab or we'll be buried alive out here."

Linich's death was not just on her hands but on her conscience. She was in command. She knew the damn storm was moving down on them, yet she had allowed her people to go after that flash of silver. And she knew why: it wasn't just the way they pressured her to explore it, it was that she feared the storm would bury whatever it was and they'd never find it again.

And that's why Lin is dead, she told herself. *One reckless command decision after another.*

By the time they finally reached the dry ravine, they were all but done in. The wind was increasing and the dust thick as fog. They had to lean into it so it didn't toss them backward. The dunes had at least partially sheltered them from the blow, but it cycled through the ravine with howling force.

She tried again and again to reach Benyon at the hab, but the storm was rolling in with ferocity, bringing a strong electrical field with it and, before long, even suit to suit communications would be compromised.

Despite the flying dust enveloping them, she knew the foothills were just in front of them. Before long they'd see them. And then she did: the dust thinned just enough so she could make out their rising spires.

She led the way out of the ravine and the wind nearly blasted her flat. It was so strong now that they had to move side by side, holding onto one another, fighting forward together. In the low gravity, you could bounce like a ball, but it also made getting traction with their boots that much more difficult so they moved slowly. Much slower than she would have liked.

The foothills were right in front of them now: fuzzy, obscure shapes in the blow like leaning tombstones. Using the GPS on her suit, she knew she could guide them right to the rover.

We can do this, she kept telling herself. *We just have to stay together and keep our heads.*

By the time they pulled themselves up the rugged slope to the foothills, the dust storm was increasing in intensity like she'd never seen before. It was an absolute chaotic hell of flying sand and particulates, the dust whirling around them in the moaning wind, sticking to their suits, caking them like mud. They had to pause in the relative protection of a tower of sandstone to scrape the debris clean.

Visibility was down to about ten feet by that point. It would be easy to get lost in the storm. If one of them wandered off even a dozen feet, chances were they'd never find them again.

Her throat dry and her heart pounding, Taiwo began to climb up into the foothills. She had gone maybe five feet when she realized the others were not behind her.

Shit!

She backtracked and there was Van Huesen, standing there, one hand on a projection of brown rock. He was looking behind him. She did not see Perchant. A dust devil engulfed Van Huesen and he disappeared for seven, eight unnerving seconds. Then he was back.

"Where's Perchant?" she asked over the comm. "Where the hell is he?"

"He's … he's gone," Van Huesen said, his voice crackling over the comm, the transmission filled with static and background clutter.

Taiwo put a hand on him so he wouldn't disappear, too, and for a brief moment in the dim, yellow light of the storm, she saw something out there that did not belong: a flash of green. Not light exactly, but more of a sparkling like sunlight reflecting off an emerald.

Or something like a huge green eye, a voice said in the back of her mind.

"It got him," Van Huesen said. "Thought I heard … then he wasn't there." He said something else, but it was lost in the static. "It'll come for us … won't stop …"

And Taiwo knew he was right: that fucking drone would keep coming and coming until it collected them all. They wouldn't be safe in the rover. And they wouldn't be safe back at the hab.

"Come on," she said.

◊

Yet, even knowing that there was no escape from such a relentless enemy, she didn't stop. She couldn't stop. Van Huesen just behind her, they threaded their way through the foothills, towering cliffs to one side, jutting rock formations to the other. Underfoot, it was rubble and loose gravel that made it hard to get a footing … at least, an expedient one that would move them away from the drone as fast as they could.

Maybe it has a range, she told herself, hoping against hope. *Maybe it will only go so far, then turn back as it was programmed to.*

But that was wishful thinking and she knew it: that thing was not some simple lawn-robo that cut the grass and picked up leaves, following exact parameters. No way. Whatever sort of AI package drove it was probably incredibly sophisticated, the cutting edge of an alien technology many millions of years old. Those who built it and left it behind on Mars, were probably long extinct.

Which is what you'll be if you don't focus. There's only now. Right now. This minute.

In the foothills with their gigantic wind-worn boulders and projecting shelves of rock, they were protected from the storm somewhat, but the air was still filled with flying grit that sounded hungry as it glanced off their helmet bubbles, as if it was anxious to chew its way in.

Taiwo kept moving, prayers she'd learned as a child cycling through the back of her mind. She remembered being afraid of the dark as a child. How her mother assured her there was no such thing as the boogeyman (despite what her brother told her—*oh, he's real, squirt, he's real, all right, and he hides in basements and under stairs and under beds, he likes to grab little kids by their ankles and get 'em in the dark and do awful things to 'em)*, and Taiwo had believed it. But there *was* a boogeyman. By God, there was. She just never guessed she'd have to go all the way to Mars to find him.

They climbed and crawled and forced their way among the huge rocks, finally scrambling up a high rectangular boulder. There, they paused a moment. Had the dust not been blowing, they would have seen the rover down below in the distance, but it was lost in the storm. But what they could see above the blowing ground clutter was the approaching storm.

"Oh God," Van Huesen said over the comm in a defeated voice.

It stretched from horizon to horizon, a boiling black mass of dust and dirt rising up easily five or six-hundred feet if not three times that. It rolled forward slowly, devouring the landscape, the sky, turning everything in its path to a howling dark dead zone. Lightning forked from it along with occasional bright flashes of light that made it look like it was burning inside.

Behind them in the distance, she saw a shadowy, scuttling form like a giant spider weaving its way through the rocks. She saw it just for an instant, but she knew damn well what it was.

It was still coming.

Nothing could stop it.

It was designed to seek out life forms and collect them in any conditions, over any terrain. The desert and rocks were no more of a barrier to it than dirt and pebbles would be to a sand spider.

Moving down the slope to the desert again was like entering a turbulent, thrashing sea, except the waters were made of sand, dust, and anything that wasn't tied down. When they reached the ground, they were lost in it again, visibility practically nonexistent.

The debris flew heavy and fine, scraping against their face plates like metal files. Their external mics picked up the sound of the storm which was a near-constant roaring like a rushing waterfall. It pushed them down to their knees and they crawled slowly, painfully forward. Death was out there with them—circling. Moving in closer. Maybe they couldn't see it, but it could see them.

Van Huesen stood up slowly, bracing himself against the blow, teetering uneasily. What possessed him to do so, Taiwo did not know: if the wind knocked him down with the kind of force it was expending, he might bounce thirty feet into the storm and be lost for good.

She reached up and gripped his leg. "Get down!" she cried over the comm. *"Get down for god's sake!"*

Through the static and interference, she heard him say, *"See it …
should … real close … we … "*

And it was at that exact moment that she saw a flash of green light,
spoking, flickering. It seemed to spin around in an arc like the lens of a
lighthouse.

"GET DOWN!" she shrieked over the comm.

But as to whether Van Huesen heard her or not, she didn't know. And
it didn't really matter: the green light seemed to swallow him and he looked
like a stick figure submerged in bubbling, emerald champagne. She had
about enough time to scream as he was yanked away into the storm.

He might have cried out over the comm, but she just wasn't sure.

Now she was alone.

⚜

By the time she reached the rover, crawling on her belly all the way,
keeping a very low profile, the dust was caked three inches thick on her
suit. Its joints were becoming inflexible. She had no choice but to pause
and scrape her suit clean, or what she could get at anyway.

Hurry! Hurry! Hurry!

Then she was at the rover, but it, too, was caked in grit. She had to
paw it aside to reach the latch to pop the door. It took several minutes of
frantic scraping. But, finally, she had it open and she climbed inside. The
windshield was clear because it was designed so nothing would adhere to it.
Outside, she saw, it was like a blizzard of flying dirt and dust that seemed
to be getting thicker and heavier by the moment.

Only when the rover was moving again did she dare relax slightly,
doing breathing exercises to calm herself. The rover crept cautiously
through the storm, wind buffeting it, making it shake and jump from
time to time. It had to get her back to the hab; it just had to. It was her
only chance.

I lost my entire team, she thought. *All of them: Linich and Perchant and Van Huesen. They'll charge me with negligence and I deserve it. I—*

That thought died in her head when she saw the flash of a green beam out there in the maelstrom. But it couldn't be. That would mean … well, that would mean that the drone knew exactly which way she was going and had circled ahead to stop her.

But it couldn't be that smart, could it?

There was no time to think it out, because this time there was another beam, this one like a bolt of red light that smashed into the rover like a fist. Taiwo cried out as the rover was lifted off the ground, tossed into the air where it came down with a jarring impact on its roof, bouncing a few times as things tended to do on Mars, then slid down and down into some sort of gully and came to rest.

Whether it was the crash or the dispersed energy of the bolt itself, she was stunned and knocked unconscious.

⸸

When she came out of it, it was in a panic of pure terror, her mind foggy and caught between dreams and reality. It took her a few minutes to come around. And when she did, she blew the hatch on the rover and crawled out onto the rusty soil of Mars. The gully was protecting her from the blow, so as soon as she crawled free, it hit her with titan force. She was knocked down, pushed back, sliding until she bumped into a rock outcropping.

Alone now, Christ, she was so alone now.

The storm raged and howled, grit and sand blasting into her. She knew there was no way she'd be able to stand and walk; the best she could do was crawl.

The hab was many miles away, but she had little choice. At least, the GPS was still working, still guiding her.

She looked out into the storm, expecting to see the green flash of the drone's eye, but there was nothing. She found it very hard to believe that it had attacked the rover, disabling it, without further plans of collecting her.

Yet it didn't seem to be around.

Had the storm driven it off?

She didn't think that was possible. It had done just fine in it before, why would it suddenly be incapacitated by it? As she crawled foot by foot, she tried to think, to reason, to find an answer. Either the drone was right behind her, stalking her, or it had left.

Maybe it needed to recharge itself. That's not impossible. Maybe it returned to the dome.

Maybe, maybe, maybe, was all she had.

After a time, she stood in a low crouch, facing away from the wind and it propelled her along in the direction she needed to go. That was the first bit of luck she'd had all day. She kept going and going, having trouble balancing at first, but finally getting her feet under her.

In this way, she found herself on the road to Habitat #2. If she could just reach it, she had a chance. Benyon had probably already called Habitat #1 and let them know the geo team was long overdue, trapped out in the storm.

She kept going.

Mile by mile by mile.

And still there was no sign of the drone. Her greatest hope was that it had returned to the dome and would bother her no more, but she knew that was too much to hope for.

It took her well over two hours to reach the hab, but she made it, stopping now and again to clean her suit of debris. But finally, she came down a ridge and there it was. She could see very little of it, of course. It was made up of five geodesic domes connected by inflated tubing that looked like gigantic vacuum hoses. There were three outbuildings and a charging station for the rovers. Carefully, she reached the first dome and followed it until she found the airlock.

Then she was in, atmosphere normalizing, scrubbers cleaning her suit.

When the interior pressure was at 90% Earth normal, the green light came on and the door slid open. She fell through the doorway onto her knees.

Benyon was there, helping her off with her helmet, asking a dozen questions at once. When she'd caught her breath and the warmth of the hab began to unlock her muscles, she swallowed some hot coffee which was amazingly revitalizing.

"Dead," she finally said. "They're all dead."

"Hell you talking about, Doc?"

So she sketched it out for him, realizing how fantastic and improbable it all sounded. He listened to her, caught between belief and disbelief, looking at her pityingly. Whether that was because of what she'd gone through or because he thought she'd suffered a nervous breakdown, it was hard to say.

"Can you get through to Hab One?"

Benyon just stood there, looking pale. "Nothing's going out. Not with the storm."

She sipped more coffee. "Listen to me: I know you think I'm crazy, but that thing is out there and sooner or later, it's going to come for us. We need to be ready. We need to come up with some kind of defense. Can you at least understand that?"

"Doc," he said. "It's just that—"

Boom. Something hit the habitat and hit it hard. The entire structure shook. The lights flickered.

"What the hell was that?"

"It's here," Taiwo said.

"Oh, Doc, c'mon. It's probably just a rock thrown by the wind."

But if it was, it came again, concentrating on the outer hatch of the airlock, pounding on it, smashing into it relentlessly. The habitat trembled. *BOOM! BOOM! BOOM!* Again, the lights flickered. The hatch wasn't designed for that sort of abuse and it sounded like it was being hit by a tank.

"Into your suit!" Taiwo shouted. *"Hurry! Get into your suit and get your helmet on!"*

Already, the warning buzzer was going off, the robo-voice warning them that they were losing pressure rapidly.

The drone was through the outer hatch now.

It was beating on the inner one.

As Benyon scrambled to get into his suit, the drone hit the hatch again and again. Then, maybe tired of brute strength, there was a flash of red light and an enormous concussion that knocked Taiwo off her feet and sent Benyon rolling. The lights were flickering nearly constantly now.

The hatch was blown free and the habitat became a tornado of loose papers, coffee cups, dishes, folders, pencils, lab equipment—in fact, anything that wasn't tied down went airborne as the pressure was lost and the storm found its way in.

And with it came the alien drone.

⚶

It was too late for Benyon.

He didn't get his helmet on and suit pressurized in time. The low atmospheric pressure made his blood boil into bubbles that ruptured his arteries and veins, killing him nearly instantly. Long before hypoxia set in because of the carbon dioxide-rich atmosphere or the abrading wind peeled the skin from his bones, he was utterly destroyed.

So much so that the drone lost interest in him.

It scanned him with its green light, but he was far too gone to make a reasonable specimen. The drone went for Taiwo. But by then, she had scrambled away, closing one pressure door after another as she fled deeper into the habitat.

The drone, apparently, had been programmed to seek out and collect its specimens at all costs, so it kept coming. It sheared through door after door, either battering them free with its claw grasper or blasting them open with the red bolts of energy.

Regardless, nothing was going to stop it.

It would keep coming until there were no more lifeforms to collect.

The doors slowed it down enough so that Taiwo could get back outside via an emergency hatch. The storm hit her with fury, lifting her up and slamming her against the habitat. On all fours, she crawled to one of the outbuildings: blast shack. This was kept well away from the habitat and was where the C-4 blast packs were kept for geo and seismic work.

It was her only chance.

Far behind her, she heard the drone burst from the habitat. By then, she had popped the perimeter door of blast shack. It was warm in there. Kept heated because cold explosives did not ignite properly in the Martian atmosphere. She unlocked one of the steel crates and removed a single bright red blast pack.

And by then, the drone was in the doorway.

It was an evil thing. Covered in dust, it looked like some horrible biomechanical machine made of broken insects—carapaces and jointed appendages, spidery manipulators and clasping chelipeds, spiky and long-limbed and terrifying. Its single green eye blazed brightly. The eye of a cyclops.

Those who had made it must have been very intelligent and as fear coiled like worms in her belly, she said over her external speaker: "Listen to me. You must listen to me. I'm an intelligent creature. I'm aware and sentient. You must not kill me. You are in error in collecting me. Do you understand?"

The green eye watched her.

The grasping claw was wide, ready to grab.

The needle was out on the other upper limb.

It was ready.

It had paused, but it was ready.

It made that terrible clicking sound.

Taiwo pulled the igniter on the blast pack. In exactly sixty seconds it would explode. It was a simple matter of stopping it, but she didn't think she'd have the chance.

The green beam hit her and it was like getting shot up simultaneously with a dozen hypos of ketamine. Her body went numb, her head spun. She was lost in a gray haze, miles beyond pain or anxiety or fear. She was and she wasn't.

But she hadn't let go of the blast pack.

When it went, it obliterated not only her but the drone. In the confines of blast shack which was made of multiple layers of titanium composites, the shock wave spread out and was deflected right back to its source. Taiwo was atomized and the drone was blown out into the storm, a loose collection of components that could never be joined again.

The storm blew for three days and by the time help arrived from Habitat #1, the red sands had covered everything, entombing it for an eternity, much like the alien dome itself.

THE SKREE

⎣⏤⏌ Λ⏤➤⟫

The city was like a badly cauterized wound, jagged and ugly and festering. Just about everything that had been standing was collapsed into hills of rubble with huge blackened craters set between. Rafe stood on the remains of a mangled bridge and studied it in some detail before the heavy fog pushed in off the river and everything was lost in a white haze.

He went back to Grassman and squatted by him, kicking some bricks out of his way. "About as bad as we thought," he told him. "It'll be dicey crossing it, but if we go around, it'll add days."

Grassman nodded. His fatigues were ragged, his face smeared with grime. His breathing was labored and trails of sweat ran down his cheeks. He looked up at Rafe with bleary eyes. "Why don't you go on ahead and leave me here to rot? Christ, I won't think less of you."

"Quit talking like that."

Grassman grunted. He reached inside his pack and found a cigarette and lit it with fingers that trembled. "I can't keep going on like this. I'm old and I'm tired," he said, blowing out a cloud of smoke. "Go find the unit and come back for me."

"That's not going to happen."

As long as there was life left in him, he was going to keep moving. Rafe would see to it. If he left him alone, things might happen. Bad things. And they'd been through too much shit now to give up.

And I don't want to be alone, Rafe thought. *Not with those things everywhere.*

"You're coming along if I got to carry you."

Grassman shook his head. "Carry me, he says."

"I will."

"Leave me. Go."

But Rafe refused. He'd always been like that—once he got something in his head and he decided it was the right thing to do, nothing would stand in his way. He shouldered his flamethrower and pulled Grassman to his feet.

"You're nuts," the older man said.

"People say that about me."

Together, Rafe holding him up, they crossed the bridge.

◊

It was bad, of course.

Entering any city these days was asking for trouble because the Skree tended to congregate in the cities where the hunting was best and the food supply the most concentrated. They were very simple when you came down to it: they lived to eat and breed. They would attack anything or anyone that moved.

Three years was all it took.

Three years ago, the city had been a productive place of men and women and children going about their lives. Now it was a hell zone, a hunting grounds. Every city in the world was like this now since the Skree came and made the human race into their livestock.

Rafe and Grassman crossed the bridge as quietly as they could. They ignored the wreckage, the abandoned cars and trucks, the scattered bones and refuse underfoot. The thing was to keep moving. The unit was on the other side of the city. They had to reach them. Grassman needed help and Rafe was going to see that he got it. He'd get him across the city whatever it took.

"Remember the post?" Rafe said in a quiet voice. "Remember how you warned me about Skip and Daytona? Not to play cards with them. How they'd clean me out. And, boy, they sure did. What a dumb, naïve kid I was. Remember that?"

"Sure. I was there."

As they walked, moving carefully through the ruined city, Rafe spoke nervously, talking about girls they'd known and drunks they'd been on, food they'd eaten and assholes they'd dealt with.

The fog off the river was heavy and that was a good thing: you couldn't see much, sure, but *things* couldn't see you either. That's what Rafe was counting on. They could use the fog as camo as they slipped through the city and out the other side.

There were burned-out buildings everywhere, some blasted to rubble. Heaps of wreckage blocked streets and they had to take a circuitous route toward their distant objective. All the destruction wasn't from the Skree, of course, but from men trying to *contain* the Skree. After they came, the battles raged for months and months, bombings and chemical weapons, urban warfare and constant firefights and skirmishes. In the end, it was all pointless: the Skree were here, breeding by the millions, and though the armies of the world killed swarms of them, in the end they overwhelmed mankind with their sheer numbers, bringing about the genocide that had gutted the world.

As Rafe studied the destruction at every quarter, he thought, *and to think, all of this just because of a chance encounter between Earth's orbit and their migration.*

As they walked, in silence now as a creeping feeling of dread pervaded them, they came across the bodies of soldiers, men and women that had died in the fighting or been grievously wounded and hadn't been able to escape. The Skree had torn them apart, scattering their well-gnawed remains in every direction where they still lay among the broken bricks and burst pipes, erupted sidewalks and telephone poles fallen like tall timber—mummified scraps chewed by rats, yellow staffs of bone, and jutting broomstick limbs. Fleshless faces stared up at them as they passed, some shriveled and blackened like bog bodies.

He was so used to such things by then, it didn't even really bother Rafe. The remains were no different to his desensitized mind than the dead leaves and trash that blew through the streets.

"Wait," Grassman said. "Just wait. *Listen.*"

There was nothing at first, then Rafe heard it, too. From out in the fog, beyond the standing walls of razed buildings which were ghostly battlements like ancient castle works: a low, almost somnolent sort of droning. The sound the Skree made as they scavenged about. Not the excited shrilling they made when they were on the trail of something to hunt and kill, but just the seemingly relaxed, unconcerned sound of them casting about.

"Quick," Rafe said. "It's coming at us."

They hid in the ruins of a destroyed house, behind the chimney and the mass of its attendant hearth. They waited there in the damp mist, breathing in and out as the droning got louder and louder and they could hear the Skree picking their way forward through the rubble … moving, then pausing, moving, then pausing.

Rafe peered around the edge of the hearth and, oh Jesus, he saw two of them skitter away into the fog. His heart filled his chest, expanding with each beat. The Skree had no sense of smell, but their eyesight was very good, even in the dark. The scientists said they couldn't hear either, but they could pick up vibrations on the ground same way a spider can sense a fly in distress in its web.

The droning sounds faded away.

Must have been our walking, he thought. *They must have picked up our footfalls.*

"They're gone," he said.

"Quiet," Grassman told him.

Rafe peered around the corner of the hearth again and a Skree came out of the fog. It was backlit by it, sketched out in gray tones—a skeletal, rawboned thing, a mantis-like form hesitating there on its four walking

61

legs, easily seven feet in height. Its jointed forelegs were held up in attack mode, their crab claw appendages open for grasping and shearing.

The cold sweat of pure, unreasoning terror running down his spine, Rafe did not dare move. The Skree's head at the end of its segmented, stalk-like neck was scanning back and forth, mandibles grinding. It sensed they were there, but it could not pinpoint them. It cocked its head like a puppy hearing its master's approach.

It made a whirring, clicking noise, then moved off into the fog.

For a full ten minutes Rafe and Grassman waited. They did not speak or shift cramped limbs; they just waited.

"Okay," Rafe finally said. "We better make tracks in case it comes back."

An hour and many city blocks later, they paused to rest. Rafe scouted ahead and found a culvert beneath a set of railroad tracks. It was safe in there, he decided. If anything came after them, he'd toast it and they could easily retreat out the other side. They rested, asses on the ground, backs up against the tunnel wall.

Grassman wasn't getting any better. He needed medical attention and sleep. But he wasn't going to get either for some time to come.

Rafe was worried.

Grassman was feverish now, his dirty fatigues soaked with sweat. Rafe had checked the bandages at his belly. The bleeding had slowed, but it hadn't stopped. That was not good. He was getting weaker by the hour. Rafe knew if he left him, he could link up with the unit in a couple hours, but he wasn't about to do that. Not to Grassman.

He was rambling on in his fever, whispering incessantly. "Seen 'em in Bayonne first … oh yes … heard stories, of course, and saw all that crazy shit on the news and internet, but I didn't appreciate it until the skies were black with their swarms. Shit, yes." He paused, breathing stertorously as if he had drifted off. Maybe he had. He came awake, shook, grimaced. "You can't even imagine it until you see it. In Bayonne, that's where we first went up against them. We had Bradleys. We tore the Skree up with our fifties and chain guns. A fucking turkey shoot. I thought, shit, this will be easy ... but for everyone you killed, a dozen, a *hundred* would take its place. They sacrificed thousands. They overwhelmed us. When we were out of ammo, God, they ripped us up. I can ... I can still hear all those boys screaming as the Skree pulled 'em apart...."

Rafe tried to get him to eat, but he had no interest. He took some water, but he wouldn't touch dry rations. Not even the chocolate—and Grassman had always had a voracious sweet tooth.

He lit a bedraggled cigarette even though Rafe told him not to, that it wasn't safe with the eyesight of the Skree. But Grassman lit it anyway, not even paying attention to anything Rafe said, as if he wasn't even there.

"Ha, ha, ha, oh shit, yes," he said, blowing out smoke. "When I was a kid, I read them comic books and watched them movies about alien invasions. There was never anything like the Skree, was there? Always bubble-headed invaders with fancy spacecraft and fancy technology ... ha, boy, were we wrong. Some say the Skree ain't even intelligent, not any more than some stupid dog...."

Rafe just listened as he rambled. The cigarette and the talking weren't a good idea, but he didn't have the heart to tell him to stop either, not in the condition he was in.

The Skree, the Skree, the Skree. Grassman went on and on about them. Like maybe they were the only topic left in the world and maybe they were. How they ate everything, even each other.

Rafe couldn't seem to remember the world before them. It was like a story he'd read once when he was a kid or a movie he'd watched: the plot fraying in his mind, the absurdities and impossibles of a world without the Skree making no sense, seeming like fiction.

They came because the migratory path of their egg cases crossed Earth's orbit around the sun. A one in a million-million chance that the Earth was in the right place at the right time. Finding a hospitable environment, the egg cases hatched shortly after they fell, millions of Skree being born at the same time, all of them existing to eat and fuck and lay more eggs. Within a matter of months, they were the dominant life form on the planet. And every day, every miserable, awful day there were more and more of them. They devoured people. They devoured livestock. They stripped vegetation and crops.

It was appalling.

There was no other word for it.

Rafe remembered a biologist on TV saying that the life cycle of the Skree was pure destruction. Like locusts, they ate everything until there was nothing left to eat. Then, he believed, they would turn on each other, slaughtering and feeding in a ritualized genocide until the world was a cemetery heaped with their rotting husks. He speculated that the migration of their egg cases—countless billions of them, he theorized, the Earth receiving only a fraction of which—probably decimated world after world and it had been going on for countless millions of years.

But they still never figured out where the Skree came from, Rafe thought, *or how it was their egg cases were ejected from their home planet to congregate in space and begin their migration.*

Grassman had finally drifted off. Thank God. Rafe decided he would let him sleep for an hour; then they had to push on. They couldn't be in the city after the sun came up—the streets would be full of the Skree.

I'll just wait it out, but I won't sleep. I can't afford to.

These were the last words he thought before drifting off from exhaustion.

◆

They moved on, every foot a struggle now because Grassman was so weak he could no longer stand up straight. Rafe had to hold him up constantly, keep him on his feet and moving so he didn't fall down. He wasn't saying much. The fever heat and sour smell coming off him was sickening.

He's not going to make it, Rafe kept telling himself regardless of how he tried suppress negative thoughts and ideas. *He just won't make it.*

But he couldn't let himself think things like that. He just couldn't.

The city was an absolute junkyard of wrecked, abandoned, and rusting vehicles. An auto graveyard. They blocked streets, were crashed into each other in tangled masses of metal, driven right through the plate glass windows of stores. People went crazy when the Skree invaded the city. Despite the warnings they'd been receiving for weeks to get out, they hadn't, and when the Skree descended on them they all tried to leave the city at once.

Some made it, of course, but not for long. The Skree saw lone cars and trucks as prey and attacked them in numbers.

"Just keep moving," he told Grassman. "One foot in front of the other. Before long we'll be with the unit and the docs will patch you up. You'll be good as new."

They came across streets that were covered in the broken carapaces and stray limbs of the Skree. Whether they were killed by men or by each other, it was really hard to know. Their remains crunched underfoot.

There were plenty of human bodies, too, most of them stripped down to skeletons by the invaders. The foul, pungent stink of death was thick in the air.

Rafe struggled on, Grassman seeming to get heavier all the time. That and the flamethrower on his back and all the other equipment made his legs ache. But he had to keep pushing on. He couldn't abandon Grassman to those fucking monsters, and the flamethrower was indispensable: if he came upon the Skree, it was the only thing guaranteed to kill them or drive them off. You could blast them into pieces with a shotgun or carbine, but the others just kept coming. If you burned them, the rest scattered. They didn't like fire.

Rafe stopped; he smelled woodsmoke.

That meant people. But that wasn't a good thing either, because a lot of them were desperate, vicious and crazy. They hunted the city in wolf packs, killing and robbing. Most of the good people were gone; the ones that remained behind were looters and criminals, or worse.

He saw fire burning in a barrel, twenty or thirty people gathered on the sidewalk before a shrapnel-pitted brick façade. They were dressed in ragged coats, hats pulled down to their eyes. There were overloaded handcarts around them, piled with disparate things, like the carts of bag ladies.

He gave them a wide berth because he knew they were junkies of the worst sort. He could tell by the way they shook and jerked, inarticulate cries shrieking from their mouths.

Screechers, he thought. *Goddamn screechers.*

That's what people called them, because they were Screech addicts. *Screech* was the street term for the toxin that the female Skree injected into the males when they mated, making the latter into submissive sexual slaves that the females devoured during sex. It was in their initial sting when they attacked humans, too. The venom amplified feelings of pleasure and satisfaction by releasing a chemical cocktail of endorphins, dopamine and other neurotransmitters in the human brain, electrifying the reward system much as cocaine and heroin did. The chemical rush was addictive and humans would cry out in lust as they were torn apart. It was reportedly like an endless orgasm, and once it was in your system, like the male Skree, you only wanted to get off. Nothing else mattered.

The high was so coveted that Screech addicts would kill the Skree to get their glands.

They were best avoided.

Rafe swung a wide arc around them, and he and Grassman were never seen in the fog. Thank God.

An hour later, they had to stop again. They were maybe halfway across the city, but there was no way Rafe could keep going, dragging Grassman with him like that. They rested under a bridge.

"We'll take a breather for twenty minutes."

Grassman nodded his head, confused and disoriented all the time now. Rafe watched him continually, knowing what was coming, but refusing to think too much about it.

Again, he told himself he would not sleep, but his body was aching, his fatigues drenched with sweat. He had to close his eyes. Just for a few minutes.

$$\mathsmaller{\text{\textdagger}}$$

Wake up!
You must wake up!
About an hour later, Rafe came out of sleep, feeling groggy and doped. He fought to keep his eyes open, but they kept shutting. He was tired. So damn tired. What brought him out of it and to complete wired alertness was an awful crunching sound like someone cracking open a walnut. His eyes opened as adrenaline surged in his blood, panic making every tired muscle in his body snap taut.

He could see Grassman's form in the moonlight about fifteen feet away and there was a Skree hovering over him. It tore at him with its jagged mandibles, the upper and lower sets shearing his flesh like scissors, snipping and cutting, blood spraying into the air and glistening on its snout.

Rafe let out a shriek and scrambled to get his flamethrower up and the Skree raised its head at the end of the narrow trunk of its neck and looked at him with its huge compound eyes. It was completely indifferent to his presence. It made clicking, snapping noises like twigs being broken, then went back to its prey. Its thorax glistened greenly in the moonlight, its wing cases trembling.

Grassman, though gored and broken, was still alive. Rafe could hear him talking to the Skree, whispering as one might to a lover deep in the night.

As Rafe fumbled to bring up the flamethrower, its mandibles flensed open Grassman's back and he moaned as if being devoured by the thing was the most pleasurable experience he had ever known. It tore out his spinal vertebrae and he let out an orgasmic cry. The Skree crushed it in its mandibles, crunching it like a dog with a meaty bone.

Rafe brought up the gun assembly of the flamethrower, the tanks on his knees, and aimed it at the Skree. It made a shrill, ear-piercing cry and he squeezed the trigger. The Skree and Grassman's remains were engulfed in flames. The directed fire seemed to swallow them in a rolling ball.

The Skree droned as it burned.

It fought and spun in a circle, waving the claws of its forelegs about as its eyes boiled out of its exoskeleton in plumes of steam. Its carapace blackened, making crackling sounds as it split open and the thing collapsed atop Grassman, blazing and snapping, a cloud of black, greasy smoke rising from its carcass.

Its death didn't take long.

Rafe watched it burn, knowing he should get away as fast as he could because its cries probably alerted other Skree, but still he stood there, feeling wounded at a very deep level.

Oh, Grassman, he kept thinking. *Oh, dear Christ, Grassman.*

⁂

He wandered aimlessly through the gutted city, its buildings—or what there was left of them—like crumbling tombstones. Many had collapsed completely, others marked only by standing walls and leaning chimneys. There were mountains of rubble he had to climb over, streets littered with human bones and grinning skulls. This was the world now: an ossuary, an endless necropolis, a boneyard monument to what had been but would never be again.

Grassman's death affected him in ways he could not adequately catalog, but one of them was that he really didn't give a damn anymore. About the unit, the world, the fucking Skree, even himself.

He tramped along through a haze of mist and wood smoke from burning structures. He toured neighborhoods that had been burned flat, limbless trees and telephone poles standing like black masts. Everything was smoldering, carbonized debris crunching underfoot.

He came across stragglers with mad, staring eyes, many of them grievously wounded, others just plain out of their minds. They didn't even seem to know that he was there. Groups of Screech junkies watched him, but did not interfere with him.

He stood atop a hill of scattered bricks for some time and thought about Grassman. How wily and crafty that old guy was, how he'd kept Rafe alive for so long with his wisdom and common sense. Without him, there didn't seem to be much point in going on. As he stood there, staring into the haze, he realized that tears were rolling down his dirty face and he wasn't sure if he was crying for the loss of Grassman or for the loss of the world.

He pushed on.

Just before dawn he came to a section of the city that was mostly still standing. The perfectly insane thing was that the streets and avenues were netted in some glistening white mesh like a millions of spiders had spun gigantic cobwebs.

He edged in closer, sensing danger but oblivious to just about everything by that point. He had a flashlight in his shoulder sack and he dug it out, holding it in his hand, knowing that using it was a very dangerous thing.

Fuck it.

He turned it on and studied the webs in some detail. They weren't webs, of course, but a network of something like silk that was strung from rooftops to the streets below, from overhangs to parked cars, from utility poles to awnings. And in it, his flashlight beam revealed pearly orbs about the size of grapefruits, clusters of them.

Eggs.

These were Skree eggs. Not just thousands of them, but quite possibly millions. He stood there, shining his light about and from where he stood at the outer edge of the network that went on for many blocks in either direction, he counted over five hundred of them in a matter of minutes. The clusters appeared to be strung on specialized silk threads like pearls on a necklace.

"Rotten, stupid, disgusting things," Rafe said out loud. "You go world to world and destroy everything. Eat everything and everyone, breeding and breeding until there's nothing left and you starve."

Yes, that's what they were: an invasive species that overwhelmed any ecosystem they were introduced into.

Time to thin the herds, he thought.

He hosed down the netting with his flamethrower, pleased at how easily it all burned, as if it was dipped in gasoline. The flames raced up and down the webs, the eggs themselves superheating and popping like blood-swollen ticks. He lit them up for about a block and watched them fall all around him before he gave up.

What was the point?

There were millions of networks like this across the world. And he couldn't waste any more fuel. The sun would be coming up and he had to reach the unit.

It was all there was now.

And all he really had.

Skree carcasses were everywhere as he reached the outer south side of the city. The army and the aliens had fought pitched battles here and the evidence was heaped in every direction—great mortuary piles of dead Skree, jumbles of limbs and shells and broken wings, all tangled into a composite whole, rotting and stinking in the sunshine. Green, slimy juice leaked from them as they decomposed, a thin yellow steam rising from the massed dead.

No scavengers dared touch them.

Not carrion crows or buzzards, vultures or gulls or ravens. Not even wild dogs or sewer rats or lowly beetles. At first, of course, these creatures went after the dead Skree with wild abandon, but not for long: they were toxic and anything that ate them died writhing in pain as if they were full of nerve gas.

Rafe walked among them in the early morning sunlight, sick to his stomach at the sight of them, the popping noises of them completely breaking apart, and the smell, of course … like a mountain of dead fish decaying on a poisoned beach.

Packs of looters watched him with hungry eyes. They seemed to be everywhere, ragged and filthy and all of them deranged in their starvation. They would kill anyone for what they carried and quite often they would kill simply to feast on human flesh. Desperation, terror, and necessity had turned them into skulking cannibals with ash-blackened faces and hollow cheeks that tunneled in and out of the wreckage from underground lairs where they lived like packs of rats.

Only two of them dared approach him and he killed one of them with his pistol. As he reached the end of the street, the corpse had already been dragged off to be fed upon.

This was the world.

This was what it had come to.

And that was bad enough, but what he found in the park was much worse. He remembered the park when he was a boy. It was a weekend retreat for working families. A place to watch Little League games, to picnic and cook out, watch parades in the fall and the fireworks on the 4th of July.

Now it was something else entirely.

As he came through the trees, he heard it. And hearing it, knew exactly what it was because he'd witnessed it before. There were hundreds of Skree in the park and they were all mating, rasping and grinding their carapaces together, hissing and droning and fluttering their wings with a terrible buzzing. The sound of their intertwined bodies was like broken glass ground under a boot on a sidewalk, like peanut shells underfoot.

None of them paid any attention to him; they were completely entranced by the act of copulation. The females were whirring and shrilling, the males happily purring with delight, their wing cases vibrating. Even the ones being devoured were experiencing exquisite pleasure, the females' mandibles peeling them down to meat and their mouthparts punching into them like the needles of industrial sewing machines.

Sick to his stomach, his nerves jangling with fear, Rafe walked past them and around them until he was free of the grinding and scraping sounds, the perfectly awful noises of exoskeletons being cracked open like eggs.

He found the unit at last.

He arrived at an inopportune moment, because they were being attacked by a swarm of Skree. Machine guns and automatic weapons were clattering, grenades exploding, men screaming out as they were ripped apart. Flamethrowers were gushing out streams of fire which engulfed Skree and the beleaguered men and women fighting them. It was sheer pandemonium and it could only end one way.

Rafe didn't even bother joining in on the slaughter. What was another suicide among the many? He sat on a grassy hill and watched the decimation. The unit had the weapons, lots of weapons, and the people that knew how to use them. But the Skree had the numbers. Dear God, so many of them. They were on the ground, massing, dying, killing, overwhelming. They were in the sky in black swarms, hundreds and hundreds of them descending, attacking and biting and stinging. For every soldier there were easily fifty Skree with more arriving all the time.

You see this, Grassman? Rafe thought. *You see what's happening?*

This, he knew, was happening all over the world. Armies of human beings fighting to the death as the already teetering human population crashed to oblivion. In a matter of months, the only ones left would be the looters and stragglers and crazies. The Skree would mop them up, pluck them from their hidey-holes like chocolates from tins until there was none left. Until the human race was extinct.

Then the Skree would turn on their own kind and begin their own inevitable fall to self-destruction.

Rafe sat there. He lit a cigarette and placed the gun assembly of the flamethrower across his knees. He laughed, he cried, he listened to the shrieks of the dead and dying and the answering screeching of the Skree as they killed and were killed. It was all funny and sad because it was so perfectly Darwinian—survival of the fittest.

After he finished his cigarette and butted it out under his boot, he cast aside the flamethrower and the rest of his heavy, restrictive gear. Then he stood up, brushing off his legs.

"HEY!" he shouted. "YOU FORGET ONE! I'M OVER HERE, YOU STUPID MISERABLE FUCKING BUGS!"

Then he remembered they were deaf as stumps. So he emptied his pistol in the direction of a dozen or so nearest to him that were preying on downed soldiers, tearing them open and feeding on the soft, warm entrails of their bellies. He stomped his feet and that drew their attention.

Two of them started in his direction, one of them dragging broken, bullet-perforated wings behind it. They moved like praying mantises, stalking forward carefully, their mandibles scraping together, their huge multi-lensed eyes gleaming like pink diamonds. Their carapaces glistened like wet gray plastic. Now and again, their streamlined, segmented bodies paused, forelegs—raptorial legs—held up defensively before them, the thorn-like spines on them dripping with human blood.

Rafe waited for them.

Like a hero in an old war movie, he had two grenades left and he was going to use them, go out in a blaze of glory and take them with him. That was his plan. The only thing his worn, threadbare mind could come up with.

Then he heard the manic droning of wings and one of them swooped down and took him from behind. He dropped the grenades as he was taken up into the sky, writhing as he was pierced by the crushing, armored crab claws of its forelegs.

⚔

How long he dangled there like a fly in a spiderweb he did not know. He woke and he was trapped in a silken network of the sort he had burned early that morning. The web strands were wrapped around his legs and arms and he was held there, spreadeagled, his entire body aching. The webbing was elastic and strong and he was willing to bet it had the tensile strength of high carbon steel.

He was not going anywhere.

Lookit me now, Grassman. Aren't you glad you're dead?

There were huge clusters of eggs above and below him. When the larvae hatched, he knew, they would eat him slowly and patiently, enjoying every delicious strand of flesh until he was no more. It would be an agonizing, lingering death that would probably go on for days.

He could see a collection of burst eggs not that far away, the grubs having hatched. Tangled in the network near to them were several badly-used human skeletons. There was a woman whose face was eaten down to a bleeding skull. She had one eye left and it was rolling in its socket.

The network shook and Rafe saw a Skree moving up it, climbing it like an ant up a blade of grass. It went to the woman, tore at her with its mandibles, stripping off a strand of meat and casually chewing it with the most appalling pulping noise.

Then it cocked its head and stared in his direction.

It was coming.

Rafe fought and strained, knowing he still had a knife on his belt. But it was hopeless. He might as well have been chained. Yet he kept at it, the network shaking with his contortions.

Then the Skree was before him and he could smell its fishy odor and the stink of human blood on its breath as it breathed through the spiracles at its sides. It studied him with its neon-pink globular eyes for a few moments and then it seized him like a mantis seizes an aphid. It was a female and he cried out as she jabbed him in the belly with her stinger.

It was like getting stabbed by a red-hot poker.

But the pain eclipsed and then faded away as wave after wave of joyous serenity washed through him. His pleasure made colors blossom in his head—purple and blood-red, juicy orange and electric indigo. One after the other, each one making him moan with ecstasy. It was like riding the hot spike of one orgasm after another, each one leaving him breathless and quivering.

The Skree began to make a chittering sound, then a high keening like a cicada that became melodious in his mind, unlocking reward centers in his brain with silver keys. As she tore into him, mandibles peeling the flesh from his belly and groin, he shook with climax after climax.

And the music.

The Skree's song, it was so beautiful, so very beautiful as she fed upon him, cracking open his bones and sucking the marrow out.

THE SOFT ONES

"**C**an you still see him?" Natalia asked.

Yuri shook his head. Even with the binoculars, the captain was gone. He hovered there, seemingly, at the outer edge of his vision like a bulky ghost in his e-suit, then he was gone, swallowed by the fog.

"Try to establish contact."

Natalia went back inside the module and tried the radio. Again, nothing but static rising and falling, droning low and then rising to something almost like the scraping of fingernails on a blackboard before fading away.

She swallowed, unsettled by it. "Captain? Can you hear me? Are you there?"

But there was nothing but that constant noise that got under your skin if you listened to it for very long. Natalia killed the comm; she couldn't bear that sound. It was like high-pitched radio static that she had heard a thousand times as a test pilot and then as a cosmonaut, yet it was worse— like forks scratched over glass or metal, and something, oh yes, something like a distant screaming—

"Natalia?"

"Nothing," she said, her mouth very dry.

Nothing, nothing, and nothing, a voice said in her head and she hated it because it made her feel weak and frightened at her core.

She went back outside the descent module. Yuri stood there with the

76

cable in his hand, a spool of it at his feet. There was over two hundred feet of it. Enough, surely, for the captain to make a thorough reconnoiter of the area they had landed in. Maybe he would find some sign of civilization: a road, a trail, a fence, a utility pole.

That's what they were all hoping for. The worst-case scenario was that they had ditched in some tropical hellhole many, many miles from civilization. That brought a needling panic to Natalia, but she had to remember that the entire resources of Roscosmos were behind the search for them, as well as those of sovereign space agencies. All the world would be seeking them aggressively. After all, a space capsule with billions of rubles in technology could not simply disappear. Certainly not in this day and age.

"He's still moving," Yuri said, playing out more line.

Natalia said nothing.

She studied the cloying, yellow mist, the steaming bogs of black water, the little islands of rank growth. There seemed to be little else. At least, what the fog would let her see.

But it had to lift, didn't it? Even in the worst jungle in the world, the fog would dissipate. That made sense. It would have to. Then again, what did she know about jungles? She was born and raised in Mordovia. There were heavy forests in the Volga Upland, but nothing remotely tropical.

Maybe this would go on for weeks. Months, for all she knew. And that wouldn't do at all. They had food and water for one week, no more. Surely by then they would be found. The emergency beacon was sending out signals every five minutes. Somebody, somewhere should be picking them up.

Any minute now, helicopters will come swooping in. If not ours, then the Americans. Somebody.

She leaned back against the capsule, watching Yuri ten feet away playing out the line. How easy it would be to get lost out there in the flooded undergrowth and miasmic swamps. But that wouldn't happen. The EVA cable was nearly unbreakable.

Something splashed fifteen or twenty feet into the fog. It couldn't be the captain. Not yet. He was out there easily a hundred feet or more. Yuri looked at her in the dim light, his face yellow in the phosphorescent shine of the mist. His eyes were very wide.

She felt a chill ride up her spine. "It can't be him," she said.

"No." He pressed his lips tightly together. "I worry about the animal life. What if there are crocodiles out there?"

She hadn't considered that.

The splashing came again and they were both at high alert. It was no crocodile—the splashing sound seemed to be that of a bipedal creature, much like that of a man moving through a pond. It was there and then gone. They listened, but heard nothing else.

And that was yet another thing that bothered Natalia immensely: why was there no sound of animal life out there? No birds calling, no insects buzzing? Everything was flat and dead save for the sound of dripping water.

And why hasn't the sun risen? she asked herself. *We've been here over twenty-four hours and it's still that weird twilight. No brighter, no darker. Just the same.*

Yuri gasped and she was instantly at his side. "What?" she asked, her nerves frayed. "What is it?"

But he only stared off into the fog.

Then she saw it, too. She tried to blink it away, but it remained: what looked like three luminous yellow eyes watching them. Then a succession of flashing colors, pink and blue and orange. And then, as if a switch was thrown, the eyes winked out.

"What in the hell was that?" Yuri asked.

But Natalia had no idea. After a time, she began to breathe again.

⸎

Their landing zone was in Uzbekistan. It should have been a simple textbook reentry and touchdown. The captain had accomplished it five or six times before as had Natalia.

But something happened up there, something that was unknown and out of their experience. As they began their hypersonic descent, the initial drag parachute was deployed successfully to slow the module. And it was bare seconds afterward that something happened. There was a blinding flash of light and the module seemed to roll, then spin.

They all heard a whining, screeching sound, and Natalia was certain that the capsule was breaking up. During those few seconds of terror, all systems on the module went black.

Then whatever zone they had passed through was over, drogue and main chutes were deployed. The ship came down, crashing through the jungle to where it now sat, on a grassy wedge of land amid the endless, misty bogs.

They were glad to be down and safe, but systems were still acting oddly—the GPS was inoperable, the radio unable to pick up anything, and the onboard computer system had shut down and would not reinitiate.

And that's where the crew was now: concerned, uneasy, and worrying (at least in the back of their minds) that rescue would never come.

$$\text{\textsinterrobang}$$

Later, after a quick freeze-dried meal inside the module, the captain said, "I don't understand you two. You're acting like children. Of course there's animal life out there. We're in a tropical ecosystem, by God. Is it really that surprising that you heard splashing sounds and saw shining eyes? There's bound to be creatures everywhere out there."

"It was ... strange," Yuri said, refusing to give into the nervous tension that Natalia knew he was feeling.

"The jungle is a strange place. That's for certain," the captain told him. "When I was out there, I heard things moving around me in the fog, but not a one got close to me or acted aggressive in any way. There's really nothing to be concerned about."

Natalia listened to them banter back and forth about it. Yuri was unwilling to come out and say how disturbed he'd been, and the captain was hardheaded, practical to a fault. He had very little imagination and didn't seem to understand fear. In fact, he was the perfect cosmonaut, in that nothing could shake him. He took even the most desperate situations in stride.

Natalia sighed. "I would feel worlds better if we could at least pick up a radio signal. A transmission. Music. Voice. *Anything*. I don't like this. It sits on me wrong." Realizing the others were staring at her, she shrugged. "There. I've said it. This is all very weird and I don't like it."

The captain told her she was letting her nerves get the best of her. That her imagination was running wild. He reminded her of who and what she was. "Besides," he said, "they'll pick us up soon, and we'll receive a hero's welcome back home, and you'll laugh over your fears. Consider this an adventure. It's a tale you can tell to your grandchildren."

That made them feel better. There was something about the captain's calm, easy, fatherly manner that swept skeletons back in closets and monsters back under beds where they belonged. Yet it was short-lived. At least for Natalia. She was not one that gave much credence to her woman's intuition, but she had to admit (at least to herself) that it was on high alert. The captain could be as pragmatic and rational as he wanted, but she could not get past the fact that deep inside she was worried sick. Something about all this just *felt* wrong.

"I wish the sun would rise already," Yuri said.

The captain shrugged. "It's this damned fog."

Natalia knew at that moment that he was concerned, too. She could sense it, but there was no point in saying anything about it. The captain told them it had been a long day and they needed sleep.

So they reclined their shock couches and made ready for sleep. The captain, worn out from fighting through the water and muck and heavy vegetation, went out almost immediately. It was not so easy for Natalia. She lay there in the dark, unable to close her eyes. She studied the fog moving against the viewport in tendrils fine as lace. There was something eerie and unnatural about it.

Several times, she almost called out to Yuri across the module because she knew he wasn't sleeping either. But she was afraid of waking the captain and what he might say to her if she did. He was the commander and she had to follow not only his orders, but his suggestions. There was nothing to worry about, he claimed, so she had to believe that.

Somehow, she drifted off.

It took time, but she slept for an hour or two, and then she opened her eyes, feeling a low-ebbing panic inside her. Near to her, the captain still slept. She looked behind her couch and Yuri was not there.

Oh, he didn't go outside, did he? Not alone? Not in this awful place—

Then she saw he was standing in the back near the hatch. He'd opened the visor and he was staring out into the foggy world which had become their prison.

Quietly, so as not to disturb the captain, she climbed off her couch and joined Yuri. He didn't even hear her coming or sense her approach. When she reached out to touch his arm, he jumped and muttered a low cry.

"What's wrong?" she asked.

He stared at her with dazed, faraway eyes, his lips moving as if he was speaking, but no words came out.

"Yuri?"

He brushed a hand over his face. "I ... I was sleeping ... I think I was sleeping." He swallowed. "I heard a voice. I must have dreamed it. It sounded like my mother. It was calling me outside."

Natalia didn't like that at all. Yuri was acting like he was still in some sort of dream state. His eyes were huge and glassy. "I saw colors in the fog—alizarin crimson and phthalo blue and burnt sienna and cadmium orange ..."

This concerned her even more because those were colors of oil paint an artist might have on his or her palette and his mother had been a painter. Natalia had seen some of her landscapes. She was quite good.

"Yuri, you're not making sense."

He seemed to blank for a moment and then he blinked rapidly and rubbed his head. He looked at her sheepishly, as if he was going to explain that he had been sleepwalking or something, then he looked out the window.

"They're here," he said.

Natalia looked. The fog was thicker than ever, moving in dank sheets and rotting shrouds. And in it, she saw eyes shining, dozens and dozens of eyes. Whatever they belonged to, there were many and they were staring at the module. There was no mistaking it.

"They know we're here," Yuri said in a low, frightened voice, "and they're watching us."

☟

Natalia suffered through a restless sleep for hours after that. Yuri mentioned nothing of what happened in the night and she didn't care for that, because his talk of voices and colors and his near-hypnotic state combined with the watching eyes left her uneasy and apprehensive.

When he was outside, she told the captain all about it, but all it did was make him angry. "You dreamed it, Natalia. That's all. Quit reading things into completely innocent events. I'm surprised at you, acting like a scared little girl. I've always known you to be made of sterner stuff than this."

There was no point trying to talk to him. He had already decided she was losing her grip on reality and had written her off as a weak-willed woman. When they got back—*if, if, if*—it would go into her record, effectively ending her career. She knew it, but it didn't bother her because she had the worst feeling that they were going to die out here in this rank, decomposing armpit of creation.

You can see it in his eyes that he thinks that, too, she told herself. *Behind the tough, authoritative demeanor, he's scared silly. He's a little boy that needs his hand held in the dark.*

But she knew he'd never give into it or admit it. His job as commander was to lead, to support, to cool rankled, nervous dispositions, and, above all, to set an example for his crew. Once he admitted they were in a hopeless, awful situation, he would fall apart, and he and command would part ways.

When Natalia stepped outside to join him and Yuri, he was hooking the EVA cable to his suit again. "I'm going to move in a different direction until I find something," he announced.

"Or it finds you," Yuri said.

The captain turned on him quickly, rage kept at a low boil in his eyes. "I've had enough of the both of you! You're acting like children and I don't want to hear any more of your silly spook stories! You're cosmonauts! You represent the elite of the Russian Federation! Start acting like it!"

With that, he moved off, Yuri playing out the line as he went. Neither Yuri or Natalia spoke. They had been chastised by their commanding officer and it sealed their lips. At least, for a time.

"He shouldn't be going out there," Natalia finally said, listening to him splashing away as he navigated the islands of tangled undergrowth and the sucking, muddy pools between. "He's asking for trouble."

"He doesn't know what else to do."

That was true, Natalia knew. If he gave into the fears that haunted him, he was finished. He would keep following standard procedure even if it led to his death.

Hip deep in the black, steaming water, he moved forward carefully and cautiously. He climbed up onto a spit of land, using dangling vines from a large, bizarre tree. It had a thick, scaly trunk that looked like some impossible hybrid between a knotted banyan tree and a backyard weed growth like a trumpet creeper. It was not lost on her that it looked primordial somehow like something out of the Permian.

The mist moved around him, vaporous and swirling, and gradually his shape dimmed in its depths and was gone. They heard him moving out there, but he was lost to sight.

Yuri played line out. "He's a brave man. A very brave man. He's convinced himself that there are people out there, but there aren't. And that he can find his way home, but he can't." He shrugged. "I suppose we should just be grateful that the air is breathable here."

Natalia felt something dry up inside her. "What do you mean by that?"

"You know exactly what I mean."

↕

Leaning up against the module, Natalia studied the enclosing fog and the hole they had punched through the jungle when they came down. She could just see the parachute canopy shrouds and suspension lines dangling in the trees, the former looking like deflated balloons and the latter like a web spun by a drunken spider.

Although the air was warm and moist, she felt cold inside, her head full of frost.

There were things she wanted to say to Yuri, but she didn't dare voice her fears, as if doing so would make them real. Everything was wrong about this place and their position in it. She thought of the strange phenomenon they'd encountered upon reentry. It was bizarre and inexplicable. She'd never heard of such a thing before, and the anxiety she'd felt up there had only increased when they'd landed down here in this green hell.

The more she thought about it, the less she wanted to think about it.

She was thankful, oddly enough, for the thick fog, because without it, they just might be able to see clearly what sort of alien, otherworldly place this indeed was.

She watched Yuri with his line, how singularly fascinated he was with the simple task of letting it out. He was trying to lose himself in it, not to think or speculate about the terrible predicament they were in. At first, she thought he was being foolish and cowardly, now she realized how very wise he was. Avoidance was all they had now and he was practicing it with great determination.

She could hear the captain in the distance, moving ever deeper into the unknown. She could imagine how terrified he was, how he wanted to give up and in to his fears. But he wouldn't. No, he had to prove his point and keep his command from crumbling.

We're all deluding ourselves. That's the really scary part. None of us has the guts to admit where we are or how we've gotten here, and the absolute horror of our situation. We just wait and pretend, one ear constantly cocked for the sound of our rescuers that will never be coming.

She heard a splashing sound out there and Yuri flinched, going board-stiff for a moment. The sound was too close to be the captain and they both knew it. Whatever it was, it came from just within the fog. Another splash followed it along with a bubbling, gurgling sort of sound.

She thought she saw shadows moving in the mist. Yuri was looking in the same direction so maybe he thought he saw them, too. Regardless, he said nothing and would not look in her direction.

The line hung limp in his hands for a few moments and she could almost hear his heart pounding with dread, then it went tense again and he fed it out.

It went on that way for maybe another ten minutes. The captain was still moving, yes, but pausing frequently as if he saw something or heard something.

Then they heard him shout.

Then he began to scream.

⚲

The scream that echoed from the fog was filled with panic and terror. It came again and again, followed by an anguished shriek of pure agony. Natalia had only heard something like that once before when, as a child, a man had slowly been crushed beneath an overturned truck following a traffic accident. It was like that—a primal sound of pain, of the body and mind and soul shrieking into death.

Yet this was somehow worse.

The initial scream froze both of them completely. For a few precious seconds, they did not move. They didn't even breathe. And then it came again and they were in motion.

"Hurry!" Natalia cried, following the EVA line out into the mist. *"We have to get to him!"*

Yuri quickly fixed the line to the module so they could follow it back and then he was just behind her, gripping it, moving hand over hand into the primordial mist, rot, and dankness. The vegetation was thick and tangled. It would have been easy even without the line to trace the captain's progress through it. It was wet and soft. Broad, fanning leaves trembled like jelly when you brushed them. She had never seen anything like it. She kicked aside a warty sapling and it broke apart, splattering like pulp.

Crooked, thick-boled trees grew around them, dripping a warm ooze like sap. Vines dangled. Green-scummed pools of black, mucky water sucked at their boots and strange triangular leaves brushed their suits, leaving trails of globby nectar.

Sweat running down her face, Natalia said, "Go easy. We don't know how deep this water is."

They followed the line through a bog of brown, bubbling mud and greasy water and into a stand of oblong toadstools that were white as corpses. They stood six or seven feet in height, nodding and dripping. More pools on the other side. They passed through them into deep mires whose dark waters were afloat with blobby tubers blossoming pallid flowers. Then into the jungle again. A clearing and then the line ended. It looked as if it had been sheared by cable-cutters.

"This … this just can't be," Yuri said. "That line is strong enough to tow a train with."

Natalia did not argue with him; she knew the tensile strength of EVA cable. The line ended at a broad green stump. She kicked at it with her boot and it splattered into mush like the sapling. Everything here was soft and gelatinous, oozing and warm. Sickening. The entire landscape was disgusting to the human mind—soft like the belly of a rotting corpse.

Keeping an eye on the line as best they could, they made a gradual sweep through the surrounding foliage of wet bushes, things like swollen seedpods and clusters of pale tubers. The mist surrounded them, drifting about them, coiling around them like serpents.

Then: *"Here!"* Yuri called out. *"Oh, dear God, right here!"*

Natalia followed his voice through the shivering fog. Globs of sap dripped on her as she moved. She brushed them away with repulsion. They had the consistency of phlegm.

She saw Yuri's ghostly shape come out of the fog and slowly take on solidity. He was standing there with a crooked scowl on his face.

The captain was sprawled a few feet away. He was dead; there was no doubt of that. He was ghastly white and oddly shrunken, shriveled. So much so that his suit looked far too big for him, like a little boy dressed in his father's clothes. His eyes had sunk into his skull, his mouth was frozen in a scream. He was covered in some sort of slime. It glistened wetly on him as if he had been dipped in snot.

"What happened?" Yuri asked. "What could have happened?"

There were round welts on his face and throat and hands. Natalia figured his entire body was covered with them as if he had been attacked by a hundred hungry leeches. And that's how he looked: like he'd been *sucked* dry.

She pressed her boot against him and there was a curious sizzling sound. It was the slime. It was corrosive like some sort of digestive enzyme. But worse, his suit collapsed as if it was empty.

Hearing the sound of slow, stealthy movement in the jungle around them, and what might have been soft footfalls gradually edging in their direction, she said, "We need to get out of here."

"But the captain—"

She grabbed Yuri by the arm. *"Now,"* she said.

There was no discussion. They followed the line back to the module, moving much faster this time. Despite their excellent conditioning, they were both panting, out of breath, their faces wet with perspiration from fighting the terrain. But they were driven. Oh, yes, make no mistake of that. Driven by fear, the ultimate motivation. They would not stop until they reached the safety of the capsule.

The dark, oily waters of the mire sluiced around Natalia's hips as she waded through a bog, the stench of decay and putrescence so overpowering, she nearly gagged. It was as if everything in the world had come here to die, to mildew and rot into mulch and fetid drainage.

Things floated by—maybe they were just plants or vegetable bulbs and maybe they were things far worse—but she did not look at them any more than she listened to the bubbling and gurgling sounds around her. The mist moved in sheets, turning, twisting, recombining and blowing into her face like the hot, moldering breath of a corpse.

She kept turning, making sure Yuri was behind her. She heard sounds splashing in the water and stumbling through the jellied undergrowth, but that did not necessarily mean it was him.

They're here, a voice told her. *Very, very close and they're watching.*

As she pushed through a bamboo-like maze of leprous fronds, she caught sight of the terrible yellow eyes shining in the dark. There were many of them. Gripped with panic that seemed to squeeze her heart like a cold fist, she turned and Yuri was no longer with her. She saw his hazy form standing knee-deep in a muck hole, tentacles of mist wrapping him up like a mummy.

"Yuri!" she said, just above a whisper.

He turned in her direction. "The colors ... oh my God, the colors ... blue and purple and crimson and orange. They flash on and off, on and off."

Natalia went over to him and shook him roughly. *"Snap out of it! Do you hear me? We're in danger!"* she shouted in his face. *"WE HAVE TO GET THE HELL OUT OF HERE!"*

He was in that weird hypnotic state again. There was no time for that. She towed him behind her like a troublesome little boy. He mumbled things under his breath, but she would not listen, could not listen. She could not let anything weaken her or they would die horribly like the captain.

Off to her right, she caught a momentary glimpse of something blobby and shapeless submerging into a dark pool. She had to keep driving them forward. In another five minutes, they'd reach the ship and there they would be safe.

"Not far now," she said, one hand gripping the cable and the other holding Yuri's hand. "We're almost there."

And then Yuri let out a short grunting sound as if he had been hit by something. His hand was yanked from hers and she fell to one knee in the moist loam. She saw him yanked back into the fog with tremendous force.

He screamed with amazing volume that rose and rose in pitch and seemed to go forever, finally fragmenting and echoing through the misty jungle. By then, Natalia was on her feet, running toward him where she saw him writhing like a puppet on a string. She stepped into a sinkhole and plummeted face first to the ground, coming up quickly, pawing black mud from her face.

She saw Yuri scrambling and fighting with distorted, elfin forms that seemed to converge from every direction, awful shapes that moved with liquid noises and hissed like vultures. Then others dropped from the trees and together, they took him down like Cro-Magnon hunters felling a mastodon.

She could not see them clearly, but none of them could have been more than three or four feet in height.

"YURI!" she cried out.

She thought she heard his voice telling her to run but it was hard to say above the rustling and squishy sounds of the little horrors ringing him, trilling and hissing and squawking. By the time she got to her feet, she saw that they had some sort of dangling trunks or proboscises. They stood up, aimed at Yuri and ejected some thick, glistening fluid at him.

He screamed even louder and began to sizzle and sputter. And before he dropped, she saw him begin to dissolve, his flesh going molten and smoking. It ran from his skeleton like wax down the stem of a candle.

Then the little creatures buried him alive in their numbers and she heard an awful slurping noise.

Her stomach in her throat, she stumbled away, making it maybe ten feet before she gasped with a sound that echoed in her head. There was one of them right before her, a quivering, palpitating horror like a slime mold in the form of a little man. It was faceless and rippling.

As it aimed its proboscis at her, she reacted instantly and kicked out at it with everything she had and it exploded into a gushing pulp that sprayed the undergrowth. Another dropped from a tree like a leech and she punched out at it. Her fist went right through it as if it was made of some crawling, mucid jelly. When she withdrew her fist with a cry of revulsion, the creature literally collapsed into a pool of slime.

She fought her way through the jungle, splashing through bogs until she saw the shape of the module waiting there for her.

Oh God, oh thank God.

Then she was through the hatch and the airlock shut with a hissing sound. She sat on the floor, wet and filthy and shaking. After a time, she began to sob.

↕

Natalia waited behind her shock couch for some time, mumbling and touching her fingers to her face, smelling them again and again. She had washed her hand in sanitizer thoroughly, yet she was certain she could still smell the revolting little monster on it. It was a warm, foul smell that stank simultaneously like hot, spilled entrails and rotting plaster.

Rescue will come for you just like the captain said, and this nightmare will end, a voice of denial told her again and again as if she was a small child in need of comfort, which she pretty much was.

She tried not to think about how dark and scary it was outside and the little manlike things that haunted it, the sloshing sounds they made when they moved, the slurping sounds they made when they fed like pudding sucked through a straw. She refused to remember it or the way Yuri and the captain had died because it was how she would die.

Outside, they were gathered and she knew it. Through the viewport, there was a flashing of light as their chromatophores lit on and off with blazing, bright colors. They were trying in their own simple way to communicate with her.

She tried not to look at the colors because they made her feel weak inside at her core. They flashed not only through the viewport, but inside her head, each one creating a different emotion—fear, joy, loneliness, exuberance, depression, on and on, on and on.

Finally, she could take it no more.

Abandoning her safe place behind the couch, she took a flare pistol from the survival supplies. She would kill them. She would burn them up. Then the others would know to keep away and she could live and die in the solitude she now craved.

She opened the airlock.

Then the outer hatch.

She saw literally hundreds of yellow eyes shining in the dimness and hundreds more out in the fog. She was a wondrous curiosity to them and they flashed colors at her rapidly like deep-sea squids, like gasoline on water, changing, shining, blending into one another.

In the sky high above, the haze cleared long enough so that she could see one large moon followed by two others that seemed to be chasing it. Then the fog closed in again and she was grateful because she was so very, very far from home.

The little men of jelly made chittering noises and high-pitched squeals.

She fired a flare into the sky because she wanted to see them, to really see them. And in its cascading glow, she did. The flare lit up the fog in flickering red bands and they became very excited, rolling and bulging and flashing colors as if she was communicating.

But she saw them clearly.

They were bloated little monstrosities like shivering globs of glaucous, aspic jelly crudely formed into manlike shapes. They stood on stubby little legs and seemed to be composed chiefly of rolls and folds of gelatinous slime, offensive quivering sacks exuding mucilaginous ooze like something you wanted to step on or kill with a stick. They pulsated obscenely like beating hearts. They looked at her with tiny, beady yellow eyes set in triangular arrangements in blubbery, seamed, ovoid heads. Their suckering mouths extended into blunt proboscises and then were sucked back into puckering holes.

They were the most disgusting things she had ever seen like gray spiders swollen to bursting from their feedings. Yet she didn't hate them, because they were something that could only exist on this wet, pulpy world.

The soft ones.

"What do you want from me?" she asked, the tears rolling down her face.

But she knew. They told her with the colors because it was the only way they could communicate with something as exotic and alien as she was. Dropping the flare pistol, she went down among them and they surrounded her like children, all of them pressing in with their slimy, jiggling flesh and pulpous bodies. More came all the time until they covered her and she sank in their fungous, gelatinous depths.

"Oh," she muttered.

They were so warm and there was comfort in their greasy bodies. And when their proboscises jabbed into her like dozens of lovers entering her at the same time, she went to sleep, becoming an oozing puddle that they absorbed instantly, gratefully.

MICE

(ᓂᓇᐤ)

1

The ironic thing was, the old woman was really nice.

That's what completely blew Charlie away. *She was so fucking nice.* When he showed up at her door with the census book and told her who he was, he waited for the usual reaction. He'd been canvassing the streets for something like three weeks by that point and it was always the same—either they slammed the door in his face or looked absolutely pained like he was not just asking a few simple questions but begging for an extra kidney.

But the old woman was different.

Right away, Charlie saw that. She smiled kindly, invited him in, commented on how sore his feet must have been with all the walking and had him sit in a comfortable chair. She said her name was Dorothy Ess and gave him a tall glass of iced tea and a slice of fresh-baked bread with strawberry jam on it that she had canned herself.

"I have questions I need to ask you," he said.

"Ah, what's the hurry? Let's chat a bit. Can I get you more iced tea?"

"Sure. I think it's the best I've ever had."

So they whiled away the hour, chatting. The chair was so comfortable he began getting very sleepy.

"Have you ever thought," she asked, "about the vast distances between the stars and just how long it might take to cross them?"

He could barely keep his eyes open. He told her he'd never thought about it.

She nodded, studying him very carefully. Her eyes were very large and glassy like those of a frog. "I do a job much like yours, Charlie. Did you know that? Often, I go house to house, too. But always at night."

"Why ... why at night?"

"Because that's when *we* always come," she told him, her face mutating into something alien and invidious.

But by then, he was too far gone. He slipped away into darkness and his life was never the same again after that.

2

When he opened his eyes, a group of people were circled around him, staring at him as if ... well, as if they'd been *waiting* for him. He'd never seen them before in his life—a thin, twitchy little guy in specs, a beefy middle-aged man with a hard face, a teenage goth girl with black lipstick and stark eyeliner, an attractive Latina woman with glazed eyes, and an old man with a white chiseled beard.

"He's coming around now," the latter said. "Give him some room to breathe."

"How many more, Soapy? How many more?" the twitchy guy said to the old man. He wore a blue work shirt with "Jibby" sewn onto the pocket.

Charlie licked his lips, tried to speak but his throat was so dry it felt sandpapered. "Where...," he managed, "am I?"

"You find out, let us know," Jibby muttered.

"Just take it easy," Soapy said. "You'll come out of it."

Charlie kept trying to swallow, but it was nearly impossible. He felt confused, his limbs rubbery. It was like coming out of a dream or heavy sedation. His hands were tingling. The most troubling thing of all was that he could see black iron bars to all sides. He and the others were in a cage, a goddamn animal cage. It looked to be about twenty feet wide, maybe thirty in length.

He blinked his eyes again and again, but it did not go away.

A single lightbulb dangled from a cord high overhead, throwing a circle of yellow light. Beyond its illumination, the shadows bunched thickly and grotesquely.

You're in some very fucked-up nightmare, he told himself. *Just wait it out. In ten minutes or so, you'll wake and you'll be in your bed shaking your head at what a doozy of a bad dream this all was. It'll pass. You'll see. It'll pass.*

But it wasn't passing and the ugly reality of the cage was not fading away, it was solidifying. He looked around at the others and most of them eyed him sympathetically, or at least, he thought as much. The guy with the hard face watched him, but there was no real compassion to his demeanor. It would have looked out of place with his steely gray eyes and smirking mouth.

"How are you feeling?" Soapy asked him.

The thing was, Charlie didn't know any more than he knew why he was here or what this goddamn place was. Looking around at the others and the barely-concealed dread on their faces, a feeling of gnawing terror filled his guts and spread out into his chest. Things were coming back: the old woman, the cold iced tea, how he began to feel drowsy as she talked. And now this. It was like closing your eyes and opening them in a morgue, finding yourself stretched out on a stainless-steel table, the glaring fluorescents overhead, the gleaming green tiles on the walls, the smell of antiseptics that just barely covered a dark, noisome stink beneath.

He made himself stop right there. He had to sort this out. Make sense of things. He had been drugged and brought to this place. But why? What the hell was it all about?

"Looks like he's ready to freak," the girl said.

"No, I'm okay," he told her.

Jibby laughed with a shrill, nervous sound. "Well, you must be the only one then."

"Stop it," Soapy told him.

Charlie sat up, brushing aside hands that tried to help him. He felt dizzy for a moment, but it passed. He looked at the others one by one, taking in the desperation on their faces.

"Where in the hell are we?" was all he could think of saying.

And their eyes told him they had no earthly idea.

3

Over the next twenty minutes, everyone was introduced. Besides Soapy and Jibby, there was Friske (the hard guy), Yee (the teenage girl), and Tamar (the pretty Latina lady). They were all friendly enough in their own way, though Friske—in keeping with his working-class tough guy routine— gave Charlie a look that said, *yeah, we're in the shit, kid, and you ain't got the balls to see it through.* But, of course, that was only Charlie's subjective impression. Maybe Friske was a real sweetheart, but his attitude was that of a grizzled old sergeant that had seen too much action (and was a little soft in the head because of it).

It seemed that for the longest time, they talked of everything but the predicament they were in. Everyone rambled nonstop about their lives and what they did and where they came from in high, squeaking voices, making every attempt to psychologically defuse the situation and the overwhelming fright that lived inside them. Yee was a graphics and design student in her first year at Eastern. Jibby was a meter reader. Tamar was an Avon rep. Friske was a plumbing and heating contractor. Soapy was a retired middle school physical science teacher.

There seemed to be no connection between any of them, save they were from the same city and had visited the same neighborhood, the same house.

Finally, Soapy said, "Not much of this makes a lick of sense. The only correlation I see is the old lady." He stroked his beard. "I'm a volunteer for Meals-on-Wheels. I deliver lunches to the elderly, the indigent, and the handicapped. It's a pleasant way to pass my afternoons and it makes me feel good to do things for those in need. Truth be told, since my wife, Regina, passed, I badly need the distraction. I brought a meal to 1061

Birch—Salisbury steak, potatoes, and beans. The old woman said her name was Doris Enderby. She was very nice. We chatted, she offered me iced tea. It was very good."

Friske shook his head. "I went to 1061, too. I was quoting a new hot-water boiler to the old lady. But her name was Daniella Ellson. I had the iced tea, too."

"No," Jibby said. "Diana Erickson. I drank the iced tea."

"Me, too," Charlie told them. "I'm a census taker. But her name was Dorothy Ess."

Soapy thought it through carefully. "Same person, different names. How about you, Tamar?"

She looked uncomfortable, perhaps more so than the others. Her big dark eyes were wet and shining. She chewed her lower lip. "Darlene Ertman. She made an appointment. I went over there to give her the spiel. I drank the iced tea as well."

Yee chuckled. "So we all drank the Kool-Aid, people."

Jibby shook his head. "It wasn't Kool-Aid; it was iced tea," he said, missing the reference.

"I was canvassing the area," Yee said before she was asked, "doing a survey." She shrugged. "Hey, dude, it paid in cash. Why not? Lady said her name was Dixie Ellerby. The iced tea was really good."

Charlie sighed. "Same lady, same initials, different name. Like it's some kind of joke."

"Either way, she got us all," Soapy pointed out. "The question is *why?*"

Nobody bothered fielding that one, because, other than them being in the cage together, there was nothing to go on.

"That old lady must be some kind of psychopath like you see on TV," Jibby suggested. "She brought us here to do something awful to us. There can't be any other reason."

Tamar was trembling, the others wide-eyed save for Yee, who rolled hers.

"Jibby, please. That won't get us anywhere," Soapy said.

And he was right, absolutely right, but that didn't stop imaginations from running wild. You could practically hear the terrible whirring of mental gears as the very idea rolled through minds, creating the worst possible scenarios of torture and defilement.

Jibby shrugged. "I'm just saying, is all. I read a horror comic when I was a kid where this weird old guy kept people in a cage and slowly starved them to death until they—"

"All right, shut up with that shit," Friske said, his eyes huge and intense. His hackles were up and he looked like he was ready to punch Jibby right in the face. "I tell you one thing—anybody comes into this cage and I'll fucking tear them apart. I'm getting out, one way or another."

"Let's just try and be calm and reasonable," Soapy said in a very sedate, tranquil voice as if he was trying to talk down a mad dog from biting him.

"Yeah, we'll see."

Friske began to slowly circle around all of them like an animal in a cage, which, Charlie knew, he pretty much was.

Tamar looked close to tears. "I just want to get out of here. I want to go home. My cat's there. I have to feed her."

"We'll get out. We just have to be patient," Charlie said, because he couldn't think of anything else to say.

Jibby laughed with a snarling sort of sound. "Listen to you sling the bullshit. A month from now you'll be foaming at the jaws like a wolf."

Friske advanced on him. "I warned you," he said.

Soapy stepped between them. "We need to settle down and think."

Yee shook her head. "I like this. This is great. A couple hours and we're ready to tear out each other's throats. Human behavior at its finest."

Friske gave her a hard look, then seemed to settle down. He slowed his breathing and slowly licked his lips. "Well, we can't all just drop off the face of the Earth without somebody noticing. My boss knows where I went. If I don't come back, he'll be asking questions."

Tamar brightened. "That's right. My boss, Peggy, knows the address of where I went. If I don't call her, she'll call the police. There's probably five messages from her on my phone now."

"Which is why the old lady took all our phones," Jibby said.

"Doesn't matter," Soapy told him. "We all went to the same place and when we don't come back or go home, red flags will go up and the police will be visiting the old lady and this will get sorted out."

Everyone seemed to relax at the idea. It was only a matter of time. They just had to wait for the wheels to turn in their favor. It was probably happening right now. When the police received missing persons reports on six people last seen at a particular address, things would happen.

Charlie swallowed down his fear, which continued to rise. He had the worst feeling that the above would not be enough, that what was happening to them was not some simple abduction but part of some much larger and darker scenario. It was just a feeling. But one he could not dismiss. Through the years, he'd had lots of them and they were invariably right.

The cops will get called in. No doubt of that, he thought. They'll knock at the door of 1061 Birch and when nobody answers, they'll get a warrant and break the door down. But inside, they won't find us or the old lady—just an old, empty house full of dust and cobwebs. In the kitchen, they might find an empty iced tea pitcher and glasses with summer flies crawling over them. But that's all. The house will be like the Mary Celeste, *empty and uneasy with ghosting memories. They might find a cup of coffee on the table, half-drained and possibly still warm, a cigarette burned down to gray ash in an ashtray. But no people. The cops will search, but they'll never find us. They won't know where to look—*

He stopped that line of thought because even though he knew it was true in many ways (or at least he *felt* that it was), he also knew it would paralyze him with fear to let his imagination run wild.

"Something on your mind, Charlie?" Soapy asked.

"No. Nothing at all."

4

Although no one liked the idea of venturing beyond the circle of light, they paced off the cage. That was, Charlie, Friske, Yee, and Soapy did; Tamar and Jibby refused to leave the comfort of the lightbulb. It was perhaps the only thing that was keeping them sane.

Charlie's guess at the size of the cage was about right.

The further they got from the circle of light, the deeper and more menacing the shadows became. But they did find a door to their cage at the far end. It was locked, of course, but that didn't stop Friske from trying to force it by battering his bulk into it again and again. Soapy tried to stop him, but he shoved him away.

Finally, red-faced, shaking, white foam speckling his lips, he gripped the bars with his big hands and shouted: "GODDAMMIT, LET US OUT! WHAT KIND OF FUCKING GAME IS THIS? LET US THE HELL OUT ALREADY!"

That didn't bring any results either.

Charlie stood with Yee, feeling very helpless. He was unnerved at how Friske's voice echoed out endlessly as if the cage was sitting in the center of some gigantic amphitheater.

After Friske had slunk back to the others, he was still standing there with Yee and Soapy.

She had her hands on the bars, peering through them. "It's so dark out there," she said. "Have you ever seen anything so dark?"

Charlie had noticed it, too. Not just dark, but black. A blackness of the sort that did not seem normal. The complete absence of any light, the way it might be in deepest space, in the ebon gulfs between the stars themselves. It was frightening.

Soapy left them there. Even his rational mind didn't want to take that one on or what it might suggest.

Yee and Charlie went over to the door, standing there, thinking. Charlie figured that sooner or later, their jailer would have to show. They would need water, food, the basic necessities of survival … unless Jibby was right and their captor wanted to reduce them to animals starving in their own waste like monkeys in the straw.

"How long do you think it'll take before the police show?" Yee asked.

"Soon, I would guess."

She smiled sardonically at him. "You don't really believe that at all."

He just shrugged.

She was way too perceptive for her own good. She was a pretty girl with her long black hair and Asian eyes, gifts from her parents, no doubt. She was smart and she was anything but naïve. He knew that, under different circumstances, he would have been attracted to her.

"Listen to them," she said. "God."

Back at the light, Friske and Jibby were arguing and snapping at one another while Soapy tried to calm them and Tamar pulled deeper into her shell. Something she kept handy at all times, Charlie had noticed, like a fiddler crab. It was getting heated. Friske was threatening Jibby, who was ranting and raving that it was all some kind of experiment designed to break them down one by one until they were slavering animals ready to kill each other for food.

"Oh boy," Yee said. "It begins."

"What if the light goes out, Mr. Tough Guy?" Jibby said. "How long you think you're going to be sane in the dark?"

"I'm warning you."

But Jibby, who was apparently already cracking up, laughed at him. He pulled his belt off and, jumping up as high as he could, used it to swat at the light ten feet up. He hit it, but thankfully it did not break. Instead, it swung back and forth on its cord, making shadows leap around them, creating an atmosphere that was that much more threatening and eerie.

"Stop it!" Soapy cried.

Too late. Friske punched Jibby in the face and dropped him. It was pandemonium. Yee had sidled up closer to Charlie. The swinging light illuminated what was beyond the bars which was ... nothing. He couldn't even be sure there was a floor out there, such was the degree of blackness. The cage might have been suspended in dead space, something which disturbed him greatly.

As the light swung back, it briefly—very briefly—lit up what was outside the door which looked to be another cage of sorts. That was weird enough, but the light fell upon something that made his skin crawl: a sort of coiled appendage that was gray, hairless, and segmented like the tail of a rat. He only saw it for a second, but it was thick around as his arm, tapering to a point. Whatever it belonged to yanked it back as the light touched it.

Charlie thought he saw a momentary glimpse of a huge, hulking shape.

His heart drummed in his chest and cold sweat broke out on his brow. He heard the creature move off with a dry, slithering sort of sound like a dozen snakes in motion.

Yee was gripping his arm by then, her entire body shaking. "Did you see that?" she asked in a weak, airless voice. "Tell me you saw that."

"Yes," he managed.

Not only had he seen it and heard it, he could now smell it—a wet, dank odor like things rotting beneath a log that was quickly overpowered by a pungent, nose-reaming phosphine stink. There, then gone.

A monster, a small voice said in the back of his head. *There's another cage and there's a monster in it, a mutation, something unnatural and horrible.*

Yee was holding his hand in a death-grip. They were both trembling.

"Oh, Charlie, what the hell was that?"

"I don't know. Something alive."

They backed away toward the others. The arguing had died down now and Friske was sitting on his haunches, rocking back and forth, muttering, *"I warned him, I goddamn well warned him,"* and Jibby sat across from him at the very outer edge of the light (that was no longer swinging). There was blood on his mouth and murder in his eyes. If he had a knife or a gun, Charlie figured, he would have killed Friske.

Tamar had buried her face in her hands and Soapy just looked angry and frustrated.

Charlie sat down next to Yee.

"Are we going to tell them?" she whispered.

He shook his head. "Not yet."

He needed time to process this in a reasonable frame of mind. What did it mean? What did any of it really mean? There were no monsters in the real world. He knew that. He believed that. Yet he had seen that thing—or, at least, part of it—and he knew it was not some trick, some rubber tentacle or such fairground bullshit. It had been real and with the smell that came off it and the sounds it made, he could not even conceive of what it might have been.

The only thing he knew for sure was that only the door kept it from them.

By this point, he told himself, *you know you're not just locked up in somebody's basement. This entire thing is bigger than that. Far worse than that. Wherever this place is, it's not part of the real world as you know it. You better accept that before it's too late.*

Yee was still holding onto him or maybe he was holding onto her. She leaned in like she was going to kiss him and whispered, "They need to know."

"They won't believe us and you know it. Besides, they're already coming apart at the seams."

Tamar was staring at them. So was Soapy.

"What are you two whispering about?" he asked.

Charlie swallowed. "Just speculating, I guess. Wondering when our jailer is going to show."

Soapy looked like he had a few ideas about that. He opened his mouth to voice them, but he never got the chance.

5

There was a sudden explosion of noise that was like thunder in the monolithic silence of the cage: a shrill whining like a whistling tea kettle or a pressure leak in a boiler. It was loud enough to blow out eardrums. It rang out and out with that high-pitched hissing sound and Charlie was certain he could feel it thrumming along his bones.

After about twenty seconds, it cut out, leaving everyone woozy and disoriented. Tamar was on the floor. She tried to sit up and vomited out a watery gruel. Soapy had a hand on her shoulder to comfort her.

"What the hell was that?" Yee asked, tears rolling from her eyes.

Charlie shook his head. His eyes were watering, too, his ears ringing incessantly. The molars in his jaws seemed to ache as if the fillings in them had suddenly expanded. It had been like standing next to a cranked Marshal amp while Jimmy Page knocked out the mother of all power chords.

The silence that followed was gigantic and encompassing. It seemed to have volume and weight that bore down on them, threatening to crush them like bugs. Friske looked shell-shocked and Jibby was still clutching his head, mouth agape in a silent scream as if it was still going on.

"Our jailer," Soapy said.

Jibby looked at him with eyes that were red with burst blood vessels. "And now things will get ugly," he said.

Nobody disagreed with him.

There was a crackling sound that seemed to come from above the cage, followed by a momentary peal of feedback. Then a voice began to speak: *"I see that I have your attention, babies,"* it said. *"That is good. That is as it should be. Now we can begin. Now we can get down with it."*

The voice was female and sounded African-American with a sultry, seductive undertone like a woman from a 1970s Blaxploitation movie. Charlie nearly giggled at the incongruity of it all.

What the hell was this about?

"Who are you?" Soapy asked.

"I am the controller, Subject One."

"Subject? Now wait a minute here—"

The voice interrupted: *"There are certain ground rules which all subjects must obey, babies. Food will be offered and you will eat it. Clean water will be supplied and you will drink it. Subjects will sleep at lights out. It is important that you remain healthy. Failure to follow these rules will result in punishment, dire punishment. Things will get heavy. Do you copy that, babies?"*

"Is this some kind of joke?" Friske said.

"You hear me laughing, Subject Two?" The voice cleared its throat. *"So*

let's stay on the same page here. Listen up. Do me a solid and follow the rules, babies. It's the only way. Lessen you want to tangle with the man and you don't want that, brothers and sisters. Can you dig it?"

Friske began shouting and swearing, just beside himself with it all. "YOU LET US OUT OF HERE! THIS HAS FUCKING GONE FAR ENOUGH! DO YOU HEAR ME? LET US THE FUCK OUT OF HERE!"

He was raging, but inside, Charlie figured, he was just as scared as they all were. This was just how he externalized it. He kept at it until he was short of breath, wound down like a toy. Then he just slowly sank to the floor, his face twisted up in a mask of pure frustration and pure terror.

"I can't let you out, babies, because there's just nowhere for you to go," the voice said. There was a cruel, inhuman tone to it. Not a scrap of sympathy in it. *"No, babies, there's just no way. We're already over a light year out from your home system."*

Nobody spoke for a moment as that settled in. What she said was clearly impossible, it was science-fiction shit. That's what Charlie told himself and he was pretty sure the others were telling themselves the same damn thing.

"Light years?" Jibby said. "Like out in space? That's crazy. It's a head game. That's all it is. She's fucking with us. Light years, my ass."

The voice laughed with a low, throaty sound. *"Don't be such a drag, Subject Three. You're bringing me down. See, we already cut out. We're swinging out to what your people call the constellation of Eridanus. Specifically, Gamma Eridani, whose fourth planet is called Metaluria. Can you dig it? Such sights your sheltered little Terran minds are going to see! It's gonna be out of sight because Metaluria, that's where it's at."*

"We've been abducted," Tamar said.

"Right on, baby, right on," said the voice.

Finally, Friske and Jibby were on the same page. They started by arguing about the impossibility of such a thing and it looked like it would escalate into violence again, but it didn't. They had come to an understanding:

this entire situation was ripe bullshit and anyone who bought into what that woman said were not only naïve imbeciles, but full-blown mental defectives.

Soapy was thinking deeply on what she had said. "Gamma Eridani is at least two hundred light years away. It would take thousands of years to get there. Hell, millions."

"With a standard drive, baby, with a standard drive. But this wagon can bend space-time. We'll reach our destination in approximately one month, give or take."

"How long is this nonsense going to go on?" Friske asked, very calm now because he had everything figured out and it gave him confidence. "No, really, enough games here. Cut the shit. I don't accept flying saucers and little green fucking men."

Jibby grunted his assent.

"Sorry to hear that, Subject Two. Real, real sorry."

Tamar was sobbing. She was not a strong person; that much was obvious. She was an attractive lady, maybe missing *beautiful* by scant inches. Chances were, Charlie figured, she'd gotten along on her looks her entire life. They were the armor she wore to conceal the numerous psychological scars and traumas that festered beneath her skin. He felt a need to put a hand on her shoulder and tell her everything would be all right. But he had the feeling she would flinch, that she did not like to be touched.

"All right, all right," Soapy said. "Let's keep our heads here."

"You tell 'em, brother. You're one cool head."

"You're right, you're right," Jibby said with more than a little sarcasm. "Let's just pretend things are fine and fucking dandy. Or, better yet, let's go to pieces like our uppity, entitled Avon lady."

Tamar looked at him, then buried her head again.

"Leave her alone, asshole," Yee snapped at him.

"What we need to do here," Soapy said, "is just calm down and think. Getting emotional and pissy won't help anything."

"Yeah, okay, old man," Jibby said, his voice dripping with contempt.

"Enough rapping, babies. Time to crash. Sleep tight and don't let the bed bugs bite."

Then the lights went off.

6

It shut down Friske and Jibby like nothing else could. Charlie and Yee pressed closer together. He could hear her breathing with short, sharp gasps. She was terrified and so was he. The darkness was exactly like that outside of the cage: completely seamless and impenetrable. Not so much as a pencil beam of light broke it up. It was bad enough for the others, but for Yee and him, it was far worse. They knew there was something awful in the next cage, something perfectly alien, and only the bars of the door kept it from creeping out into the dark among them.

"I told you they'd turn the lights out," Jibby said. His voice was smug, yet filled with underlying terror.

"What's the point of this? What can possibly be the fucking point?" Friske asked.

Soapy sighed. "It may be to teach us a lesson. Our captors might be flexing their muscles to show us how strong they are and how weak we are."

Jibby laughed with a short, grunting sound. "It's a game. Just a sick game."

But Charlie figured Soapy was right: they were being punished. Maybe if they just quit arguing for a while the lights might go back on. But he didn't see that happening.

Nobody spoke for a time and then out of the darkness there came a perfectly awful slithering sound, a soft and sliding noise like an especially large snake was moving in their direction. Charlie's breath locked in his throat. He felt helpless, perfectly helpless. Inside, he was a little kid again and the sound came from beneath the bed or from behind a closet door that had not been shut properly.

"What the hell was that?" Jibby whispered.

No one dared answer. Then it came again, not just that dragging, coiling sound, but an investigative noise of something touching the bars, brushing against them in the direction of the door, as if it was trying to find its way in.

Charlie and Yee were shaking. The cage had filled with that rank, fetid odor and that overpowering chemical reek.

"Do you smell that?" Soapy said.

"Part of the game," Jibby maintained.

"It's not a game, baby. You better understand that right now. This is deadly serious ... you dig?" the voice said, echoing through the cage. *"We have a real long way to go and we won't be there for a long while yet. The real bummer is that some of you won't survive the trip. It's a downer for sure. So go to sleep on that, babies. We'll chat again in the morning."*

Though there were things they were all thinking—dark and dire things—nobody said a word. They were completely at the mercy of the voice and they knew it.

It was a long night, or period of darkness, or whatever it was. Nobody slept much. Charlie and Yee tried, but it was hard to relax with thoughts of what was in the next cage. They could hear Friske whispering under his breath from time to time and Jibby grumbling. Both Soapy and Tamar were silent.

The good thing was there were no more sounds from the next cage and that weird smell had died away.

Even though there were no pillows or mattresses, everyone did sleep eventually. Slept or were *put* to sleep.

7

In what passed for morning in the cage, the light was back on. It wasn't much, but it was something. At least they could see again. Everyone woke up to it, groggy and disoriented, backs stiff from sleeping on the floor.

"If they want me to be a good, happy animal, they better give me a piece of carpet or something," Jibby said. "I'm too old to sleep on the floor."

There were a few grumbled assents to that.

They all stood around, stretching out their muscles, but not really speaking because there really wasn't much to say by that point. Charlie watched them furtively. He didn't think their spirit at large was broken quite yet, but it was coming. There would come a time, and not so far away, when not even Soapy's pragmatism could hold them together.

He kept thinking about what the voice had said—*The real bummer is that some of you won't survive the trip*—and it disturbed him to no end. What did that mean exactly? And why were they referred to as *subjects?* Maybe he really didn't want to know.

Tamar had pulled away from the others and was sitting with her back against the bars, humming incessantly with her face held in her hands. She was in a bad way and Charlie knew it. Very close to a full-blown nervous breakdown, and it wouldn't take much to put her over the edge.

"Why doesn't she stop that?" Jibby said, a nervous tic making the corner of his mouth jump.

Friske stood with him. "Yeah, it's getting on my nerves."

"She's been through a lot, as we all have," Soapy told them. "Let her get her comfort anyway she can."

"Fuck that," Jibby snapped.

Where (or how far) it would have gone from there was anyone's guess because both men were looking for a target to take their fears and frustrations out on, but Yee defused it by saying, "Look!"

Charlie saw it and thought he was hallucinating: in the corner there was a curtained cubicle. They all went over there and discovered it was a toilet and a sink. Sanitation had been taken care of. Funny, but he knew it hadn't been there a few minutes before. He remembered casting an eye in that direction.

Not there, he thought. *Then there. Just like magic.*

But no one was interested in looking a gift horse in its proverbial mouth, so they accepted it. Gratefully, they emptied their overflowing bladders one after the other.

When it was Charlie's turn, he remembered that just before Yee called their attention to the cubicle, he'd felt an odd sort of tingling along his forearms and at the back of his neck. Interesting.

The next revelation followed in short order.

Another light, this one at the far end of the cell, came on, revealing a table set with food and drinks. No one hesitated. There were pitchers of ice-cold orange juice and milk, urns of hot coffee and tea. Platters of scrambled eggs and sausages, muffins and Danishes, oranges and apples. There was no disguising the fact that all food groups essential to human health and wellbeing were represented.

"Good morning, babies," came the voice from the darkness. *"I see you're all refreshed and ready to greet the new day. More power to you. That is as it should be. Eat and drink. Enjoy yourself."*

And was it Charlie's imagination or was there an undercurrent to her voice? *Enjoy yourself… while you still can.* Yee gave him a worried look and he was certain that she picked up on it, too. Soapy took a cup of tea over to Tamar, who seemed to have no interest in it. After some time and a lot of soothing words, he got her to drink some and finally even eat a muffin. It had reached the point where she would need to be mothered.

Everyone, save Tamar, ate a very hearty breakfast. Charlie figured it wasn't so much out of hunger, but out of the need for comfort and something to pass the time with. A welcome distraction from worrying over their unknown and quite possibly perilous future.

He sat cross-legged with Yee and ate. Neither said much. The food was very good. They ate as much as they wanted and the amazing thing was, no matter how much orange juice they drank, the pitcher never emptied and the juice remained ice-cold, the coffee never cooled.

But eventually, as fat and happy as they could hope to be, breakfast was over. Then it was time for ugly reality to insinuate itself once again.'

"What do you think?" Yee asked him.

"About?"

"About all this and particularly what she said last night about that planet, Metaluria." She lowered her voice. "And how some of us might not survive the trip."

He shook his head. "I don't know."

"I wish she'd just tell us what they want from us and why they abducted us. I mean, what are they going to do to us when we get to the planet?"

These were all the things Charlie had been asking himself and he didn't like any of the answers he came up with. "Whatever it is, they apparently want us healthy."

"That makes me think we'll be used as lab rats. *Subjects,* as she says, for something awful."

He had thought of that one, of course. His mind had not missed the opportunity to torment him with images of alien laboratories, experimental surgeries, and dissections. He stared long and hard into Yee's dark eyes. She was pretty and he wished they were alone. It was his hormones talking and he knew it, but he had a strong feeling she was thinking the very same thing. Desperate situations, common trauma, would often bring people together in the strangest ways. Besides, it would have been something to do to kill the oppressive, endless boredom. Thinking that, he smiled, because it reminded him of his former girlfriend, Jael. She had a way of saying very off-the-wall kind of things like, *I'm bored, Charlie. Want to have sex?*

He smiled and chuckled at the memory.

"What?" Yee asked, a playful smile on her mouth as if she had read his mind. "What is it?"

He was going to lie, then decided there was no point. The cage was all about honesty, now wasn't it? He told Yee and she laughed. She was not miffed or offended in the least.

"Let's take a walk around our cage," she said.

They did, around and around and around again. No one even asked them what they were doing. Everyone was sucked into their own little worlds. Soapy sat with Tamar, speaking softly and gently to her, trying to pull her out of her shell. Friske and Jibby stared into space, each nurturing their private frustrations and resentments.

Charlie and Yee enjoyed each other's company. Had it not been for the situation, it would have been nice, it would have been fun. But even this slight diversion had to come to an end and it did.

In the worst possible way.

8

It was the noise again.

That same high-pitched shrilling that sounded even worse this time like a screeching fire whistle. It dropped all of them to their knees with its single sustained note that seemed to get louder by the second until they actually cried out from it.

Then, like last time, when they were all sufficiently debilitated, it cut out, leaving them on the floor, gasping and nauseous, tears streaming from their eyes. It was several minutes before their hearing returned. No one threw up this time, but it was close. Very close.

"What the hell was the point of that?" Friske said, clenching his teeth. *"Did you hear me? I said what was the fucking point of that?"*

For a time, there was only silence. Then, a sudden peal like feedback and the voice began to speak. *"Well, brothers and sisters, the time has come for one of you to move, groove, and get down with it! Are you reading me, babies? The time has come for one of you to make a great sacrifice! Now, cats, understand that this isn't my doing … it's the will of the man. Things are about to get very real and very ugly for one of you."*

Everyone looked at one another. What the hell was this about?

Yee and Charlie held hands; it was an automatic thing. Soapy stood with Tamar, holding her up like she was little better than a doll. Jibby and Friske looked up into the darkness above like a couple stunned frogs waiting to be netted. They had both lost their cocky, contrary attitudes and looked plain scared.

"What is it you want?" Soapy finally asked.

The voice uttered a brief, husky chuckle. *"That's what I like about you, Subject One. Righteous to the core."* The voice chuckled one more time, then it said, *"Now are you ready, babies? Then let's get on with it. Subject Three, please step forward."*

Everyone knew who that was. The blood drained from Jibby's face. He looked to Soapy as if he could straighten it all out.

"What do you want with him?" Soapy asked.

More feedback. *"Subject One, you will not interfere with protocol. Now, Subject Three, step forward. You wanted out of the cage and this is how you get out, baby. Step forward before you piss off the man."*

A heavy silence hung in the air. Nobody knew what to say, what to think, how to feel. None of them believed for a moment that he was being released. Not here, in deepest space.

"Don't do it," Charlie told him.

"No interference," the voice said and this time there was an edge to it that was anything but playful.

Jibby was so scared it looked as if he might pass right out. His entire body was shaking with tremors that seemed to pass through him in waves.

"Step forward, Subject Three. Time is wasting."

Jibby shook his head. "I won't! I won't do it!" He looked frantically at the others. "I haven't done anything! I haven't done a goddamn thing!"

He tried to grab hold of Friske, but he was shoved away. Yee and Tamar stepped back when he got in too close. Only Soapy took hold of him and stood strong with him. Seeing his bravery, Charlie did the same.

"No more fucking around, babies. No more."

There was a flash of blue light that was directed at Jibby. His eyes went suddenly blank and he marched forward. Soapy and Charlie could not hang onto to him; they were completely paralyzed. All of them were. Rooted to the floor, no power in their arms or legs. They couldn't even speak.

Jibby moved to the far side of the cage and Charlie heard the creaking of the door as it slid open. There was a terrible slithery sort of noise from the other cage followed by something that sounded like Jell-O, gallons of it, dumped to the floor. That same fetid, revolting stink rose up along with the overpowering odor of ammonia. It was so strong, Charlie's eyes watered.

Tamar made a gagging sound.

The door closed and the paralysis was lifted. Everyone dropped to the floor. Whatever had held them was so strong that when it released them, their limbs went to rubber.

It took a few minutes to recover. When they did, Charlie, followed by Soapy and Yee, went to the door. It was closed, but there was a soft yellow light coming from the other cage. Charlie gripped the bars and they were so hot, he yanked his hands away.

In the murky yellow light, he could see Jibby in there. He was on his knees, speaking in a low voice. Though he couldn't make out what he was saying, Jibby didn't sound afraid. The tone of his voice was very casual. If anything, he sounded doped. Then he held up his hands as if to embrace a loved one, his mouth wide like a glistening open wound.

Then Yee made a sound like a short, sharp cry of disgust and that stink of bleach became so strong that Charlie's head spun. But he saw what came next—they all did.

A glutinous, flaccid wave of dirty green gelatinous flesh rolled out of the darkness. A formless mass that seemed to inflate like a balloon pumped with hot gas. It slithered and rolled like a gigantic amoeba, stretching, rippling, taking shape and putting out a dozen long muscular tentacles that were pink and gray and purple. They wormed in the air.

"GET BACK!" Soapy shouted.

Charlie moved away from the bars as one of the tentacles wound around it with fleshy contractions, making a sizzling noise as it gripped the uprights, an acrid steam rising from it in lazy tendrils.

The light in the cage obscured things, so he couldn't see the exact scope of the creature, but he thought he saw eight or ten red eyes blazing in the darkness, ropy convolutions, and that green pulsating mantle—or part of it—inflating and deflating as if it was breathing.

Jibby screamed as the tentacles wrapped around him like garrotes, squeezing, tightening until blood flew from his mouth. Bones snapped. His flesh ruptured. The tentacles compressed him like a juicy mango and he exploded into a flotsam of pink tissue awash in a sea of blood.

Then a rubbery sort of proboscis extended from the creature, its end big around as the mouth of a barrel. It opened, revealing teeth like gleaming fishhooks. What happened after that, Charlie didn't know because he fell away with the others, sickened and overwhelmed with physical horror.

From the other cage, there was a slurping noise followed by meaty chewing and slobbering sounds. All of them perfectly vile. Then the yellow light dimmed and went out entirely.

By then, Charlie was on the floor beneath the lightbulb, holding onto Yee. Nobody said a damn thing because there were no words that could possibly make sense of what they'd seen.

And Charlie, sweating and shivering, thought, *they let us see because they want us to know exactly what's going to happen to each and every one of us.*

9

In the days to come, he did things without thinking about them. Seeing Jibby die like that had thrown a great switch in his head, shutting everything down. It must have been some psychological self-preservation sort of thing, a firewall that could not be breached in order to save his sanity. Whatever it was, it was the only thing that kept him from becoming a raving lunatic.

You couldn't see something like that and not be changed. You couldn't go through something like that without being altered in just about every way.

But, eventually, due mainly to Soapy's patience and Yee's unfailing support, he came out of it. The ice melted and he was able to feel again. The trauma was still there, of course, but the shock had faded.

The same couldn't be said for Friske.

Rugged, ornery, working-class tough guy that he was, something inside him—something which probably had always been very fragile beneath the layers of attitude and machismo—was broken. He stared into space. He mumbled. Tears rolled from his eyes. He shook uncontrollably. Now and again, a bit of the old, pissy Friske would emerge and he'd ball his hands into white-knuckled fists and grumble *kill 'em, I'll kill every one of them* … but that would fade quickly enough and he'd submerge deep into the black waters of his own dementia.

He was in a similar state to Tamara, who was safely tucked as far into her shell as she could get.

Three days after Jibby's death, Charlie said, "In most situations, you can have a plan, something to work toward, but in this place … what's there to plan for? There's no way we can get out of this."

"We can't give in," Soapy said. "We just can't."

He was really something. He had to be the most optimistic guy Charlie had ever met. Part of it was his personality, but much of it was probably his age. Charlie figured he was at least seventy. And you didn't survive that long without fighting your way through one problem after another. It made you tough and seasoned.

We're fucked, Charlie thought. *We're absolutely powerless and completely fucked, but still he hangs on. How in the hell does he do it?*

They had discussed the situation from every perspective and come up against the same gray wall every time: there was no fighting this and no possibility of escape.

"My roommate has a snake," Yee said. "A ball python. At first, I was like, no way, not a snake. But it's a pretty laid-back thing. It never bites or anything. She keeps it in a heated cage and feeds it white mice. I always felt sorry for the mice. What a life. Kept alive to feed a snake. What a shitty existence." She laughed dryly. "But we're the mice now, aren't we? We were abducted to keep their fucking pet healthy. What a concept."

They'd all been thinking along those lines, of course, but it was painful to hear it put into words.

"We shouldn't jump to conclusions until we hear more," Soapy suggested.

And as much as Charlie respected the man, he wanted to punch him right in the face for such childlike denial of reality.

The food was brought twice a day, but they just picked at it. Enough to sustain them, but no more. Tamara would eat if you brought food to her mouth, but it was nearly impossible to get Friske to take anything. And nobody wanted to get too close to him, because he reacted violently.

Finally, the voice gave them a lecture. *"You're being a real drag, babies. The man don't want you to be sick, he wants you healthy. You have to eat so you can be plump and randy and ready. You dig? You gotta get with the program."*

Yee sneered. "In other words, you wanna fatten us up for your monster! Yeah, let's eat as much as we can so we're nice and round and juicy! That's the way the monster likes us!"

"Now you're digging it, Subject Five," the voice said. *"You're in the groove, baby. You're down with it."*

"That was sarcasm, you fucking idiot."

"Not my bag, baby. I don't get off on that negativity, so turn it down." The voice laughed with that low, seductive sound. *"Brothers and sisters, let's get real here. Let me lay it on you like this. We went through one hell of a lot of trouble to capture the organism in the next cage. And ain't nothing we won't do to keep it fat and healthy. See, babies, that's why we stopped by Earth. Got to keep the larder well-stocked for the long trip. You digging this?"*

"But we're intelligent beings," Soapy said.

"In whose book, baby?"

"You can't treat us like this. It's immoral, it's unethical." He was clearly exasperated at the voice and he wasn't bothering to hide it anymore. "What kind of monsters are you? How can you consider yourself intelligent when you have no conscience, no principles, no moral integrity?"

The voice laughed with a terrible mocking sound. *"Oh, baby, don't be such a hypocrite! Your so-called enlightened society feeds itself by exploiting other life forms! You call it agriculture, but some might call it murder on a fantastic scale."* The voice laughed again. *"Sounds to me like your so-called moral compass swings in only one direction."*

Soapy tried arguing the point, but the voice was gone. There was simply no way he was going to convince their keepers that what they were doing was wrong. He said little after that. He sat on the floor with his back up to the bars and it was painful to see; they had finally broken his spirit.

Yee and Charlie went and sat by him and it took some time to get him to come around, but when he did, he simply shook his head. "You can't call yourself intelligent if you use intelligent beings as livestock. Whatever these aliens are, they're culturally much lower than we are. They have no sense of right and wrong. They're no better than that thing in the next cage."

There was no arguing it.

Charlie had always thought vaguely in the back of his mind that beings from another world would be advanced not just technologically but ethically. Maybe he'd watched too much *Star Trek* as a kid, but he expected more, much more. These bastards were just savages with big brains.

Several hours later, the voice spoke again. *"We have considered your argument, Subject One, and it is not without merit. Unfortunately, we reject your hypocrisy."* This was followed by a moment or two of tense silence. Then: *"Subject One, step forward. It is your time, baby."*

10

After that, there was darkness without light, without hope, without sanity. Soapy had kept them grounded. He had kept them together with his easy way, his wisdom, his pragmatism and optimism. Without him, the cage felt very empty. Maybe it had always been empty, but now they felt it like never before.

Friske was in his own world, as was Tamara. It was pointless to try to communicate with either. Though, strangely, now and again, Charlie found that she was watching him and there was something in her look that told him she was not only very aware of what was going on, but maybe knew more than he did about it.

He'd seen that look more than once, but every time he recognized it as such, her eyes would glaze over again and become positively bovine.

"What now?" Yee said. "What do we do now?"

The mother of all questions with not one single good answer. Charlie had been asking himself that ever since he woke up in the cage and he was no closer to an answer now than he had been a week ago. So he just said, "I don't know."

Yee was holding onto him very tightly. "There's nothing and I know it. We just wait our turn, I guess. What a shitty outlook on life."

In the dark, they kissed and it was nice. They spent the next ten minutes kissing and it only got better.

"Funny," he said. "I've been waiting for you all my life and I had to find you here."

They shared a brief laugh at that.

"I've never been good with relationships, attachments, any of that stuff. I've been told I'm cold and distant … but I don't feel cold or distant about you." She put her head on his shoulder. "I hope when it's our turn, we can go together. I couldn't stand to hear it happen to you and not be able to do anything about it."

"I feel the same. Who knows how much time we have left?"

"Then let's quit wasting it."

She pushed him down on the floor and then her tongue was in his mouth and it felt better than anything had in a long, long time. And when she lowered herself on his erection, it was … *exquisite.* That was not a word he thought he'd ever used before, but nothing else fit. Being with Yee, being in her and part of her, entwined, hot flesh pressed to hot flesh, was unbelievably exquisite. Physically, there was release, of course, but psychologically and spiritually they had attained new heights.

And as good as it all was, even perfect in many ways, it only made him realize how much he cared for her and, yes, even loved her. It had been building in him for some time and he had pushed the feelings aside again and again, because this was no place for such things, yet it had happened quite naturally whether he wanted it or not.

And now I'm going to have to watch her die, he thought, feeling like he had been cut open deep inside. *This girl I've searched for without ever realizing that's what I was doing, I found her here in this awful place. And now that I've found her, I'm going to lose her.*

Lying there together, inhabiting a zone that belonged only to them, she said, "Tell me what you're thinking, Charlie."

Did he dare? Yes. Why not? "I was thinking that I love you. Does that sound crazy to you?"

She kissed him. "Not at all. I'm just as crazy as you are."

And that's how they spent the night—or period of darkness—wrapped around one another so tightly they were practically living in the same skin. They talked about their lives and admitted all those things they had never confessed to another living soul. But it felt right. They spoke of many things except the ugly reality of what was coming next.

11

Three days later, they took Friske.

Something had been going on with him all day: he paced incessantly around the cage, muttering and mumbling, carrying on conversations with people who were not there. He refused to eat. Something had taken hold of him and it would not let him go.

There was no point talking to him or trying to calm him down. He was out of his head. As the day wore on, his delirium ratcheted up until he finally threw himself at the door leading into the other cage.

"FUCK YOU, SOAPY! *FUCK YOU!*" he shouted. "I WON'T DO IT! I DON'T CARE WHAT YOU SAY! I WON'T AND YOU CAN'T MAKE ME! DO YOU HEAR ME? *YOU CAN'T FUCKING MAKE ME!*"

What that was about, neither Yee or Charlie understood, though he was certain that there was another level to Friske's madness, that he was hearing things they could not, perhaps being tormented by the voice of Soapy who was trying to entice him into the cage.

The aliens could do anything they wanted, Charlie figured. If they could make things materialize out of thin air (like the food table and the curtained toilet), paralyze people and make their livestock walk into that other cage against their will, then surely, they could cloud minds and make you hear things that just weren't there.

Finally, the voice returned. There was a wet sound as if its owner was licking its plump lips: *"Subject Two, step forward,"* it said.

Whatever was left of Friske by that point came completely apart. He shook and jerked with spasms of pure terror as if he had just swallowed rat poison. Oily sweat beaded his face and loops of drool hung from his mouth which was alternately grinning stupidly, scowling with disbelief, and wide with a suppressed scream.

"Not me! Not me! It won't be me!" he yammered, spit flying from his mouth, hands bunched into fits. *"I'm not the one to go! Do you hear me? I'm not the one!"*

The voice was unconcerned and unmoved by his melodrama. *"Subject Two, step forward,"* it repeated.

He fell to the floor, shaking his head violently side to side. He went right at Charlie, seizing him by the collar of his shirt and shaking him. *"Do you see? Do you see? Do you finally fucking see, you little shit?"* he shrieked in Charlie's face, white spittle foaming at the corners of his mouth. *"They want blood and they will have blood! We're just meat! We're sustenance! That horror fills its belly with us! But why should it be me? Why should it fucking be me when it can be you or your little whore here?"*

"Friske, stop it! Goddamn it, stop it!" Charlie yelled at him, trying to break his grip which was like that of a sheet metal press.

Friske dragged him to his feet and when Yee tried to intervene, he shoved her to the floor. He dragged Charlie toward the door to the other cage. He was completely deranged. There was no talking sense to him, no reasoning. He was a violent, cornered animal whose life was threatened and he reacted in kind.

"HERE! HERE! HERE! THIS IS WHAT YOU WANT!" he screamed at the top of his lungs. *"TAKE HIM! TAKE YOUR FUCKING SACRIFICE!"*

But the control voice wasn't having it: it wasn't Friske's place to make the selections any more than one hog could choose another hog for slaughter. The same blue light that incapacitated Jibby flashed brightly, then a beam of it focused on Friske's head.

The result was immediate—he seized up, his limbs going rubbery and Charlie fell to the floor. Friske was very much aware of what was happening. Tears rolled from his eyes and his mouth hung open like that of a red-faced, bawling infant.

The cage door creaked open and Friske lumbered forward like a wind-up toy. Charlie felt a searing wave of wet, plastic heat that seemed to envelop him like Saran Wrap. A smell that was high and sickening came with it—that decomposing stink tinged with ammonia, yes, but also a feral odor like that of a zoo: glands and wet fur and reptilian musk.

By then, Friske was in the other cage and the door had slid closed again. That same dirty yellow light illuminated what happened next, not literally but almost figuratively with its gloom and crawling shadows. Charlie watched with terror-bright eyes.

There was a sudden hissing sound like gas escaping from a leaking valve and a monstrous, grotesque shadow converged on Friske, a small portion, it seemed, of a gigantic fleshy mantle that pulsed like a beating heart. Charlie saw that same ring of luminous red eyes that made him weak in the stomach, but set in the center of them like a sun with its attendant planets was a huge, globular gold eye that shined like wet metal.

Then something like a sea of bubbling ooze seemed to engulf Friske just as a flurry of writhing tentacular limbs closed in on him, roping him tightly like dozens of fat-bodied vipers. With a whirring motion, they sheared him from his skin like a sweet from a dirty wrapper and he looked momentarily like a red, peeled grape before he boiled alive in the thing's clutches, steaming and popping, becoming a bubbling lava flow of flesh.

Charlie didn't see anymore.

By then, Yee's hands were on him, dragging him away from the cage door. The yellow light slowly dimmed as if without a spectator there was no need for it.

As Yee held onto him, Charlie clenched his jaws tightly, his stomach rolling over at the slurping, sucking sounds coming from the cage of the beast.

12

For an hour, maybe two, there was silence in the cage. Yee and Charlie sat with Tamara, holding onto her the way a traumatized child will hold onto a favored pet, drawing relative comfort. He didn't know why they went to her any more than Yee did, but there was a magnetism to her, a draw. Sitting with her and holding onto her seemed necessary.

Charlie felt doped as if he'd been shot up with something, but he knew it was just the aftereffect of seeing Friske die horribly. Regardless, he couldn't string together a single coherent thought in his head. His mind was whirling, spinning hopelessly on an axis of pure horror.

Yee had been tough up to that point, he knew, remarkably, admirably tough, but she was shut down now, too. There really was no hope. There was only acceptance of an ugly death. Their lives had been lived and now they would end much as the life of a steer in a stockyard.

And it's not fair, he told himself again and again. *It's just not fair. We're human beings. We deserve more than this. Much more.*

As he thought that, holding one of Tamara's hands as Yee held the other, he nearly laughed out loud. Death was death. There was nothing fair about it. The Grim Reaper was a sneaking, underhanded, backstabbing prick and he always had been.

"Do you remember your lives?" Tamara suddenly said. "Do you remember your friends? Do you remember your moms and dads? Do you remember how it felt to run in the spring sunshine when you were a child after a long, cold winter? Do you remember how it felt to be in love? To breathe clean air and know freedom?"

123

"Tamara, you—"

"Yes," she interrupted him. "I've been watching. I've been seeing."

"But you haven't said anything," Yee said. "We thought … we thought … I guess it doesn't matter what we thought. I'm glad you're with us."

"I've never been away. Not really." She stared off into the cage. "I was sorry when Soapy died. I liked Soapy. He was a good, decent person. But I honestly didn't care when Jibby went or Friske. There was nothing worth saving in either of them. But you two—" she squeezed both of their hands firmly, warmly "—you have something worth saving. Something good, something *human* that the Metalurians can't steal from you. Do you understand what I'm saying?"

Charlie understood, yet he didn't understand a thing in the larger sense.

Yee said, "There's no hope. There's just no hope."

Tamara was silent for a moment. Finally, she said, "But there is. A microbe on a slide, if it could reason, wouldn't think it stood a chance against the omnipotent scientist that put it there or stares down through a lens at it, holding its life and death in the palm of his hand. But if it's a disease microbe, a deadly microbe … and if it escapes, if it gets inside him, it can cause all kinds of damage, now can't it?"

"But how can we do that?" Yee asked.

"Let's find out. The voice will call me next."

Charlie swallowed. "How do you know that?"

"I know."

After that, Tamara closed her eyes and would not speak again, regardless of how hard they tried to get her to. It was a day of revelations, regardless, and she gave them hope because something in her was so very confident.

13

In the morning, bare minutes after the light came back on, the voice began to speak and Charlie reached out for Yee and held her in his arms.

Again, and for the last time, he thought with such clarity that he was not certain it was his thought at all, but maybe something broadcast into his head as if he was tuned to some freakish psychic network.

"All right, babies, all animals need to be fed and so does ours. So dig this: Subject Four, step forward and let it begin! Let's get down with it, get our groove on, cats!" the voice said, sounding excited. *"As was once said: turn on, tune in, and drop out!"*

Charlie would never forget what he saw then: Tamar stood up, pushed back her long dark hair, and looked down at Yee and him, offered them the thinnest of smiles, then willingly, serenely stepped toward the door.

He wanted to go to her, to stop her, to talk sense to her. He wanted her to resist as the others had resisted, but in some way he could never understand, she had been waiting her entire life for just this moment.

"Oh Christ," Yee said.

The door opened and Yee stepped into the other cage. The animal, as it were, was on her immediately, hungrily, and she fought against it as any living creature would fight against its own death. And that's where things began rather than ended.

Yee went stiff next to him as if she'd been plugged into electrical current. So did he.

"I ... I can *feel* her," she said. "I can see through her mind...."

And Charlie could, too. He was tuned right into every second of her agony and then what came after it, feeling, knowing, existing through her and *as* her. The animal did not simply devour Tamara. No, it was much more complex than a simple feeding. It identified her and assimilated her. It pulled her into itself and there the two communed, became one and the same, a seamless human/alien hybrid.

This was what it had done with the others, he knew. It absorbed them, made them part of itself, their characteristics—both mental and physical— melting into it and becoming it.

Communion.

That's what this was.

It was at first unpleasant, for Tamara felt herself drawn into the writhing bulk of the creature. She was physically, organically, grounded within the thing: its smells were her smells, its life was her life, its biology was her own. Her humanity was leached of nutrients and cast aside.

The beast was not just a dumb animal; it was an intelligent creature. It was a mother. It was pregnant. Tamara could feel the bursting, blossoming masses of eggs drowning her; the larva suckering to her flesh; the progeny crawling over her and through her in an insane violation of body, mind, and spirit.

The tactile sensations of the animal itself were light years beyond that of a human being. She could sense the anatomies of minds; smell the musk of psyches; taste colors and textures; see through the veil of this dimension and into others.

Tamara knew she should feel horrified and repulsed and demented by this grotesque reality, but she did not feel that way at all. She struggled with the imagery that would explain who and what she was and why it should offend her, but these things no longer existed as such. Yet there was still a spark of humanity in her. It blazed up as a low flame, but burned brighter and brighter by the moment.

As her mind communed with that of the animal, she did not die as such. She explored her host with her new mind, feeling it, sensing it, knowing it as surely as a mother knew her child's own crib. And as she learned it, something that was now part of herself, she recognized its weaknesses and latent vulnerabilities.

She began to kill the spawn, the larva, the young.

As seemingly indestructible as the beast was, its cherished young were vulnerable. If their life cycle was completed, they would hatch and spin themselves in membranous sacs. But that time was distant. They lived off the nutrient-rich secretions of their mother which were a complex stew of enzymes, lipids, proteins, and hormonal discharges. Without the secretions, they would die.

Tamara, racing through the creature's anatomy, began fouling the secretions with poisons drawn from the host organism itself. The eggs began to boil with venom. The larva within squealed in pain.

The mother fought back, of course, but Tamara was like a virus invading it, corrupting it, filling it with disease and decay.

These were the things that Charlie and Yee experienced vicariously. By then, they were at the door watching it happen.

The creature looked at them with panic and rage and hatred, but mostly confusion and disorientation. It made a screaming, gagging sound ... or its own approximation of the same.

"TAMARA!" Charlie shouted at the horror and it squealed back at him with volume.

The dying animal was a huge and seething mass of green flesh, a thrashing and fungous thing that was pulsing and screeching and pissing out rivers of black filth. It was making a mad mewling sound combined with a human screeching of absolute agony. Its massive, gelatinous body was pulsating and rupturing open, all those eggs popping like soap bubbles, spewing tissue and slime and the mangled fetal remains of its spawn into the steaming, boiling pit of its blood and oozing plasma. Wave after wave of sickening heat blew from the beast.

It was dying.

It swayed this way and that, tentacles flailing, a mutation of plastic flesh that was running and suppurating with black corruption. It sheared open like a veil and a mountain of eggs spilled out and the thing was drowning in them, in a reproductive sea of bile and slime and yolk.

"KILL IT!" Yee screamed with total satisfaction and happy, mindless bloodlust. "KILL THAT FUCKING THING! KILL 'EM ALL, TAMARA! BY GOD, KILL THOSE FUCKING THINGS!"

The cage was now a bubbling, smoking soup of flesh and looping appendages. The alien animal was melting into a river of putrescence, sinking into a mire of itself and it vented a final, primal scream before sinking away into that hissing ocean of tissue and blood and burst eggs.

And moved no more.

Of course, there were repercussions. The alien animal was rare and bound for a Metalurian zoo and now the *man* was deprived of his primary mission. He had failed because he had underestimated the survivability and wrath of humankind.

And he was not happy about it.

Charlie and Yee felt a sort of static charge in the air rise up. Whatever sort of energy it was it crawled along the backs of their arms and ran up and down their spines, making their synaptic networks jangle like wind chimes.

As they watched, the bars of the cage (which probably only existed in their minds in the first place) disappeared, fading from existence. There was that sharp stench of bleach similar to what the creature had put out, but now it was stronger—it made their eyes water and burned their throats and nasal passages.

And this presaged the appearance of the man as he stepped into the light.

Except he was an *it*.

Charlie and Yee shrank from it, not just because of its monstrous appearance but because they could feel the absolute power and absolute dominance coming from it. It waited there at the edge of the light, contemplating them and what it would now do with them.

At its top there was a blue-green shell that looked less like a carapace and more like something abstract fashioned from papier-mâché, ridged and sloping forward. Beneath this, its body seemed to be a mass of thorn-like protrusions and feelers and pulsing bubbles. It had limbs of a sort, long sinuous members ending in hooked digits and fine, thrashing tendrils. All of this was supported by a fleshy sort of vertebral column that splayed out on the floor into extended webby suckers upon which it stood.

It had a bulb-like head from which grew eight or ten stalks that terminated in glassy eyes of varying sizes that were perfectly round and perfectly silver. Set around each of them like eyelashes were long, segmented vines, pink and palpitating.

This was a Metalurian.

This was the architect of their pain and suffering.

It swayed from side to side as if there was something wrong with it. Some sort of discharge dripped from it.

As terrified as Charlie was of it, he wanted to charge it, to tear it apart with his bare hands. But judging from the chemical stink rising from it, mere touching it would have been agonizing to human hands.

There was nothing to do but stand with Yee, holding onto her as the Metalurian decided their fate and how they would be punished.

Then something happened.

The Metalurian gave out a harsh rattling followed by a squealing, metallic grinding noise. Its flesh began to blacken as it shook and vibrated, its many tendrils withering away. Then it fell over like a post, exploding like a rotten gourd, pulp and crawling things flooding away from its broken shell.

It was dead.

"The virus," Yee said with absolute certainty. "Tamara became a virus that destroyed the beast and infected the Metalurian. It has to be. It's in the air. Harmless to us, but like Ebola to that thing."

"*Right on, baby, right on. A disease microbe, like Subject Five said,*" the voice told them, making that smacking sound as if it was wetting its lips. "*You done beat the man at his own game. He cut out for good.*"

Charlie and Yee looked at each other. "What now?" he asked.

"*It's up to you, baby. The man is gone. Now you tell me what to do and it happens. Out of sight.*"

Yee said, "Take us back home."

"*Far out, baby. Let me turn this buggy around and make it happen. Sit back and enjoy the ride. It's gonna take some time to reach point of origin, but the trip is going to be a gas.*"

Charlie and Yee sat down. They kissed each other and held onto one another. They could hear Tamara's voice: *Do you remember how it felt to run in the spring sunshine when you were a child after a long, cold winter? Do you remember how it felt to be in love? To breathe clean air and know freedom?*

And yeah, they remembered all right.

LIFEFORM

When the planetary survey ship *Galatea* was blindsided by a freak magnetic burst twenty million miles out from Beta Hydri-4, it limped along at sub-light for two long months. Its plasma core was neutralized. AI systems fragmented. Life support was on auxiliary that was gradually failing.

As Captain Sheng put it, "We are, people, in a word, *fucked.*"

Finally the ship fell into an eccentric orbit around the unknown planet, that began to decay almost immediately. Plotting a navigational seat-of-the-pants trajectory, Sheng brought the ship down. It came in hard and fast like a bird dropping from the sky. It clipped a mountain range that ripped away its aft thrusters, punched a hole through the thick jungle growth and finally crashed in a rocky valley.

Bennet survived.

And only because of his anti-grav harness. The rest of the crew were mangled in the wreckage. Anny Stillman was still alive, but just barely. Bennet pulled her free, though he could barely stand himself. He got her maybe forty feet from the carcass of the *Galatea* before its conversion reactor went up like a blazing sun. If it hadn't been for their e-suits, they would have been fried like strips of bacon.

But they were alive.

That was something.

Alive and marooned on an alien world.

Castaways.

⇂

The only ray of light in his dismal situation was the hope that the *Galatea's* hypercom distress signal would be picked up. But even if it was, he knew damn well it would take a rescue party nearly a year to reach the planet. Beta Hydri-4 was an easy twenty-four light years from Earth. The *Galatea* had been out further than any ship before her. The Beta Hydri system was to have been their last survey of a seven-year mission. Afterward they were going home to a hero's welcome on Earth and the colonies.

So much for that, Bennet thought.

The atmosphere on Four was Earth-comparable, the suit told him, so he stripped away his helmet and Anny's. The air wasn't bad. Not exactly fresh, a gassy sulfur smell to it. But it would do. His suit had water for five days and there were protein-rich crackers in the survival pouch. After that, he either found food and water or he died.

⇂

The heat was going to be a problem.

The days were nearly three Earth days, and it was hot, the sun a giant yellow disk in the hazy sky. He needed shelter, but Anny was in too precarious a condition to move. He had uplinked with her suit, and it told him she had internal injuries and a concussion. Without proper medical care, it put her chances of survival at a depressing 7%. Her nanos were working on her, but there were limits to what they could do.

Though he didn't like leaving her for any length of time, Bennet took a brief tour of the surrounding area, which revealed only sand and rocks. No signs of animal life. He climbed a tower of stone and saw desert scrub to the west and thick jungle to the east. To the north were more mountains. They looked like serrated purple diamonds. South, it was misty and he suspected that's where the water would be.

He went back to Anny and held onto her the way a child holds onto its teddy bear. She was the only comfort he had in a very ugly reality, and she was fading fast.

"You've got to pull out of this, girl," he told her. "I need you. I can't … I can't do this alone."

On what he figured was his third day there, the shadows began to lengthen and things began to cool. The less water he lost to sweating, the better off he'd be. As he held Anny, whispering to her, he thought of his daughter in New Paris. He had been a fool to sign up for a seven-year jaunt. He was missing so much with her. If he had no other reason to survive, she was it. He had to see her again. Her name was Sherry and she was ten years old now. He'd missed most of her childhood.

"And for what, Anny? For what? So I could come out here where people don't fucking belong? So I could die on this piece of rock eight parsecs from home?"

Twilight seemed to last forever on Four. If the stars came out, he wondered what they'd look like from this alien world.

When night came, it came fast. It went from a hazy twilight, with weird orange shadows crawling over the rocks, to absolute blackness. He couldn't see the stars through the heavy cloud cover, but he did see the luminous ghost of first one moon, then another.

With the helmet lights of his suit, he tried to get some water into Anny, but it just dribbled down her chin. He kept holding onto her through the long night. He heard weird cries in the distance and a high shrieking that faded away. There was animal life out there, somewhere. As his eyes adjusted to the dark, he thought he saw shadows slipping around him. Every time he turned on the helmet lights, there was nothing.

Imagination.

That's what it had to be.

The wind moaned like ghosts among the spires of rock and ancient draws and gullies, but other than that it was dead quiet. The stillness was unsettling.

When the sun finally came up after some sixty-three hours of night, Anny was dead. He'd been holding her corpse for many hours.

That was it then.

He was alone.

⚬

There was work to do.

There was no time to feel sorry for himself. He carried Anny's body back to the wreckage of the *Galatea*. It was easy enough to find. The debris of the ship was scattered for a city block in either direction from the impact site. Something about it all disturbed him, but he wasn't sure why.

But there were other matters to attend to.

On a low, sandy hillside covered with pink ferns that overlooked the valley where the *Galatea* lay, he dug a shallow grave of maybe four feet and gently placed Anny in there. There was absolutely no doubt that she was dead; her suit confirmed it. He took her survival pouch, water bladder, and her sidearm, a pulser, then laid her carefully in the grave inside her e-suit. She was an old friend. He mumbled a half-remembered prayer from childhood over her, said goodbye, and covered her in dirt before he began sobbing like a baby.

"I wish I could do better," he said, the memories of them together like blades cutting him open inside.

He found a large crystal like bright blue quartz and marked her grave with it.

That was it.

There was nothing else he could do.

⚬

He decided the decent thing to do was to bury the remains of the crew, what he could find of them or those that hadn't been incinerated.

It was something he'd been putting off for days.

The Beta Hydri sun was blazing and he was stripped down to a t-shirt and flight pants. The debris was everywhere as he stepped down into the little valley which was more like a great circular depression. The closer he got to the burned-out hulk of the *Galatea,* the more of it there was—sheets of metal and shards of plastic, singed composites and spiderwebbed sheets of glass, sections of piping and spears of conduits, bent struts and unrecognizable assemblages of machinery and electronic components. The heat had been unbelievably intense and many materials were fused into a common whole.

A lot of it could be used to survive with, he decided. He could make weapons and water jugs, shelters and various implements if he was creative enough. There were small laser cutting torches in the survival pouches. He could use them to fabricate and weld if he was stuck here any length of time.

As he looked around, he kept expecting to find human remains, but other than a few stray bones, the ruptured remains of e-suits, and a scattered boot or two, there was very little.

He got a sudden chill up his spine, realizing this was what had bothered him earlier when he looked down into the little valley—the lack of human remains. Now he began to look in earnest among the wreckage, kicking at suspicious mounds of sand and performing a detailed grid search from the dead ship on outward.

Where the hell are the dead? They were here. I remember seeing them.

When he had pulled Anny free from the burning ship, there had been smoldering bodies scattered everywhere. Not only that, but limbs and torsos, all manner of human remains.

Now it was all gone.

More so, meticulously cleaned up.

Panicking, beads of sweat rolling down his face, he began running around, seeking something, *anything.* He stopped, overheated, his head spinning. He had to remember that he knew nothing of the animal life on

Four. Things might come out of the ground at night for all he knew.

It's just nature taking its course, he told himself, because attributing it all to "nature" made it sound very antiseptic somehow, like rain falling or wind blowing. Neutral. Much better than the idea of nameless carnivorous monsters haunting the night world of Four.

Scavengers, that's all.

Bennet had been trained in not only surviving on alien worlds but in the psychology of encounters with potentially hostile alien lifeforms. He knew he had to keep his head. Logic was what was needed, not runaway human imagination with its instinctive menagerie of spooks and goblins.

Thinking this way made him feel better.

Besides, he had two fully charged pulser weapons. Nothing could stand up to their pulses of energized particles: they could burn through five inches of tempered compo-steel.

He had to keep his head.

That was the important thing.

⚶

As he made his way from the valley, he nearly tripped over a bone in the sand. It was a human femur, completely fleshless. There were scratches drawn down it as if it had been raked by claws. And, worse, teeth marks like the bone had been punched by an awl … or a series of them.

This stopped him.

His theoretical scavenger didn't seem so harmless now. Particularly with what he found next: groupings of large anvil-shaped tracks, each with the impression of a single curving claw like the blade of a scimitar. The tracks were sunk deeper than those of his boots. Whatever left them was big and dangerous. It was bipedal. He knew that much.

And it has a marked appetite for human remains, Bennet thought. *What happens when it wants more?*

He made it out of the valley quickly.

Before night came again, he needed a shelter. One that was defensible. He needed to be ready.

◊

He remembered one of his instructors saying that in a survival situation, there was no such thing as paranoia. Particularly in unfamiliar terrain. To stay alive, you had to use not only every ounce of intelligence, experience, and creativity you possessed, but you had to listen to your instincts and learn to trust your intuition and gut sense.

And Bennet's told him that whatever left those tracks was a monster.

He gathered his gear—there wasn't much of it, two survival pouches, his e-suit and helmet, two pulsers, some odds and ends—and moved south.

It was a two-hour walk through the hot, baking deadlands of Four. All the way he thought of what had been at the remains of the *Galatea's* crew. He wondered if whatever was out there was watching him, tracking him, sizing him up for the kill. Maybe it was just a scavenger, but he wasn't about to bet on it.

He passed through a vale of crowded blue-green scrub, climbed a rise, and there before him was a completely different world. For as far as the eye could see, a misty run of bogs and thick green vegetation, floating islands of orange reeds and steaming emerald marshes. There were tall moss-shrouded trees growing out of sucking black pools, spreading canopies of indigo foliage fine as spiderweb lace. He saw plants like giant orchids, their flowers vivid orange and ruby-red, violet and crystal blue.

It was like an Eden of life after the dry, dead badlands (as he began to think of the general crash area). Everything here was alive, full of vitality. The air was warm and moist, filled with perfumes of sweetness, sourness, and running sap. There was a decayed stink beneath it that was common to all jungles regardless of the world—things dying and rotting, giving birth to myriad lifeforms. He saw creatures that might have been insects. They hopped and swam and leaped in the trees.

But best of all, he saw a clear bubbling creek running through it all.

He left his things near a thick pink bush in which toad-like creatures with tails jumped about comically, often colliding in midair. His water bladders were seriously diminished, so he slung them over his shoulder, took a test kit from one of the survival pouches, and made his way toward the creek.

It was a precarious journey.

He followed forested islands through the bogs, being very careful of each step he took. He encountered no threatening wildlife, just lots of small skittering things that vaulted away at his approach. A few bat-like insects dove at him, but when he swatted at them, they veered off.

Finally, the creek.

Just the sound of its rushing waters was refreshing. There was something infinitely soothing about it to the human animal. He wanted nothing better than to submerge his face in its clear, cool waters and drink deep, but for all he knew it was filled with toxic chemicals that could have burned a hole in his throat.

He sucked up some in a syringe and let the kit earn its keep. In roughly ten minutes, it told him the water was safe to drink. Finally, a break! It was actually rich in minerals and devoid of dangerous microbes.

He dropped to his knees and dipped his face in. Oh, it was deliciously cool. It felt amazing on his throat, washing away days and days of dust and crud. For whatever reason, it had a slight lemony flavor to it that made it that much more thirst-quenching. After he'd swallowed a good quart of it and washed up, he filled both bladders and was actually feeling content and calm for the first time since the crash.

Standing up and studying the terrain in all directions, he caught a glint of silver in the distance. The verdant growths of Four contained just about every color of the rainbow in vibrant hues, but nothing silver. Whatever it was, it looked metallic.

Can't be metal ... not here.

He had to know.

The only way to get over there was by crossing the creek, so he stepped in. The bottom was made of flat well-worn stones, no muck, so it was easy to make the crossing. The creek was about fifteen feet wide. The water came up to his hips and felt wonderful soaking him to his skin.

He moved through the crowded vegetation, climbing one low hill after another. Then he saw it.

Sitting on a hilltop, nearly engulfed in vines, was what had to be a ship.

*

It had been there a long time. At least twenty years or so, he guessed. From its design—bullet-shaped with sleek aerodynamic fins—he thought it was an Earth ship, though definitely not a FTL star clipper or even an interplanetary vehicle, more likely an escape pod or a lifeboat. It was probably twenty-five feet long, though much of it was covered in thick, thorny growths. Using the knife on his belt, he sawed away tendrils and gnarled shoots until he exposed the hatch and found the ship's trail board. 1261-VS, it read, which meant nothing to him ... yet he was certain he'd seen a ship like it somewhere.

He had to get inside. That's all there was to it.

There was an old-style manual hatch gear. He blew the lock and corroded lid off it with the pulser. The gear was in good shape. He slid the pin in place and started cranking. It was tough at first, but gradually the hatch opened. When he had two feet of clearance, in he went. The airlock was open.

It was small inside, narrow, claustrophobic. There was dust everywhere, but no human remains. The survival equipment bins were empty; same for the weapons locker, but he did find some rain gear that was still sealed. He learned that the craft was indeed a lifeboat. It was from a warship called the *Prion.* He thought the *Prion* was a photon cruiser from the days of the Imperian Wars, which would date the lifeboat at least forty years.

Despite many harsh seasons, the structure of the lifeboat was still viable. A little cleaning and sprucing up and it would make a fine shelter. With the hatch cranked shut, nothing out there could get at him.

It was a plan.

"I dub thee *Robinson Crusoe*," Bennet said, the sound of his own voice startling in the close confines.

He laughed at his own jangled nerves. Then he heard something outside that was anything but amusing—a sort of rustling noise like something sizable was coming through the brush, something that cared not a whit how much noise it made.

He pulled his pulser and crept to the hatchway. He saw a huge shadow pass before it. Whatever it was, it was making a sniffing/snorting noise like a bloodhound casting for scent. He heard its footsteps—*thump, thump, thump*—as it moved toward the ship. It made a low growling in its throat.

He still hadn't caught sight of it, but it was close now, very close.

It's looking for me, he thought with a chill. *It has my scent.*

He didn't know that to be true, but his instinct was convinced of it. It had tracked him from the dead lands and now it had found him. His breathing was rapid as the creature growled out there, pausing and making an occasional grunting noise. He could smell its hide which was gamy and rank. But worse than that, far worse, was the foul stench of its breath—a fetid, sickening effluvium of burnt flesh, marrow fat, and human meat, the stink of what it had been feeding on in combination with all the rotting things it had dragged up from the marshes.

It tore at the growths veiling the ship. It clawed at the hull. The sound of which was like knives scraped over steel.

It paused.

He could hear it breathing with a rasping, terrible sound.

It's listening for you. It knows you're close.

Bennet waited.

It waited.

Then with a growling expulsion, it stuck the end of its snout through the door. Bennet saw a black chasm of knifing yellow fangs longer than steak knives. Hot putrescent breath filled the lifeboat. The creature roared and snapped, spitting out ropes of saliva. It couldn't get in. The two-foot opening of the door wouldn't allow for its torpedo-shaped head or its heavy, bunched shoulders.

It raged.

It snarled.

It tried to corkscrew its hulking body through the opening, but it was no good. Bennet aimed the pulser at it with a trembling hand. He would end it now. Get rid of this damned nightmare while he had the chance.

Then it withdrew.

It circled the ship, clawing at it, butting it and making it shake. Despite his fear, Bennet got in the doorway with the pulser in his hand. When he saw it out there, raging and tearing up the foliage and knocking down trees, howling with a cheated wrath, it was worse than anything he had imagined. It slashed and roared and whipped its skeletal, serrated tail about.

Dear God ...

It was a huge predator the size of a Kodiak bear. He couldn't say what it was biologically, not reptile exactly or mammal or insect ... more of a chimera than anything else, at least by Earth standards. Its flesh was a shiny metallic blue, knobs and rungs of bone thrusting out from beneath. It was bipedal, as he thought, and its body plan reminded him of a T-rex, but not the way they really had been, but the anatomically-incorrect versions from the 19th and 20th century, the upright tail draggers.

But, of course, it was certainly no T-rex.

It was plated and scaled like a medieval warrior in armor and chainmail. Thought it had two spurred legs, it had four arms that were like triple bony rods, two huge claws sprouting from long, narrow chitinous-looking paws. Its neck was an elongated thick trunk. It could raise its head up on it or lower it beneath the level of its shoulders, though jutting it forward seemed to be its natural stance.

It stood there, glaring at him with brilliant red compound eyes like those of a fly. Saliva dripped from its mouth.

They watched each other: predator and prey.

Then it charged, filled with primal wrath. It would not be denied this meal it had tracked. Bennet fired the pulser. His aim was off. He sought to core its head, but the searing blue pulses struck the animal in the shoulder, knocking it backward. It howled with pain and anger. Its shoulder was a blackened, smoking mass of disrupted tissue.

Bennet took aim again.

The beast charged two or three feet, then darted away into the bushes. He could hear it cutting a hole through the jungle, splashing through ponds and crashing away.

That was his first encounter with it.

But he knew it wouldn't be his last.

⚶

The lifeboat became his redoubt. It was his castle, his island in the stormy sea of Beta Hydri-4 (which he had now named Anny's Planet because it just seemed like the right thing to do). He brought his gear there, odds and ends from the wreck of the *Galatea,* any old scraps that might prove useful in the future. He cleaned it out, rigged an internal manual hatch gear, and set about the business of learning to survive on the planet. He had plenty of water, but his food rations from the survival pouches were getting dangerously low.

He had lost quite a bit of weight, partly from his diet and partly from the godawful heat of Four. He spent a lot of time coming and going and he was always armed. The pulsers were great, and they were self-charging (he had a solar charger if worst came to worst). But if one of them broke down, there was no way in hell he'd be able to fix it. Like so much of the technology he used, it required an extensive support system for upkeep and repair.

He just hoped they'd rescue him before things got too bad. Maybe that was wishful thinking, but it was all he had to hold onto.

There was always the threat of the chimera beast. He'd had no more encounters with it, but it was around and he knew it. He saw its tracks. He found the bones of things it had devoured. Sometimes he could smell it. And even more disturbing, he could *sense* it watching him.

Very often after dark, he could hear it roaring in the jungle.

When the long night set in, he never left the ship.

$$\text{\textpdagger}$$

He began venturing further and further into the bog lands in search of food. He discovered a fruit that looked like a large red pear. Famished as he was, he bit into it and burned his tongue so badly that he couldn't taste anything for three days. After that, he used common sense and brought the test kit with him. There were lots of fruit and berries, beautiful juicy-looking orbs of brilliant scarlet and bright orange, emerald green and bright yellow. But none of them were fit for human consumption. Purple berries that looked like grapes contained a deadly neurotoxin and green ones contained a corrosive juice whose chemical composition was similar to hydrochloric acid. A spear tip dipped in either would make a formidable weapon.

He found berries that made good medicinal salves, ointments, and even analgesics, but nothing edible.

So the fruit and berries were out. He found tubers and shoots he could eat, but most were tasteless. Same went for seeds. He tried fishing, but there was nothing in the creeks remotely like fish, only fat-bodied amphibians that hid in the mud. When he caught one, it exuded a glandular cocktail that smelled like skunk spray. It was so strong it made him vomit.

There were animals, some as large as rabbits or woodchucks, but the pulser entirely destroyed them and they were far too fast to creep up on and spear. He set traps, but they were too smart for that. He discovered large packs of weird bird-reptiles that looked like a cross between roosters and small dinosaurs. They were ferocious if you got anywhere near them. He killed one out of desperation with the pulser and its roasted carcass smelled remarkably like barbecued chicken. But when he tried to retrieve it, the others charged in and ate it.

Things were not looking good.

If the *Galatea* hadn't burned up, he could have lived in luxury off her stores for two years. But with the way things were going, if he didn't find a food source and soon, he would be dead in two months.

Much less, in fact.

He made a package of protein crackers that was supposed to be used for two meals last for over a week. It had been a month by that point, and he was emaciated, malnourished. His belly hadn't been full since before the crash. When he sipped water from the creek and saw his reflection, he nearly cried out—he was a bearded skeleton, grubby, eyes bulging, cheeks sunken. A living stick man whose clothes hung off him like shrouds.

The beast, by that point, was the least of his worries.

He was starving to death.

$\int$

What happened during the next week was a blur. Bennet lived like an animal, grubbing roots and gnawing on shoots, lapping water from the creek on all fours. He was dizzy and disoriented, delusional and confused. He hallucinated freely. He never left the lifeboat for days on end, and when he did, he had trouble finding it again. He saw members of the *Galatea's* crew and had long conversations with them. They all told him the same thing: there was a secret on Anny's Planet, a secret to survival. He only had to find it.

He lost himself in the marshes, crawling on his hands and knees from one lush island of vegetation to another. Shrunken and filthy, his clothes worn to rags, his face pocked with insect bites, he lay down finally, ultimately to die.

Then he smelled something.

In his last hours, a certain lucidity came to his mind and he saw himself for what he was—a dying animal. Rescue would not be coming for him any more than it had come for the crew of the lifeboat. Death was here. He did not embrace it, but he accepted it.

That's when the scent came to him. One that certainly did not belong on this terrible world so far from home. He dismissed it. Another smoke ghost, a phantom. As his perception narrowed and something inside him struggled for the ultimate release of oblivion, his mind was giving him a pleasant dream to sleep on.

But the scent grew stronger.

It became deliciously overpowering.

His eyes flickered open. His mouth watered. The scent was so strong, its source had to be very close. It was coming from a wide, still pool not twenty feet away. Mats of yellow-orange fungus grew on its surface. They were moist, sparkling in the sunlight.

His body little more than a withered rack of bones, he forced it forward one last time. Every inch made his muscles ache and his joints cry out.

He reached a shaking hand to the water. He extended the skeleton key of one finger into it and it was warm. It made his flesh tingle. He dipped his entire hand in. He felt no pain. The waters were invigorating. He pulled himself forward, sliding into the depths of the pool like an alligator. The pain in his limbs faded. His mind seemed to gain focus. Clarity.

You fool, he thought, *this is it. This is what you've been looking for. This was what all those people you imagined were telling you: this is the secret, the secret of survival. Your mind was channeling fantasies, trying to tell you what it already knew or sensed.*

Bringing his face up from the fortifying waters, he saw Anny's Planet as he'd never seen it before. Instead of viewing it as some sick, starving, rheumy-eyed dog, he saw it with the bright, clear eyes of an organism that wanted to stay alive and knew exactly how to do it. He sipped the waters. They were curiously sweet with a citrus aftertaste. He felt energized. He drank more and felt that much better.

Still weak, but on the path to strength, he waded over to the floating fungus. There was that delightful odor again—fizzing, sweet, refreshing. By God, it smelled just like the orange soda he'd loved as a kid. Even as an adult, there was nothing quite like it. He brought his face to it. Yes, *yes!* There was no doubt of it. He breathed it in. It was delicious, cool, fermented, and sweet.

His mind was clear enough by that point to know that he needed to test things with the kit before eating them. But reason had no place now; instinct ruled. It lived and breathed in every cell. It knew things his thinking brain could never understand. He tore away a juicy hunk of fungus and shoved it into his mouth.

Jesus.

The flavor was exactly like orange soda. It fizzed in his mouth. The fermentation tingled the back of his throat. The amazing sweetness launched cluster bombs of endorphins in his head. God, it was orange soda and orange creamsicle smoothies, candied orange fruit wedges and orange frosting, cool-sweet orange sherbet and ice-cold glasses of fresh orange juice. It was all things orange, whether natural, chemically-enhanced, or artificial.

Now he knew the color of survival and the flavor of rejuvenation. It was his favorite color and his favorite flavor. And why shouldn't it be? This world had recognized his plight. Somehow, someway it was accommodating him.

Either that or you're dreaming, still lying there, close to death.

But he didn't believe that.

He was alive.

And in some impossible, inexplicable way, more alive than he'd ever been in his life.

In the weeks following the discovery of the orange fungus and the reviving pool, he felt himself changing. Yes, he was stronger, certainly more alert, definitely more capable, but it was something else, too. He thought differently. He didn't dream about rescue. His thoughts were centered on staying alive, on conquering this world. When he thought about the future (something he seemed to be doing less and less of by the day), he saw himself here on Anny's Planet. A king in this trackless wilderness.

I belong here, he thought one day. *I've always belonged here.*

Not that he didn't long for company, especially Anny and his daughter, but, oddly enough, he was coming to terms with his solitude, making it part of him. Not a disadvantage, but an opportunity, in that it gave him the time and space to plumb the depths of his own mind and get to know his strengths and weaknesses in detail for the first time in his life. To look at what he was and what he wasn't objectively.

To learn that, all things considered, he was not a quitter, a loser, but a winner.

And more importantly, a survivor.

⚬

At night, mostly at night, he could hear the enraged cries of the beast coming from the jungle. They were the sound of wrath and rage, yes, but also of hunger and … was it his imagination or was there something almost melancholy buried in them? A very human despair, a marrow-deep loneliness that externalized itself as fury?

It couldn't be, yet something deep inside him responded to the pain of the creature. His subconscious mind sensed something there that his conscious, thinking brain could neither recognize nor understand.

He had hoped that the beast, like all animals, would lose interest in him given time. It would move onto greener pastures where the hunting was easier, follow some instinctual migration that would take it far away. But, of course, that didn't happen. The beast kept after him with a very human sort of tenacity. He couldn't understand it. The planet was rich with game. Why was it so focused on him?

Because it can't get you, he thought.

There could be no other reason. But that would imply that the beast had some sort of pride. That was ridiculous … wasn't it?

Regardless, it kept coming, circling the lifeboat in the dark watches of night, shrieking and screeching, ramming its mass into the hull and making the ship creak and groan and tremble. Sometimes its cries were so loud, so ear-jarring, that it seemed that the floor plates of the lifeboat rattled.

Bennet was tempted to open the hatch and burn it down with a pulser, but, no, he wasn't about to go after it at night. That was suicide. He fully planned on killing it, but it would be on his terms, not its.

So far it hadn't shown during the daytime since that day he found the lifeboat. But that didn't mean it wouldn't. He figured it didn't like the heat of day. But desperation might draw it out of hiding one day when he was out foraging.

He had to keep that in mind.

Maybe it was time to start stalking it rather than being stalked by it.

Because, ultimately, one of them had to go.

But as much as he wanted to kill the beast, his primary occupations were foraging for food and taking dips in the exhilarating, cool, lemony waters of the reviving pool and eating the nourishing orange fungus. Ah, the sweet drunken bliss of it. The beautiful addiction. It never ceased to taste as good as it had the first time. The amazing thing was, if he decided in his mind that it tasted more like orange custard or orange cupcakes on a given day, the more it tasted like what he imagined.

It was insane.

It was impossible.

Yet it always seemed to accommodate his fantasies and cravings. He wondered, and not for the first time, if he had been a fan of cherry or blueberry flavor if it wouldn't have become these things that first day until now.

After a morning of foraging, he always sought the pool. Its waters were like fresh lemonade, so wonderfully cold and sweet. But when he swam in its depths, the waters only seemed comfortably cool.

Strange.

He spent hours there, tripping away his mind on the flavor of orange smoothies and orange cheesecake and orange sweet rolls, bathing in the rejuvenating waters of the pool and washing away his thirst with cool sips of water. *Nature provides, nature provides.* Afterward, he would lie naked on the ground and sun himself like a lizard on a rock. It seemed like the perfect existence. And the more he lived like that, of and for the planet— *Anny's Planet, remember, Anny's Planet*—the more he wanted to. His old life was becoming increasingly bleary in his mind; he was having trouble not only remembering the faces of people that were important to him, but simple things like the blue skies and gray seas of Earth.

As he lay there ruminating one day, watching multicolored insects the size of sparrows flitting about from bush to bush, he noticed something that at first disturbed him, then amused him.

His skin.

By God, his skin was different. It shone in the sunlight, and that was because it had now formed into overlapping scales. Not rough and scaly like human skin exposed to heat and dryness, but smooth and silky like the flesh of a snake. Now wasn't that something? It had happened gradually. So gradually, he wasn't even aware of it.

Lying there, he ran his fingers across his other arm, across his chest and legs and neck, reading them like Braille. How smooth and glossy he was. The scales were a beautiful yellow that glistened in the sun.

And then he knew: he was adapting. The planet was making him part of it, evolving him into a new life form that was perfectly adapted to the environment. And now that he thought of it, why, yes, it had been going on some time. Ever since dipping into the reviving pool, he slept better, he breathed better, the sun no longer bothered him as it once had.

He was remade, renewed.

And it was that very day that he discovered the tracks of the beast.

⸭

He found them in the worst possible way.

He'd been thinking that it had been some time since he had visited Anny's grave. Though it seemed like much of his former life was becoming oddly indistinct, she remained bright in his thoughts and was on his mind nearly all the time. Before he fell asleep at the end of the day, he often carried on imaginary conversations with her.

One sunny day after a dip in the reviving pool, he decided he would make the hike and visit her. He brought his pulsers with in case the beast came for him. He never went anywhere without them. It just wasn't a good idea.

Though the heat didn't bother him like before, he was still pretty done in by the time he got to her grave. He looked out over the wreckage of the *Galatea* and it made something sink inside him. After a time, he climbed the hillside to Anny's grave and cried out at what he saw: it had been opened. Something had dug down to it and taken her remains.

"NOT HER! NOT ANNY!" he shouted. "WHY COULDN'T YOU LEAVE HER AT PEACE? WHY THE HELL COULDN'T YOU LEAVE HER AT PEACE?"

But he knew. Oh yes, he knew very well. Because he had a terrible, sadistic enemy that delighted in his torment. Which proved that not only was it psychotic in mind and evil of disposition, but it was intelligent. Only an intelligent, twisted mind would know how best to hurt him and get under his skin.

He sank to his knees, raging, then sobbing.

Then he looked around and in a little dip on the other side of the hill, he found her bones strewn in every which direction. Her skull had been shattered, ribcage cracked open, femurs broken, vertebrae tossed about ... in fact, it looked like something had not only eaten her (the bones were punctured with teeth marks), but kicked her skeleton to pieces and then stomped on it like a little boy having a temper tantrum.

He put them back in the grave piece by piece, then filled in the grave.

He found the tracks of the beast easy enough; it made no attempt at stealth. It very much wanted him to know who had defiled the grave.

It was time, then.

The confrontation between them had been coming for months, and now it was time to initiate it.

⸎

Bennet had never been a hunter. He had never stalked game of any kind. Such a thing was foreign to him, yet once he found the anvil-shaped tracks he followed them. Stayed with them. Through soft sand and mud, undergrowth and bog, he never lost them. And even when he did, he cast around like a bloodhound until he found them again, tracing not only the prints but the path of the beast through the soft jungle, the broken fronds and upturned leaves and scraped hanging vines.

He had never, ever realized before how simple it was to follow the path of an animal if you knew what to look for.

I can find it anywhere, he thought. *It can't hide from me.*

And especially now that another sense had been activated in him to new, unparalleled heights: his sense of smell. Where it seemed that mere weeks before, the planet, depending on the terrain, either smelled dry and hot or wet and rotting, now there was another odor that he instinctively recognized as the natural stink of the beast itself. It smelled of age and yellow time, reptilian musk and a blackness he associated with evil.

Everything I hate is embodied in that smell. It is the spoor of the thing I must kill before it kills me. Because there will never be peace as long as it lives.

"What I do now, Anny, I do for you," he whispered to himself.

Though he had definitely gone native (the idea of which did not disturb him in the least), he was not so far gone that he did not appreciate the level of technology he had access to. Pulsers in hand, he prepared to kill or be killed.

The trail of the beast was from last night, he figured. It was much more active in the darkness and he had frequently found the scattered remains of creatures it fed upon.

He followed it for well over two hours before he found the beast's lair. In a long, narrow valley there was a crevice in the cliff face, and he knew that was its nest. The valley was filled with thorny undergrowth that would have sheared him open painfully had it not been for the smoothness of his scales. The thorns brushed against him, skidding over his flesh like broomsticks on ice.

From the foliage, he watched the cave mouth for hours, trying to come up with a plan to kill the creature. Something which, hopefully, would not involve him fighting it face to face. The pulsers would kill it, but if it got the jump on him, it would tear him apart.

So stealth and ingenuity were required.

Then, as he waited in ambush, the beast left its lair. At first, Bennet thought it sensed him and was coming after him. But it moved off at a leisurely pace, its armored hide gleaming in the sun. Now and again, it would pause like a man sniffing the air on a fine June morning, lifting its bullet-shaped head up on the trunk of its neck and opening its mouth, its tongue lapping about. After a time, it moved off into the thorn forest and he saw it climbing up out of the valley. It let out a cry sometime later from a great distance.

Now.

Bennet crawled out from his hide and scampered among the undergrowth and thorn bushes until he reached the crevice. What he was doing was dangerous as hell, and he knew it, but he was on the vengeance trail. He would go in there and destroy anything he found. Leave a little calling card of sorts that would enrage the beast and bring it right to him where he would then kill it.

The cave beyond the crevice stank like old blood, rotting hides, piss and excrement. There were human bones strewn everywhere and Bennet knew without a doubt that they belonged to the crew of the lifeboat. He even found the remains of their ragged uniforms with name tags still intact— Summers, McKeeghan, Kita, Blaski, Raisani. How they had suffered, he couldn't even guess. But the beast had gotten them, one by one.

He found a circular nest of dried grasses, ferns, and scraps. This was its bed. He kicked it about, scattering it everywhere.

Guess who came calling, bitch?

Amused with himself, he pissed where it slept. It was immature and unnecessary, but he took great glee in it.

Before he left, he found another filthy heap of rags that he identified as another uniform. The name tag was gone, but it stank like the beast. Why was this one separated from the others? And why was it placed almost reverently atop a flattened heap of rocks?

Then Bennet knew.

There was no way he could know, but he did. The uniform belonged to the captain of the lifeboat and it was still held in veneration by the beast because ... *because the beast was the captain.* Oh, it was mad, but once it occurred to Bennet, he couldn't get it out of his head. Just as the ecosystem of Anny's Planet was changing him, evolving him, it had evolved the captain into a monster. He had fed on his shipmates, so that was no wonder. There was no way to understand the mechanism at play here and Bennet's knowledge of evolutionary biology and the planet's natural forces were minimal.

Not feeling quite so hateful, but stunned and disoriented by revelation, he stumbled from the cave into the bright sunshine, feeling an ache of dread in his belly.

And the beast was waiting for him.

⚰

There was no hesitation.

It saw him coming out of its lair and charged.

Bennet, ten feet from the mouth of the cave, had about enough time to gasp. The beast came at him, back legs pistoning, claws held out for disemboweling, jaws wide, dagger teeth gleaming, saliva hanging in foul ropes. It was a primeval monster of savagery and wrath and hatred.

It made it five feet in his direction before he fired. The particle bolt from the pulser in his right hand seemed to glance off the beast's armored hide, leaving an ugly black, burned patch and nothing more. But the bolt from the pulser in his left hand caught the monster square in the chest and knocked it back.

As it roared with hunger and agony, Bennet fired nonstop, blazing blue bolts cutting it into pieces like a surgeon's knife. They blew its chest into flaming fragments, incinerated its arms and severed its legs and nearly vaporized its head. When it hit the ground with an echoing cry of rage, it was soon dead, smoldering and smoking and popping.

Bennet realized then, breathless and woozy, that he had pissed himself. But the amazing thing, the truly amazing thing was that the burning carcass smelled … *delicious.*

After that, as they had said once upon a time, the cotton was high and the living was easy. Bennet had no enemies. Anny's Planet was Eden. He was lord and master. In the weeks after the beast's death, he still thought about Anny all the time, but the idea of his old life and the crash of the *Galatea* became even murkier in his memories.

Now that the beast was gone, he didn't even seal the hatch to the lifeboat. What was the point? He made fires during the long night, but after a time, he didn't even bother lighting them. Being outside in the night with that glittering diamond field of constellations above was enough.

He ate well, learning to effectively hunt and trap the rooster-dinosaur creatures of which there were hundreds. They were delicious. He took a daily dip in the reviving pool which made him feel better than he ever had in his life. He drank gallons of its cool, citrus waters. He learned to dry and macerate the orange fungi and mix it with the water, creating a delicious, fizzy orange drink. He even dried the fungi out and made candy.

All he lacked was company.

But he found less and less need for that as time passed. His life was serene, peaceful, well-balanced. Each day was a wonder and each night a joy. He couldn't have asked for more.

But all things come to an end.

It began with the terror. One warm, lazy afternoon as he sunned himself near the pool, he heard a hissing, screeching sound like steam from a high-pressure valve. Only it was so loud that it made the planet seem to shake. The noise grew in intensity, echoing like thunder, booming and squealing.

Whatever it was disturbing his idyllic lifestyle in Eden, it was coming from the sky. He quickly darted into the jungle out of absolute primal fear. As he did his, he saw a monstrous silver machine come out of the clouds and set down in an open meadow. Figures in red suits came out of it, three of them. They pushed into the jungle, calling out in some unfamiliar language.

Bennet was terrified.

Invaders, an old and rarely heard voice told him. *Invaders come to kill you.*

By that point he was very good at hiding. He set up an ambush and when the invaders stepped into view, he sprang it. He jumped on them, hacking and slashing until they were on the ground bleeding. He had been so fast, so deadly, so perfectly adapted to his environment, they hadn't stood a chance.

He left their remains to cure into jerky under the hot sun. Safe once more, he crawled into the cool, green-smelling undergrowth. Wrapping his skeletal tail around himself, he slept.

SLITHID

ᐱₒᐁᐟᐁ

 adis Cera was the third planet of Kappa 1 Ceti in the constellation of
 Cetus. A hot, misty world of invasive tropical jungle, its atmosphere
 was breathable, but saturated with deadly spores and pathogens.
Perpetually dark, covered in dense layers of clouds and seething vapor, it
rarely saw the light of its brilliant yellow star. It was some thirty light years
from Earth, one of the Agency's farthest outposts. It consisted of a single
experimental station hewn into the green hell of the southern hemisphere.
For a scientist, it was a wonderland of discovery. For anyone else, a good
place to slowly go mad.

⚱

Some fifteen minutes after the *Vagus-3* touched down, Sarnov led his
relief team through the rolling fog to the outer airlock of Tartarus Station.
They wore e-suits and helmets for protection. Long, crawling shadows
moved around them, half-glimpsed shapes pulling back into the mist at
their approach.

"Still nothing, sir," Gilling said, looking very grim in the lights of his
helmet. "Not picking up a thing."

Sarnov didn't like any of it. They had been in hyperspace for twelve
weeks, frozen in their cryo chambers, and the first thing that greeted them
upon waking was an urgent message from the Agency: no communication

from Tartarus in nearly two months. Not good. Not good at all. The *Vagus-3* was a resupply ship. They were bringing tons of essentials to the crew on Sadis Cera ... except there didn't seem to be a crew.

Their lights playing over the airlock, Sarnov felt weak inside. He had been a deep-spacer, a soldier and a security man for years, seeing his fair share of death and violence, but the outpost made him uneasy.

Whatever it is, he told himself, *it won't be good.*

When the *Vagus-3* had finally fallen in orbit around the planet, he had hoped they'd get a signal from Tartarus. Maybe their hypercom equipment had broken down. But there was no signal. And now, on the ground, there was not even a sign of life.

"Shall we?" Rice said. She was impatient by nature. Wired and twitchy, waiting was not her strong suit.

Inside his helmet, Sarnov nodded. Gilling, Rice, and Sato queuing up behind him, he opened the airlock. After decompression, they stepped into the station and the hatch closed behind them with a jarring echo like a tomb door slamming shut. There were no lights.

"What do you make of it, boss?" Sato asked.

But Sarnov had no answers. The station was like a coffin at midnight, its lid sprung. The sight of it gave him the same sense of superstitious terror that he could not think his way around. It was on him and in him.

The darkness was just as black as squid's ink and like it, he worried that something terrible was using it as camouflage. Something that had wiped out the crew and was now waiting for them with long yellow teeth. Their lights picked out a long corridor with an arched overhead.

"Not exactly inviting," Gilling said, the understatement of the year.

Sarnov looked over at Rice. Behind her faceplate, she offered him the cold wooden grin of a puppet.

She feels it, too, he thought.

"Okay," he said. "Let's do this. I want weapons in hands. Nobody fires without my order."

His knees full of water, he stepped deeper into the station.

Though the lights were off, that didn't mean the station was dead. Its AI package was still abundantly alive, an autonomous nervous system pumping fresh water into pipes like blood through arteries, bleeding off waste, heating rooms, providing air for breathing like respirating lungs. It hummed and clanked and whirred. It was very much alive.

Rice consulted her scanner. "We've got life support, Captain. Should we take off our helmets?"

"Negative. Not until we know what's going on."

Maybe some kind of pathogenic microbe had gotten in from the seething petri dish of Sadis Cera and infected the crew. If that was it, then it could still be very active. Sarnov was not about to take the chance.

"I don't get it with the lights," Gilling said, flicking a wall switch. "None of these work."

"Maybe the generator's down," Sato said.

"The backups, too?"

No, it did not make sense.

Sarnov led the way forward.

There was something shuttered and menacing about the darkness around them that the mere lack of light could not explain.

"Over here," Sato said.

He was standing before a junction box … or what had been a junction box. The switches were shattered, connections severed, even the housing dented and banged-up.

"Looks like someone went after it with an axe," Rice said. "Almost … well, almost like they wanted the station dark."

"Why would they want that?" Sato asked.

But that was a question nobody wanted to field. Maybe Sato was not feeling the cloying atmosphere of dread in that station, but the others were picking up on it, Sarnov knew. It was like being plugged into some circuit of terror. Inside his suit, it crawled up his spine and over the backs of his arms. His scalp was tingling as if it had been peeled back.

He began to tell them to keep together, but his throat was so dry, he could barely speak. Terrible thoughts massed in his head like maggots, slinking and crawling, bursting free from cold, pearly eggs.

They came to a bend in the corridor. Sato took the left fork and stopped right away. "Jesus," he said.

They all saw it—a body. But one that had literally erupted as if it had swallowed a grenade. It was splattered in all directions, meat and tissue stuck to the walls in clumps, blood like red spackling dried on the ceiling. Whoever it was, man or woman (and there was no way to tell), they had died violently as if they'd been flensed with a hot knife, their remains glued to the floor in a coagulated pool of blood and gristle.

Gilling turned away. "What in the hell happened here?"

A pulser weapon would burn a body, but it wouldn't make it explode like that in some catastrophic anatomical eruption. The body looked like a deep-sea fish exposed to traumatic decompression, and even that didn't quite cut it.

Rice squatted down by the body and read it with her scanner. "It's not telling us anything we don't know—necrotic, dead for many days, complete destruction of its systems—but it does say that it was a man. If he had an identity chip, scanner's not reading it."

Sarnov stood there, his anxiety deepening into a chasm inside him. Thoughts drummed in his head, suggestions, ideas, each one bringing a greater fear with it.

Rice stood up. "Captain, I'm picking up motion moving in our direction ... biosigns all over the place. Whatever it is, it's definitely not human."

Now they could hear its approach: the slapping of bare feet like a swimmer coming out of a pool. They waited with pulsers in trembling hands, their suit lights illuminating the corridor just before them. A dark shadow moved in their direction with an odd, uneasy side-to-side locomotion and then it stepped into the light—an aberrant, malformed thing that initially looked like a walking mass of palpitating tumors.

"Hold your fire," Sarnov said, his heart like a cold brick in his chest.

The creature—manlike in that it had two arms and two legs—stood there, breathing with a wet, squeaking sound like a balloon inflated to the bursting point. It was a bulging, tumescent thing of quivering corpse-white flesh that seemed to be composed mainly of oval, pulsating sacs, dozens and dozens of them. Blunt, fleshy tubes grew from its distorted head and face, wriggling like worms. It had a single suppurating eye the color of bile, lips rotted away from its mouth, exposing a sardonic grin of pink gums and gnarled teeth.

When Sarnov noticed that the sacs were inflating, he gave the order: "Fire!"

They opened up, the bolts from their pulsers hitting the creature and making it blaze like a match head. It seemed to erupt like a fusion bomb, glowing bright blue like a gas flame, before collapsing into a blackened, twitching mass.

"What in the fuck was that?" Sato asked, staring at the smoking, sputtering mass before them.

Gilling stepped back, leaning against the wall like he was going to be sick. Rice tried to read the remains with her scanner, but it was no good.

"We," Sato breathed, "should get back to the ship and call this in, boss."

"We can't do that. Not until we search this place for survivors," Rice told him.

She was right, and Sarnov knew it. They couldn't tuck their tails between their legs and run, much as he wanted to, not until they were sure. Despite the worm of horror eating out his guts, there was protocol to be followed.

Tell them, a voice said in the back of his head. *Tell them before it's too late.*

But he couldn't. His voice had dried up in his throat and he found it difficult to string together a single coherent thought. He wasn't going to say a word until he was sure. Not until he was 100 percent sure of what they had gotten themselves into.

"All right," he finally said. "Let's go."

◊

It was like moving through the passages of a ghost ship, a black and godless void where anything might jump out at you from the shadows. The fear crawled up Sarnov's spine like black, hungry ants and he had all he could do to keep it at bay. They all felt it and he knew it: no one spoke, no one made a single joke or told a single off-color story; they bunched together like kids in a spook house, frightened every second.

He wanted nothing better than to call this off, but he was bound by duty.

You don't really think any of them are left alive, and you know it, he told himself.

There would be no one to help or save. His crew wasn't here to play hero or savior. No, their job in this situation was strictly undertaking, counting the dead and viewing the carnage.

Sato's face in his helmet had a pinched, stiff look to it, his eyes wide and staring as if he was shellshocked. Gilling was pretty much the same, save that every time he looked at Sarnov it was accusingly, as if to say *C'mon, Captain, we're a merchant crew, we're not trained for this shit.* Only Rice seemed motivated to find out what the hell this was about. But that wasn't surprising. She was basically fearless and curious as hell by nature.

They came across two more bodies in staterooms that looked like nothing more than splattered red grapefruit pulp. Something terrible had gotten to them.

Or got into them, Sarnov found himself thinking without a trace of hope.

Rice was leading the way now, checking rooms one by one, her helmet lights splashing over the walls and floor, revealing very little. They came across a set of bloody human footprints, long dried, in one of the corridors, and a bloody handprint on the wall. That was about it.

But, inside, Sarnov knew better than to hope that this nightmare was over. The fear that gripped him would not let go. It squirmed in his belly and moved through his chest in hot waves.

Rice stopped and they nearly collided with her.

"Two individuals just ahead," she said, her voice beginning to crack with the fear the others had been feeling for some time. "Biosigns right off the map."

Sarnov licked his dry lips. "All right. Hold your position and be ready to fire."

Rice had just started to pull back to them when something stepped from a darkened doorway, something the scanner had completely missed: another creature. It was an inhuman living carcass, a huge pulsating torso made of breathing sacs that looked oddly like small, membranous-skinned breasts. They quivered like rotting melons infested by larvae ... except where the nipples would have been there were bright pink eyes.

As the thing inhaled with a grating, gravelly noise, the sacs were sucked into its swollen, bleached-white body. When it exhaled, they popped free again like fleshy water balloons with a sort of rubbery, stretching sound.

Five-feet away, the thing grinned at her with its shining, exposed gums and peg-like teeth. The multitude of tubes rising from its face and neck hung limply, like sawn-off hoses. Again, a single eye stared back, wriggling in its puckered socket like a fat white grubworm.

"RICE!" Sarnov cried, unable to get a shot at the thing with her in the way.

She hesitated for just two or three seconds, perhaps mesmerized by horror, and that cost her. The carcass inflated like a bladder until it looked nearly twice its original size and then with wet popping sounds, it ejected its sacs at her—they flew through the air like balls, dozens of them hitting her and adhering to her suit like barnacles where they pulsated and swelled. They all heard her scream over the comm as she tripped and fell, trying to rise up, her hands flailing.

"Eggs," Sato gasped. *"They're fucking eggs ... "*

They clung to her like polyps, expanding and throbbing. Made of some opaque gelatinous tissue, there were vague, coiling, embryonic things inside them. She was in unbelievable agony and before anyone could get to her or the mutant horror that had infected her, something absolutely inconceivable happened: the eggs began to melt into her suit. One after the other, they passed through its outer shell without leaving so much as a rip or a pinhole.

She began to thrash and jerk, writhing like she had grabbed a high voltage line. Beyond her faceplate, they could see her contorted face, yellow as cheese, begin to crawl and ripple on the skull beneath. And then the helmet began to fill with what looked like expanding bubbles of seafoam, except they were eggs, a multitude of them … clumping gelid eggs like frogspawn. Her face was buried beneath them.

By that point, everyone had pulled back. They all liked Rice, had served with her, struggled with her, and laughed with her, but *this*, this was a nightmare. Her suit began to bulge as if it was being pumped with helium. The faceplate of her helmet cracked open about the same time her suit burst with a gushing profusion of eggs. She was buried in a snot-like web of them, but beneath it, incredibly, she still moved.

The walking carcass that had ejected its ova at her stood there, its entire body palpitating as more eggs pushed out of its flesh. Its head thrashed from side to side, hands clawing in the air, its jaws snapping open and closed. It was making a high-pitched wailing sound as if it was singing its death song.

Gilling opened up first with his pulser and the others followed suit until the creature blazed up and broke apart on the floor like a bag of burning leaves, hot embers of it blowing through the air.

Meanwhile, Rice's torment was hardly at an end.

Beneath the mountain of eggs, she was still struggling. Steam rose from them like boiled blood. Then her fingers broke through the mass, wiggling like white silken worms. She was a blind, inhuman thing squirming in primal ooze as she clawed her way free, her flesh the same deathly white as the carcass, her hair gone, her neck and face a profusion of suckering white tubes. As she stood, eggs bulged from her like gigantic tumors and one eye which was as white as a newborn maggot irised open.

Sato screamed at the sight of her. The dozens and dozens of eggs at her torso were expanding, jiggling, making ready to eject.

Sarnov fired and the others joined in. They did not stop until she was a smoldering black mess on the floor, popping and sputtering.

"Now it begins," Sarnov muttered over the com.

Both Sato and Gilling were absolutely distraught, nearly hysterical with the horror of it all. Sarnov knew that they were both near the point of mental collapse, but there was no time to talk to them or tell them what was going on because more of the carcasses were coming. They could hear them moving up the corridor in their direction, hissing and screeching.

"Christ, boss, we gotta get back to the ship," Sato said.

Gilling kept shaking his head inside his helmet, his eyes huge and blank. He was grinning, frowning, grimacing, his face a map of his emotions which were chaotic and ever-changing—hatred, terror, disgust, and a darkness edging closely to madness. "Rice ... oh God ... Rice ... she, she—"

"Yeah," Sarnov said. "But we need to concentrate on staying alive. Let's go!"

They followed along as he moved down the corridor, but he knew they were coming apart at the seams. He was holding them together with spit and a prayer, and that would soon not be enough. Though he hated himself for thinking it, he almost wished that the carcass had gotten one of them instead of Rice. He needed her spunk and attitude, not these two wallflowers that were gradually withering away, pulling deep into themselves like little boys fearing monsters under the bed.

"They're coming for us," Gilling said and his voice sounded dry enough to cough dust. "Do you hear? They're fucking coming for us!"

Sarnov heard, all right. Of course, they were coming for them. The station was full of those creatures and they would never stop until they were burned down by a pulser. That was a given. He could hear their slopping footsteps, the chattering of their teeth, their squealing cries.

But he had to keep his head: everything depended on it. He had briefly looked at the layout of Tartarus Station before leaving the ship. If his memory served him, the corridor they were in was basically where the crew lived, the doors to either side belonging to their quarters. Ahead, would be the galley and rec room, beyond that, the labs and warehouse. And it was there they'd find the EXIT airlock.

They had to get there.

But before them was a darkness that seemed darker and more threatening than any darkness he had ever seen before. As he moved down the corridor, guided by his helmet lights, Sato and Gilling seemed like black paper cutouts clinging to him, afraid to get more than a foot away. In his mind, he could smell their fear-stink and it was sour and yellow. The dark ahead and behind seemed filled with the wailing and guttural noises of the carcasses.

They're converging from every direction, he thought. *And we're trapped between them.*

It was an awful idea and patently real. The darkness was alive with gorgons and night-terrors. And the scanner had burned up with Rice.

"Gonna ... gonna get out of this shit-show," Gilling was muttering under his breath. "Gonna quit the service, go back home ... go back home and stay there."

His voice was low but Sarnov could hear him over the helmet comm. In the light and security of the ship it might even have been somewhat comical, but there was nothing funny about it here: he was cracking up when he was needed most.

Sato said, "Boss ... oh God, what are we going to do? I can feel them closing in on us."

He had no more said that when two of them stepped out of the dark before them, both gravid with eggs, pulsing and swelling, dripping slime, seeming to liquefy as they moved forward, oozing clots of jelly that plopped to the floor. Their heads shook back and forth as if they were in terrible torment, the multiple slithering tubes where their faces and heads should have been waving in the air like sea grass in a current.

Gilling screamed and fired. His hand was shaking so badly and he was so riven with terror, that his first shots went wild. They hit the walls, they burned holes in the ceiling. Then he walked the stream of bright blue pulser bolts onto his target, and blasted a carcass quite literally into flaming pieces. By then, Sato and Sarnov had reduced the other one to blackened wreckage at the very point where it was preparing to launch its eggs.

Gilling screamed again, tripping over his own feet as he fell backward, hitting the floor.

In his light, Sarnov saw that one of the arms of the thing Gilling had blasted was still alive. Its fingers scratching over the floor, it pulled itself forward. Distended like the arm of a waterlogged corpse pulled from a river, it foamed with slimy white goo, putting out dozens of the tube-like growths which seemed to be inflating and deflating as if they were breathing.

With a cry of disgust, Sato cremated it.

$\mathwork$

The galley.

They made it there, about a dozen carcasses patrolling the passages, seeking them out, but seeming not to know where they were exactly. They were still out there, shrieking and raking the walls with their claws, making those repellent juicy sounds that Sarnov didn't even want to think about.

"We'll wait here until it settles down," he told them. "Then we'll make for the labs and get out."

"Let's just go now!" Gilling said.

"Not yet."

Gilling looked tragically disappointed behind his faceplate, fragile and worn, his eyes huge and wet. Beads of sweat rolled down his face and there was tic in the corner of his mouth that made his lips twitch constantly.

Sato quietly moved about the galley, exploring. He found the remains of least five bodies that had exploded, lots of withered black things like desiccated plums that must have been eggs. It was sickening, like some human slaughterhouse. But at the same time, Sarnov understood that the carcasses had a definite life cycle: they reached a point where they were so bursting with eggs that they literally erupted whether they had a host to pass them to or not.

"Quiet," he said over the comm.

Outside, one of them was shuffling around, making wet garbled sounds as he or she or *it* scratched at the door. After a time, it went on its way, moaning and rasping.

"Boss, look at this," Sato said.

He was over at the other end of the galley and to get to him, Sarnov had to step around burst corpses with their stuffing hanging out, heaps of remains, and brown eggs like rotten apples fallen from trees. He accidentally stepped on one of the latter and it mushed under his boot like a soft mushroom.

Sato was looking at a shriveled, dead-gray object on the floor. It was about three-feet long and looked suspiciously like the tentacle of some marine animal, in that its underside was set with suckers, each of them about the size of an old-time fifty-cent piece. Yes, it looked very much like a dried-up, well-muscled tentacle, but the dead narrow eyes at one end and the wide mouth of interlocking, spiked teeth beneath them ruined the illusion.

"Don't touch it," Sarnov said.

"I wasn't about to, boss. What the hell is it?"

Inside his helmet, Sarnov cleared his throat as bile began to rise up his esophagus. "It's a Slithid worm," he said.

Sato stared at him through his faceplate. His mouth hung open and his eyes did not blink. "No, no, no," he said. "That's not possible. They're extinct. I read all about it. Drones sprayed the whole of Sadis Cera after the first landing team was wiped out."

"Well, they missed a few."

Sarnov explained that he'd had his suspicions when they found the first body. Once you saw the remains of an egg-zombie explosion, you'd never forget it. Fifteen years before, he'd seen such a thing on Lykonis, the second planet of Wolf 1055 A. The entire station had been wiped out. He'd been part of the cleanup crew and it was a nightmare that never left him.

"The Slithids are awful things, and we still don't know much about them," he said, his voice dropping an octave. "Nobody knows how they get places, but they show up on planets light years apart. Some of the big thinkers back in the colonies have speculated they wormhole from place to place. Who knows? Way beyond my pay grade."

He looked across the room to see if Gilling was listening in, but if he was, he gave no sign of it. He sat on the floor, rocking back and forth like a traumatized child.

Sarnov went on, explaining the life cycle of the Slithids. "They look for hosts and lay their eggs on them. Right away, the hosts mutate into those things out there, walking incubators that keep the Slithid eggs warm and nourished. They seek out other hosts and eject eggs onto them. And those eggs somehow split into more and more eggs. Eventually, the eggs hatch and that's what we're in the middle of: a mass hatching."

"Jesus."

"Yeah."

Across the room, Gilling was on his feet. They both heard him over the comm, *"No, I ain't waiting for that! I'm getting the hell out of here!"* And then he quickly went to the door and out of it. By the time Sarnov and Sato got there, both calling over the comm for him to come back, he was already moving up the corridor, his boots thumping on the floor.

Immediately, the anguished wailing of the walking carcasses spiked to a feverish pitch.

"GILLING!" Sarnov shouted over the comm. "GET BACK HERE! GET BACK HERE, YOU IDIOT!"

But he was too far gone to comply. He was a simple machine fueled by dread and driven by fear. He had barely made it twenty feet when one of the egg zombies came out of the darkness, jerking and contracting, a dripping, oozing sewage of decomposition.

By then, it was too late for either Sarnov or Sato to do anything.

There was something intimately unpleasant about listening to someone die over the comm, their death screams in your ears, reverberating through your skull with the sound of shattering white glass.

Sarnov and Sato were forced to listen to every excruciating moment of Gilling's end. A brace of shrieking, slobbering egg zombies joined the other and completely cut off any chance of escape he might have had. They slowly advanced on him, puffy white things pulsating with bubble-shaped ova that leaked a leprous yellow placental fluid as they came to term. The eggs were obscenely alive—jiggling, expanding and deflating like pumping hearts, inside each a lively, twisting, sinuous form.

Sato had his pulser in his hand, but he never fired, any more than Sarnov did. There was no way to do so without the risk of hitting Gilling. And the idea of charging in there to rescue him was beyond human conception, not with the active state of all those eggs.

The ring of egg zombies closed in around him, reaching out with dead-white fingers, but they never got him.

Suddenly, they just stopped as if they'd hit a wall. And for a few brief seconds, the exterior mics of Sarnov's suit registered only the skin-crawling popping and fizzing sounds of the carcasses, and the tissue that dropped from them like congealed jelly.

Even Gilling's manic screams died out.

And it was in that momentary pocket of silence that the worms came.

Sarnov saw one coming out of the wall near Gilling and for a few seconds, he had no idea what he was even looking at: this was not the flaking, dead thing he'd seen on the floor of the galley curled up like a dead snake or the mummified, fragmentary remains he'd seen scattered everywhere on Lykonis after the biocon teams sprayed chemical weapons.

No, this Slithid was alive, plump with vitality—a swollen pink worm nearly as long as his arm and segmented like the tail of a scorpion. It swam right through the metal-composite wall as easily as a man passing through a patch of mist; there was absolutely no resistance.

It undulated up and down like a dolphin rather than side-to-side like a serpent. As it moved, the air around it crackled and flashed with tiny blue arcs like static electricity. With each winding motion, droplets of clear goo foamed from it, bubbles scattering in every which direction, some popping against the ceiling. Its yellow eyes protruded from their sockets with each stroke, and its mouth opened like a filter-feeder, rows of teeth like surgical needles jutting from pearly white gums.

Sarnov became very aware of the pulser in his hand and a voice in the back of his head that screamed *Kill it! Kill it! Kill it! Kill the damn thing!* But that was impossible, for as the egg zombies pulled back at its appearance, it wound itself around Gilling's helmet like a blubbery tentacle of pink meat.

By then, of course, it was not alone.

Dozens of others came out of the walls and ceiling, swimming in the galvanic ether around them like maggoty eels, their segments fat with eggs.

Within bare seconds, Gilling was covered in them. They wound him up like yarn, their ovipositors pumping out eggs that literally filled his suit. Again, like the walls, it was no barrier to them. Gilling screamed wildly until his mouth sounded like it was filled with wet leaves and his suit inflated to the bursting point with eggs. Just before its lights went out, his helmet filled with eggs like roe, then his face was buried in them.

The faceplate cracked open from internal pressure as did his helmet, his suit erupting with a mountain of slimy, viscous eggs that gushed from it like lava from a volcano, spilling out in a pool that drowned him.

And then if it could have gotten worse, it did: the carcasses began ejecting their eggs and they flowed in a gelatinous storm down the corridor like the gigantic disembodied eyes of thousands of toads, spinning and enlarging and finally bursting open with a splattering afterbirth and disgorging immature worms that crawled over the floor and walls and ceiling and squirmed in the air, covering everything like grave worms coveting a rotting corpse.

Just before Sarnov turned and ran, he saw Sato get engulfed in layer upon layer of eggs.

↑

After that, Sarnov's mind folded up in his head as he ran and stumbled, trying to escape the eggs and their septic spawn. The infestation of Tartarus Station was complete. Dozens of eggs covered his helmet and he blew its seal and tossed it down the corridor. He could smell the worms and their hosts—a sweet, sickening rank odor like gangrenous flesh.

An immature worm dropped onto his cheek. It was cold and fleshy. It seemed to dig into his skin with tiny hooks and the pain of their attachment burned like acid. He stripped it away and crushed it in his hand. It let out a thin, mewling cry like that of a newborn kitten.

He knew that Sato would be coming for him now, or what he had become—a living incubator, a lush, greening hothouse of eggs and larval young.

He knocked two more worms away from him, all the while thinking of the one that had ridden his face, that unclean noxious horror that made his blood feel contaminated simply by contact.

It's nothing! It means nothing! You got rid of it, you killed it, it didn't have time to inject eggs into you! Just reach the ship and get out of here!

A clutch of eggs fixed themselves to his left glove, then his right. He stripped them off and just as he did, two egg zombies came down the corridor toward him, quaking and pulsing, shambling masses of living pulp and gestating eggs, faces crawling with those writhing tubes and swollen orifices, grinning with peeled mouths.

He burned both of them down and leaped over their smoldering remains, the stink of which was like greasy burnt feathers.

Just as he burst from the airlock into the nightmare darkness and cloying mists of Sadis Cera, an egg the size of a baseball struck the back of his hand and clung, throbbing and bleeding a serous juice. With absolute revulsion, he clawed at it, tearing into it with his fingers and then it was gone ... but not really gone: he could feel it inside his arm like a huge bubble.

Sarnov screamed as he vaulted through the gagging, foul mist. More eggs found him. One settled in his hair and he crushed it in his fist, thick fluid squirting between his fingers, the unborn worm trying to slink away like a fat slug before he smashed it to paste. Several others stuck to his suit and he smashed them with his fists.

He fell to one knee, batting away eggs and swimming worms, looking back and seeing a swarm of eggs floating from the open airlock of the station. It looked like a child blowing bubbles. He emptied the pulser, vaporizing as many as he could and then he was running again.

The ship, just get to the fucking ship! Don't think, don't reason, don't speculate! Get there and load yourself with drugs—antibiotics, antifungals, and antiparasitics! You have a chance! You have just one fucking chance and you better make good on it!

Yes, yes, yes. A quick liftoff and into orbit, then call the Agency on subspace and they'd be here in days with drones to hit Tartarus Station with fusion weapons that would boil it into the ground.

He made it.

Inside *Vagus-3,* he laid in an emergency trajectory and before the anti-magnetic core cut him loose from the planet, he'd dosed himself with everything in the med-kit.

His heart pounding, his brain filled with white noise, he realized that the ship was filled with eggs and worms. They came right through the outer shielding and inner bulkheads. The worms, many of them quite large now, sparkling like living powerlines, swam through the air, chasing each other, knocking eggs out of their way.

The ship was not lifting off.

Of course not, he realized in his panic. It wouldn't until he was safely strapped into his couch. Safety protocol. Now there were eggs clustered to the panels in great throbbing masses like limpets and bivalves sticking to beach rocks.

He let out a hysterical scream as he saw Sato there—or what he judged to be Sato—looking in the viewport with one eye like an oyster suppurating with diseased blood. He was bone-white, his face wriggling like deep-sea tube worms, a nest of squirming hoses and fat polyps. He was a great sac of ova.

Eggs stuck to Sarnov and he couldn't peel them away fast enough as they sank into his skin and his body began to swell, cracking and snapping and realigning itself. Things crawled from his face and worms filled his throat.

Fight it, fight it, fight it—

He slumped into his chair as the eggs inundated him and the worms drilled into him relentlessly. He reached up one shaking hand and touched his face, and it felt like congealing jelly. Buried alive in eggs, running with drainage, and bursting with blunt lively tubes, he couldn't seem to remember what he was fighting for.

Sometime later, he crept from the ship, carefully mothering his young.

HELLSCAPE

ᗯᴏᴏᴧᴗᴛᴊᴏ

1

The commander does not know how long she has been hanging there, dangling like a juicy fly in a spider's web. It could be hours or days or weeks for that matter. There's no way to know. Her head is whirling, spinning, and her thoughts—when she has them—are dashed against the walls of her mind, breaking like fine crockery, shattering into fragments that blow around in her skull without form or substance.

She hangs three feet off the ground from a milky sheath of threads that bind her wrists. It's like spider silk, warm and sticky with great tensile strength. Even using every bit of her strength, she cannot break it. It stretches, but instantly snaps back into place like a rubber band.

There are horrific stabbing pains in her legs and a crawling, prickly heat at her scalp. Her uniform is sweat-soaked and soiled with grime and dried blood.

When her eyes open, she sees the horror before her. This is a slaughterhouse where the aliens dismember their human prey. On the ground there is a fetid, red sea of spilled viscera, shattered bone, and fleshy waste. Thrumming scavenger insects like blue millipedes crawl through it, feeding and breeding in the carrion depths. Nearby is the head of a woman with the top of her skull opened, stringy red hair matted with blood and brains. The inside of her cranium has been licked clean as a jelly jar: not one scrap of gray matter remains.

Sickened, the commander closes her eyes and when she opens them, one of the aliens materializes before her, a leggy nightmare shape with pincers and an armored exoskeleton. It's ghostly-white like a termite queen, its plates vibrating, its mouth making clicking and hissing noises. Multiple, brown gelid eyes study her.

At its horned feet, mutilated human forms lacking limbs worm about on their bellies, begging for mercy. The alien treads over them, sees that the commander is awake. It seizes her with its chelipeds and brings its palpitating stinger to bear: a black, gleaming spike that is easily a foot in length.

As she screams, the stinger is jabbed into her belly, her legs, and her groin until she grows limp. The alien, drooling now with acidic secretions, moves in closer ...

2

When the *Hesperion* hit, it broke open like a carton of eggs and all the baby birds came crawling out, dizzy, disoriented, groggy, barely able to stand. They crawled free in their e-suits on an alien world that was equal parts sand, dust, and blowing grit.

They were in a fix, and Ramsland told them as much. Four of them were alive and whole, but three of their team were dead and two others were wounded so horrifically they were beyond help. They could not be moved. And there lay the problem: the *Hesperion* had been downed by an Imperian warship, so it was only a matter of time before they showed looking for survivors to torment.

Doc McGhee did everything he could for the wounded, but much of his equipment was damaged in the crash, so he couldn't uplink with their nanos to begin intensive medical procedures. Which, of course, meant that Ramsland had a very ugly command decision to make. Did she abandon the wounded or did she keep her people there, in which case they would all die when the Imperians showed?

"We don't have much time," King said. "They'll be swarming down on us any minute now."

Her troops looked at her, awaiting her command. Damned if she did and damned if she didn't.

"Doc?" she said.

He shook his head. "The trauma, the shock … no way. They'll never wake up."

"Then we don't have a choice," she said.

The others stared at her, relieved that they were going to escape and evade, but secretly hating her because she was going to leave the wounded behind. Doc said they wouldn't wake up. She hoped that was true because no one had ever survived capture by the Imperians.

She looked down at the mangled, still breathing bodies of Pent and Sarwani. God, they'd fought by her side in a dozen engagements. They were not only her comrades, but her friends. And now she had to leave them for the Imperians.

The *Hesperion* had been one of two forward recon ships of the fleet, sneaking into Imperian space ahead of the main body. The other was the *Nyx*. Rescue would arrive, she hoped, but that might be days or possibly weeks. And if Imperian Raiders attacked and pushed them back, it might never come at all.

She looked over at Brightman. "Try one last time to raise the *Nyx*."

"Captain, I advise against it," King said. "Even encrypted subspace chatter will be like a homing signal to the Imperians. Trust me, they're listening."

Ramsland nodded. "Do it anyway."

Brightman tried. Nothing but static even on the secure and emergency channels.

King was getting anxious. "Okay, we need to move, Captain. *Now*. We have bare minutes. The Imperians have a beam on us and they'll be here soon."

She sighed. "All right, move out. We continue mission. We stay alive."

Doc McGhee shook his head. "But—"

"I'm sorry," she said. "But if we don't get out of here, we're all dead and you know it."

King led Brightman and Lee out the hatch into the dry heat of Epsilon Reticuli-2, the sun blazing and white above them. They had to wear sun goggles against the glare, but the air was breathable. Far to the south there were immense tropical forests, but Ramsland's crew were in the dry, dead lands of the equator, many hundreds of miles from any sea or river system. This was Imperian terrain: arid and hot.

Once Ramsland got her bearings, she led the others into the rocks beyond the crashed ship. They were tall, jagged structures with plenty of deep pockets to hide in. They were made of some quartzite matrix with prismatic green hexagonal crystals jutting from them like emeralds.

They had barely hidden themselves when King looked up from his microscanner and said, "They're coming ... the Imperians are coming."

3

Somehow, someway, the commander gets one hand free and that's the beginning. The aliens are buried in the sand because the sun is high and hot and they avoid it. She reaches up and wipes pooled sweat from under her eyes, a sticky web of blood from her mouth. Then she touches the top of her head and it's slimy and soft, like a jungle mushroom.

What does that mean?

Good God, what does that mean?

Beyond the remains and riven human anatomy, she sees the crewmen the aliens have dismembered, peeled, and scarified with their relentless, torturous cuttings. Dead eyes in diseased faces look to her, bleeding mouths call to her, stumps and protruding bones reach out to her. One of them watches her with eyes like rotten egg whites that cry serous tears. She hears voices that scrape and scratch.

Why did you let this happen?

Why didn't you get us out?

Look what they've done ... look what those evil monsters did to us....

The voices kept imploring her, crying and screaming and demanding until her mind falls into a whirlpool of blackness, sliding in and out of a delirium dream state, a hypnagogue of graveyards and battlegrounds haunted by distorted alien insects that pick away at the dead.

When she opens her eyes again, the alien toxins have subsided. She remembers the pen knife in her shirt. Sawing, carefully sawing, she cuts through the cobweb sheath that holds her wrist.

She drops to the ground.

She's in great pain, every inch of her aching from abuse, but she plans on escaping while the aliens are buried in the sand, dormant and senseless. This is the only chance she'll get.

She crawls over to a crewman who is not insane yet, or not very.

"C'mon," she says. "We have to get away now. It's our only chance. I'll carry you."

"But I like it here," he says.

"You need to come with me."

"But they're so nice to me."

He doesn't seem to realize that the aliens have taken his legs; he's too stoned on their toxins. They'll take his arms next, then his—

But there is no time.

Quickly, she crawls out onto open ground, away from the jutting rocks, then she starts running.

4

High overhead, an Imperian Raider made two passes over the wreckage of the *Hesperion*. It looked like a gigantic, multi-barbed arrowhead of glittering blue metal. It hovered for a moment or two, then banked off to the west.

"That was close," Lee said.

King grunted.

Like Ramsland, he knew better than to be optimistic. The Imperians would be coming in numbers. When they moved in on the ground, they came in armies like driver ants, destroying anything in their path. It was how they operated, how they fought. They would charge in with hundreds and thousands, overwhelming the enemy, sacrificing countless of their own to get at them, to get close enough to tear and dismember.

Lee looked more than a little frightened. "Captain? What are we going to do? What's our plan?"

"Escape and evade," King told him. "Wait for the fleet. See if we can find a sign of the *Nyx*. And in between? Kill as many of those fucking monsters as we can."

"But we're only a handful. We'd better find somewhere to hide and lie low. We don't stand a chance against them."

Ramsland didn't say anything. She turned briefly and looked over at Doc McGhee, and something passed between them. They were both thinking the same thing—King was too ready to fight and Lee only wanted to hide. Brightman was unsure, caught between these two opposing poles.

King was filled with bravado. "Listen to me, kid. We're better off fighting to the death than being taken alive by those fucking things. You can't reason with them, you can't expect mercy. They're killers. Cold-blooded killers."

"I'm just saying we should find a good, safe place to wait this out until the fleet arrives."

"You're a coward," King said, as if it really was no surprise at all. "You have the luxury of choice; I don't. You see, I've tangled with these monsters before, I've seen what they can do. I was on the ground after they finished with the Ceti colonies. I wish you'd been there. I wish you could have seen what I saw. They slaughtered every last one, kid. Men, women, and children. They cut the men into pieces, they disemboweled the women. They nailed children to the walls of houses and watched them bleed out. Before they left, they took the heads of the colonists. Even the heads of infants. And do you know why? Because they consider human brain a delicacy. That's what we're facing. So you might want to rethink your sudden turn of pacifism."

"Okay," Ramsland said. "That's enough."

King. He was really something. A good warrior as far as that went. But he had all the humanity, all the sympathy of a black widow spider. Not that what he said wasn't true, it's just that there were better ways to make his point.

She looked out over the planet, the heaped rocks and towers of stone, the sand dunes shifting between them, the endless hard-baked salt flats left over from an ancient sea. The wind was hot and gritty, everything eroding into spinning clouds of dust.

"I'm getting strong signatures," King said, studying his microscanner.

Ramsland watched the wreck of the *Hesperion,* the sky, and the blowing sand with her scope. She didn't see anything. She knew they had to get out of there, but where to? That was the question. She supposed they could move across the dunes to the next heap of rocks and then to the next one after that, leapfrogging until they got to the cliffs in the distance, hope for a cave or a gully, something that would shield them and be defensible.

"It's going up and up," King said.

Lee and Brightman visibly tensed.

Ramsland saw it through her scope: mounds beneath the sand in the distance popping up like bubbles, like buried beach balls, until there were eight or nine of them. Her throat got very dry, her spine wet with beads of rolling sweat. The mounds moved, gaining speed and throwing up plumes of twisting dust. They converged on the *Hesperion.*

"Diggers," King said in a low voice. "Goddamn diggers."

Ramsland saw one of the mounds explode into blowing sand as a form burst from beneath: a jagged head like a flattened-out helmet and huge foreclaws. Then the creature fully emerged, a massive corpse-white exoskeleton of plated armor, skittering jointed legs, scissor-like mandibles, and those lethal claws that looked like the blades of scythes.

Imperian diggers.

The rest emerged like their leader, fanning out with clicking, chitinous sounds. Their mandibles rasped and hook-like mouthparts gleamed like fangs.

King immediately brought up his chain gun, but Ramsland shook her head. Killing them would amount to suicide. It was better if the Imperians thought they all died in the crash. It was the only chance they had.

Like the exaggerated alien ants they resembled, the Imperians quickly moved toward the *Hesperion*. They communicated with grating, stridulent noises punctuated by a high-pitched trilling and a staccato *zit-zit-zit* sort of sound.

Regardless of its intent, it made human flesh crawl. Everyone automatically pulled closer together, hands on weapons.

"Nobody move," Ramsland whispered. "I don't care what you see or hear, don't you dare move."

It was good advice because the Imperians wasted no time in their grisly business. They dragged out the mangled corpses from the ship and then the injured. Without hesitation, they tore them apart, scattering anatomy in all directions with manic rage and sadistic, childlike glee. The injured began screaming and there wasn't a damn thing to be done for them.

Other than King, everyone looked away when they cracked open skulls with their pincers to get at the brains they relished, slurping and chewing with a sound no one would ever forget.

Then they made a sweep around the general area, apparently searching for stragglers. After about fifteen tense minutes, finding nothing, they dug back into the sand and disappeared.

"I'm going to kill them," King said, "every last fucking one of them."

5

The aliens want her back.

They don't like it when their livestock strays. As night closes in, they're out in numbers, seeking her out, ships passing high overhead with scanning biosensors trying to track her.

But the commander's not stupid: every time she hears the rumble of their approach, she digs down deep into the sand and hides. There's not much of use on the planet, but there's lots of sand.

Somehow, she needs to get south, far south to the greenbelt where she can hide in the jungle. Water will be there and probably edible plants. No doubt there will predators, too, hideous alien monsters, but she'll have to use her cunning to avoid them.

One thing's for sure: she can't survive in the desert.

With that in mind, she begins the long walk south, hiding, sneaking, trusting her instinct.

Her first obstacle is the weather—not just the merciless heat and dry dusty grit blown into her face, but the sudden sandstorms that engulf her, spin her around, re-sculpt the dunes until she's not sure whether she's coming or going. They abrade her exposed flesh and fill her hair with sand that gets down the neck of her suit and makes her back feel like it's blown with hot ash.

It's not the smoldering wind and incinerating hot sand like cremains blown from the mouth of an oven that she fears, it's the sudden weird, inexplicable storms. The sky goes dark and looks oddly like smoked glass, shooting out purple and green forks of lightning that strike the ground randomly with bright, deadly flashes of plasma. It's hot enough to turn the sand to crystal that crunches underfoot.

There are pools of loose mica sand that seemingly have no bottom and there are voracious ticks (for lack of a better word). She doesn't know what they really are. They're about the size of marbles, but repellently soft like slugs. They come out of pockets in-between the dunes, swarming, massing, covering her with their leggy, pulpous bodies. They immediately bite into her exposed flesh, sucking blood until they are swollen like large, juicy grapes that splatter into brown pulp when she smashes them.

Night finds her still moving, relentless in her need to escape the horror of the aliens. The landscape by thin moonlight is rugged and pitted like old hide. She hears unpleasant rustling sounds from the rocks and slithering noises from things that swim in the sand sea. For well over an hour, something follows her, *creeping in the shadows. It makes a guttural croaking like a frog.*

After a time, it leaves.

Then she's alone without even unnerving lifeforms for company. Exhausted, dehydrated, her head pounding like a drum, she keeps going and going.

The aliens will never catch her.

Never.

6

When the microscanner assured them that there were no more diggers hiding under the sand, Ramsland led what was left of her command out into the suffocating heat of the planet. It was tough going, climbing one shifting dune after another, sliding down into the valleys between only to begin their climb yet again. The dust blew, sand glancing off their uniforms, faces beaded with sweat.

After a time, they reached another rock outcropping where they huddled in the shade. The good thing was that there had been no more Imperians. The bad thing was how long could they go on like this, hiding like mice. If properly rationed, they had enough food and water for a week. There was more aboard the *Hesperion,* but that was definitely a dangerous jaunt.

We might try it at night, Ramsland thought, *but even then, it's going to be risky.*

For the time being, they hid in the rocks and waited. Night was some eighteen hours away yet, the days on Two being so damn long. There was nothing to do but rest and hope for the best because they were in a very, very bad situation.

She watched the landscape which was primarily a series of dunes in constant motion, cresting and shifting, breaking down, building up, rolling gradually like waves at sea. Dust clouds and sand storms propelled by the hot wind blew over them, gathering like fog, whipping around and then dissipating. That wind howled like something alive, something wicked and sentient, occasionally stopping, leaving an eerie void of silence in its wake.

How long can we possibly survive? she asked herself again and again.

If the Imperians didn't get them or they didn't die of thirst or hunger, the climate would destroy them. How long could the human mind listen to that awful wind without fragmenting?

Though the heat was punishing, she was grateful for it because there was no way the Imperians could get a heat signature from them in that oven. But when night came, it might be different.

"This waiting in this goddamn heat is killing me," Lee whispered.

"Get used to it, son," King told him. "There's other ways to die here and you won't like them."

Brightman was shaking despite the temperature. "Oh God," he said.

"Just relax. Everyone relax," Doc McGhee said, patting Brightman's arm. "Fear and anxiety will do us in just as quickly as the enemy."

He had already asked Ramsland if he could hand out some tranks to calm everyone down, but she was against it. They had to be alert and in fighting shape; they couldn't afford to let their guard down. The pharmaceuticals of their individual e-suits had been disabled. She didn't need anyone relaxing too much.

King's microscanner activated with a low, muted beep. "I got something," he said, adjusting it. "A sig ... biological ... it's saying there's a human being out there. Due east."

Everyone perked up. It had to be someone from the *Nyx*. There was no way it could be anyone else.

"Getting closer," King said.

"We need to go help them," Lee said.

Ramsland shook her head. "Absolutely not. Not until we know what this is about. Could be a trap."

They all knew what she meant: the Imperians could control human beings via a parasite. They might send out someone to draw them out.

She studied the dunes with her scope. The others were doing the same.

Nobody spoke. The tension held.

"Should be visible any second now," King announced.

"There!" Brightman said.

Yes, Ramsland saw them now. It was a man in a dirty fleet uniform and he was running, scrambling up dunes and sliding down them, losing his footing in the soft sand, tripping, falling, crawling like an insect and then on his feet, running again.

"Something's after him," Lee said. "You can see that."

"And we don't want what's after him to be after us," King breathed.

His flight took him into the general area of the *Hesperion* crash site. No one had to say how dangerous that was. But there was no way to warn him. Now he saw the wreckage and stopped. Slowly, slowly, he walked among the scattered debris and saw the remains of the crew baking in the sand.

"Can't we do something?" Brightman said. "Signal him somehow?"

"Not without drawing attention to ourselves."

Lee made a deep moaning in his throat. "Captain, c'mon, we can't let him die out there!"

But that's exactly what she was going to do because there was no longer a choice in the matter: mounds had risen all around him. He saw them and tried to run, moving in a haphazard course toward the nearest dune.

But he never got there.

The mounds came at him from every side, speeding under the sand and, even at that distance, they heard his scream compete with the feral growl of the wind.

A mound hit him and he pitched over.

There was blood soaking the sand. He tried to get away, but his feet had been severed and the best he could manage was a sluggish crawl as he continued to scream. The diggers showed no mercy. Without ever revealing themselves, they went after him like buzzsaws, sectioning him until his legs were gone and he was nothing but a writhing torso jerking with spasms in the hot red sand. Then they sliced even that in half, then quartered it. His head seemed to jump from the stump of his neck in an explosion of gore, spinning across the sand and then it was pulled under like a drowning swimmer and was gone.

That was it.

When the mounds disappeared, Ramsland put her scope away. The others, save King, had already done so.

Brightman and Lee were staring at her. She knew they blamed her for the man's death. But if they had gone to help him, it would have been them lying in pieces out there.

They didn't seem to understand the horror of the Imperians, but they would. God help them, given time, they certainly would.

7

About the time the commander thinks she's the only human being left on the planet, she's found by a group of fighters from another crashed fleet ship. They live a desperate life like freedom fighters or partisans: hiding, fighting, scavenging, killing any aliens they find. She's drafted into their legion and lives with them, as them.

They are led by a hot-blooded, angry warrior named Morrik, who outranks her. He lives only to kill their oppressors. He stalks lone aliens and then attacks them with his little army, hacking them into pieces. She is with them again and again as they kill the enemy.

One day, he makes a speech: "EVERY ONE OF YOU MUST FIGHT! YOU MUST DESTROY THOSE CREEPING MONSTERS! THERE IS NO OTHER REASON FOR EXISTENCE! KILL! KILL! KILL! THINK OF WHAT THEY HAVE DONE TO US! TO OUR BROTHERS AND SISTERS! WHEN THE FLEET ARRIVES, WE SHALL BE HEROES! IF ANY OF YOU SHOW ANY COWARDICE, I WILL KILL YOU WITH MY OWN HANDS! BELIEVE THAT!"

So together they wage war on the aliens and the fight for survival goes on and on in Morrik's little war of attrition. The fleet will be coming, he assures them. The idea that it might not does not enter into his mindset, his patriotic ideals and world vision.

They will be coming, oh yes.

They wouldn't abandon them on this godforsaken planet.

No way.

They wouldn't do that.

8

Walking, walking, walking.

Despite the heat, Ramsland decided it would be best to get them as far away from the wreck of the *Hesperion* as possible. Sooner or later, she feared, the Imperians would make a detailed sweep, seeking out stragglers, and they needed to be well away when that happened. So soon as the sun was not directly overhead, they walked.

The landscape, of course, was monotonously repetitive. A few hills of rocks, sand seas in-between, an ocean of dunes cresting and breaking in every direction.

If we make it out of this it will be by sheer dumb luck, she thought.

She had King scouting ahead with his microscanner, pathfinding for them (if it could be called that) and looking for any signs of trouble. What worried her most were the diggers, so pulsers never left hands. Everyone was ready to start shooting at a moment's notice.

Sweating, struggling, and generally miserable, they pushed on.

About an hour into it as they rounded a spire of stone and mounted yet another dune, the sky a white haze, King came back, panting and puffing.

"Some sort of encampment ahead," he told them. "Abandoned, by the looks of it."

"What's the scanner say?"

"No Imperians, but human remains."

Just another little something for general morale, Ramsland figured. But much as she wanted to give it a wide berth, she knew couldn't. They followed King down the slope of a dune and into a little valley with sharp outcroppings of black rock that jutted like broken teeth. The dust blew hard down there for a few minutes, but when it stopped, they saw.

"God," Lee said, turning away from it.

Ramsland counted the remains of five people, three men and one woman. One of them, tossed away from the others, looked blackened as if he'd been exposed to searing heat like a pulser beam, the blood and fat boiling out of him and coagulating into a tarry pool. But it wasn't a pulser, she knew, but the terrible venom delivered by an Imperian bite.

What was left of the man had dried and cured in the sun like beef jerky.

"Take a good look," King said, his chain rifle balanced on his shoulder. "This is what your enemy does with captives."

The others had been heaped in a loose pile. All of them had been meticulously flayed, the skin peeled from them no doubt while they were still alive. The sand was red from their blood. All of them, of course, had been beheaded.

"Look at this," Doc McGhee said, searching around at the outer edges of the camp.

Half-buried in the sand was a blasted, broken carapace from an Imperian, its limbs scattered in all directions. It looked like melted plastic.

"Pulser hit," King said. "In fact, I'd say this digger took about three pulser bolts simultaneously."

"They got one of them, anyway," Brightman said.

King's sunburned face grinned sardonically. "And we'll get a few more before this is done."

Ramsland ignored him. This was hardly the time for *rah-rah-rah, go team go!* They were on an alien world with dwindling supplies and only luck, cunning, and perseverance would see them still alive in a week. No amount of self-deluding patriotic bullshit would save their hides.

"We better get out of here," she said.

They began to do just that … and then, suddenly, King raced into the rocks, shouted, swore, and came back dragging a man by the arm. He dumped him before them.

The man was stick-thin, terribly emaciated, his skin a burnished brown from the relentless baking sun. His uniform hung in strips and flaps. He looked up at them with glazed eyes, his mouth opening and closing like that of a gulping fish.

"Looking everywhere for you guys," he finally said. "If we stand together, we've got a fighting chance."

Sure, he was from the Fleet, a *Nyx* crew member, another human being in this dreadful place, but no one went to him. No one dared get close to him.

"He's been crabbed," King said.

There was no doubt of it. His head was bald and there was a parasite clinging to it with six spindly legs, its gray thorax pulsating. It had beady black eyes and something like spiny crab claws. Ramsland knew that the Imperians used them on their human pets. With the parasites—not surprisingly known as *crabs*—they could control their captives, make them do anything they wanted and, more importantly, communicate with them.

Lee looked from Ramsland to Doc McGhee. "What are we going to do with him?" he asked. "Can we get it off him?"

Doc McGhee shook his head. "Not with what I have in my medi-kit. Its feelers are dug right into his brain. We try and pull it off him and it'll kill him."

"And there's easier ways to kill him," King said, bringing his chain gun to bear.

"You can't," Brightman said.

"The hell I can't." King towed him over closer to the crabbed man. "He's just a zombie, you idiot. There's nothing left in that shell that's remotely human. Can't you see that?"

And that was bad enough, Ramsland knew, but what was worse was that he was uplinked with the Imperians. They knew exactly where he was and were listening to all that was being said.

"Captain?" King said.

"Toast him," she muttered.

The others drew back as King raised his weapon. He was smiling, his eyes shining and crazy like those of a mad dog about to bite. Beads of sweat rolled down his face in the dry heat.

"Hey, c'mon now," the man said. "I'm human like you. Please don't do this, don't—"

King squeezed the trigger and two bright blue chain pulses struck him. He blazed up like was stuffed with gunpowder, becoming a blackened thing that broke apart in the sand like cigar ash.

"Let's get the hell out of here," Ramsland said. "They'll be coming for us now."

Dutiful, but despondent, they followed her up out of the valley. King led them on at an accelerated pace now. They had to find somewhere safe before the Imperians showed.

9

Sometimes she feels so alone, like a single star in a black sky. Her head throbs and her eyes water and her lips dry out until they are cured like strips of jerky. It's the heat. The awful dry atmosphere of the planet. This is what she tells herself again and again. She feels weak and terribly fragile as if she's in the depths of some wasting illness that is slowly, inexorably sucking the life out of her.

God, where's Morrik and the others? Where are the fighters? Why have they abandoned her?

She has never been religious in her life, but now she prays—for escape, for rescue, for anything to break the pattern of her suffering. She's like a little girl again, trapped in a nightmare, disturbed, delirious, afraid of everything and everyone. Sometimes, out of the darkness, she hears her own airless voice calling out for her mother to take her home, to please take her home away from the creepy-crawly aliens, away to some place safe and warm where she can sleep in a soft bed.

Her head throbs constantly.

It feels like fire burns in her legs.

And it goes on and on and on....

10

The first Imperians came about two hours later. As everyone hid behind a low shelf of black, volcanic rock, King's scanner went wild. Not just one signature, but two and three and four and five and six—a small-scale swarm by the looks of it.

"Oh shit," Lee moaned. "Oh God."

"Stand ready," Ramsland told them.

"Aye-aye," King said.

For the first time in days, he looked really alive. As if he had been waiting for this moment—and he probably had been.

Ramsland watched dozens of mounds moving at them as the diggers sped in their direction under the sand. It was only a matter of time before it came to this.

Now five or six mounds exploded into spinning dust devils and the first wave of Imperians appeared, ghostly-white, multi-legged, and determined. They made a guttural hissing as if it was some sort of war cry.

Everyone fired simultaneously and the Imperians were ripped into flaming debris, burning carapaces and twitching limbs cast in all directions, pungent black smoke rising from them in whirling clouds.

Ramsland watched as dozens more emerged.

The wind blew the sand and dust from the burst mounds at them in sheets, obscuring their attackers. Shrieking and shrilling, the Imperians pushed in, completely suicidal. And she knew that they would pile up their dead by the hundreds to get at them. They had no concern for their own lives. There was only the greater hive to them; individuality did not exist for Imperians.

They burned down at least thirty of them, but that didn't even slow the advancing enemy. They were everywhere now, swarming, blood-lusting, droning. Several made it into the rocks. King killed two of them and

Brightman a third.

But one of them survived, appearing out of the fog of blowing sand and dust. Lee was down, blood webbing his face and one of them crouched over him.

There was no way Ramsland could fire; he was just too close to the beast. Its white exoskeleton was plated and heaving, sharp, erect spines rising from it. It hovered over Lee on spurred legs, its foreclaws pinning him down, immense mandibles like sickle blades poised to scissor him into pieces.

Shit.

Lee screamed as the stinger at the rear of its palpitating abdomen jabbed into him again and again like a hypodermic needle, injecting him with paralytics which reduced him to a helpless, breathing slab of meat.

He was like a spider stung by a wasp: lying there, doped and grinning. The Imperian seized him, its foreclaws peeling him like a grape, shaking him like a terrier with a rat in its mouth.

Then its fangs sank into him.

The effect was immediate: the venom was like acid and he swelled as if from anaphylactic shock, his flesh blackening and bursting open with gouts of steam as the blood, fat, and connective tissue within went to hot bubbling jelly.

Ramsland fired.

The pulser blast cooked the Imperian from the inside out. It superheated like a tick held to a flame, and its exoskeleton exploded into shrapnel.

They were among them now in numbers, blasted shells and ruptured skulls and limbs piling up. The stench from their burning remains was unbearable. It seared her nostrils and throat.

In the blowing sand, swirling dust, and the black smoke of burning Imperians, it was hard to know where anyone was.

Then she saw King.

He wasted three Imperians and when a horde of them moved at him, he tossed a thermal grenade and threw himself to the ground.

WHOOM!

The blazing kinetic energy broiled and blew his attackers apart, leaving a smoldering heap of body parts scattered over the ground and a flak of flying debris like tossed gravel. The heatwave singed Ramsland's eyebrows.

There were too many of them now to stand against. They would be totally overwhelmed by their creeping numbers any second now.

She jumped through the haze of smoke and dust. Doc McGhee was down, most of his left arm torn away. She hoisted him to his feet and tried to drag him off. She burned down two Imperians that stood in her way and then a pincer darted at her face. She turned away from it at the last second, but it scraped against her cheek like a hot poker.

She fired instinctively.

The bolt knocked the Imperian back and Doc McGhee, barely conscious by that point, screamed in agony as he was yanked from her grip by another alien that seemed luminously white, practically glowing. There was no way she could shoot without hitting Doc. Not that it mattered, for its barbed mandibles closed on his throat, neatly snipping off his head and spraying hot blood into her face.

She stumbled backward, tripped over a burning Imperian exoskeleton and then she was crawling through the broken anatomy of a dozen more, their acidic secretions burning her hands. Her pulser was gone and she didn't even remember losing it.

She saw King, fighting on and on, killing one Imperian after another. He whirled, jumped, fired, ducked under slashing claws. Then he spotted her and came running over.

"Captain!" he cried, reaching out his hand for her.

And then something hit him.

An Imperian ripped him open with its claws and he shrieked with a combination of pain and rage that the fighting was over for him. Its mandibles seized his head and cracked his skull like a walnut, blood and brain matter flying through the air in a clotted mist.

As Ramsland watched helplessly, the Imperian battered him down with its foreclaws, leaped on him and bit him repeatedly until he became a blackened, blood-gushing mass of meat that finally, ultimately, erupted into a shapeless red pulp.

She saw his chain gun and crawled to grab it, but it was kicked away from her. She looked up and an Imperian was standing over her on its jointed legs that looked as if they'd been fabricated from white metal. It didn't have feet as such, of course, just black curling thorns like cat's claws where they would have been. The armored plates of its abdomen and thorax were fluttering as if with excitement. It watched her curiously with red eyes like glistening beads of blood, its head cocked to the side. She could see the tubercles and sawblade spines set atop it.

"So get it over with," she said.

The rear of its abdomen was throbbing, the stinger dripping neurotoxins. Its foreclaws with their deadly pincers hovered inches from her face. Its mandibles opened, revealing the fanged mouthparts beyond.

It made a warbling sort of noise followed by a droning, then *zit-zit-zit* that went right up her spine.

It reached for her.

Clutched her in a death grip like a vise.

Then its stinger pierced her again and again.

Her head spun, her body going to rubber, and she fell face-first to the ground, going out cold.

11

For days her head has been filled with an awful smell and now she sees its source: decomposing bodies are scattered about. Most of them are headless and all of them have been cut into pieces, de-limbed and eviscerated, their remains left to decompose or dry to black leather in the arid, hot climate.

This is what she sees when her eyes open, truly open for the first time in many days.

She is still hanging by her wrists.

With a sinking feeling in her belly and then an explosion of terror, she realizes that she never truly escaped. That Morrik and his rebels were merely a hallucination. She was still in this horrible place. Still a captive of the Imperians.

And worse, oh dear God so very worse, she has no legs. They have been cut off.

12

A nightmare. A godawful nightmare. Ramsland told herself that that's what it was. A hallucination. The result of a starved body and a mind twisted by the ceaseless deprivation of Epsilon Reticuli-2. Much as she tried, she could not wake up, could not break through the walls of her delusion.

Tell me what I want to know.

There was an Imperian inquisitor before her, a bloodlessly white arthropodal horror, a machine-like insect with a plated exoskeleton and jutting sharp ridges of bone. Spined and multi-limbed with infrared eyes that burned into her, it spoke with a clicking-hissing voice that became words she understood in the depths of her mind because of the parasite that was attached to her bald cranium.

Tell me why you humans invaded.

She tried to explain that they had not invaded, that the Imperians had attacked human outposts and colonies, that they were merely fighting back, but the inquisitor could not comprehend such a thing: the Imperians had the right to destroy, enslave, and feed upon all other lifeforms. Why did she not understand that? And why did the Imperians not understand that humans *always* fought back when they were threatened. It was their way. They were not about to be slaughtered by alien horrors with no reprisals. They would not take shit from insects, from fucking bugs.

Tell me about your world. Tell me about the rich food sources we shall find there.

Oh no, no, no, no, she wouldn't tell this monster about Earth and the colonies. No goddamn way. Already, she could envision the swarms of

Imperians coming from the skies in their raiders, descending on the cities, exterminating human beings, enslaving millions as workers and beasts of burden, using the majority as livestock.

Tell me of the multitudes.

But she would not. She could hear the voices of every man, woman, and child in the galaxy calling out to her, pleading with her to never, ever give them up. That there was something much larger at stake here than her own life. So even when the inquisitor began slicing her apart with a laser scalpel, she would not tell. She screamed and writhed and bled, but she would never tell.

Even contorting on the ground, an armless, legless, and faceless freak, she would not tell them what they wanted to know.

TENTACULOID

ˡ⟩ᵥᵗᶠ⁻ˠₒᵃₛᵥ

When Kattrix woke from hibernation, she was stiff as a board, her limbs about as supple as frozen drumsticks. She lay there in the tube, breathing in and breathing out, thinking and not thinking, aware of herself and not aware at all. She was a speck of dust blown from one dream to another.

Remember, she told herself. *You must remember what it's all about.*

Everything was distorted and muddled. She was here in this freezing tube on the *Ceres*, coming out of the black sleep. She was a child in the colonies, waking up in her little bed in her little house on the dry seabed of Eridania. She was here, she was there, she was nowhere. It all faded, combined, whirled about in her head as her body slowly woke up, shaking off the somewhat unsettling effects of metabolic suspension. She felt a painful pins-and-needles sensation from her feet right to the top of her head.

The hibernator was monitoring her physiology, everything from heart rate to blood gases, injecting her with specialized pharmaceuticals that relaxed her and brought her body carefully out of its deep freeze state.

She tried to speak, but her mouth was all rubbery and her tongue was limp. It felt like she'd just gotten a shot of lidocaine to the gums.

It would wear off.

She'd been frozen a half-dozen times, and you just had to be patient.

But that was a year or two … never for a century—

The thing that bothered her was that Captain Buhari was not there, talking her through it. The system was designed so that the commanding officer thawed first, followed by the exec officer. The idea was that the two of them could then decide whether to wake the others, in case of malfunction. As Biosciences officer, she would have been thawed with the second batch, when the *Ceres* was six weeks out from Kepler-452b.

Where were they?

Where was Buhari and First Officer Macini? Chief Medical Officer Ptocek and Chief Engineer Zhao?

What if they're dead? What if they're all dead? a paranoid voice asked her. *What if you're alone on this damn ship? What then?*

But she knew the terrible answer to that. Unless there had been a system failure, she had been frozen for over 150 years. Everything and everyone she had known was long gone. And if she was the only survivor, it meant she would spend the rest of her life in solitude. The *Ceres* was designed for a one-way trip.

The hibernator detected her spiking anxiety levels, shooting her up with a mild sedative that relaxed her instantly. She smiled. She giggled. All was right with the world. The idea that she was some fourteen hundred light years from her home system made her feel warm and fuzzy inside.

Gradually, the feeling of eager optimism faded. Thirty minutes later, she was completely thawed, her body temp normal, metabolism stable. The peripherals released her.

She sat up very slowly. There was dizziness for a moment or two, but it faded. Gradually, she swung her legs out of the hibernator. The ship was pitch black. There was a red emergency light above the pneumatic door leading into Cryonics, but nothing more.

She was confused, terribly disoriented.

God, it's cold.

None of it made sense. Cryonics was, of course, colder than the other areas of the ship by design, but it wasn't this cold. She was shivering. Her limbs felt numb.

She stepped out of the cryo chamber and it took her a moment or two to adjust to walking again. She began moving around, taking small, easy steps. *There*. She was nearly out of it. Stretching, bending, working all her muscle groups, wandering about naked. She needed a uniform. It was waiting for her in the locker near her hibernator.

Now it was just a matter of finding her way there in the darkness.

⟊

Once she had her insulated uniform and boots on, she felt worlds better. The sensory package in them uplinked with her nanos and warmed her up. She found the emergency locker and a small flashlight whose beam was nearly bright enough to light up Cryonics.

What she saw she did not like.

There were some forty freezing tubes on the *Ceres* and many of them were empty. As she walked down the rows of them with her light, her hand shaking, she looked into each and every one. It made no sense. Buhari and Mancini were still frozen, as were the other senior officers. The empty tubes belonged to colonists and other support personnel … almost as if they had been thawed at random.

Swallowing down her apprehension, she accessed the communicator on the collar of her uniform. She hailed on all frequencies, but there was nothing. It was unsettling. The power seemed to be out, but life support was still functioning.

And I'm alone in the cold and dark.

She shook that from her mind because she was not alone, not really. She could thaw the others at any time. But she wasn't going to, not just yet, not until she figured out what the hell was going on.

That was it. She couldn't let paranoia take charge of her. It just wouldn't do. Remain calm or all was lost. She was trained for every eventuality. She was a professional.

Follow procedure.

Yes, that was the thing. Using the communicator in the collar of her uniform, she tried to connect with the ship's cyberplex which ran everything. *Nothing.* It was like it wasn't even there … but that was crazy.

Breathing in and out slowly, she went over to the Cryonics door. It did not open automatically. She had to work it manually. She pressed the button and it opened with a swishing sound.

She stepped out into C-passageway, panning her light around, pushing back the enclosing, suffocating blackness. The passage was long and empty. Other than that, nothing seemed amiss. Yet she felt her anxiety rise again until it was almost a physical ache inside her. As she moved up the passageway, she became aware of an odd, unpleasant odor to the chill air. She couldn't say what it was exactly, only that for a moment it was terribly pungent, nearly sickening, a stink not unlike an infected wound. There, then … gone.

You're letting your imagination run wild, she told herself in a very cool, clinical voice. *Keep it in check.*

She swallowed and made it to the end of the passage, feeling very much like the child she had once been that was afraid of the dark. *And the things that haunted it.* But she suppressed that immediately; things like that had no place in a reasoning mind.

She reached the door at the very end and stopped dead.

In the beam of her light, she could see a dark handprint on it. She knew instantly that it was blood. Crusted, dried blood that was many, many days old, if not many weeks.

Her heart was pounding now. Her mouth felt very dry. This was exactly the sort of thing she had been afraid of finding. Before she went any farther, she again tried the communicator of her uniform. But it was dead. *Offline.* Something. She tried the intercom on the wall. After a few seconds of manic fiddling, it lit up.

Thank God.

"This is Lieutenant Tieg in C-passageway. Please respond immediately."

Her voice was carried through the ship, echoing and echoing like a scream down a well. It faded away finally into what seemed bottomless dark abysses and she started breathing again. The sound of her own voice in the silence was disturbing.

The little girl inside her, the very one that was afraid of the dark, kept whispering.

(that was stupid, Kattrix, now it knows right where you are)

She dismissed that and worked the door until it opened. D-passageway was before her, seemingly endless. She moved down it quickly, the darkness thick as molasses around her. In her gradually escalating fear, it almost seemed that she could feel it brush against her like a living thing.

At the end, she paused.

There was a smear of blood on the bulkhead. It looked almost black in her light. There was more of it on the galley door. Her breathing was faster by then, her heart beating uneasily in her chest with painful thumps.

Do it, she told herself. *You have to do it.*

She worked the pneumatics manually and the door hissed open.

⚮

The first thing she noticed was that awful smell again. This time it seemed to be even stronger: not just a death room smell of infection, but like something that had lain moldering in a grave for weeks. Swallowing, she told herself it was her imagination because nothing could smell like that on the *Ceres,* particularly in the cold. Her wrist sensor told her it was 38°F. The bacteria of decay didn't do well in chilly temperatures.

Besides, what could smell like that on the ship?

But she knew, oh yes, she knew. And until she found the others, that was exactly where her mind was turning.

The situation was more than a little dire. Common sense told her that she should wake Buhari and the others immediately. But the first thing he would ask was if she had searched the ship for the others and what would she tell him?

I wanted to, Captain, I really did, but I was scared. Oh yes, scared to death, because I had a really, really bad feeling in my gut.

She knew she had to calm herself. She couldn't let fear control her. The most important thing was—

Oh, Christ ...

As she stood there, thinking, she'd been panning the galley with her light, taking in the rows of empty tables, the banks of food synthesizers on the far wall, the sinks and coffee machine ... and that's when she saw all the blood. And it wasn't just a handprint or a smear this time. In fact, it looked as if someone had emptied gallons of the stuff on the floor beyond the tables and right up the wall where it glistened darkly in her light beam.

Though it was the last thing she wanted to do, she made her way over there, her stomach rising into her throat.

The blood was long dried, but she could still smell and taste its coppery tang on her tongue. Not just blood either, she saw, but cast-off scraps of meat, sinew, and scattered red-dyed bones, most of which had been snapped as if something had been after the marrow in them. Her light beam picked out a loop of entrails hanging from a bench, the shattered remains of a ribcage, the staff of a femur, a badly worried pelvic girdle.

She stumbled back, feeling woozy and light-headed, pressing a hand to the wall to support herself so she did not go down.

Somebody had not only died here; they'd been slaughtered like a steer.

The light revealed a broken skull, vertebral segments scattered like dice, and a single blanched eyeball glued into a crusty pool of blood. Pushed under one of the tables was a boot with a stub of bone sticking out of it.

She turned away.

Enough.

She had to get away. She had to wake the others.

⚓

All the way back to Cryonics, Kattrix was certain she was not alone in the darkness, that eyes were not only watching her, but something unknown and unseen was actively stalking her.

Knock it off, she told herself, with little conviction, *you're imagining things.*

Maybe, maybe. But if she was, who had more of a right? There was no getting around that somebody had been murdered in the galley. Hell, not just murdered, but slaughtered like a sacrifice to some ancient, malefic god.

D-passageway was empty, yes, but filled with jumping shadows that crawled over the walls with reptilian gyrations. There was something terribly oppressive about it that weighed down on her, threatening to crush her. She expected that at any moment something would jump out at her.

Twice, she stopped because she smelled that awful pungency again, only this time it was much stronger. The smell of yellow age, dead flies, and dust, the way a mummy pulled from a sarcophagus would smell.

As quickly as it overwhelmed her, it vanished.

She had a plan, and it was not only reasonable but sensible: she would thaw the others so she wasn't so painfully alone in this goddamn mausoleum, then she was going to open the weapons locker and arm herself with a pulser.

She came around the bend of D and stopped so quickly she nearly fell over, a high-pitched cry escaping from her throat. A black, creeping terror made her nerves and ganglia stand straight as pins.

There was a woman hanging not ten feet from her.

A section of cord had been attached to a strut over her head and noosed around her throat. Her neck was broken, head cocked to the side. Her face was green and puffy, eyes set in black hollows. Her tongue bulged from between her lips as if she had regurgitated it.

She was one of the colonists, Kattrix knew as she stood there, her heart pounding and ice-cold sweat running down her face.

The woman wore one boot and from her chest on down was mass of blood. She had been eviscerated, her entrails dangling out.

But it wasn't possible.

Kattrix knew it just wasn't possible.

She'd been down this passageway ten minutes before and there had been no body.

Think! she commanded herself. *You must think! There's a reason for this! There must be a reason! You're turned around ... you're in a different passage ... you're—*

But, no, it wasn't true.

The body wasn't here before and now it was which meant someone or something had *put* it there.

Kattrix tried to control her breathing. She couldn't lose control. She had to continue with her plan. And to do that, she had to get back to Cryo.

But before she did, she quickly examined the cord looped around the woman's throat. There was something unusual about it. In her light, she could see it was made of some transparent, elastic material that looked oddly like tissue, some sort of living tissue like gut.

That's insane. You know it's insane.

Enough. Keeping close to the wall, she sidled past the body, refusing to put her light on it for fear she would see its face grinning down at her.

Moving quickly now, she started toward Cryonics, feeling so loose inside she thought she might unravel. When she was twenty feet from the body, she heard a loud thumping sound and nearly screamed.

She spun around with the light and saw that the woman's corpse was swinging back and forth violently as if it had been pushed, its single boot thumping into the wall.

Kattrix ran.

⚓

When the door to Cryonics was closed and locked behind her, she finally started breathing again. Her back to it, she slid down to her knees, incapacitated with fear. Her entire body was trembling. But she knew it wouldn't do; it just wouldn't do.

(*hide! you must hide! hurry! hide yourself before it finds you!*)

Steeling herself, Kattrix climbed uneasily to her feet, playing her light around, making sure there were no unpleasant surprises awaiting her. She refused to think about what she had just seen. The captain and his staff would work it out.

Cryo was large, the hibernators arranged on three separate tiers. She walked among them until she found Captain Buhari's. It was a long metal tube with a port near the top through which you could view the sleeper's face. Even frozen, he looked confident and ready for anything.

She entered the code and the hibernator made some clicking sounds, something like a low breathing caused by the release of gases ... and then a red light blinked on and off.

MALFUNCTION, the screen told her.

Kattrix entered the code again and went through the thawing procedure exactly as she had been taught and drilled on dozens and dozens of times.

MALFUNCTION, it said again.

Though it was cold and the vapor of her breath was visible every time she exhaled, she began to sweat. Her jaws were locked tight, her stomach like a clenched fist.

Desperate now, she tried Mancini's freezing tube, followed by Zhao's and Ptocek, punching in the codes perfectly.

MALFUNCTION.

MALFUNCTION.

MALFUNCTION.

"No," she said, shaking her head. *"No."*

As a creeping dread consumed her, crawling over every inch of her skin, it began to feel like reality as she understood it had ground to a halt and she was swaying uneasily at the edge of some yawning abyss of madness. Nothing was working right. Even the tubes were not responding. It was as if some sentient, malevolent other had arranged things to maximize her anxiety.

Stop, she told herself. *You have to stop and think rationally.*

Yes, that was it. She had to approach this logically, not as some addle-brained child. Cause and effect, cause and effect. But it was the *cause* that was giving her the most concern. Life support was operational, but there was no power. The hibernators were functional, yet they did not respond as they were designed to. And yet some of them had opened and released colonists, but not all of them.

She looked for some sort of pattern that would make sense, but found nothing.

(you saw the remains ... one body was torn apart, the other was disemboweled and hung up like a trophy and you know what that means, don't you?)

She clutched hands to her head as if she was trying to keep her skull from flying apart. "No, no I don't."

(think, Katt! think! there's a dark mind with a dark agenda behind all this ... you are not alone on this ship ... there's another here watching you!)

Of course, on the most primitive, childlike level it made a certain amount of sense: something evil had boarded the *Ceres* and thawed the colonists for fun and games—tormenting them and breaking them down one after the other with fear before it hunted them down for sport and slaughter.

It made sense, yes, but the more sense it made the more she had to reject it, or she was going to come apart at the seams. She panned the light around, more certain than ever that she was not alone. She could feel something closing in on her—from the left, the right, behind her ... in fact, wherever the light wasn't, *it* was.

(watching you)

The darkness seemed to rustle secretively around her. She thought she heard the sound of low, steady respiration behind her, but there was nothing there when she put the light in that direction. Then, from one of the upper tiers of hibernators, there was a noise like a stick dragged along the wall.

"Is someone there?" she heard her voice ask. It came out of her automatically, unbidden, as if she was begging for reassurance.

Dark shapes seemed to be gathering around her. She spun this way and

She couldn't be sure as she fought to slow her breathing and the flesh that crawled at her spine.

(maybe you did and maybe you didn't ...think about it: if the entity can hijack the ship's systems, then maybe it can hijack your mind as well)

Was that what was happening here? Was it playing with her? Not only making her see things that were not there, but carefully maneuvering her through the *Ceres* to a waiting kill zone? What she might have thought were her ideas, might not have been hers at all.

(for all you know, Kattrix, it might have made you punch the wrong codes into the hibernators....)

She banished the voice from her mind. She wasn't about to carry on some insane conversation with her eight-year-old self.

(you mean the one that was terrified of the dark?)

"Shut up," she said under her breath.

This was ridiculous: she had a real enemy out there; she couldn't be fighting against her own psyche. It was a sign of deteriorating mental health.

She moved up the passage.

⟊

(you better be careful, Katt)

(real careful)

(it's close now)

(it's drawing you in)

But Kattrix refused to listen, because she was tired of that damn voice tormenting her. She was not a child; she was an adult. She was independent and mature and she had a pulser in her hand, goddamn yes.

The voice seemed to fade as she asserted herself. She kept moving down the corridor, playing her light about. In her mind, the corridor was a black hole leading down into the fetid darkness of a spider's lair, where some horrible thing awaiting her with gleaming fangs and the mouth of a leech that would suck her soul away. Or, at least, Little Katt wanted to give her

that with the light, seeing nothing but the enclosing blackness. It pushed in from every side as if it was trying to smother her. Before she had some kind of fear-induced breakdown, she was going to walk over to the weapons locker and get a pulser. At least then she'd be armed. It was only about twenty-five feet away. She'd be there in seconds.

Cryonics was a large circular chamber with windows that looked out into the passageways and decks. As she moved toward the weapons locker, shadows moving around her, she caught her reflection in the window, the glare of the light.

Her heart seized in her chest.

There was a formless black shape coming up behind her. She swung around yet again, but the light found nothing. Standing there, barely able to keep on her feet by that point, her heart pounding and a trickle of sweat rolling down her spine, she played it around in every direction.

(do you see it? it's here! it's in this room with you! it's right ... THERE!)

But there was nothing, just a tangle of shadows like coiling snakes dissolving away. Then she saw a rolling cloud of vapor. Something was there, oh dear God, something was right there only she couldn't see it, just the white clouds of its breath as it exhaled.

Now the vapor was coming from six or seven different locations as if whatever was there had more than one mouth.

Kattrix screamed and ran stumbling to the weapons locker. She typed in the code to open the lock, fumbling it three or four times. Then a pulser was in her hand. She scanned back and forth with the light.

She could hear something breathing—it was over here, then over there. It was on the second tier of hibernators, then it was right in front of her.

She let out a cry and fired.

A blue sword of light cut through the darkness, hitting one of the windows and burning a hole right through it. There was a scratching, clawing sound like rats running up the walls and then only silence.

What now?

Oh, what now?

But she knew. There was only one thing left to do and it was dangerous as hell: she would have to make her way to the upper level to the bridge and observation deck. She might be able to access the ship's log manually from up there and find out what was happening.

It was the only chance she had.

As she made her way down C-passageway, the ship seemed to open around her like the jaws of a trap. It was waiting for her, the door to every cabin and every walkway thrown open like the lids of coffins. Each one held nameless horrors that would seduce her and destroy her.

If she gave into any of them, it was all over with. An immense irrational fear had completely consumed her now and she was moving utterly by instinct. And it was this, more than her rational brain, that smelled things that certainly had no odor: the flat, metallic smell of the ship, deserted and lonesome; the hot, coppery odor of recent death; and the stink of the entity that haunted the *Ceres* … a foul, moist, rotten stink of evil and corruption.

Pulser in one hand, flashlight in the other, she moved down the passage, her breath dry and rasping in her throat, her eyes staring, her flesh clutching the musculature and bones beneath in a death-grip.

She heard secretive sounds behind her.

In front of her.

In fact, wherever she was not looking.

Everything was riding on what she did and didn't do, she knew. Never had she held such deadly responsibility. If she stopped now, if she weakened now, the entity would never stop. It would thaw the others one by one and kill them for its own amusement. She had no time to consider the *hows* and *whys* of the situation, how this creature could be or why it had boarded the *Ceres* in the first place. It was here and it was evil.

That was enough.

Before her now was the elevator that led to the deck above, but she

wasn't about to risk getting trapped in it. Not when her enemy seemed to know how manipulate the ship's technology for its own ends.

There was an emergency crawlway at the end, designed to be used if the power failed. Sucking in a deep, cool breath, she opened the hatch and jumped back, expecting something yellow-eyed and noxious to leap out at her.

But there was nothing.

The crawlway was a tube, tight and claustrophobic. The light revealed nothing but the ladder leading up. Rung by rung, she climbed higher and higher, feeling the dead weight of the ship pressing down on her. The atmosphere in there was like that of the *Ceres* itself—bleak and hopeless, rotting black with malignance—only concentrated, tearing the heart out of her until she wanted to curl up somewhere and whimper.

(careful, careful, Kattrix … it's watching you)

She banished her childhood fears, more or less unsuccessfully, and opened the hatch at the top. She leaped out, rolling across the deck, coming up with her pulser and light. She heard a scraping sound down the passageway, but saw nothing. But there was a dark cabalism in the air and she could feel it seeping into her like poison. The atmosphere reminded her of tombs and closed-up cellars.

Move!

Yes, there was no time for imagination or ruminating. Time was running out on every front and she knew it. She'd made it this far, but she had a very strong feeling that her enemy was slowly, inexorably closing in for the kill.

(listen, Katt! do you do you hear it?)

She did and she didn't. Part of her was certain it heard a low, guttural, growling sound coming out of the blackness at her, but another part was convinced it was her imagination. She cast her light around, but saw nothing.

Then she nearly fell over as the light momentarily picked out something like a membranous scuttling shape. It was there, then gone.

Did I see it? Did I really see it?

that impression.

Regardless, as she inched forward, seeking the emergency crawlway that would take her to the next deck, she realized she had never seen a darkness like this before. The pen-sized flashlight put out something like two thousand lumens, but it barely seemed to scratch the dark before her.

The gloom seemed to be strung with cobwebs that broke against her face. The corridor smelled damp and unpleasant like a musty cellar. The flashlight beam flickered, making her tighten her grip on the pulser.

She stopped because just ahead there was a noise that literally made her skin crawl: the sound of respiration, but rubbery and creaking like a breathing leather sack inflating to the point of bursting, then deflating.

She thought for a moment she saw a distorted silhouette pull back swiftly into the shadows. It seemed like it was there, then it broke apart, blowing around like dandelion fuzz.

(you're real close now, Katt)

A smell blew out at her—like mildew and rotting vegetables that quickly changed to the stench of stranded marine life: briny, sun-washed, bloating, and putrescent.

Little Katt was mumbling nonsensical things in her mind, disjointed words and phrases punctuated by a droning, mindless humming.

(you you you should listen, Kattrix)

(you should listen before it's too late)

But she didn't want to listen because it was just her fears and paranoia being channeled through a younger version of herself, one that she suspected lived in darkness and was evil and black at its core like a rotten apple.

(it came aboard, Katt, because the ship disrupted its twelve-hundred-year migration from the Cygnus arm of the galaxy, where its home star is located— Deneb ... it comes from the seventh planet, a dark, dark world of black, steaming methane seas and nitrogen clouds and rains of sulfur dioxides ... it's an evil place where sunlight is unknown. Its world was poisoned out, so the Tentaculoid left, seeking new life forms to subvert, to conquer, to feed upon, and exploit for its amusement ... and it found us, Katt, and now the games begin)

211

(a monster, Katt)

(it's a monster that can adapt to any environment)

(and it's hungry, God, how it's hungry)

Kattrix gasped as the words of Little Katt faded in her head. There was no way her subconscious mind could know all those things unless they were placed in her mind by the very thing that stalked her, the entity that would thaw the colonists one by one like a hungry man taking meat from a freezer.

The breathing was much louder now and she gasped at the sound of it. The idea of the Tentaculoid and what it was capable of filled her with a horror that was not only psychological, but physical. She wanted to scream. She wanted to throw up her guts at the repulsion she felt.

She heard a wicked cackling in her head.

(oh my poor, poor Kattrix, you're so naïve)

(you think you can escape it)

(but you can't escape it any more than a fat, juicy steak can escape the plate that holds it or avoid the knife that will cut it—)

She heard a slithery sort of sound from the welling darkness ahead that the flashlight simply would not touch. She froze in place, her temples and ears thumping with blood. Little Katt giggled again, but this time whatever was using her voice to torment Kattrix did not even attempt to hide its sinister nature: it was actively alive and malevolent.

(silly stupid little bitch, you should cower now, because I am coming to claim you ... I will rip you apart and suck the quivering mind from your skull and you can't possibly stop me)

Inside, Kattrix went cold as ice as her core temperature plummeted. The Little Katt voice was not some frightened reflection of her childhood: it was the *thing* itself. The Tentaculoid. Its laughter was like shattering glass in her brain and she pictured it, some metaphorical image of the thing that haunted the dark: it was huge and monstrous with the bloated, well-fed body of a spider and the shrieking, lunatic head of Little Katt on a sprung Jack-in-the-Box neck, its long tusk-like fangs dripping with poison.

And she knew at that moment that if she did not move and move right now, that the terror inside would weld her to the floor, making her into a quivering, spineless thing that would wait for the Tentaculoid like a human sacrifice.

"SHOW YOURSELF!" she screamed at it.

And the volume and force of her voice seemed to make Little Katt's malefic laughter momentarily shrink inside her head. She heard that slithering sound again. Like a thousand snakes woken from hibernation, unreeling themselves and moving in her direction. The panic jumped inside her.

Then the flashlight began to dim.

She shook it, rapped it off the wall, but it did no good: the beam was weakening and she knew the Tentaculoid was responsible—it wanted the corridor to be as black as the toxic alien sea that it had spawned in.

Refusing to let fear own her, she moved forward and then stopped again. The floor and bulkheads of the corridor were dripping with blood as if they'd been washed with red paint. It pooled on the floor, moving in her direction.

Her flashlight picked out a stray leg, then an arm, both neatly stripped like castoff chicken bones from a feast. Ahead she saw a vertebral column and then a ribcage, a pelvis cracked like an eggshell. Then something came thumping and bouncing in her direction: a decapitated head. Its white face was hooked in a scream and spattered with blood like freckles. From the long red hair, she knew it belonged to Dr. Ptocek, the Chief Medical Officer.

Then her light went completely out.

The Tentaculoid was coming, skating forward over the sea of blood. She could smell its foulness and, worse, she could feel it. She began to scramble backward, even though a hysterical voice in her head promised her that she would never escape. It would not be allowed. Her terror was at its peak and she was ripe for harvesting.

Something down the corridor flashed at her and then flashed again.

But it wasn't ordinary illumination.

This was something else: bioluminescence like that of a deep-sea creature. It flashed again and again in what seemed a pattern and each time it did, she saw more of the creature itself. *Flash:* she saw a towering medusoid shape of translucent white jelly. *Flash:* she saw a gelatinous, grotesque monstrosity of crawling, vermiform polyps. *Flash:* she saw the thing gliding at her, dozens of suckerless, vitreous tentacles writhing like feeding worms.

Then she jumped back out of sheer panic, turned and ran just as something slashed at her out of the dark and ripped a shank of hair from the back of her head.

Running, running, running. Completely out of her mind, incapacitated with fear, but moving, not taking time to think because *it* was right behind her and the hunt was on. She needed to find an emergency crawlway to take her up or down; anywhere but here. But how the hell could she find it in the dark? Her flashlight was out and even the emergency lights had gone dark. If she had the time to feel along the bulkheads, she could find one of the crawlways, but there was no such time.

Unless—

She spun around and fired the pulser twice. One blue bolt burned a trench in the bulkhead, but the other hit something that roared with pain. The corridor echoed with its agony and was saturated with an awful stink like burned plastic.

(that won't save you, you dirty little bitch)

She started running again and something hit her in the back. She was thrown five feet and crashed face first to the deck. Thankfully, she didn't lose her flashlight or her pulser. She rolled away, scrambling to her feet. In the strobing bioluminescence of the Tentaculoid, she realized she was wet with blood. Not her own blood, but the blood the creature had siphoned from Dr. Ptocek and sprayed at her. It had been like being hit with a stream of water from a fire hose.

The Tentaculoid advanced, a blackened area near dead-center of it bubbling and giving off an oily smoke. As it moved forward, it gave off a weird clicking and whirring noise as if it had clockwork guts: the sound of cogs meshing and teeth locking.

She turned and fired two more times.

It was all pointless and she knew it: she was tired, near to exhaustion. She would never get away from the thing and she had no time to find a way. The corridor was perfectly circular and soon she would be right back where she started from.

The Tentaculoid fired another high-pressure stream of blood at her. It completely missed her, striking the bulkhead like a sudden summer squall. Not just blood, but gummy tissue and bone fragments and what might have been teeth.

But in its light, she saw the emergency crawlway and fled down it as fast as she could, leaving the Tentaculoid on the deck above her where it let loose with a wet screeching at being denied its chosen victim. On the lower deck, she ran again down D-passageway, darting through the door into the galley.

In the doorway, she paused, pulser in hand.

It was going to come for her now and she knew it. She wanted it to think that it had her cornered. When it filled the doorway, she would blast it repeatedly with the pulser, then slip out the back way. It wasn't much of a plan, but it was something.

Now she saw its flickering, mad bioluminescence lighting up the crawlway further down the passageway. It forced its fluorescing bulk down it like dough squeezed from a tube. Then it was out, waiting there, massive and pulsating, breathing from a dozen expanding and deflating blowholes. A blubbery thing with a thousand moving parts, translucid and nearly crystalline-looking. It had taken on a slightly yellowish tinge now and she could see through its flesh which was like that of a comb jelly.

Within, there were odd red and orange structures that might have been organs and corkscrewing purple tendrils that might have been some type of rudimentary circulatory system.

Then it was coming, seeming to flow forward on a raft of sparkling slime.

Kattrix retreated inside and waited for it to fill the doorway.

Which it did.

It was flashing pink and then gold, as if it was confused. Several long, smooth tentacles entered the galley, searching around, sweeping over the walls. Kattrix was hiding behind a table, near the back of the galley, within easy reach of the rear exit.

It moved forward with a slopping, oozing sort of sound. Now it flashed red as if it was angry. It made a screaming noise and began flinging chairs out of the way, overturning tables and benches.

(*I know you're there, Katt: I can smell you … oh, when I find you I'll pin you down and have my fun with you … I'll give you a memorable death, in and out, in and out, the old inny-outy oh yes oh yes …*)

Kattrix couldn't take it anymore: her entire body was trembling, her heart banging away in her chest. Her jaws were locked tight so she didn't scream and tears squeezed from her eyes.

(*Kattrix?*)

The Tentaculoid got closer and closer.

(*oh, Kattrix, where are you?*)

When it was twenty feet from her, she brought up the pulser and gave it one bolt of charged particles after the other, drilling burning holes in it, crisping polyps, and blasting flaming bits of it in all directions.

It smoldered and shrieked in her head, but it kept coming. Nothing could stop it. It would take a hundred pulsers in unison to destroy it and even then, that might not be enough.

(*YOU CUNT YOU MISERABLE CUNT*)

(*WHO DO YOU THINK YOU ARE*)

(*WHO ARE YOU TO DENY ME*)

(MY FUN)

(MY FOOD)

Kattrix screamed in mad terror because she knew deep down that there was no escaping this horror. It would keep coming and coming until she was too tired to fight and then it would have its fun. Then it would violate her and tear her open and bathe in her blood and suck the meat from her bones.

She ran out the back exit with the creature trailing her and a voice in her head, one that was her own, said, *it's like a sex act to that monster, don't you see? The terror it creates is like foreplay and the pain that follows is heavy petting and the murder, the physical destruction of it victim, is the climax.*

Maybe you should consider that.

The terror.

It feeds on it.

But there was no time to think. Once again, the beast pushed her into mindless, directionless flight down the corridor, legs pumping and lungs rasping, hot sweat steaming on her face.

⸙

Why isn't it following me? Kattrix asked herself just a few minutes later. *What is it doing? What does this mean?*

She waited there in the corridor, her back up against the wall. She was shivering from the sweat drying on her in the frigid temperatures. But she had time to think, to plan. The question was: why was it giving her that time? She didn't know, but she suspected that it was part of the game. Her fear would escalate if she didn't know where it was or when it might strike. The fear of the unknown was the greatest fear of all and she could feel it gripping her, pushing her stomach up into her chest, tightening her windpipe so she could barely breathe, forcing cold sweat from pores that rolled down her face in beads.

That was exactly what it wanted because fear, *human* fear, was like a drug it was addicted to, that it needed to mainline and saturate itself with. And right then, it was stoned on it, practically overdosing.

And that made her think: *What if I cut it off? What if I wasn't afraid? What if I forced it to go cold turkey? What then?*

Those were the questions that flew through her mind, each one as unfathomable as the other. Even if she wasn't afraid—something which seemed unimaginable—it was still a deadly predator. She knew she could hurt it, but she didn't think she could kill it.

At least, not while it was strong.

Instead of being afraid of it, she suddenly found herself hating it. She was filled with omnipotent rage that made her shake with anger. It had killed innocents. It had turned the mission to Kepler-452b into a horror show. And, maybe the worst of all, it had reduced her to a sobbing, terrified weakling. She wanted to kill it, to blast it into fragments.

The fury inside her made her boil.

And as it did, as the terror deescalated, the flashlight came back on. Just like that.

The fear it creates is its power! Without it it's weak—

Something shrieked from the other end of the corridor. Not something but some*one*. Someone had cried out. She could hear them shouting. The flashlight in her hand, she went down there, being as careful as possible.

The Tentaculoid was suddenly there, appearing like a ghost. At the sight of it, she gasped and her light dimmed as fear gripped her again and she felt her guts go to water. The terror that surged in her completely incapacitated her, leaving her pale and shaking.

The creature flashed cold chemical light and she saw a man bare feet away from it. He was starting this way and that, confused, out of his mind with fright.

"CAPTAIN! CAPTAIN BUHARI! WAIT!" she called out. "YOU'RE MAKING IT STRONGER!"

But if he heard her, he gave no indication of it. He was locked in a fight for survival, trying to stay alive just a few more seconds. He was lithe, quick, and athletic, but it wasn't enough to save him and she knew it. He didn't understand that at its core, it was a game, it was sport. He was the fox the hounds had cornered so red-coated dandies could shoot him down.

He just didn't get it.

And no amount of spry athleticism could save him from the Tentaculoid and its appetite. He was meat on the hoof and now it had him, its scintillant incandescence telegraphing its intent. *Flash:* the Tentaculoid was in front of him, a palpitating bag of jelly encircled by its own corkscrewing tentacles. He saw it, let out a cry in the consuming darkness, backpedaling away from it. *Flash:* it was behind him, a dozen slobbering mouths opening to suck the meat from his bones. He darted to the left. *Flash:* it was there, too, a towering oily mass of shifting tissue, putting out countless saw-toothed limbs. He made one last valiant attempt to get away. *Flash:* its tentacles coiled around him with a rubbery squeaking.

Kattrix was already charging down there and as she did so, two things happened: her flashlight dimmed and went out again, and when she brought up her pulser and squeezed the trigger, nothing happened. A tiny red warning light blinked on and off. Low battery.

She skidded to a stop.

There was no way the pulser's charge was down—she should have had dozens of shots left.

(but you don't, Kattrix ... because I make the rules)

Little Katt giggled in her mind like a warped, sadistic child tormenting a helpless puppy. The laughter grew louder and louder, ringing through her skull until it felt like it would explode from sheer internal stress. She dropped to one knee, her dead flashlight and pulser hitting the deck.

The laughter finally faded and the deranged voice of Little Katt began to hum offkey in her head.

(poor, poor Kattrix ... trying to be a hero)

(but wait)

(oh yes ... just wait and watch what I do with my wriggling little toy)

(watch closely)

219

The Tentaculoid was no longer flashing its photophores. Now it glowed with a steady pale, blue neon light, illuminating the end of the corridor and what was in its clutches.

"No," she sobbed. "Oh, dear God ... *no* ... "

The Tentaculoid took an obscene delight in her watching. Whatever their relationship was (and the idea that they actually had one disgusted her), she was special and she knew it. The others, she had no doubt, were slaughtered indiscriminately: stepped on like ants, swatted like flies. But it was different with her and that was probably the scariest thing of all.

(yes)

(it is different, Kattrix)

"No, no, no!" she said, clutching her hands to her head as if this would shut it out, make it not so.

(oh yes, my little thoroughbred ... I'll run you to death and when you can't take any more ... I'll use you ... I'll break you ... I'll fill every one of your holes ... I'll drown you in my seed ...)

(and I'll do it out of love)

"NO!" she shouted, out of her mind at the very idea of it. "NO! JUST KILL ME! PLEASE JUST KILL ME LIKE THE OTHERS!"

Little Katt laughed hysterically. But it wasn't just in her head this time. It echoed up and down the corridor, it bounced off the floor and ceiling, gathering, reverberating, directed at her like a hypersonic weapon. The laughter shrilled and fragmented, cycling out of the Tentaculoid itself, from a dozen blubbery blowholes.

"PLEASE! I'M BEGGING YOU!"

(is that)

(is that how it works, Kattrix?)

(do lovers beg each other??)

(is that part of the game???)

(it excites me)

Kattrix was sobbing uncontrollably now. All the toughness, resolve, and independence she'd once prided herself upon was gone. She was broken. A simpering, cowering cur waiting to be whipped by her master. She groveled, she whimpered, she shook with terror.

"Please, please, please don't hurt him," she begged. "Take me ... violate me ... tear me to pieces, but, please, oh dear God, please don't ... hurt ... him...."

This made it pause. It held Captain Buhari like a child preparing to pull the wings off a fly. It flashed red, flickering.

(because you love him)

"No, I don't! I barely know him! I ... I ... I ...."

(YOU ARE IN LOVE WITH HIM)

Kattrix let out a scream because that monster was digging through the most secret depths of her mind. Love Buhari? No, not *love*, not exactly. Just a crush, maybe even an infatuation, but nothing more than that. He was an amazing man. Strong and handsome and desirable, but, but—

"It's not like that!" she cried, even though it *was* like that and she had kept it secret, even from herself because, well, because he was married and his wife was a biochemist, one of the crew of the *Ceres*.

(NOW YOU LOVE ME)

(ONLY ME)

(NOW I ALONE LOVE YOU)

(I DESIRE YOU I WANT YOU YOU'RE MINE)

The Tentaculoid dangled Buhari in the air, one tentacle noosed around his throat, another wound around his legs and a third held inches from his face, a single claw unsheathed for the gutting.

"Please don't kill him," Kattrix mumbled. "Take me, just take me."

It seemed as if the creature was actually considering her request. It was still glowing with that pale, abyssal blue, but it was also flashing again— blood-red, rose-pink, vibrant purple, back and forth, back and forth, as if it was not only confused but rioting with emotions.

It doesn't understand, a voice in her head explained. *Self-sacrifice is an alien concept to it. It knows hate and pride and gluttony and lust, but finer, higher concepts are beyond it.*

"Please," she said.

Buhari, though he was battered and broken, dripping with blood and no doubt in considerable pain, still put his crew before himself. "LIEUTENANT! LIEUTENANT TIEG!" he shouted. "RUN! DO YOU HEAR ME? KATTRIX, GET AWAY! GET AWAY NOW!"

His voice saying her name made her feel warm inside, but there was no time for that. She began backing down the corridor after picking up her dead pulser and flashlight, feeling it was important to do so.

(stay! you must stay! Kattrix, do you hear me?)

(stay! you must be part of this!)

(I want to be inside you ... and I want you inside of me ... together ... joined ... knowing what I know and tasting what I taste and hungering as I hunger ...)

Seeing Buhari inches from death, but still noble, indomitable, and selfless, made her ache inside and the ache quickly became anger. "FUCK YOU!" she screamed with all the volume she had.

The Tentaculoid flashed a brilliant ruby red and tore Buhari apart like a straw doll. His legs were ripped free and then his arms. Off came his head. His torso was split open and his stuffing strewn in every which direction.

Betrayed and jealous, it was coming for her now.

⸙

As Kattrix ran, the Tentaculoid stayed with her. If she sped up, it sped up. If she slowed down, it slowed down. It kept an easy twenty-feet between them, no closer, no farther. It was part of the twisted little game it played, she knew. Just a game, that's all. That's all it could possibly be—*it can't be anything more, not love, not that, not some insane alien obsession*—because she couldn't let herself believe it was anything more; the idea of that monster harboring feelings for her was an obscenity.

(I'm coming to get you, Kattrix)

(I'll catch you then kiss kiss)

(me so horny)

It had extended two seeking limbs to either side now as it followed her at high speed. Each was tipped with a single silver claw and it scraped them along the metal bulkheads, throwing showers of sparks like a locomotive grinding rails.

Kattrix felt herself slowing now.

This just couldn't go on. She was exhausted—physically, mentally, and maybe even spiritually. Everything inside her felt as if it had been drained off. She felt cold, white, and empty. Though her survival instinct demanded that she keep going, she simply couldn't. Let it have her. Let it destroy her at every level. Let it play its evil game and use her for sport. As long as it ended, as long as it just finally ended.

Now she was barely moving.

Just sort of shuffling along, those very things that kept her motivated all these many years shutting down one after the other. She awaited the burning embrace of the Tentaculoid. Her lips still quivered and tears still ran from her eyes, but she could no longer feel any of it. Anguish had become a perpetual state of being.

She turned to her fate.

The Tentaculoid was gone.

She stood there, mindlessly staring at where it should have been but was no more. Laughing with despair at the futility of it all, she stumbled back drunkenly, bumping into the fire extinguisher in its breakaway bracket. She put her back to the bulkhead before she fell down.

This was it.

It would come for her now.

And then it did.

It was right in front of her: a gigantic, rippling mass like an alien jellyfish composed mainly of slime and watery, bubbling tissue. Its bulging, quaking surface wriggled with stubby tentacles like a sea anemone. As she stared hopelessly at it, they flashed bright orange and red and metallic blue and chromium yellow, then becoming semi-transparent like petroleum

223

jelly. Suckering mouths opened and closed, exhaling white rolling clouds of vapor in the chill atmosphere of the *Ceres.* Dozens of longer, glassy tentacles slithered over and around it, busy and undulant like a nest of maggots on a greening corpse.

Two of them wound around her legs. A third constricted her right arm, the pulser dropping from her fingers. She didn't fight; she hung limply in its grip. She ignored the gag reflex that the feel of the Tentaculoid inspired—it was like being caressed by thawing meat. She didn't even wrinkle her nose at the sharp chemical stink that it secreted.

Little Katt once again giggled in her head, except this time it was more of a wizened cackling.

(I've got you, Kattrix)

(you belong to me)

(and you'll never ever get away)

Kattrix said nothing. She waited. *It* waited. It was so very smug, so sure it had won the game. She was weak and defeated.

Little Katt kept snickering.

The Tentaculoid made slushy, slopping sounds like entrails poured into a bucket. Slime gurgled from its many orifices. Then with a moist tearing sound, it split open lengthwise, revealing a pink, puckering slit like a vagina made of wet, well-chewed bubblegum. From it, came what at first looked like a long, glistening, pink worm. It was easily as thick as her wrist where it emerged from its orifice, tapering to a fine point which began to explore her.

(Kattrix my toy my pet my lover)

The vermiform organ brushed against her ear, the tip exploring her ear canal, then withdrawing.

(me so ...)

It stroked her hair, flicking aside a few locks.

It traced the bridge of her nose.

(... me so horny ...)

Caressed her cheekbones.

Licked against her lips erotically, leaving a snot-like strand of jelly.

(all mine now ... I will explore you as I have the cosmos ... I will love you ... I will plumb your depths and know your secrets)

Now the worming organ pushed up under her uniform shirt, toying with her bellybutton, feeling like the cold nose of a dog. It located her breasts and took its time squeezing them, sliding between them, and flicking her nipples. Then, again, it withdrew. It found the heat between her legs and nested there, its obscene length coiling and pulsing.

Through all this, revolted and terrified, Kattrix did not move. She was docile as a mouse. A plaything to be handled and nothing more. The Tentaculoid held her loosely. It had won and claimed its prize. There was no need for violence, not at this stage.

She waited.

A single word appeared in her brain: *now.*

When she moved, the creature was caught off-guard momentarily. Her free arm swung out and her hand grabbed the fire extinguisher in one quick, fluid movement. She depressed the trigger and coated the worming tendril and its orifice in foaming white CO_2.

She had found its weak spot.

Its soft white underbelly.

The pink tissue beneath the protective layers of blubber was its Achilles heel. It screamed. It screeched. It tossed Kattrix. She thumped against the ceiling and hit the floor.

The Tentaculoid in agony could no longer hold its liquid shape as the CO_2 seared its delicate anatomy.

(YOU CUNT YOU MISERABLE CHEATING WHORE)

It took off down the corridor, leaving a hissing wake of steam and slime. In some unknown way, she had mortally wounded it and the ship seemed to tremble with its wailing cries of pain.

The flashlight was working again.

The green READY light of the pulser glowed.

Without hesitation, Kattrix picked them up and, cradling the fire extinguisher in the crook of her arm, gave chase.

The rules of the game had forever changed.

And her odds had never looked better.

⚉

She followed the trail of slime that sparkled like diamonds. It was easy enough to do. The Tentaculoid had left a great quantity of it in its flight. As she went after it, she began to believe it was not anything so simple as a secretion but blood or ichor, some life-giving, life-sustaining fluid that the creature was losing in copious amounts. It had that same unpleasant chlorine stink to it like the monster itself.

Though Kattrix was exhausted beyond anything she had ever known before, something was on fire inside her—wrath, hate, the need for payback. Whatever it was, it energized her, it fed her, it made her feel … for the lack of a better word, *mighty*. It was as if her body was made of iron now, her ligaments and tendons leather thongs, her muscles steel springs, her guts cement.

She felt invincible.

For the first time since waking in Cryonics (and maybe for the first time in her life) she felt like she could not be beaten, not be overwhelmed or outthought.

I'm coming for you this time, you sonofabitch, she thought.

Even the cruel, demented voice of Little Katt had fallen silent and she figured that was because the Tentaculoid was grievously injured and could no longer afford the expenditure of energy. It needed time to heal, to lick its wounds, but that was one thing it was not going to get.

The slime trail led to the lifeboat bay and she figured that was the creature's lair. It was probably where it initially entered the *Ceres* through ways she could not even guess at.

But it was here.

There was a standing order on the ship that no one could enter the bay without a suit, so she went to the locker and pulled one on. Outfitted against a sudden loss of pressure, she went through the airlock into the lair. The lights were off, of course. She panned about with her light, fearing she was stepping into a trap.

She took no chances.

She tethered herself with an EVA line so she would not get sucked out of the ship in case the creature decided to blow the main hatch.

Why wait? she asked herself. *Beat it to the punch.*

She punched in the code and a red light began flashing, a warning voice counting down the seconds until the atmosphere was bled from the bay and complete decompression occurred.

Little Katt had said the Tentaculoid was a monster that could adapt to any environment, true, but Kattrix was willing to bet that took strength and energy, two things it probably didn't have at a premium at that moment.

As she moved deeper into the bay, the flashlight picked out globes about the size of beachballs that dangled from the overhead by fleshy threads like spider silk.

Oh God ...

As she studied one in detail, she saw it was an egg sac. It was transparent as a plastic bubble, and inside was a curled-up leggy horror: a fetal Tentaculoid cooking in an amniotic brine of plasma. It was easily one of the most repulsive things she had ever seen. One of them was bad enough, but the idea that it was a mother and could breed was sickening beyond belief.

She heard the creature screech in her head with rage and hate and ... *terror.* It knew what she was going to do and it went mad at the very idea of the destruction of its young.

But by then, she was firing the pulser, burning the sacs one after the other. They exploded as the bay doors opened, erupting with clouds of tissue and fluids that froze instantly into ice crystals. She destroyed ten or twelve of them before the Tentaculoid interfered.

She saw it hanging there like a spider, a translucent medusoid of squirming polyps and tentacles and puckering mouths with what looked like hundreds of threads dangling from it, spreading out like hairs in the zero gravity. Ribbons of slime hung from it that were pink as its insides.

(OUR LOVE BUT OUR LOVE—)

Oh, it was good right to the end, thinking it knew something of human emotion but only imitating it for its own foul ends. It was something that should never have existed in the first place and existing, should never have been allowed to escape the black tomb of its home world.

Like a squid siphoning up water to jet-propel itself, the Tentaculoid inflated to three times its size and charged at her with amazing speed. She fired three times and three bolts of energy blasted into it, shearing off tentacles that swam through the ether like sea snakes. Ripped open and bleeding pink discharge and rivers of slime that froze instantly, it struck her and she went spinning end over end in her suit. She bumped into the ceiling, was deflected and thumped against a bulkhead.

But with a hand on the EVA line, she righted herself and the Tentaculoid was coming again. She fired four more times, each blazing blue bolt a direct hit that shattered the creature into an agitated vortex of flesh and slime and innards.

(YOU YOU YOU DON'T DARE)

(I AM TENTACULOID I AM ETERNAL)

She finished it off with a dozen more particle bolts that sheared it into blackened pieces and chunks of drifting ice. It was as dead as such a thing *could* be dead. As she dangled limply on her tether, its remains were sucked out into dead space until there was nothing left in the bay.

She followed the tether back to the airlock and closed the bay doors. In the airlock, she could barely stay on her feet. When pressure was normalized, she fell to her knees and crawled out into the ship.

It was some time before she had the strength to remove her suit and begin the long walk back to Cryonics.

WHEN YIGGRATH COMES
⌊⊐⌐ ⌐↘⎰⎰⎯⫯⎰⊏ ⌐⌐⌐⍀⟋⫯⎰

The jumpship *Bartholomew* touched down on Gamma Eridani 4, about two clicks from the Terran outpost on Centipede Ridge. It was dark out there. Darker than dark, the sort of unrelieved stygian blackness only found on alien worlds countless parsecs from Earth and the colonies.

The sun had set some six hours previously, and with GE 4's eccentric orbit, it would not rise for another five days.

Riger, the First Officer, led the others out into the methane-heavy, poisonous atmosphere—Doc Kang and two techs, Sealander and Wise. The landscape before them was a crazy-quilt of rises and hollows, sharp-crested waves of rock that looked like dunes, and tall, narrow pipes of stone. The rises weren't so bad, just a little trippy in the low gravity. The hollows, on the other hand, were filled with a congested thorny vegetation that pulled and snagged at their suits. Overhead, triple-winged cartilaginous birds called Trinary Qualaks shrieked in the murky sky. They were also known as *piss-mongers,* owing to their unpleasant habit of directing streams of corrosive urine at anything which startled them ... which was pretty much everything.

Riger led the others over a razor-backed hillock, and there was the outpost sitting atop the ridge in the distance. It looked like an interconnected series of multi-storied black boxes. There had been no contact with the survey team in six weeks.

229

Riger got on the comm with the *Cosmo* which orbited some four hundred kilometers above. "It's dark, real dark," he said. "Not picking up any life signs down here either. It doesn't look good."

"All right," Captain Cawber sighed. "Go in, but go in careful."

"Aye, Sir."

"Keep your eyes open, mister. God knows what kind of mess you're going into."

Riger stood there, studying the outpost. He wore a shiny green enviro-suit known as a Lizard Skin, eyes fixed and worried behind the bubble of his helmet. Like the others, he carried a pulser weapon.

In the black sky, there were occasional phosphorescent blue-white streaks caused by bursts of ionized xenon gas in the nitrogen-rich atmosphere. They looked like a sort of tubular lightning.

He led them up Centipede Ridge to the compound. The outer fence wasn't energized. Everything was down.

Just for the hell of it, he tried to raise the survey team again, even though he knew it was hopeless. The outpost was called Starlight Station, but why anyone had called it that with the constant heavy cloud cover and hydrocarbon smog of GE 4 was beyond him.

"Well?" Sealander said over the com. "We going in or what, sir?"

"When I say."

It was a terse reply that shut Sealander up. Riger understood his anxiety. He was scared. They were all scared. And for that very reason, they weren't going in until he had a good feel for things. Twenty-third-century technology told him there was nothing alive in Starlight, but his instincts were what he trusted.

"Okay," he finally said. "Lead us in, Sealander."

"Shit," Sealander said.

Wise giggled.

Sealander got to the main hatch, scanning it with the lights of his helmet. "She's not pressurized, First," he said over the com. "Airlock is blown."

Riger and the others came across the compound, nearly hopping in the low gravity. The shadows around them were deep, sinister pools. The beams of their lights slashed about like blades.

They went in.

⚔

"Can you get some lights going in here?" Riger asked.

Sealander shrugged inside his suit. "Sure. Probably. Generator's down. According to specs, there should be four backup systems. Funny none of them kicked in."

"Maybe somebody shut them off," Wise said.

"Now why in the hell would they do that, son?" Doc Kang asked.

Wise had no answer to that. At least none he was willing to share. The kid had imagination, real imagination, and sometimes that was a benefit, Riger knew. But not in a situation like this. What you needed here were level-headed nuts-and-bolts types. An imagination could be lethal.

If it was up to me, he would have stayed behind.

But the choice of the landing crew wasn't up to Riger. Captain Cawber picked who he wanted and that was that.

Sealander was studying the layout of Starlight. The graphics were displayed on the inside of his helmet bubble. "Looks ... looks like the power core is below. If we follow this corridor, take a left, then another right, we should see the hatchway at the end."

"Maybe we shouldn't split up," Wise said. "I mean, not just yet."

"C'mon, kid, and zip it with that talk," Sealander said, leading him off.

"All right, Doc," Riger said. "Let's you and me find central control."

He led the way, his helmet lights casting a blue-tinged illumination before him. Kang followed. Crazy, knife-edged shadows swept around them. They checked a few rooms on their way to central, mostly labs—geo and bio—and an emergency supplies closet. They saw no one or any indication that anyone had been there in some time.

"What do you make of it, Doc?" Riger asked when they paused at the station canteen, their lights scanning row upon row of empty tables.

Kang shrugged. "Not really sure. I mean, let's face it, if anyone was still alive, they would have picked up our transmission."

Riger felt his throat tighten. "But there were fifty people here ... they can't all be dead."

"Can't they?"

He was right, and Riger knew it. It had been six weeks since the distress call was received. That was a lot of time. Anything could have happened. That's what worried the hell out of him.

"At the very least," he said, "there should be some bodies."

Kang shrugged again. "When I first joined the service, I was a medic on an ore-crusher, the *Dolly B.*, making the hop from Proxima D and E to the uridium refineries on C. There was an ore camp called Crater Valley. Automated but for five hard rock drillers. Nobody had heard from them in weeks, so we sent down a rescue party. You know what they found?"

"Not a thing."

"Exactly. Those boys were gone, just gone. Point being, things happen way out here, First. Bad things. Things you can't even imagine."

Riger had heard plenty of tales like that in his time. He didn't even bother commenting on it. Doc was always going on about something. He didn't believe men and women belonged out this far.

Riger called in to the *Cosmo,* told them there was nothing to report. Not yet.

They moved down the silent corridor, then up a metal flight of steps. The sound of their footfalls echoed out and came back at them, making it sound as if they were being followed. Had Riger been an imaginative man, he might have told Cawber that the atmosphere of the station felt corrupted, contaminated by something namelessly bleak and horribly noxious. It seemed he could feel it invading him like a disease. The station was deserted. He was sure of that, yet it didn't feel as deserted as it should have under the circumstances. It felt unpleasantly *occupied.* But by what, he could not say.

⇕

Five minutes later, when Sealander came over the com, Riger nearly jumped. "Hate to say it, First, but Wise was right: somebody shut everything down. And I mean everything. Not just power, but life support, water recyclers, atmospherics, everything. About five and a half hours ago, from what I'm reading."

Riger felt something chill inch across the back of his neck. *That would have been just after sundown,* he thought.

"Can you power it up?"

"Sure, I can cold crank the pile, but it'll take fifteen, twenty minutes to cycle it."

"Do what you gotta do."

"Aye."

Riger was standing in the cabin of the chief biologist, a woman named Freeman. As he swept his light around, he saw nothing out of the ordinary and maybe that's what spooked him. There should have been something. Even a few drops of blood would have been reassuring.

It's so damn quiet, so damn empty.

"First! Over here!" Kang called over the com.

Riger rushed out into the corridor. Kang had ventured ahead into central control. He had his light on a form pressed up against a bank of instruments. Whoever it was, they wore a yellow e-suit and bubble helmet. Both were old in comparison to the Lizard Skins of the *Cosmo* team.

"Who is he?" Riger asked.

"I don't know. Can't get anything out of him but gibberish."

"Scans should have picked up his life signs."

"Yes," Kang said. "They should have."

Inside the helmet bubble, the bar lights revealed a middle-aged man whose eyes were huge and white, unblinking. His face was contorted through pain or terror, his mouth trembling. Every time he started to speak, it became quickly incomprehensible.

"Can you shoot him up?"

Kang nodded. He pulled a hypo from his medical kit and found the port on the man's suit. There was a low hissing as the medication was transferred. Right away, he relaxed. He blinked his eyes slowly and licked his lips.

"You ... you got the distress?"

"Yes," Riger told him. "Who are you? What happened here?"

"Pelan," he managed, his eyes dopy and glazed now. "Geophysics, Starlight Project."

"I'm Riger and this is Doc Kang. We're from the DS clipper *Cosmo.*"

"Deep Space, eh? Deep Space boys." His face hitched suddenly as if he had been jolted. "It ... it ... there's so much."

"Take your time," Doc told him.

Pelan nodded. "It was Henley, you know. George Henley. George and I were friends. Then he found the site, the ancient city by the dry ravine. That's where it started. It was Phyterian. There was no doubt. We ... we always thought the Phyterians were wiped out by climactic upheaval. But that wasn't true. No, no, no. George proved it. The extinction event ... it was the relic. The relic George found buried in the ruins. The relic ... oh dear God, *that awful relic ...*"

Riger and Kang were kneeling by him now.

"What relic?" Riger had to know. "Tell me."

Pelan was breathing hard, nearly hyperventilating. Cords as thick as the roots of an oak sapling stood out in his neck. "That city ... it was abandoned sixty thousand years ago. That was the time of the event, you see. The extinction event. The relic. George found the relic. That's why *it* came back, the entity, Yiggura, Yiggrath ... the Phyterians had many names for it." He was sobbing now, his eyes darting about madly in his head. "The relic ... the relic called it ... old as the universe, pestilence old as the Big Bang, the primary cosmic generation. Don't you see? Don't you see how late it is? *It's here! It's here now! It watches us and calls out to us!*"

"Dr. Pelan, you need to calm down," Kang told him.

"He's raving, Doc," Riger said, shaking his head. "He's not making any sense."

Pelan went rigid in his suit. "Goddamn you, listen to me! The Phyterians worshipped the thing! The relic was holy to them! When George found it in the ruins, Yiggrath came! Dark matter entering the visible spectrum! It had to exist! It is here now!"

"He's goddamn hysterical," Riger said.

Pelan scrambled to his feet. He started this way, then that. When Kang tried to get hold of him, he shoved him aside. He was shivering and shuddering. In fact, he was *vibrating* rapidly like a pneumatic hammer. It didn't seem as if the human body could move like that. He vibrated faster and faster until his boots rattled on the deck plating.

"What the hell is happening to him?" Riger asked.

"I don't know," was the best Kang had to offer.

Pelan looked like a man being electrocuted … slowly. He was holding onto two modular desks as the clonic tremors rolled through him faster and faster. His voice, high-pitched and wavering, was frenzied: "D-d-d-dark matter … an ecosystem for s-s-such things … the great spiral intelligence … born of gravitational force … anti-matter into a subatomic particle storm of l-l-living, breathing hate … writhing anti-creation, the absolute *negative* … the black fog of wrath … it can … it can … it can be broken down theoretically, empirically, m-m-m-mathematically … the writhing shadows … the tenebrous spiraling sentience … do you see? Do you see? The voices … God help us … the voices … *seven* … it differentiates, it assimilates … it accelerates … it expands … *eight … eight-point three point one-five-seven point nine-three … yes, yes, I hear it, I hear it!* The time is now—matter into energy into malignance … the hungering star-jelly … no longer entombed … now is the time of the turning, accept me and see me and stare into the primordial riven wastes of chaos! *Five … five … five … six … seven three … point nine-three-one squared … point point six point six point six point six six six SIX SIX SIX SIX SIX—*"

There was a loud, fleshy eruption, a very, *very* wet eruption of blood and tissue and boiling matter. Pelan was launched into the air, his suit making a horrendous, grisly popping sound, instantaneously expanding to three or four times its size like a helium balloon inflated to bursting in a microsecond.

He hit the floor with a wet, gelatinous sound like jelly in a plastic bag. The inside of his helmet bubble was splattered bright red. What was inside his suit was no longer recognizably human. It slopped and rolled with turgid, convulsive waves. Droplets of blood glistened on the seams.

Kang went to him right away, though he was obviously beyond hope. He pulled the pressure locks of the suit and unzipped it. He cried out as Pelan's anatomy surged out at him in a wave of red, mucid pudding that nearly engulfed him.

Riger pulled him to his feet.

"Like … like he underwent some massive systemic decompression," Kang said, his voice shrill and panicky.

The only thing Riger could really do was call it in. But when he tried, he got static. A heavy, droning, listening sort of static that bothered him in ways he could not put into words. It sounded as if there was something just beneath it, a low and unearthly sort of respiration as if he was hearing the planet breathe.

"I don't get it," Kang said. "Comm was working just fine ten minutes ago."

Yes, it was, wasn't it? Riger wanted to say but didn't dare. He was in command, and he had to act like it. His skin was literally crawling now, and it had nothing to do with what had happened to Pelan. This was something else, something that ran much deeper. An instinctive sort of fear. He had the feeling that they were being watched, coldly appraised by an inhuman intelligence that was icy and cruel.

"Got a mountain of pure copper just over the rise, Doc. Sensors picked it up. It can play hell with communications."

Kang nodded, but it was obvious he wasn't buying it.

Riger tried the comm again, and this time the static was so shrill, it hurt his ears.

"I don't like this," Kang said.

"Me either, Doc."

He tried to raise Sealander and Wise. At first there was just dead air, and his heart began to hammer. Then, "Yeah, First. Sealander here."

Thank God. "I want both of you up here right now. We're finishing the sweep, then we're heading for the *Bart.*"

Silence. A crackling. "Shit, sir, we're almost done here. Another five minutes and we'll have this place lit up like the Fourth of July."

Five minutes, five minutes, Riger thought. *Do we even have five minutes?* He didn't know. He just didn't know.

Confusion and uncertainty were settling into him, becoming a gnawing anxiety. It wasn't like him. He was generally a strong, secure sort of leader, but moment by moment, he was feeling weaker. It was this place, this awful place. It was sucking the life out of him.

"All right, five minutes. But no longer."

"You got it, First."

"At least the suit-to-suit comm is working," Kang said.

Or being allowed to work, Riger thought.

⚓

They found George Henley's cabin next. The walls were pasted with prints of the Phyterian city. It looked like a nightmare labyrinth of black basalt, narrow and crowded, sharp pinnacles rising high above that looked like fangs. There were maps, too. One laid over the top of another. From them, it was easy to glean that the city was only a few hours away.

"Look at this," Kang said.

Photos. Grainy blow-ups of something that looked like an immense, craggy skull; not one of white bone but something perfectly alien made of a mottled, bluish material that almost looked like some sort of metal.

There were shots of men standing by it, which gave it scale. It looked to be fifteen or twenty feet in length. It had a grotesque, exaggerated, goatish appearance like the skull of a ram that reminded Riger of Medieval prints he'd seen of the Black Goat of the Witches' Sabbat. The idea made him shiver. *The Devil, the Devil, way out here.* Regardless, the skull was hideous, chambered with hollows and exaggerated jaws, two immense cylindrical horns rising from its apex.

"Makes me think of ancient Egypt on old Earth," Kang said in a dreamy sort of voice. "That thing looks like the head of Anubis, the jackal-headed god of funerals and mummification."

Riger didn't know about any of that, he only knew the image of the skull made him feel uneasy, nervous … *expectant.* Disturbed. The skull was dead, of course, but the feeling he got was that it was not dead *enough.*

Kang pushed the photo print closer to him. "That's the relic," he said with something like religious awe. "That's the relic that summoned Yiggrath, the unborn and undying, the endless, deathless shade from the black seams between time and space."

Riger just stared at him. "What in the hell are you talking about? Pelan never said any of that."

"I … I don't know." Kang looked confused. His Adam's apple bobbed up and down like a monkey climbing a grapevine. In the lights of his helmet, his skin was sallow and diseased, his face running with beads of sweat. "I don't know why I said it, First."

Riger turned away from him. There was a loose, repellent cast to his features. It disgusted him.

Kang found a personal tablet hidden beneath more prints of the city. As soon as he touched it, it activated a halo-journal entry. A narrow, wizened face was projected before them.

"There can be no doubt," said the dour voice of the image, *"that what we now know of the Phyterian civilization and what we thought we knew are in direct contrast. For decades we believed that the Phyterian race were destroyed by an extinction event known as the Primary Cataclysm. This being a climate-*

altering release of methane gases via unprecedented and devastating seismic activity in the Southern Hemisphere in the region known as the Plain of Glass. These deposits were locked in intercrustal pockets during planetary cosmogony.

"At the PC—Primary Cataclysm—level of sediments we see evidence of a mass extinction of the sort Earth experienced at the close of the Permian. Namely, that ninety-five percent of GE 4's organisms perished. This PC Boundary, as it's known, occurred some sixty thousand years ago. And it was at this time that the Phyterians, a squat bidepedal toad-like race, also went extinct. Before that time, the planet was rich in biodiversity—herd animals such as the Hesperhippus and Bonditherms, the massive quasi-reptilian Crotacoils, numerous species of land-dwelling Prycops and Megacytes, aquatic helix worms and fishlike Icthydonts, as well as plant species such as the Tyrannophytes and Nyctaderms, thousands of species of seed pods, club mosses, and fungi. The list is endless.

"Now, no one can refute that the Primary Cataclysm occurred, but we now know there was another extinction vector of much more terrible potential. What this was is difficult to explain, but the finding of the relic skull by Phyterian priests known as the Accylardu-dek-despoda, or the Sect of the Gashed Ones, was the catalyst for what was to come. The skull—if I may be so bold as to apply such a descriptor—is not formed of bone as we understand bone, but of a spongy material that has so far defied analysis. I believe it is the material remains of a creature not from the space that we know and understand, but a denizen of the dark world, a creature of dark matter, a thing of dark electromagnetism from a parallel anti-universe. How it died, I cannot say, but I think that it was in a transitive interdimensional state between the exotic physics of its universe and the known physics of our own.

"The Phyterian priesthood called this entity something that can be reproduced phonetically as 'Yiggura' or 'Yiggrath'. The skull was the key. It opened the gates between two spheres of reality, it channeled the pestilence that claimed the Phyterian world, a life form that feeds upon mass death, upon mass extinction. A living representation of the skull. That is a theory. That is a guess. But based upon glyphs in the dead city and my own assumptions, I believe it to be true."

That was the first entry. Succeeding entries became more and more nonsensical, lacking lucidity or any linear logic until they became little more than the ranting of a disturbed mind.

"Doc, we don't have time for this," Riger said.

"Then we better make the time."

He queued up the next entry.

The image of Henley reappeared. It was the face of a man close to madness—staring eyes, twitching mouth, trembling lips, a voice that was high and scratching, nearly hysterical.

"The skull, the skull, the damned skull. It is in my dreams, it shadows my life. It compels, it owns, it possesses. I am not who I was. I feel I am being appropriated by a godless horror from some loathsome dimensional pit of insanity. The skull is not bone. It is dead but it lives. It is warm under my touch, pliant and fleshy. There is memory in it, memory of this world and a thousand others, exterminations and extinctions and genocide. I have touched death and death has taught me its secrets."

The next entry showed an image of what looked like a very old man. His eyes were bloodshot, his mouth contorted into a grotesque grin.

"Now the others do not scoff so much, eh? They do not think that George Henley is so mad after all, do they? None will dare approach the cursed ruins of Kry-Yeb, the dead but dreaming city of the Phyterian Empire. I have returned the skull to its tomb beneath Kry-Yeb, though distance matters not to such a thing. It appears to me, it haunts my dreams, it beckons to me. But I will not go there. I will not lay my hands upon it and view the carnage of dozens of worlds turned to poisoned, toxic graveyards. I will not!

"It is only the blazing light of the sun which weakens the skull and its potential. I fear the coming of night.

"The others? Oh yes, they feel the thing now and they know it calls forth another of its kind for soon will be the time of the great dying, the mass entombment, the sacred and profane interment of all that walk above the land. The time of the skin-turning is at hand, may God help us all."

The final entry was of a broken, stick-thin old man whose back was bent and whose hair had gone a shocking white. One eye was closed, the other wide but glassy, a deranged glistening orb.

"There is no escape. With great, pitiful futility, Dr. Pelan and the others have sent out a distress call. That which waits in ravening darkness only laughs. Soon will come the night, the night which lasts five Earth days. When the sun again rises, we shall all be dead. The signs of the coming of Yiggrath, the unborn and undying, the endless, deathless shade from the black seams between time and space, are many. There is a curious red haze in the sky and branching green lightning at the horizon. The winds are hot and dry, the winds of pestilence, the breath of the embalmer. No one can be sure of anything now. As another darker, malefic dimension intersects with our own, electronics and machinery fail. Time is turned back upon itself so that now is yesterday and five minutes ago is two weeks hence. The space-time continuum is tearing open and I alone can see what is waiting to creep out."

(later)

"It is full dark out now and Yiggrath comes. I hear the others out there, the crew of Starlight Station. They are driven to a mad frenzy, screaming and crying out, shrieking in the night like animals being butchered as they fall into the hands of the living god. And out the window ... yes, it is Yiggrath rising high and black and diabolic above the station. His horns brush the dark spiral holes between the stars.

"It comes! It comes!

"Inside, oh God oh god, the hour of the skin-turning ... "

"Shut that damn thing off!" Riger ordered.

"That's it," Kang said. "That's all there is."

⚶

They were getting out, back to the *Bartholomew* and up to the *Cosmo*, away from this planetary haunted house. Riger wasn't going to bother searching for anyone else. They needed to come down here with a large search party. There was no way he could handle it with four men *and why the hell didn't Sealander have those fucking lights on yet?*

As he hurried Doc Kang down the corridor and then down the metal steps to the first level, he tried to call into the *Cosmos*. That static, that damned static. It was as if there was no ship up there. All he was getting was the drone of the planet itself, the echo of atmosperic electrical activity.

Then he heard Captain Cawber speaking.

"Cosmo!" Riger cried. "This is Riger! We're coming back up, sir. What's going on down here is more than we can handle."

He expected Cawber's usual stern rebuttal, but what he got was much worse: "All right," the captain sighed. "Go in, but go in careful."

What in the hell?

"Captain? Captain? Are you reading me?"

"Keep your eyes open, mister. God knows what kind of mess you're going into."

This was the transmission from earlier, after the crew landed with the *Bartholomew*. Riger had everything he could do not to begin laughing maniacally. What was this? What kind of sick fucked up joke was this?

"Time is turning back upon itself just as Henley said it would," Kang mused in an airless voice. "Now we'll be delivered into the hands of the living god."

Riger wanted to hit him, to knock him down so he would quit spouting such nonsense.

But it was not nonsense.

For *something* was happening. Reality—the reality he had long known—was disassociating itself from Starlight Station. He felt a hot, bright sort of delirium open inside his head as time became elastic, stretching and sagging and reinventing itself. Now the corridors were too long, stretching into black, stark infinity. He felt that if he followed them, if he ran blindly down them in hysterical terror, he would fall off the rim of the universe and plunge into the ravening darkness that Henley had mentioned. Yes, it was here, it was now, it was happening. He could feel the physical parameters of the station begin to alter, squeezing him from all sides, the walls oozing and

242

bubbling, the angles in the corners warping, intersecting, splitting open to reveal sinister, eldritch vistas beyond time and space.

"We don't belong out here," Kang said, his face pale as spilled milk behind his helmet bubble, his eyes huge and white like goose eggs. "Out here in these awful spaces where darkness is endless and insanity takes physical form. Do you see that, Riger? Don't you see the terrible, horrendous mistake we've made by exploring deep space? It wasn't *our* idea at all! From the very crude beginnings of Sputnik and the Gemini missions, we were summoned into space, driven into it like herd animals, compelled to come out here where *they* would be waiting, the living gods!" He reached out for Riger, clawing at him. "Don't be a fool! Open your eyes and see, really *see!* It's always nightfall out here and and and *seven* ... this planet is a trap, a trap! We followed the dark creek into the black black ... *eight* ... river which spills into the ocean of stars and now we see the malign shapes that hide behind them like a child behind a blanket! Here flesh and matter and time and cold intellect intersect and and and—" He began to shake, trembling and jerking, thumping against the wall. Vibrating now. Like Pelan, *vibrating.* "The ... the coordinates ... *eight-point three point one-five-seven point nine-three* ... oh God, oh God, oh God ... here now it becomes! The stars are stripped away and the blackness of the cosmos opens like a great, hungry mouth and and and and *five ... five ... five ... six ... seven three ... point nine-three-one squared ... point point six point six point six point six six six SIX SIX SIX SIX SIX—"*

Kang's voice became a funneling scream as he vibrated madly and there was a deafening, fleshy *pop!* as he exploded inside his suit. He bounced off the walls, hit the ceiling, and fell at Riger's feet, the inside of his helmet filled with a bubbling, sloshing red mire of macerated tissue and blood.

Riger ran.

He got on the comm and called, *shouted* for Sealander again and again but there was no response. Just that static squealing in his ears, louder and louder, shrilling, screeching, making him cry out. He ran toward the entrance and there was Wise, Wise waiting for him.

"WISE!" Riger cried. *"WISE!"*

Then his hands were on him and he could feel the soft give of the man's Lizard Skin and Wise pitched over, his suit breaking open from the extreme internal pressure it had undergone and what was inside, splashed over the floor.

That's when Riger knew.

That's when he *really* knew. Wise was sprawled there on the floor in a soup of his own anatomy, a husk of pulp and raw wet matter. He had been birthed from his e-suit like a slimy fetus from an infected placenta, wearing the globular jewels of his organs on the *outside,* wrapped in the moist pink tentacles of his intestines. *The turning, the skin-turning.* It was how the living god received his worshippers, how Yiggrath welcomed them into his church—he turned them inside out

Riger stumbled out into the poisonous atmosphere of Gamma Eridani 4, standing and falling, rising and tripping on rubbery legs. His mind was flying apart inside his head like wheat chaff.

This is … this is … this is the hour of the turning.

He looked up and screamed, for Yiggrath had come. He/it/she towered above him, a glossy obsidian-black gargoyle rising a mile or two or three into the hazy, flickering auroral neon-slashed sky. Its jagged, spectral wings spread from horizon to horizon, its titanic body flickering and sparking with a soft blue lambency. The rising spires of its horns seem to brush the clouds. It grinned down at him, its snout opening like a monstrous bivalve that could have swallowed the stars.

Riger screamed no more; he was struck dumb with awe at the cosmic horror of the creature, of Yiggrath, the unborn and undying, the hyper-relativistic nightmare, the multi-dimensional living god that threaded the galactic magnetic field like a needle.

Bathed in its frozen shadow, everything around him began to spin and whirl, pulled inside out and broken into a blazing cyclonic storm of energized particles like droning phosphorescent corpse-flies that seemed to move around him and through him at light velocity and perhaps beyond until he was certain his head would split open like a jelly-filled gourd. And then, *then,* as his mind sucked into a black hole inside his cerebral cortex, he saw an enormous, endless plain of glittering stars forming chains and pulsating nebula and nightmare constellations that no man had ever seen and lived to tell of.

And as his eyes seemed to explode from his head, his voice rambling on and on and on—*eight ... eight point three point one-five-seven point nine-three*—he saw the trans-galactic gulf and its throbbing pulsars and glowing strata of stars split wide open, coming apart like a jigsaw puzzle in an alien spectrum of light and he saw worlds, a million-billion dead worlds blackened into cinders in some geometrically perverse, impossible anti-space where multi-faceted triangles and polygons and trapezohedrons hopped like frogs and a milky, writhing incandescence crawled, a monstrous worm a hundred light years in length. And as his voice screamed out the coordinates of his own approaching destruction with a sort of manic and rapturous mad glee—*five ... five ... five ... six ... seven three ... point nine-three-one squared ... point point six point six point six point six six six SIX SIX SIX SIX SIX*—he knew what Yiggrath wanted him to know: that the universe, the third dimension, was all synthetic, it was a simulation, a twisted vision, a hallucination that the beast had dreamed and now had grown bored with.

This is what Yiggrath wanted Riger to understand, the lurid joke inside the punchline hidden in the hysterical cackling iridescent chaos of known space, the seed it planted in his head as his skin began to turn.

SANDTRAP

As soon as the distress call came in like the shrill whine of a jungle bird, Jarvey started cursing under his breath, calling the *Cimarron's* comm every name he could think of. Way out here, a distress signal was trouble. Big trouble. The sort of trouble he could do without, thank you very much. But he had his duty—to God, country, and Company, not necessarily in that order—and he would do it. It was his job and nobody could ever say he didn't do his job.

Bartel yawned and pulled his headset off. "What you got there, smart boy?"

"Kiss my ass," Jarvey told him, having listened to his bullshit for the better part of six months now. He had all he could do not to go over there and kick Bartel's ass sideways. Would have, if he wasn't afraid of what he might catch. "It's a distress signal."

Bartel nodded. "Hey, you're good. You ought to do this for a living."

Jarvey ignored that, running a track on the distress call. Way out here, on the dirty backside of the Ursa Major cluster, Christ knew what they were letting themselves in for. He watched the viewscreen, the scattering of stars out there, all that black emptiness between. Gave a man ideas. Those fathomless voids planted dark seeds in a man's mind, things that came back to haunt him in his sleep.

"So where's our distress signal coming from?" Bartel asked, finally pulling his boots down from the navigation console.

"From my asshole."

Bartel rubbed his hands together. "Again? Well, you better get your ass to Biomed."

"Why don't you just shut up so I can concentrate here?" Jarvey snapped. "AI's running it. I'll know in a minute."

"Close or far?"

"Jesus, Bartel. Climb off my ass already. Gimme a minute here." Jarvey brought up a few diagrams on his screen. "You never did tell me, Bartel ... how old was your sister when your daddy got her pregnant with you?"

"That was my brother, not my father. Get it straight."

The gibes were flying back and forth by the time Tyden made the bridge, came up the companionway wiping sleep from his eyes. Tyden was a big man with a red beard and a tattoo of a four-leaf clover on the back of his left fist. When things got tense or scary, he would kiss it, wish for luck.

"Okay, girls," he said, "you can discuss your marital plans later. What the hell's going on up here? Alarms going off and what not. Jesus."

"We got trouble," Jarvey said, chewing the words with distaste. "We got big trouble."

Tyden knew it was a distress signal, but he wouldn't let on. "Well, can it wait? I was taking a shit down there."

Bartel giggled, started punching coordinates up on the screen, knowing what was in the offing and making ready.

Tyden saw Jarvey wasn't amused. "C'mon, what do you got?"

"We got us a distress signal from about five parsecs out, pretty weak. I had to boost it just to grab hold of it, see what it said," he told the skipper.

"Five parsecs ... shit, take us six weeks to make that at full steam. Whoever sent it will be toast by then. You figure on that?"

Bartel tapped a finger to his balding head. "Goddamn, that Jarvey is one smart cookie. Didn't I tell you he was some kind of smart cookie, Cappy?"

"You did."

Jarvey went on. "I locked it to ... Zeta Ursae Majoris, Mizar ..."

He went on to tell them the basics. Zeta Ursae Majoris, a.k.a. Mizar and 79 Ursae Majoris, was a second-magnitude, hot white star of the A2 spectral type with a very pronounced magnetic field. It had a companion, Mizar B, and was the second star in from the handle of the Big Dipper. The signal was coming from the fifth planet, a place called Andros. It had been overflown by drones, but never visited by a manned craft.

Not until now.

"Okay send a beam home, tell 'em we're diverting for a distress," Tyden said. Then paused. "Either of you boys have a problem with that?"

Bartel said, "Hell, no, Cappy. I always wanted to hang from the Big Dipper as a kid."

Tyden nodded. "Go ahead, Jarvey, get it off your chest."

Jarvey shook his head. "I'm just saying how it's none of our business is all. Way out there? Who in Christ's name would be way out there? Distress is saying it's an Earth ship ... but who knows? Could be a trap. Could be something else waiting for us, trying to draw us in. We're a long way from home with no backup, that's all I'm saying."

"You ever think of anything but your own ass?" Bartel put to him.

"No, and it's kept me alive this long. We're six months out, is all I'm saying. All we're supposed to be doing is running the deep circuit, salvaging satellites and wrecks. We shouldn't be stirring up any shit that's none of our business."

Tyden took off his cap and slapped it against his leg. "None of our business? Goddammit, Jarvey, there's people out there. Men and women that need our help. They're a long way from home, too."

"C'mon, Cappy, it's dangerous jumping out that far."

"Don't you goddamn well tell me about dangers, mister. Hell, I've been on deep probes that went on six years. I think I know my business."

"Yes, sir."

"When you were still pumping the neighbor's beagle, Jarvey, I was out *here*. When you got the first hair on your girly balls, I'd already pulled three tours at the Wolf 359 station and mapped out UV Ceti with Barnes. Now boost that distress, put a beam on it and tell 'em we're coming. Bartel, lock in a course. I'll meet both of you at the tubes. Rig for hyperspace...."

⚡

They were stiff as lake ice when they got out of the cryotubes six weeks later, just standing there, working the kinks out of their backs and the knots out of their joints. Jarvey was punchy, still not liking this pigfuck any farther than he could throw it. Six weeks off course. Damn. He'd been hoping he'd wake up, see Centauri A in the viewscreen topside. But he knew that wasn't what he'd see at all.

"Goddamn freezers," he grumbled. "They play hell with my insides. I had the shits for a week straight after that pull last month. The cold interferes with my lower regions."

Bartel laughed. "This guy and his rectum. It's all he thinks about."

"Kiss my ass." Jarvey turned to Tyden. "I'm serious here, Cappy. Last time, I could barely digest my food. I had to hold everything in my mouth until it was soft."

Bartel ate that up. "Way I hear it, that's not the only thing you hold in your mouth until it's soft."

Tyden laughed and Jarvey raged and it went on for some time. Bartel giving Jarvey a hard time about his mother and sister and their curious sexual peculiarities. The barnyard lineage in his family.

"All right, girls," Tyden finally said. "Let's go see what Andros looks like."

⚡

Five minutes later, they were watching the planet on the viewscreen, a huge crusty ball the color of beach sand. Jarvey told them it was roughly the size of Earth with comparable gravity, but a slightly eccentric orbit that barely made it parabolic. It was hot, dry, and rocky, a hazy desert from what the sensors told him. Atmosphere was primarily hydrogen with some helium and ammonia, clouds of methane, various hydrocarbons. Possibly some subsurface water. No terrestrial life showing up on the biosensors, but the components were there. And life had been logged on much more hostile worlds.

"We still getting the distress?" Tyden wanted to know.

"Pretty week, but it's there," Jarvey told him. "Still no voice, just auto-beacon. Could be just the machinery operating down there."

Bartel was watching Andros, thinking things that surprised even him. It was just another world and he'd seen plenty … yet there was something about it that held you, made you want to look and wish you hadn't. The planet was tan and brown and drab, mottled like the flesh of a mummy. It looked like a sandstorm caught in a snow globe, a spinning lifeless sphere of suspended dust and dirt and suffocating heat, an orb of withered fruit. You looked at it and it looked at you and it made your throat go dry, your palms sweat, your chest feel tight … because, well, it *really* did seem to be looking back at you. Like a haunted, disembodied eye.

He had to look away.

Jarvey saw the way he was acting, but didn't have the wind in his throat to comment on it. Both men were watching that world watch *them* and knowing that Andros was more than a dead world, it was a graveyard.

"Okay," Tyden finally said. "Let's set this beast down.…"

⸎

When the boarding ramp was pressed down into the warm, shifting sand, Jarvey was right behind Tyden, weighed down in his bulky e-suit, trying to juggle all the equipment he was carrying. Right away he did not like the place. The endless panorama of desert broken only by occasional outcroppings of jagged rocks and leaning towers of stone. The heat shimmering out there, how the sky and land merged into one at the horizon, both that same color of dirty sand.

The terrain was monotonous, repetitious, like some gigantic matte canvas where the artist had gotten bored, duplicating the landscape every quarter mile right on to infinity. You could lose your mind out there, never knowing if you were a hundred feet from the ship or a hundred miles.

No creativity or originality anywhere. Nature had just slapped this place together with odds and ends left over from other worlds, called it a day.

No, Jarvey did not like it.

Staring out there, adjusting the magnification on his helmet viewplate, he could see how topography like that could suck your mind dry. Just seeing it made something curl up in his head.

"External temperature, seventy-three degrees Celsius," he said, reading the scanner strapped to his arm. 163 fucking degrees F. Without the climate controls on the suits, they'd drop in minutes. He took some more readings. "Wind ... negligible. Same old, same old. Hydrogen, helium, methane ... picking up some metals and salts in the soil. Nothing on bioscan, but I'm getting heavy interference when I try subsurface. Reflections from those ores, probably."

Tyden walked out into the sand drunkenly, trying to get his legs under him. The suit was heavy in near-normal gravity, and the sand of Andros was soupy, his boots sinking into it up to the ankles with each step he took. "This stuff is like snow. Bartel, you pack the snowshoes?"

Bartel shook his helmeted head. "Negative on that, Cappy."

Jarvey moved in a loose circle, getting used to the sand, how it pulled at you, making each step a chore. Not like beach sand, he decided, but more of a fine silica, slippery and sluicing. He watched the sand, saw currents moving through it, little eddies and turgid waves that fell into themselves.

Bartel came up to him, linked an arm with his own. "I don't know about you, honey, but I want a refund. This place doesn't look like the brochures at all."

Jarvey shrugged him off, almost went on his ass as a result. "Christ, this goddamn suit ... feel like I'm loaded here."

"Takes some time to get used to," Tyden put in, holding a scangun above his head and trying to lock on the distress.

"Oh, just take it off," Bartel said. "I'll run naked with you."

"Fuck off."

"Quit talking dirty to me." Bartel stood there, wavering uneasily as he settled into the sand.

Jarvey felt positively claustrophobic. The e-suits were day-glo orange, bulky and cumbersome. They were actually designed for low-gravity environments, but the freighter and salvage crews weren't given anything better. The expeditionary forces had light, adaptive environmental suits. But they were expensive, so the Company outfitted its boys in e-suits that were old ten years before.

"I'm locking that beacon," Tyden said, taking a reading from the scangun. "South-southwest ... about two klicks from here. You copy that?"

Jarvey checked his scanner. "Aye, I'm getting it ... picking up some low-level telemetry, pretty garbled. I'll link it with the *Cimarron's* memory plexus, see what I get." He worked the scanner on his arm, started getting feedback from the ship right away. "Okay ... distress is from a ship called the *Burnam,* United Mining. Geolab, drilling rig. Had a crew of six ... getting some log entries, most of it's lost ... here we go, last entry we're picking up was that the *Burnam* was pulling a geo survey of the Gamma Majoris system, which definitely puts them in this general quadrant."

"Any reason for ditching?" Tyden wanted to know.

"Not that I'm tapping into ... most of the logs are damaged or wiped out." Jarvey gave up. "What the hell is a mineral cruncher doing way the hell out here? I didn't know the independents were jumping out this far."

"Polycrystals," Bartel said. "Big money fast. What's United care if they lose a few crews along the way?"

Tyden told them United was going to be fined when word hit the Agency. Commercial survey crews weren't allowed out this far. And that made sense. If something happened to them, they were marooned. Case in point, the *Burnam.*

They started walking, Tyden in the lead, moving through the shifting sea of sand. Clouds of methane drifted over them and threw gigantic shadows, blocking the light of the blazing sun overhead. The landscape shimmered and rippled and surged. As they stepped down, pockets of ammonia and chlorine gas puffed from the soil in yellow vapors.

"Watch for sinkholes," Jarvey said. "Picking up hollows here and there."

They adjusted their scanners and kept moving, trudging across the nightmarish territory that went on and on, even the rock formations looking identical. Andros made Death Valley look positively appealing.

"Keep pushing, people," Tyden said. "We got a long way to go. We got us a ship to find."

⚟

They found it about an hour later.

Out in the middle of a rippling, endless sand flat. Rolling dunes in the distance hemmed them in from all sides. The wind had picked up, blowing a thick ground fog of methane around their legs, obscuring everything. But they saw the ship, they saw what was left of the *Burnam*.

It was scattered for a quarter mile in all directions.

Jarvey knew that no one could have survived such a wrenching impact. Studying the debris, he was thinking that it looked like maybe there were a dozen ships out there, all trying to rise from the ocean of sand. Gleaming, hooded projections of riven pressure hulls. The sharp wings of stabilizers. The blackened tubes of thrusters. Shards of metal poking from the sand like half-buried razor blades that were probably the remains of cabins and superstructure, the bulkheads that had once fused them into one. Wreckage dispersed everywhere, metal and plastic and synthetic alloy twisted into corkscrews.

Tyden said, "What a fucking mess ... those poor bastards." He pointed out beyond the sand dunes toward a vague run of serrated bluffs far in the distance. "Adjust your viewshields ... a crystalline mountain range, like diamonds and just as hard. Ship must have come in rough, hit that range and it had the same effect as an iceberg on an old ocean liner. Sheared her right in half, ripped her stem to aft and dumped the pieces down here."

Jarvey figured that was exactly what had happened.

The *Burnam* must have been crippled, perforated by meteors maybe, her drive seized. They looked for the first place to set down they could find. Boosters must have failed after entry and the ship came in like a bullet, those crystal mountains gutting her.

Yet looking around at the wreckage ... he just wasn't sure. Every scrap and fragment were gouged and abraded, looking like something had chewed it all up and shit it back out. Hardly scientific, but he couldn't help thinking it.

Tyden said, "Well, we better look for remains."

∲

They spent the next hour doing just that.

The sand flat was a ship's graveyard, masts and spirals of metal jutting like tombstones and monuments. There was something unnerving about searching through the mangled wreckage. It got inside them, hit them on a personal level. Like sorting through the aftermath of an ethnic cleansing. They felt like they were defiling some sacred burial ground.

But they found no bodies.

Not so much as a scrap of bone or the scorched rag of a pressure suit.

Nothing.

But there was blood. They found it on pieces of metal, on spirals of plastic and plates of hull planking. It had gone black in the poisonous, scalding atmosphere of Andros. Just stains now, but there all the same. And a lot of it.

"The bodies must have burst on impact," Jarvey said. "There might be pieces of them up on that range. Who knows? But all this blood, nobody crawled away from this mess. You know that much."

"But we should be seeing *something,*" Tyden said. "A piece of bone, a shard of skull … maybe the odd limb."

"Maybe what's left is buried in that sand," Bartel suggested.

"No, there should be something, dammit."

The wind was throwing sand around now, a fine grit that peppered their suits and viewplates like powdered glass. The methane fog was hissing from the churning ocean of sand in whirlwinds, in tornadic mists. Dust devils skimmed along the debris, whipping particles in all directions.

Jarvey didn't care for where any of this was going. He suggested that the corrosive atmosphere of the planet may have dissolved human remains on contact. But Tyden wasn't buying that either. He pointed out that the crew's pressure suits would not dissolve, even a full blast from a pulser couldn't burn them up completely. There was blood … a lot of blood … but no flesh and no bone and no bits of suit. It didn't wash.

Bartel's face looked tense behind his viewplate. "C'mon, Cappy, what are you saying here? Scavengers? The remains were *dragged* off?"

Jarvey swallowed thickly, looking for movement among the wreckage. Nothing. Nothing at all.

"I'm not saying that at all," Tyden said. "Just that … well, none of this fits and you know it."

"Let's just hoof it back to the ship," Jarvey said.

"Negative." Tyden passed the scangun in a wide arc, looking for something but not saying what that was. "We institute a grid search. A kilometer in all directions. Let's go."

⚶

They found no bodies.

No bones.

No fragments of suits.

But what they did find were funnels. Funnels maybe ten feet in diameter that were dug down into the sand a good fifteen feet. They were perfectly uniform as if they had been channeled by some machine. Jarvey and the others found no less than ten of them out on the sand flat, just east of the wreck site. And as they started searching, they found that more had opened up among the wreckage itself.

"These weren't here before," Bartel said, staring down into the mouth of one. The sand began to erode at its edge and he almost lost his footing, went tumbling down. "I would have seen these."

Tyden said, "Yeah, we all would have. These are recent ... and I'm thinking they're just a little too symmetrical to be of accidental origin."

Jarvey was thinking the same thing, and it was making him sweat inside his suit. There were reasons for it, he was certain, just like there were reasons for the missing remains of the crew. You thought about it long enough, you might even come up with something ... and, then again, if you thought about it long enough, your brain might just burn up like a falling star. Or maybe you'd wish it had.

Tyden was curious about the funnels, planned on figuring them out one way or another. And like baggage cars hooked to a train careening off a bridge, Jarvey and Bartel had no choice but to follow. They counted no less than twenty-six funnels. Most of them were new.

"Crazy shit," Bartel said, teetering in that poisonous wind. "You turn your back, they open up. How come it doesn't happen when you're watching?"

And Jarvey found himself thinking, *because that would be too goddamn easy. If we had explanations, then this dead hellhole couldn't work our nerves the way it is.*

"Bartel?" Tyden said over the helmet-to-helmet channel. "What the hell are you doing?"

Jarvey looked over at Bartel. He was up to his calves in the sand, sinking steadily like a man in quicksand. He just looked at them like they were crazy and then he seemed to get it. With a crazy, strangled cry, he stumbled free, falling onto his hands and knees, the others helping him to his feet.

And behind him, where he'd been standing, the sand was moving.

Not just moving, because it was always moving a little, but twisting and churning like something was stirring it from underneath. A shard of metal from the *Burnam* trembled and then sank from view like a stone into a peat bog. The sand began dropping away, swirling like water now—a foot, then two feet, then five and ten, a perfect funnel forming. Then the whirlpooling motion ceased. A pebble dropped into the funnel, some grains of sand.

Nothing else.

"Well at least I wouldn't have gone very far," Bartel said, trying to make light of it and failing.

There was something very unfunny about these funnels.

Jarvey scanned it, couldn't find anything beneath it but more sand, some hollows lower down, maybe caves or subterranean chambers. The scanner seemed to think these were natural in origin.

"Could be just some weird geologic or seismic activity," Tyden said, throwing that out, seeing if anyone wanted to try it on.

Bartel just said, "Sure, that's all it is."

Jarvey kept scanning. "There *is* some geothermal activity down below … movement down there like the crust is in motion. I can't tell you much more than that. But if you want my opinion …"

Tyden looked at him, very stern behind the face shield of his helmet. "Yes?"

"I think we should make for the ship … this sand and what's beneath, it's a little on the unstable side. I'm still picking up sinkholes from time to time, but they're moving. Filling up, opening somewhere else."

"Keep an eye on it," Tyden told him. "I want to check something."

Tyden led them away from the crash site and up over the dunes. It was hard going, the sand moving with gentle, rolling undulations like water in slow motion: moving, cresting, surging, then falling back into itself. Filling pools and overflowing, becoming breakers that rose up incredibly slowly, freezing in position, then gradually eroding back down again. Even the big dunes were in subtle motion, oscillating so slightly the eye could not follow their progress, but Jarvey and the others could feel it just fine. That sluicing action played hell with their sense of balance, tipping them this way and that, carrying them gradually back down the dunes inch by inch if they stood in the same place for too long.

An ocean, Jarvey thought, *it's a goddamn ocean of sand.*

When they had reached the peak of the last of the dunes, they passed down through a hollow of methane mist that swallowed them alive like fog at sea. They climbed back up over a pebbly rise, found some stable high ground. The wind was howling up there, throwing sand and pulverized bits of rock in sheets, obscuring visibility. It would blow and kick up, then settle down long enough for you to see where you were. The sand on their view shields sounded like fine hail on windowpanes.

Tyden stood there, running the scangun over the hills rising before them. They were sharp and jagged like the spines of a buried saurian, some rising hundreds of feet, others barely poking up out of the sand. There were tall tubes of rock, huge boulders, flat tables of stone juxtaposed between.

Beyond the alien mountains, there were the high peaks of that crystalline range that Tyden figured had sheared the *Burnam* open. They rose in sharp, triangular and conical protrusions, caught the sun and broke it up into prismatic rays of purple and red and indigo, dazzling and blinding. The men had to turn up the filters on their view plates so as not to go blind, such was the intensity.

Climbing into the foothills above them, squeezing up between slats and towers of rock, Tyden scanned the crystalline mountains. "Pure crystallized carbon," he said. "Some impurities ... boron, nitrogen ... but amazingly pure. Diamonds. Jesus, a mountain of diamonds."

Bartel and Jarvey stayed below, both silent, no gibes or smartass comments, just silence. They listened to the wind and sand on their external speakers and waited, just waited.

Jarvey looked behind them. He could see the graveyard of wreckage sticking up out of the sand flat, the wind whipping up storms of grit that raged and then dissipated.

Then: *"Hey!"* Tyden called out to them, up among the rocks. "Get up here, you two!"

Bartel led the way.

Same as Tyden, squeezing between shelves of rocks, crawling over tablets of stone, through hollows worn into boulders the size of two-story buildings, and finally among all those weird, cyclopean towers.

"Look at that," Tyden said.

Jarvey wasn't sure what he was seeing, but it made his skin crawl.

About fifty feet above them, there was a leaning spire of rock with a flat boulder at its base. Suspended between these by ropy filaments was something like a cocoon, a translucent green and flaking thing, hollowed out and ragged. It looked like it had been up there a long time. It flapped and trembled in the wind. Jarvey thought it resembled a giant green spider with those reaching tendrils anchoring it in place.

"What the hell is that?" Bartel wanted to know.

Jarvey scanned it. "I'm guessing … a pupa," he said uneasily. "Scanner's saying it's made of unknown proteins in a complex arrangement, some lipids and glutinous waxes … organic in nature. A chrysalis. A chrysalis shell."

"You saying something came out of that?" Bartel asked.

"Yes. Same way a butterfly or moth would...."

That didn't go down really well, for this thing was twenty feet across at least. They could see the chamber within, the shiny material in there, each wondering what could have crawled out.

Up above, suspended from a dozen rocky hollows, were other empty chrysalids. At least a dozen.

"We better get to the ship," Tyden said.

⚬

It was a long walk back through the shifting sands and methane fog, the billowing sand. They crossed through the wreckage as fast as they could. The wind kept at them, pushing and pulling at them, trying to knock them flat at times. About the time they made it out of the wreckage, Bartel started screaming.

When they looked, about fifteen feet behind them, he was caught in a spinning whirlpool of sand. It was moving counterclockwise and at such a rate that he could not escape it. He spun like a top, gradually corkscrewing down into the sand as a funnel opened up around him and the sand drained away and him with it. By the time they got near to him, he was up to his waist in it, his arms flapping and his body gyrating.

They couldn't even get to him.

When they got close, the pull of the maelstrom nearly sucked them in, too. Well, Tyden, anyway. True to form, Jarvey was keeping his distance. Tyden gave up soon enough.

"Just ride it down!" he told Bartel who was plain out of his head with panic.

The funnel had dropped maybe ten feet now. Bartel was up to his chest plate in the spinning sand. Then the funnel emptied out. It was perfect and proportional and the sand drained away to unknown depths, freeing him. Dizzy and shaking, he went to his knees.

"Try crawling up," Tyden said.

"Gimme a minute … my head's spinning."

Finally, down in the pit, he got up, wavered uneasily. The point of the funnel was maybe a foot across. The sand was sloppy and sinking. He started to climb back up, digging handholds in the earthen walls. He made it maybe seven, eight feet and then the apex of the funnel was in motion again. Sand was being sucked away, dropping down through a hole that had opened below and was widening. As the sand was displaced, Bartel was moving back down. He crawled and climbed as fast as he could, but he simply couldn't keep up with the displacement from beneath.

He was being pulled down and there was nothing that Tyden and Jarvey could do but watch his descent.

Tyden was on his belly, reaching an arm down. "Climb, Bartel! Climb up! Grab my hand! Grab my hand!"

But he was moving steadily downward, fighting and clawing, shouting for them to help him. "Get a rope or something!" he yelled. "Get a goddamn rope down here!"

But they didn't have any rope.

And Bartel began to scream.

It was a wailing, shrill cry that echoed through the helmets of Tyden and Jarvey, bouncing around in their skulls and making them feel every horrible moment of his terror.

And then—

And then they saw it.

The hole had widened like the mouth of a barrel, sand boiling from it in a churning, cyclic action. Bartel slid down farther and farther, then the sand fell away and they saw what haunted the empty spaces below—what was digging away the sand, displacing it at a frantic pace, and drawing its prey down like an antlion burrowed in beach sand.

Jarvey let out a cry.

It was like some huge, hairless spider or maybe a beetle. A dirt-colored, insect or arachnid with a body like a segmented barrel, a nightmare arthropod with clicking crab legs and hooked mantis spurs, serrated jaws moving side to side and a forest of spearing thorns looking for something to impale. It was in constant motion, making a high, keening sound, exhaling vapors of methane and spitting globs of acid.

And then it had Bartel.

Its mouth was moving, all those thorns puncturing him in a hundred places like the busy needles of a sewing machine until he was shredded and soft and digestible. It pulled him into its snapping mouth that chewed side to side and up and down, interlinked jaws coming from all directions.

Tyden shouted, pulled the pulser from his belt and aimed it at the beast. The pulser hummed and a saber of blue light found the horror in the pit, made it glow and sizzle, X-rayed it, turned it red and white and smoking, made it crisp and flake and give up its ghost in a pall of greasy smoke. Then the beast fell into itself, ashes and embers and popping coals.

The funnel collapsed, burying it in sand, nearly taking Tyden with it.

Jarvey took hold of his ankle before he fell into the creature's grave and yanked him back, away from the funnel that was now just a depression in the sand.

"We ... we gotta make that ship," Tyden said, gulping air and panting, his face wet with perspiration.

Both threaded with panic, that's where they went.

⚜

Andros was a world of disappointments.

When Tyden and Jarvey got to the desert bowl where they'd set the ship down, they had a little problem: the ship was gone.

"Where the hell is it?" Tyden wanted to know. He moved in circles, looking and seeking, arms up in the air, demanding answers. "It was right here! *I know it was goddamn well right here! Wasn't it here, Jarvey? Wasn't it?*"

Jarvey, his flesh puckered with gooseflesh now, said that it was. He wanted to speak, but he was having trouble breathing. His mouth was dry and his throat was closing up on him. He worked the scanner on his arm. "It was here ... *it's still here.*"

Tyden looked at him. "What the hell do you mean?"

"It sank." Jarvey was breathing hard now. "It's below us, about a hundred feet down."

That brought silence for a moment.

Jarvey waited.

Tyden looked up at the blazing sun of Mizar, felt it consume him in heat, baking him inside his e-suit. He got out his scangun and aimed it at the ground, confirmed what Jarvey had said. He started to say something, then shut his mouth.

"Those chrysalids," Jarvey said in a defeated, empty voice. "What got Bartel ... it must come to term up in those chrysalids, then burrow down into the sand. Must be part of its life cycle."

"Sure," Tyden said.

"Alive, but doesn't register on bioscan."

Tyden didn't care about the creatures, but that was because he was a fool, because he had no imagination. As awful as they were, they were truly exceptional. The sand was their sea, their environment, and they were perfectly adapted to it. Amazing, completely amazing.

Jarvey figured they had created the ocean of sand on Andros. Like earthworms devouring loam and organic decay and shitting out topsoil, these things chewed solid rock and passed out sand. You could not hope to wear out such a fixated, insidious enemy. The sea of sand was probably full of life, an insane alien ecosystem.

He started telling Tyden about it, but Tyden wasn't listening.

He didn't give a high happy shit about the natural history of the planet.

He was a man used to making decisions, but now that had been stripped away from him. There was nothing to make decisions *with*. Options, technology, command—it had all been stripped away from him by this hot, noxious, eroding world of dust and sand.

He fell to his knees, began to dig with his hands like he might actually reach the ship below.

Jarvey just stood there, not certain what he was feeling by that point, but thinking, his mind turning hard and telling him just how long the air and water in the e-suit would last him. And it wasn't long.

Tyden was digging and digging, his mind gone now, maybe temporarily and maybe for good.

Jarvey should have gone mad with him, but he didn't.

He just watched.

For six months he'd taken shit from Bartel with that mouth of his. The insults. The bullying. It went on and on. Tyden could have put a stop to it, but he didn't. And now look at him: digging in the sand like a little boy that had lost his big, shiny marble. This was retribution. This was fucking karma. Big, tough, in-charge Tyden was pissing his pants.

Jarvey smiled behind his polycarbonate viewplate. He felt like laughing at the absurdity of it all. And especially at Tyden himself, great fucking gob that he was. "If you dig for six, seven weeks, Cappy, you might find that ship of ours."

Tyden looked up. His face beyond the viewplate boiled with rage. *What was this? Goddamn defiance, and from Jarvey, that pissing little worm?* He climbed to his feet, swayed in the sand like a swimmer on a wobbling diving board. "What the hell did you say, mister?"

"I said, you dig six, seven weeks and you'll find the ship," Jarvey told him, amused by it all. "Only problem is, we'll be fucking toast by then. And you know why? You know why, big boss man? Because you had all the answers. Because you were in charge and you wouldn't listen to me when I tried to save your miserable bacon. Big brave fucking Tyden puffing out his chest so he could impress Bartel. Now ain't that something? Ain't that just something? Like one turd trying to impress another with its smell."

"You better stop right there," Tyden warned him.

"Oh, but I ain't going to stop, big boss man. I'm just telling you the truth, you stupid sonofabitch. Because you were in charge and you had all the fucking answers, bright boy, didn't you? And now we're never getting off this dirty rock, this goddamned Andros. We're trapped in this fucking dust bowl and it's your fault! You hear me, *it's your fault!* If we're lucky, real damn lucky, we'll get sucked into a funnel like Bartel! If not? Then we'll slowly suffocate and get pulled down into the sand and maybe, just maybe, a hundred fucking years from now, the sand will spit our bones back up! *And it's your fault, your goddamn fault—*"

Tyden couldn't take it.

Not from that yellow squeeze of piss Jarvey.

He vaulted at him, stumbling along, but getting to Jarvey long before he could get out of the way. Then they were swinging at each other, screaming at each other, going at it tooth and fist. Only thing was, in those bulky e-suits it was about as ridiculous as ridiculous got. Absolutely comical. Like trying to square dance in suits of armor. They both went down on their asses twenty seconds into it.

They said nothing for a time.

The wind blew and the sand shifted and the sun blazed overhead. They could feel the nightmare gravity of that sterile world pulling them down into the sand, interring them in a tomb of grit.

"Well, Cappy, you got any orders for me?" Jarvey finally said.

"Go to hell."

"I'm already there, thanks to you."

Tyden's hand went for his pulser. He was so over the edge by that point that he would have burned Jarvey down where he sat rather than listen to his mouth, listen to all the petty gripes and recriminations he had been storing up all these months. His hand went for his pulser, but never got there.

And that was because the sand began to move.

They thought at first it was the creatures, opening up funnels beneath them, getting ready for lunch. The sand shifted and rippled, trembled with minute oscillations like it was thrumming with current. Jarvey got to his feet and so did Tyden and they tried damn hard to stay there, but the sand really started moving, rolling and seeping and sluicing like secret rivers that tossed them around, knocked them into each other. The sand was liquid and gushing, sculpting mounds that lifted them up and hollows that dropped them down.

Jarvey's feet slid out from under him and a cresting wave of sand nearly buried him. Tyden tried to ride another and it lifted him up where he balanced uneasily on its apex, and then it just dissolved beneath him. The entire sand sea was in motion, rising and swelling and stirring like soup in a pot.

It wasn't the creatures this time, but some weird geologic phenomenon that was no less frightening.

Jarvey took hold of Tyden as the whirlpooling sand spun them around. A great, billowing wave of it lodged them on its crest as it rose up ten, then twenty feet, carrying them away like a couple surfers riding an immense breaker toward a beach. Only on Andros, the beach *was* the ocean and the world and everything else. The wave carried them over that undulating desert, past cones of rock that would have sheared them wide open. Then it crested, fell apart, and they were dumped in the slushing sand again. A storm of wind-driven grit and dust blew over them.

"You all right?" Tyden asked him, digging his way out of a dune that had nearly buried him alive.

"Yeah. Just fine."

They looked around.

They could not say how far the wave had carried them. Maybe a few hundred yards, maybe a mile. The terrain they had known was gone now, swallowed by the sand, reinvented and reshaped by the surf itself. Looking around, they could not say where they had even originally touched down or where the wreckage of the *Burnam* might be.

They climbed atop a shelf of rock, trying to get their bearings. All around them was a rolling field of sand dunes, some twenty or thirty feet in height, pockets of methane caught in the dips between them like patches of ground fog. The sandstorm had subsided somewhat.

Jarvey consulted his scanner. "That diamond mountain is about three klicks straight ahead," he said. "If you feel like doing some climbing, Cappy. About thirty feet below us is the wreck of the *Burnam.*"

Behind his viewplate, Tyden looked hopeless, angry, exhausted, ready to fold up and have himself a good cry. But he recovered quickly enough. "Okay, let's climb out of here. It's not like we have anything else better to do."

Jarvey laughed and sat in the sand. "Why? I like it here just fine. This is as good of a place to die as any."

"C'mon, Jarvey, quit being such a fucking quitter."

"Sorry, but my old team spirit has dried up and blown away. I kind of like this place."

"You're useless, you know that? Just goddamned useless!"

Tyden started climbing up the nearest dune, taking out his rage on the sand itself, clawing and digging his way up. He got to the top and flipped Jarvey the bird and then he was gone. Jarvey could have raised him on his helmet mic … but why? What was the point? He'd never liked the sonofabitch anyway. In fact, he'd never really liked *anyone* his whole life. Always nosing into your business and imposing themselves on you, making demands and always, always wanting something.

Jarvey had only wanted one thing his entire miserable life: to be alone.

To just be alone.

If it hadn't been for the lack of food and oxygen and the randy wildlife, Andros wouldn't have been so bad. Just the wind blowing and the sand moving. Like having the beach all to yourself and there was something calming about a beach, now wasn't there? Made you want to stretch out and take a nap, feel the sand pulsing around you like jets of water, slowly taking you down to a place of utter peace. A place you could close your eyes and just … go … to … sleep.

Which was exactly what Jarvey was doing.

Then Tyden came over the comm: *"Jarvey! Get your ass up here! I mean right goddamn now!"*

Jarvey shook himself out of his stupor. The sand had nearly covered him, like maybe it knew he wanted to sleep.

Something about that scared the shit of him.

⚶

It was quite a task getting to Tyden.

Stupid bastard was standing on top of a knob of rock, pointing madly at something just below him. Jarvey had to climb one dune and slide down a hill of sand until he reached the next. Then climb again and again, one dune after the other. And every one of them in motion, moving and eroding even as he mounted them. Every time he paused to rest, the sand began drawing him down into its quicksand belly. By the time he got to Tyden, he was out of breath, sweat running down his spine, his breath hot inside the helmet. And all the while, the methane fog blew in scanty patches and that glowing orb of sun slowly basted him.

This had better be fucking good, he thought as he crab-crawled up to Tyden.

When he pulled himself onto that knob of blackened rock, he dragged himself to his feet. "What?" he said. "What the hell is it?"

Tyden pointed down in a pocket below them.

What Jarvey saw looked like an elongated silver bullet with wings and a conning tower. Jesus, it was the *Cimarron.* It was the goddamn ship. It had been buried down a hundred feet, but that weird sandstorm tidal wave had brought it back up. Unearthed it like a precious antiquity and peeled the sand from it. It was there waiting for them.

"We aren't going to die here, Jarvey. We're getting off this goddamn rock and right now."

"Yeah ... sure."

"What the hell's wrong with you?"

But Jarvey was not even sure himself. It seemed all too coincidental. That the ship would get vomited back out and close enough that they could actually find it. Looking down at it, he just shook his head inside his helmet. This was too pat, too easy, too something.

He looked out across the dunes, the jagged outcroppings of rock that thrust from them like the digits of a skeleton, the monotonous expanse of the landscape. So dreary, so empty, so impossibly dead. He was feeling what he'd felt when he'd first seen the planet from above, that there was something terribly wrong about Andros; it was not just a desert planet, but a crypt. An immense sandy crypt where the galaxy buried its dead.

He hated it.

He hated this world like nothing he'd ever seen before. It was not right, not normal, just haunted and bleak and deranged. A graveyard of blowing sand and dust and flying shit. If you were to stand like he was for any length of time and just stare at what was out there—and more importantly, what *wasn't*—it would suck your mind dry, drain it with its awful sterile uniformity.

"C'mon, Jarvey ... what the hell's wrong with you?"

"It's a mirage," he said. "The ship's not really there. It's a fucking mirage."

"It's no mirage, you idiot. The scangun sees it, too, and it don't believe in mirages."

Tyden started down the slope.

"No!" Jarvey shouted through his mic. "It's a trap. Can't you see that? Can't you see that it's a trap? The sand is trying to draw us down there, it wants us to go down there so it can—"

"You're out of your fucking tree, Jarvey."

And, yes, Jarvey figured he was. Mad and raving, just plain crazy, but that didn't make him wrong. Looking down at the ship in the hollow, he knew it was a trap, it was bait set to draw them in. It wasn't natural, not on this world, for the ship to be sitting pretty like that in a carefully excavated pit. The pit was too uniform, too squared off ... like a grave. Yes, it was like a grave that had been meticulously dug.

But Tyden was going down there.

And then so was Jarvey. What choice did he really have?

The sand of the slope carried them down without them having to do much but maintain their balance. It was slippery and gliding like it was made of silica. They rode down there and then the ship was right before them, huge and gleaming and built for speed. A silver bullet designed to tame the black wastes of interstellar space.

Jarvey didn't want to go in there, but when Tyden opened the hatch, he did.

Then the sand was gone and it was just the ship. That great fine ship that would carry them away from this nightmare world. They got out of their e-suits and went to the bridge, seeing the desert out there through the viewscreen, endless and shifting and stark. Just like Jarvey had originally thought: a place that could drive you mad.

"Buckle in," Tyden said.

The displays lit up. The engines began to rumble. The ship shook as the core was released and the jets began to whine with life. It was really going to happen. They were really going to make it. Then the lights flickered and the displays went black, one right after the other.

Tyden switched to backup.

Nothing.

"She's dead," Jarvey said in a low, wounded voice. "The sand got her. It flooded the vents and thrusters and breathers. Whole goddamn ship is fouled with sand. Do you see, Cappy? It *was* a trap! It was a fucking trap! This goddamn hulk ain't nothing but a coffin and we're nailed shut in her!"

Tyden looked like he was going to hit Jarvey or maybe just batter his own skull off the bulkhead. He was capable of just about anything other than accepting the clusterfuck fate had tossed them into. His face rioted with emotions. A man in a box, a man in a cage, a man pushed so far in a corner that his ass had a crease. He looked over at Jarvey with absolute hatred, then something like bewilderment.

"Face it, Cappy," Jarvey said. "This is all she wrote. This is the end of your command! This is the grand silly-assed punchline that'll leave 'em laughing in aisles! Ain't it rich? Ain't it just rich?"

And maybe it was, but Tyden could not laugh. Something about being buried alive in the hulk of the *Cimarron* for the next ten thousand years or ten million years had just squeezed the humor out of him.

Jarvey, however, thought it was hilarious. "What's the matter, Cappy? You ain't got no sense of humor?"

And then the ship began to move, but it had nothing to do with the engines. It began to shake and vibrate, slowly corkscrewing its way down into the sand. It was sinking. Sinking again and this time it would not surface. Not for another millennium at least.

Tyden unbuckled himself. "We gotta get off her, Jarvey! She's going down! She's going down and she ain't gonna stop until she drops down a mile and maybe two!"

Jarvey did not move. "Get off her into *what* exactly? The sand? The wind? The poisonous atmosphere? C'mon, Cappy, just sit tight. We got life support for a couple months aboard her. But out there? Not a damn thing."

But Tyden wasn't about to argue. The ship was moving and he was getting off her and that's all there was to it. Jarvey heard him climb into his e-suit and stumble off toward the air lock. A minute later, the outer hatch opened and Tyden dove into the sand that was swirling and spiraling around the ship like some whirlpool in a desert, a whirlpool of quicksand.

Jarvey just sat there, watching it all. "You asshole," he said over the mic, certain that Tyden could hear him.

Through the viewscreen, he could see Tyden fighting through that slopping, sluicing sea of sand. He sank right up to his hips in it, but kept fighting and actually made it free through sheer brute strength and abject terror. He pulled himself out of the pit, but he didn't get very far.

One of those funnels opened right beneath him.

It was the same as what had happened to Bartel. Jarvey not only saw it, he heard it over Tyden's open mic. The poor bastard shouting and screaming and begging for help and there was none to give him. And when the creature showed itself, Tyden tried to get his pulser out, but it fell from his fingers with the dizziness and Jarvey heard the creature devour him until the man's transmitter was pulped along with his body.

The funnel filled back in.

Jarvey started laughing. "You never were too bright, Tyden."

All around the ship, one after the other, the funnels began to open up. Not five or even six, but twenty and thirty, fifty and sixty, and then a hundred. Twice that many. The creatures were coming up out of the sand with skittering fans of spidery legs, spurs and needles and whirring mouthparts. So many of them that Jarvey actually screamed at the sight of them. Like kicking over a rotting log and exposing a colony of ants. It was like that—a multitude of busy, creeping motion that buried the ship even as it sank and the viewscreen went black.

Jarvey shut it off; no sense wasting battery power.

"Go ahead, you silly bastards!" he cried out at the creatures. "Do your best! You'll never get in! You'll never tunnel through that shell! Ha, ha, ha!"

But they kept at it some time and it nearly made Jarvey lose his mind:

the sound of those limbs and needle-filled mouths scraping and scratching against the metal hull. It was unbearable, shrill and echoing inside the coffin of the ship. You could not escape it. It got inside your head and under your flesh.

Then it stopped.

Stopped completely and there was only the sound of the sand grating against the hull. It was a relaxing sort of sound like beach sand thrown against the side of a house. You could go to sleep with it.

Jarvey sat there on the bridge, trying to come up with some sort of plan. For even in a madhouse—or a buried casket—you had to have one. And when it came to him, he began to laugh. Laugh at Tyden for being such a great, goddamned idiot. The ship had battery power that would last upward of two months. The food and water would last one man almost twice that long. And the air would be recycled to infinity, or nearly. And in that time, Jarvey could get to working on the breathers and vents and engine ducts, clean the sand out of them. It would be something to do. And if and when the sea spat him back onto the surface, he would be ready to blast off.

Goddamn, it was a plan and it made sense.

Tyden had called him a quitter, but he was no quitter.

Jarvey cracked a fart and laughed until his eyes watered. "There's your final salute, oh Captain! Ha, ha, ha! I'll have the last laugh now, you fucking moron! I'll get off this rock next week or next month and when I get back home, I'll tell them! I'll tell them all about you, you fucking turd! I'll tell them how you folded under pressure, how you pissed your pants and ran off! Your name will go down in the history books as a coward!"

Jarvey danced around the bridge, laughing and joyous ... and then he hit the floor. *Hard.* He tried to stand, but he went down again. His head was reeling with dizziness and that was because the ship was no longer slowly sinking, no longer moving with a lazy corkscrewing motion, but spinning faster and faster until it felt like Jarvey's guts were going to come up the back of his throat.

Steeling himself, he crawled across the floor and clicked the viewscreen.

It flickered on. It showed a storm of sand cut through by sunlight from above.

Oh no, oh Jesus not that ...

Jarvey tried to tell himself it was just a big hole the ship was sliding down. One that would take it deep before bringing it back up again. But he knew it wasn't so. The ship was caught in a monstrous, immense funnel, spinning around like a top just like Bartel when he had gone down and Tyden, too. But that didn't mean that ... it couldn't mean that—

The ship shook and went still.

On the viewscreen, Jarvey saw the great funnel that the ship was caught in. It must have been several hundred feet deep, possibly more. He could see a circle of light far above like a man looking up from the bottom of a well.

The ship trembled.

Something huge scraped along its metal shell. A scratching sound like knives dragged over the hull. An immense and spurred foreleg fell over the viewscreen, blotting it out. The ship began to groan and creak as an immense pressure was put upon it, as the mother of all those funnel creatures took hold of it and began to squeeze it. Rivets popped. Seams sheared open. The hull's integrity was breached.

The lights went out.

The *Cimarron* truly became a coffin.

Jarvey let loose with one wild, whooping scream as that impossibly massive, gigantic creature crushed the ship like a tin can in its jaws, smashing everything inside to pulp. Including him.

Then it began to chew.

And the funnel began to fill in.

But Jarvey was right in the end.

The remains of the *Cimarron* did come back to the surface a week later. And just like the *Burnam,* they looked like something had chewed them up and shit them back out. And there was a very good reason for that. Just like the *Burnam,* there were a few bloodstains, but nothing else.

And all around the field of wreckage, the sand drifted into dunes and the wind howled and Andros was a graveyard.

TOMB ON A DEAD MOON

With the shadows falling over its face, the moon looked like a skull—haunted and deathless, peering from the grim basket of darkest space. And as the *Centurion* pulled in closer, that dead moon seemed to be grinning at them, bone-white and morbidly amused.

But that was all just a trick of the light, Hallas pointed out, created by the ship passing from the dark side to the light side of the moon combined with those murky clouds blowing through the atmosphere.

Hallas. He was good at pointing out things like that. Great at reason and cold logic, at sweeping away shadows and creeping bogeys. You could mention how patches of fluctuating radioactive mist looked like wraiths rising from some cosmic tomb or how the wind shrieking through a deserted Martian canyon sounded like lost souls calling your name ... but in every case, Hallas had the answer. There was nothing under the bed or in the closet that he could not explain away.

But this time, he just wasn't up to it.

For regardless of what he said and how much sugar he poured on top, that damn moon still looked like a death's head. Brice was thinking it, and so was Tamyln. Like maybe that moon was waiting for something. Maybe for them. And maybe it had been for a long time.

Brice knew he didn't like it.

He had no reason not to, but it was there all the same: that almost instinctual sense of apprehension and superstitious fear. The way a house deserted for decades and tenanted by shadows made you feel. You couldn't exactly explain *why* it made you uneasy, it just did.

A house was just a house and a moon was just a moon.

You could keep telling yourself that, sure, but something inside you knew better. Like seeing a bloody head in a bucket. It was just a head, sure, but someone or some*thing* had cut it off, now hadn't they? And if this moon was a severed head, then Brice figured he was waiting for it to open its eyes.

"She's an ugly old girl," Tamyln said. "Atmosphere is black ... dirty-looking like the smoke from an old-time foundry stack, I'm thinking."

Brice was thinking that, too.

The clouds were gathering thick and dusky now, kind of like a funeral veil being pulled over a skull's face. And Brice just couldn't help the things circling in his head, all those macabre thoughts, but that old lonesome moon just sort of inspired such thinking, now didn't it?

"All right," Hallas finally said, rubbing the sleep from his eyes. "Shoot that probe, Tamlyn. Let's see what kind of guts this thing has."

Tamyln did and they watched the probe penetrate the cloud cover, its beacon blinking red all the way down, sending telemetry back to the ship. Then it just disappeared in that shrouded darkness like a burning cigarette dropped into an abandoned well.

"What you got?" Hallas asked.

But Tamlyn was just staring at the viewscreen, seeing that moon and letting its image fill him, making him think things and by the look on his face, they weren't good things.

"C'mon, Tamyln," Hallas snapped. "Get your ass in gear, for chrissake. What're you reading down there?"

Tamyln sighed and studied his screen. "Atmosphere ... hydrogen, helium, carbon dioxide, suspended clouds of sulfuric acid. Okay, getting an impact reading now ... yeah, um ... same old shit, boss. Chondrite rock ... primarily iron-magnesium silicates, trace amounts of titanium and alkali metals. Just your average ball of shit and dust."

"But why out here?" Hallas wanted to know.

And that was the question.

The moon was caught in a hyperbolic orbit on the outer edge of the Alpha Tauri system, which in itself was unusual, for there wasn't a sizeable planetary body for nearly fifty million kilometers. But there it was, ominous and somehow unsettling, caught in the far-flung pull of Aldebaran, which was nothing but a blazing orange pinhead at that distance. It didn't make much sense ... a moon way out there.

Unless maybe it wasn't a moon at all.

"I suppose we could log it as a dwarf planet," Tamlyn said.

"Let's just call it a mystery and wormhole our asses out of here," Brice said. "I don't want the *Gladiator* worrying about us or anything."

The *Gladiator* was the *Centurion's* sister ship. A good three weeks out yet.

"I'm copying that," Tamlyn said, stroking his black beard. "I don't like the look of that thing, and I ain't ashamed to admit it."

"Oh, for the love of Christ," Hallas said. "What's with you two? Your brains didn't thaw out yet from the hibernators? You're acting like a couple of kids in a cemetery on a dare."

"Feeling that way, too, boss," Tamlyn admitted. "Because if I've ever seen a cemetery, it's that goddamned moon."

Hallas didn't like the way they were acting.

But Brice didn't blame Tamlyn, and he sure as hell did not blame himself. There was something spooky about that moon, and he could feel it right up his spine, whether Hallas liked it or not. Maybe they'd just been out too long, and maybe they were getting spooked by deep space. It happened sometimes, and who had a better right than them? Hell, nobody had ever been out this far, some 65 light years from Earth in the very backyard of the Hyades star cluster. Aldebaran, or Alpha Tauri, formed the celestial eye of the Taurus the Bull constellation as seen from Earth. But you didn't want to be thinking about that, how Aldebaran looked from good old Earth, and especially when you were on the *Centurion* and wouldn't see that warm blue planet for something like seventeen months at max hyperspace.

"Maybe ... maybe we should wait for the *Gladiator,* boss," Tamyln said. "Just a thought."

Hallas glared at him. "Are you out of your mind? Why should we share it with them? Boys, there's a pot of gold down there, and I know it. Finders keepers, eh?"

"I'm with Tamlyn, sir," Brice said. "I don't like this at all."

"Well, tough shit. I'm in charge, and we're going down there ... got it?"

They both knew there was no point in arguing.

"Glad you see it my way," Hallas finally said. "All right, Brice. Find us a place to set this crate down. Time to go calling, way I see it. Oh, you girls want to bring your trick-or-treat bags along, it's okay with me. We find any ghosts, I'll scream right along with you ... "

⚓

It wasn't much better on the surface.

Brice was still feeling it ... like something leggy and hairy was climbing up his spine or unfurling its legs in his belly. Even in his e-suit, which was warm and self-contained, he was shivering. He didn't even have enough spit to wet his lips.

"Not picking up any spooks out there," Tamlyn said. "At least, not yet."

No, not yet.

Brice had seen some pretty forbidding worlds in his time, but this place had them beat. It was blasted and gouged, a twisted landscape of impact craters and jagged crevices, brooding slab-like headlands of black basaltic crystal and high razor-toothed mountains that looked sharp enough to slit open the sky's belly. All that blown by pockets of poisonous mist gray as cigar ash.

And dark and brooding and forbidding. The sort of dark that made you tense with every step like you were waiting for something to jump out at you or take hold of you with cold dead fingers.

Goddamn place was creeping Brice out, and he hoped it was just in his head, but he wasn't so sure about that. Because there was something *disturbing* about that pile of rock and he couldn't get past it. He hadn't liked the moon from above, and he sure as hell didn't like it from ground level either. The atmosphere was somehow loathsome, somehow invasive ... it seemed to crawl right inside you and curl up in your belly in a black, seething mass, like it never planned on leaving. And there was something frightening about that.

"I was in a place like this before," Tamyln said over the comm in his typical monotone. "Sure, I remember it well."

"Where?" Brice asked him.

Tamlyn didn't say anything for a moment. He just stood there, his helmet lights washing his face down with a dull illumination. "Back home when I was a kid, the Dry Valley colony on Rigel Four. Sure enough. There was this hollow about two klicks from town, full of these old ruins ... some city of stone, nobody knew who built it. Towers and arches, things like pyramids. Place was ten million years old, they said. People said it was haunted by something. We used to go down there as kids, see if we could scare the shit out of each other ... and you know what? We always did. This place reminds me of those ruins. Gets under your skin, you know? Like you're being watched."

Brice didn't say anything to that.

What could he say? He wasn't sure if what he was sensing was a feeling of being watched exactly. But it was something like that. A sense that this place or something that inhabited it was acutely aware of their presence and had been since the moment they dropped into orbit. He didn't know what that was or where it was hiding, but he could feel it ... in the rocks, in the mist, in the shadows that slithered around them. Oh yes, it was there, all right, waking up like a hungry cat after a long nap and he had to wonder when it would show its teeth. Maybe it was death itself. Because with all those towers and weird pilings of stone around them like tombstones and monuments, it felt very much like death or maybe something even beyond death. A nameless oblivion you couldn't exactly put a name to or would ever want to.

"Wish we'd waited for the *Gladiator,*" Tamyln said.

And Brice wished that very thing himself, for he had the oddest feeling that when the *Gladiator* arrived, it was going to find an empty ship. But no people.

Hallas was walking around in a circle with his scanner. It was beeping, which meant it had a fix on something. "Damn," he said. "I'm picking up some structure just over that rise. Scanner's thinking it's not natural in origin."

Tamlyn sighed inside his helmet. He did not look pleased.

And Brice was thinking, *I'll just bet that sonofabitch isn't natural in origin.* He'd been waiting for something like this, the keys that unlocked the graveyard gates, and everything that was lurking behind them.

But it would do no good to argue. Not with Hallas. He was in command. Maybe the *Centurion* was a mineral prospector and Hallas was just a geologist, but he was also an opportunist and a scavenger. If there were ruins out there, he'd want a piece of them, or any goodies they might be hiding from his hot little capitalistic fingers.

Greed was how the shit got deep enough to drown a man, Brice knew.

They energized their anti-grav harnesses and, one by one, floated up into the sky. They gradually climbed the face of the ridge, which jutted up nearly two hundred feet. With their array of helmet lights and wrist spots, they looked very much like fireflies rising into the night.

And then they were over the cliff, and to a man, they felt something heavy and dire settling into them. Something that would never, ever let go.

Ten minutes later they were looking up at a pyramid.

It was perfectly triangular, fashioned out of some weird blue-green stone with a circumference of nearly half a mile, three times that in height.

Its surface was dusty, encrusted with patches of grit and debris. But not enough so that you couldn't make out its color in the lights or see that it was smooth like the surface of a mirror. Shiny, slippery even, as if it had been meticulously polished.

Brice could see himself in it. And everywhere he looked, it was carved with bizarre figures that might have been alien letters or glyphs, but crowded and overlapping. So busy they gave him a headache just looking at them.

Hallas was examining them very closely.

"Looks like the entire thing is scratched with those figures," he said. "I wonder what it all means ... the scanner can't make heads or tails of it. It's not even sure if it's a language."

But the scanners, which were uplinked to the *Centurion's* data banks, were failing them in more ways than that, because they couldn't even tell them what the tower was made of. Not stone, not metal, maybe some type of plastic polymer. Maybe.

Brice only knew he didn't care for the structure. Like that entire goddamn moon, it didn't sit on him right. And those letters or whatever they were: why did he have the oddest feeling that he had seen them somewhere before? Somewhere a long time ago?

"Those scratchings," Tamyln said. "Almost look like runic letters from old Earth."

"Out here?" Brice said.

Tamlyn just shrugged inside his suit. "Not saying they are, just saying they *look* like 'em."

They kind of did, but Brice wasn't going to admit to that.

Tamlyn was always reading weird shit, and you didn't want to get him going with any of it and especially not on this damn rock.

"Scanner's saying it's hollow," Hallas said. "But there's no way in. That's funny."

"Oh, it's all funny, boss," Brice said before he could really stop himself. "This whole fucking thing is funny, don't you think? A moon where there couldn't possibly be a moon and the only thing on it is this goddamned tower. Why do you think that is?"

"Take it easy, Brice. It's probably some kind of monument or sentinel put down here a million years ago."

"And maybe it's a warning. Maybe it's telling us to get the hell out."

Hallas turned to him. "You want to pack your pussy-ass back to ship, Brice, you go right ahead. But if there's alien artifacts in there, you don't get a cut. Me and Tamlyn will take full shares."

Tamlyn stepped in-between them. "Maybe Brice is right, boss. This whole set-up is damn weird and you know it. I'm looking at this thing, and I don't like the shit it makes me think. Maybe we ought to leave it alone, you know? Maybe this is Pandora's Box, and maybe we don't want to lift the lid."

"Jesus H. Christ," Hallas said. "You two kill me. Look at this thing! It can't hurt you! It's something left by some ancient civilization—"

"Yeah, just this and nothing else," Tamlyn pointed out.

"—and inside there might be a fortune! You know what museums and collectors back home will pay for alien artifacts? And if there's the remains of little green men in there … *shit!* Forget it! You two want out, then get back to the ship. I'm sick of the both of you."

But Hallas couldn't leave it there.

He had to give them that same tired lecture they'd heard about a hundred times by then. Ten years before, he'd been a geologic engineer on a rock crusher called the *Hermes*. They'd been mapping planets in the Pollux system, doing a low-atmosphere fly-over of the fourth planet, when lo and behold, set down there in the jungle just as thick as threads in carpet, was a city made of glass. Captain asked for volunteers to explore it. She got three. That was it. Out of a crew of twenty, she got three. The rest didn't want to drop down there. They'd been out almost four years by then and they were tired, just worn out and sick of it all. Besides, that steaming yellow jungle was tangled and rotting and pissing an acid rain, and inhabited by some especially predatory wildlife. Well, those three that went down with her found the remains of some crablike ETs in that city that were unknown to science and now the four of them were so goddamned rich they had their *own* mining company.

"I missed out on that one because I was stupid and lazy and just plain afraid to go down to that hellhole," Hallas finished by saying. "But not this time. I won't fucking miss out on it this time. You two want to go back to the ship and put on some skirts, you go ahead."

It was an old story with Hallas, but it worked.

Nobody was going back. Maybe both Brice and Tamyln figured they were about to wade into some shit that would bury them alive, but they weren't going back. Greed. It was a funny thing. Like death. And madness.

For the next hour they circled the structure, looking for a way in. Anything. Hallas even tried to melt his way in with a pulser, but no dice. A pulser could burn through six inches of poly-composite faster than a drill bit through cardboard, but it couldn't even touch this stuff. The scanner told them that the pulser hadn't even warmed it up. Which made Hallas both very frustrated and very excited, because maybe he couldn't get in, but whatever that tower was made of, the formula for the stuff was going to be worth billions.

"I hate to be the one to say it, boss," Tamlyn finally said, "but we're pretty much screwed here. We can't cut this stuff or chip it and I'm starting to think even a military-grade pulser couldn't do it. Maybe we ought to call her quits."

Hallas didn't want to, but he was thinking the same thing.

But Brice changed his mind.

"Over here!" he called. "Look at this!"

Tamlyn and Hallas went over to where he was leaning up against the tower. They both saw it: an opening. There was a perfectly circular opening in the pyramid and one big enough to drive a truck through.

"No way we overlooked this," Tamlyn said.

"Well, we must have."

But Brice was shaking his head. "We didn't. It opened up while I was leaning against it. I *saw* it. There was a pinhole and then it opened into this."

Hallas had his scanner out. "This goddamn thing's saying there ain't no hole there at all."

Which means it's got about as much sense as you do, Brice thought.

"Well, there's only one way to find out," Hallas said.

He went in.

⇩

The pyramid was completely hollow. It went up and up as far as their lights could reach. There was nothing inside but those high walls and a flat stone floor that gradually sloped down to a massive round passage like a drain in a basement slab.

They stood at the edge of that hole, panning it with their lights. "Artificial for sure," Hallas said. "I'm reading bottom at about a hundred and ninety feet. You copy that?"

"Aye, I do," Tamlyn said.

Brice knew what was coming next.

There was no way in hell Hallas would leave now, not without finding out what sort of goodies were below. Greed was eating a hole right through him. He was dreaming of vast treasures.

Maybe he was right.

And maybe he was terribly wrong.

"We better get out of here," Brice said. "That door closes back up, we'll never get out of here."

Hallas just shook his head. "It won't close, for chrissake. Besides, you opened it, I'm thinking, by triggering some kind of switch. Maybe by leaning against the wall ... pressure-sensitive or something. We'll be fine."

But Brice honestly did not believe that.

Because whatever was down that shaft was not anything remotely good. It was not treasure or artifacts. It was something cursed and ancient. He could not have known that for sure, yet he did. Some archaic sensory network inside him had woken up and it was ringing his nerves like a bell.

What he had felt while orbiting the moon and what he had felt ever since they stepped on its surface was much worse here. It was alive and sentient and electric.

Standing there, feeling that unnamable malevolence filling him, drowning him, he felt physically ill. Like he needed to vomit or scream and maybe both at the same time.

"Let's go," Hallas said.

They energized their anti-grav harnesses and stepped over the lip of the passage. First Hallas, then Tamlyn, and finally Brice. One by one, they drifted down and down into that vaulted blackness, their lights splashing over the perfectly smooth walls of the chasm.

Long before they reached bottom, Brice began to do something he hadn't done since he was a child.

He prayed.

⚚

Below, there was a tunnel that led off into smothering darkness. Hallas led on and the others reluctantly followed. It was made out of that same shiny blue-green material like smoky glass. And like the entire structure itself, there were no seams, no places where any of it had been joined together, as if the entire thing had been carved from a single block of the same material.

The tunnel went for about a hundred feet and then opened into a massive amphitheater that was oval in shape. It was easily a hundred feet from the curving ceiling to the smoothly sloping floor. Every inch of the place was scratched with the same symbols as the exterior. There were no artifacts as such in there, no mementos of some long-gone race. There were only a series of convex pylons made of some lusterless metal like dirty bronze. Some of them were as tall as the men themselves, others came only up to their knees. Not two were the same height and they seemed to be arranged in some arcane, unknowable sequence. There were fifteen of them leading up to a great circular mirror on one of the walls that was roughly as large as the opening that had originally let them into the pyramid.

"Doesn't make any sense," Hallas said. "This is it? This is all there is?"

"Unless that's a door or something," Brice said, studying the mirror.

Tamlyn was walking in circles, panning the pylons with his lights and with his scanner. "It does make sense," he said. "According to the scanner, these pylons are arranged pretty damn systematically." He stepped among them and stood before the mirror. It was made of some indigo glass … or something like glass. The scanners said it was some type of plastic, but weren't certain if there was anything behind it. "You want my opinion, boss?"

"Damn right I do."

"Then I'm guessing these pylons will open up that mirror or door or whatever it is. Must be some way to manipulate them … by touch or pressure. Christ, who knows?"

Brice was standing in front of the mirror himself now. He brushed a fine layer of dust from its surface, or as much of it as he could. The glass looked very thick. He got the unsettling feeling that it was a window, and that any moment he'd see a gigantic, distorted eyeball staring back at him.

He wanted to run.

He had an awful sense that not only were they being watched, but that something malefic was even then reaching out to them, picking their brains, leading them in directions that would benefit it and only it in the end.

"What are these here?" he said, wiping at the mirror with his glove. "On the glass … more symbols. They look like …"

Tamlyn was studying the symbols now, too. And as he did so, he was making funny sounds in his throat like maybe he couldn't breathe. He yanked a cloth from his pack and began madly wiping the dust from the glass.

"Look!" he said. "Do you see it? Do you see this?"

They did.

The edge of the mirror was encircled by etched disks with triangles set inside them. In the center was a huge circle with an inverted five-point star set in it. More of those weird letters at each point.

Brice swallowed. "But that's … that's a—"

"Pentagram," Tamlyn said in a shrill, uneasy voice. "And all around the outside there, pentacles."

Brice was stepping away from them now. "But those are from old Earth … symbols of witchcraft, the black mass. Not out here, they can't be way out here."

"Sure, they can," Tamlyn said. "They can be here if maybe these symbols *originated* outside the Earth and were later brought there."

"That's crazy," Hallas said.

"The evidence is right here," Tamlyn pointed out.

Hallas shook his head. "But by who?"

"Or *what?*" Brice muttered.

Tamlyn shrugged. "Who knows? But maybe witchcraft and all that business has its origins out among the stars, on alien worlds. Maybe it was all brought to Earth during the dawn of the human race."

"Now that *is* fucking crazy," Hallas said. "Who brought it there? A bunch of witches on broomsticks for chrissake?"

"You're not getting it," Tamyln said.

And maybe he wasn't or didn't want to, but Brice was getting a pretty good inkling by then. Maybe he was way off base here, but he was putting together a few things in his mind and they left him pale. For what if what we knew as witchcraft and sorcery and all that business were just remnants of some impossibly ancient alien religion brought to Earth by extraterrestrials a million or five million years ago? And what if these ETs schooled our primitive ancestors in their rites, taught them about their gods? Things like the Black Goat of the Sabbath and the horned devil and all that could have been nothing more than terrestrial symbolic representations of alien deities, images the human mind could identify with and pass along. If all that was true, then this could be a shrine or a temple.

Maybe this place wasn't either of those exactly, but it had powerful religious significance. He could almost feel some diabolic energy here waiting to be unleashed, waiting to be worshipped.

"What are you saying, Tamlyn? That this is some kind of church, some kind of altar?" Hallas said, still not buying any of it.

"No, not exactly. This is something else entirely." He was studying those symbols again. Finally, he tapped his finger dead-center of the pentagram itself. "You see what's etched here at the very axis of the star?"

They did. It looked like a staring eye with three hooked protrusions or whips emerging from it at right angles to one another.

"Yeah, what of it?" Hallas wanted to know. "More gobbledygook."

But Tamyln shook his head. "The Yellow Sign."

"The what?"

"The Yellow Sign. The symbol of Hastur."

Hallas was getting impatient. "And what the hell is that?"

So Tamlyn told them.

Hastur was an incredibly ancient Earth deity that was worshipped in Hyboria and Samaria. He was a sort of pagan devil, a monstrous evil that would drive you mad to look upon. He was known as The Unspeakable One and was referred to in eldritch grimoires as Him-Who-Is-Not-To-Be-Named.

"And according to legend, Hastur was imprisoned in a tomb on the Dark Star." Tamlyn started to laugh then, but it was an eerie and discordant laughter. "Don't you see? *This moon is the Dark Star and this place is Hastur's tomb ... *"

Brice wanted no part of this.

"Look!" Hallas said.

The pylons began to glow with a grainy red illumination. And then the mirror, if that's what it was, began to melt and liquefy and run.

Before any of them could move, a titanic vortex of black howling wind came blasting through the chasm where the glass had been. It was vicious and merciless and destructive. It was more than a wind, but a venting of ovens and atomic piles and sentient black matter. And it had eyes. Two red, burning eyes.

Brice barely had time to scream.

ф

When he came to some time later, Brice was in the tunnel that led to the amphitheater. That wind must have carried him along and dumped him there. He came to, senseless and confused, and the first thing he did was to cry out. The sensors of his suit told him that its shell had not been compromised.

He was safe, then.

He scrambled to his feet, madly calling out on the comm for the others. But there was no answer. Just that heavy, ominous silence and the grave feeling that he was not alone and never had been.

He kept going, making for the passage that would lead him up and out of this place. Then he saw an e-suit lying in front of him in his lights. Tamlyn. Brice went to him, tried to turn him over, but as soon as he did, he saw the damage.

Tamlyn's suit was pitted with thousands of tiny blackened holes. And inside, flaking ash in the shape of a man.

He'd been cremated.

Brice stopped thinking then. There was only the ship and the stars beyond that would lead him away from this madness. He finally reached the chasm and drifted up with his anti-grav harness. At the top, he stepped onto that sloping floor and right away saw that Hallas was waiting for him.

"Why didn't you answer?" he screamed into his mic. "Why didn't you fucking answer me?"

Hallas stepped forward with a deadly intensity, the lights of his suit shut off. And long before he got there, Brice knew that what was facing him was not Hallas at all.

Stark terror shattered inside him. *"Get away from me! Goddamn you, get away, get away—"*

He pulled his pulser and fired. A blue spear of light punched a hole right through Hallas. But what came out was not blood, but a glittering black mist that opened like a corpse orchid. Brice fired again, this time shearing off Hallas' left arm. More of that black mist surged out, sparkling and oily, not flesh exactly and not gas, but something in-between. An alien ectoplasm that slithered out in ropes, connecting with the other black material and becoming a living, crawling plexus with blazing red eyes like dying suns.

Brice hobbled over to the door, but it closed up on him.

He felt a wave of heat strike him and he went to his knees, struck mad and sobbing, turning back to look upon the face of his god.

Whatever it was, it reached out to him and took him, and his own lights showed him what was behind the helmet bubble. Something black and viscous and burning, a living funeral pyre devouring itself. More of it oozed from the ruptured suit by the moment. He saw faces flickering in that fleshy excrescence—Hallas, Tamyln, a thousand others popping like bubbles. All of them screaming his name.

This was Hastur.

Something that was not to be looked upon and something that was not to be named. Brice's mind went with a single manic scream as he saw that thing and felt something like a thousand, ten-thousand, frozen needles piercing him at the same time.

A cold so terrible it burned with the light of stars.

⚓

From three parsecs out, the *Gladiator* picked up the directional beacon of its sister ship, the *Centurion*. Beckett, the captain, ordered the ship full ahead for the moon and when they'd fallen in orbit around it, he just stood there, staring at it on the viewscreen.

"Goddamn moon, way out here," he said. "What do you make of that?"

At the comm, Pearson swallowed, shook his head. "It shouldn't be here at all."

Harms stood there, staring out at the dead moon. His eyes were fixed and glassy. His mouth kept moving, but no words were coming out. Nothing but a dry sibilance of air.

"What's eating you, mister?" Beckett said.

Harms' face was covered with tiny droplets of perspiration. He wiped them free with his hand. "I ... nothing, sir. Just got the heebie-jeebies, I guess. Been out too long."

Beckett understood that, because the moon was getting to him, too. Although it made no rational sense, he was thinking it looked like a skull grinning up at him from a bone pit. A skull that had been picked clean by vultures. But he wasn't about to tell his men about that or the way it made something crawl in his belly.

"We've all been out here too long," was all he said. "But the *Centurion's* down there and that's where we're going."

"Sir...," Pearson said. "Beacon's coming in strong from the *Centurion*, but she doesn't answer. Just static. I'm getting no life signs from her and, shit, magnetic pile is out. She's dead."

Swallowing down something thick in his throat, Beckett said, "All right, we're setting down."

They strapped in and the *Gladiator* homed in on the beacon, cutting through the murky atmosphere and dense gray mist. She set down about fifty yards from the hulk of the *Centurion*. On the viewscreen, her elongated globular shape made her look like the husk of a dead caterpillar.

"Nothing, sir," Pearson said. "She doesn't answer."

"Must've had some kind of malfunction and ditched," Beckett said, almost as if he was trying to convince himself of the fact.

Harms, at the comm, said, "Wait! Scanners picking up movement! Two forms moving in our direction. E-suits, all right."

"Thank God," Beckett said. "Thank God."

"But ... sir, no life signs." He looked at the captain, worry etched into his features. "Bioscanner says those suits are *dead.*"

"Bullshit. Just a malfunction." He turned to Pearson. "Hail them."

Pearson did and what came over the speaker was an angry, hissing static with something buried in it that almost sounded like screaming voices.

"Funny …" Beckett said.

"That's not the suits, sir, it's the background noise of the moon itself."

On the viewscreen, the two figures in E-suits were closing in on the *Gladiator.* They were waving their arms in greeting. Beckett noticed that they cast no shadow in the lights of the ship. None at all. But he shook that from his mind. A trick of the atmosphere. *Something.* For a moment, he thought he saw red luminous eyes glowing inside the helmets. But he shook that away, too.

Both Pearson and Harms stared at him with something like abject terror. The bridge seemed to be suddenly filled with creeping shadows.

"Sir," Harms said, his voice barely above a whisper, "still no life signs from the suits. Bioscanner is reading inorganic. They're dead, those suits are dead, their life support isn't even functioning. There's nothing alive in them."

But Beckett would not listen. Not to them and not to what screamed inside his own head. "Malfunction, that's all. Man the airlock.…"

At the hatch, there was the booming of fists. Not a hurried rapping, but a slow and mechanical cadence. It echoed through the ship like the gong of a funeral bell.

Pearson began to scream.

The ship shook and vibrated, the air steaming with the sudden intrusion of icy cold. Lights flickered and bulkheads crawled and voices screeched as something like a black, living mist filled the ship, intersecting time and space and matter, ripping them open, inverting them, casting them to the four energized, seething winds. Beckett shrieked as he was literally pulled apart, turned inside out, broken into blazing subatomic particles, and then crudely slapped back together again. Within a matter of seconds, the ship and those who crewed it had their atoms mixed. When it was over, Beckett and the others were melted and mutated, their shattered and disassociated anatomies jutting from the bulkheads and decks, split faces locked in screams that would never end.

♦

Later, there was silence on the dark star.

As there had been in the beginning and would be in the end. A breathing, claustrophobic silence that brooded across the gouged and cratered surface of the dead moon. Towers of rock and glittering shelves of stone rose like monoliths. Beneath them were the *Centurion* and the *Gladiator*. Both lifeless and abandoned like the broken carapaces of insects.

Nothing lived on the moon now.

Nothing occupied it but shadows.

Nothing was entombed there.

Whatever had been imprisoned for so many years was free now. And it set out in a formless black appetite to devour time and space and the guts of the universe itself.

HOST

When the steering cable on the rover snapped, the wheel went crazy in Booth's hands, spinning like a top. The rover fishtailed, swung to the left, then the right, jumping the ditch on the side of the dirt road and finally coming to rest when it smacked into an old binya tree. The impact threw him back in his seat and he sat there, breathing hard for a few minutes. The restraining belt around his midsection had jerked so hard it was like he'd been punched in the stomach.

"Shit," he muttered under his breath. "Goddamned ... *shit.*"

A few other expletives flew, but not many. He knew better than to get himself worked up over mechanical failure. No sense wasting the energy. The planet had a subtle, sneaking way of sucking that right out of you like everything else; you didn't need to do it to yourself. It was the climate—damp and tropical, a true green hell like the Amazon basin back on old Earth.

Booth stared out the windscreen at the binya that had smashed in the front end of the rover. They were everywhere on the planet. Technically, they were trees, but they all looked exactly the same: like thick-boled, flat-topped stumps. Their bark was so thick and impervious you could break an axe blade trying to chop into one.

But it had stopped the rover.

That was one good thing. Otherwise, the damned thing would have plunged down the hillside through the tangled brush and gone right into the seething red swamp far below. And that would have been another special kind of hell.

He'd once seen a rover dragged out of one of them. The corrosive waters had melted the tires, peeled the paint off its shell, and turned the driver inside into a bubbling heap of jelly.

Booth sighed and tried the uni-comm, but it was dead. The battery was probably crushed by the impact. He had his communicator badge, but it wouldn't carry back to Outpost #4. Too damned far.

Still swearing under his breath, he climbed out of the rover and grabbed the survival pack from the back and looped its strap over his shoulder. When he was back on the road, he was miserable right away. The sulfur swamps stank like rotten eggs and there were tendrils of gagging yellow mist in the air.

And I've got a six-mile walk back to camp, he thought.

As he started trudging up the road, the heat bearing down on him and countless multi-colored insects buzzing around him, he was imagining what Troutman was going to say when he learned he'd cracked up the rover. A real piss-fest. It was sheer mechanical failure, but old Trouty wouldn't care about that: the planet made him absolutely miserable and he was always looking for someone to take it out on.

Well, fuck him, Booth thought.

The road twisted and turned through the heavy purple jungle of thick undergrowth—spidery, squat palms and broad-leafed ferns, egg-shaped seedpods leaking vinegar-smelling nectar and orchids so brightly red they would blind you. An amazing profusion. The jungle was unpleasantly pervasive on the planet, growing constantly. The dozer from #4 had to constantly push it aside from the roads or it would grow right over them.

Booth paused.

Already his shirt was soaking wet, perspiration running down his face. He swallowed a salt tablet from the survival pack and washed it down with a swig of water. If he had to be stranded, why at midday in this stagnant wet heat?

He started walking again.

A pack of sauriks burst from the bush twenty feet down the road, scaring the hell out of him. They looked like Earth lizards but they walked upright. They hissed at him and crossed the road into the jungle on the other side. They were pissy by nature, but essentially harmless. They were toothless vegetarians, but if you startled one, they'd shoot a toxic brew from their glands like a skunk that was nearly impossible to wash off. Its putrescent stench would cling to you for days.

They were colloquially known as *shit lizards*.

Booth sighed and got his nerves under control. Pollux was a bright orange platter in the sky, beating down on him.

He walked on.

At least they were only shit lizards. There were far worse things on the planet, but most of them, thankfully, only came out at night. The idea of being out here at night when all the nasty wildlife came out like slime polyps and fangworms made him feel weak in the belly.

But now was not the time to worry about such things. He'd be back at #4 long before sundown. Going up a hill and down into a misty hollow below, he remembered that there was an emergency station less than two miles from him. It would mean cutting off the main road, but it provided food, water, and shelter for people in his situation. If he went there, he could call for a pickup.

Trouty wouldn't like it, of course. *Those shelters are for extreme emergencies,* he'd say, *not because some idiot cracked up a rover and was too lazy to walk back to camp.*

To hell with him, Booth decided. It wasn't healthy for any man to be out here in this heat and humidity. Last thing he needed was to get some kind of sunstroke. Such things could be very dangerous on this godforsaken world, leading to brain fever and disorientation. People had wandered off into the jungle with it and never been seen again.

Screw that. He was going to the shelter.

He knew that if he cut down through the jungle, he could easily take an hour off his walk, but that would mean walking through the slime of rotting vegetation that stank like corpses and was often four or five inches deep, crawling with bloodsucking ticks and balloon leeches. And that didn't even take in the acid-spitting viper plants and mud eels—

Wait.

What the hell was that?

He paused atop another hill, swatting at a swarm of flying mites, staring out into the jungle, heat waves rising from the decomposing vegetable matter.

He listened.

I heard it, he thought. *I know I heard it: a woman sobbing.*

But that was ridiculous, of course, way out here.

Then he heard it again. It was definitely the sobbing of a woman punctuated by low cries of pain. It had to be coming from just ahead. Following the snaking road through the dank forest and down into another misty hollow, he found her. He wondered briefly if it was some kind of hallucination. The vapors from the swamps could do that to you if you breathed enough of them.

But she looked real enough.

A young woman, maybe in her twenties, curled up on the side of the road. She was wet and slimed as if she had crawled through the knotted vegetation, fighting her way through the ooze of the jungle floor.

"Hey!" he said, moving toward her. "Hey!"

She jerked as if surprised, her eyes huge and glassy, her mouth a crooked gash, lips pulling back from white teeth. There was something more than a little shocking about that, such a hungry look, the way a reptile looks at its prey. But it faded quickly enough and was replaced by ... incredible beauty.

Booth stood there, breathless, head whirling in the stifling heat. His mouth was dry. His heart thumping. The sweat that ran from him feeling momentarily cold as ice. But this woman, my God, she was the most perfectly beautiful woman he had even seen—from her perfect olive skin to her huge dark eyes to the black hair that fell to her shoulders.

He was stunned.

Then something seemed to click in his head and whatever had gripped him, held him spellbound, lifted and his head cleared.

"Are you all right?" he asked her. "What are you doing out here?"

She simply looked at him with her huge eyes, saying nothing. She wore a ragged Agency uniform, scientific class, her face smeared with grime. She looked like she'd really been through it. He gave her some water, but she was only able to drink a little bit before she started coughing and gagging.

Her name tag said "Forest."

"We need to get you out of here," he said. "Can you walk?"

She just stared at him, as if she didn't know how to speak. He wasn't sure what to do with her. *Forest, Forest.* That name echoed in his head—*two weeks ago, you remember, the bio-survey team from Outpost Seven that went missing. There was a botanist with them ...*

"You're from Seven," he said.

Again, she just looked at him.

She was traumatized, in shock. Maybe she even had a nervous breakdown. Out here, alone apparently, surviving for two weeks in the jungle. That would explain her emaciated look.

"Can you walk?" he asked her again and got the same dumb silence. Her left leg looked wrong, twisted beneath her. He examined it. There was no doubt about it: it was broken. That complicated things. It meant he'd have to carry her. No easy thing in the heat.

After he explained his own plight, he said, "I'm making for an emergency shelter. I'll take you there. We can call for help."

He tried to pick her up, but she shrieked with pain. She shook her head, then held out her arms warily to him.

"Piggyback?" he asked.

She smiled as if it was exactly what she wanted him to say. He got his back to her and she put her arms around his neck. Thankfully she was petite and half-starved, so she didn't weight much. Still, in that awful heat, it was going to be tough going.

"Just hang on tight," he told her, standing up. "I'll get you there."

And he swore for a moment he could hear a black, moonstruck sort of laughter echoing from the cellar of his mind and a voice that said, *Don't worry. I'll never let go.*

The long walk began.

It was just as punishing as he thought it would be. Ten minutes into it, the sweat was pouring out of him in rivers. His lightweight khaki uniform was soaking wet, his face dripping. Walking to the shelter alone would have made for an unpleasant adventure, but carrying Forest turned it into a fight for survival, every step hard labor. The good thing was that old Trouty wouldn't bitch at him when he found out he saved the life of a missing biologist from Outpost #7. Hell, Booth might even get a commendation or a pay bump for it. But that was later. Right now, it was a pleasant fantasy like the air-conditioned shelter with its endless supply of ice-cold lemonade.

Fifteen minutes later, he had to pause a moment, lean up against a stout binya tree. His head was spinning in the heat, his eyesight blurring. His rider said nothing, clutching him tightly like a little girl riding on her father's back.

Wait till I get back to Four, he thought. *I'll be an effing hero.*

But that seemed so far away. He just had to make it to the shelter. In another twenty minutes, he figured, he'd see the turn off that forked from the main road. He was living for that moment.

As he walked, he kept an eye out for wildlife. The last thing he needed was to run into any predators. He didn't even have a gun with him and he was certainly in no condition to fight or protect Forest. He just had to hope for the best. Most days, you never saw much. The animals were out there, watching, but most wouldn't approach a human. He was told it was the otherworldly, completely alien smell of humans that drove them off.

Maybe it was.

And today, he was really stinking, so maybe that would put out a barrier they wouldn't cross. He could only hope. The only thing he could smell was the damp rot of the jungle itself, the sulfur stink of the swamps. There was an occasional sweetness, too, like vanilla, that seemed to be coming off of Forest. In the foulness of the planet, it made him almost giddy.

The heat of the sun was unbelievable.

It bore down on him in waves that he could practically see. Combined with the torrid heat seeping from the ground it was like being slow-roasted in a convection oven. He was so utterly miserable that his head was filled with a haze and he couldn't seem to think his way around it or string together a single rational thought. He was melting, turning into a pile of ooze of the sort that came out of the jungle floor when you stepped down on it.

He was feeling tapped, weak, his knees wobbly, but he kept pushing forward. There was only Forest and she had put a strange sort of spell on him. In the back of his confused mind, he desired her, lusted after her, hoped she would never, ever let him go.

Funny, but as he walked down the misty road, he remembered his mother's root cellar back in Ohio when he was a kid. It had a secret, dark smell to it, an earthy odor of black soil and decomposing humus, the way he imagined a deep grave would stink. Mom kept her canned vegetables down there and he was always the one sent to get some snap peas or cucumbers. One time he discovered a spider hanging from the light bulb in a very large web. There were dozens of fly carcasses strewn about the top of the shelf under the light and dozens more in its web. The spider was huge, the size of a walnut, swollen with the juice of the flies it had drained. As he stared at it with rising disgust, it was feeding on another fly that was still horribly buzzing its wings as its life was sipped away. It was only doing what spiders did, of course, cleaning up pests, but it offended him to the point that it showed up as a monster in his dreams for years to come.

Strange he would remember that now, so many years later.

Feeling as drained as one of those flies from so long ago, he said, "Not long now. Not very long."

And from the cellar of his mind, once again he thought he heard that laughter like shattering glass and the sweet voice of a little girl. *No, not long now,* it said. *Not long at all.*

The thoughts dimming in his brain, mixed up, tripping over one another, he noticed that the jungle was no longer so vibrantly colorful. It was always such a bright shade of purple with reaching, brilliantly red and orange fan leaves, that now it was startling in its paleness. It looked bleached as if the color had been sucked out of it.

You need rest, he told himself. *You need water. You're not thinking right.*

But then he saw the fork and moved quicker, motivated at the idea of the survival shelter and all it offered. God, he was so weak. His muscles ached and his head pounded. He was dehydrated and disoriented. Just a little farther, a little farther. Forest seemed to grip him tighter and he thought he felt her lips on his throat and her tongue, as if she was licking away the salt on his skin.

The road to the shelter was downhill and that made it a little easier. He kept moving, one foot after the other, and now he could hear the sound of water bubbling. It was from a spring-fed creek that rushed past the shelter. The water was pure and clean and drinkable. Oh God, he couldn't wait to plunge his head into it and clear out the cobwebs so he could think clearly and stop the pounding in his head and the hot pulsing of his temples—

He fell to his hands and knees not ten feet from the shelter. He'd made it. Dear God, he'd made it. But he was so weak, so drained, that he knew he'd have to crawl to the doorway and drag Forest with him.

But there was the creek.

Oh, listen to it bubbling and surging. He pulled himself to it and Forest held on tightly. He saw his reflection in the water—haggard, gaunt, his eyes bulging from his head—and that of Forest, her beauty having melted away, revealing her true nature: a white, bloated thing like a gigantic termite that clung to him with spurred legs, its proboscis buried in his throat, its swollen, segmented body pulsating obscenely as it sucked away his blood.

He tried to scream, but he was too weak.

She was mounted upon him, making slobbering sounds as she sipped away his life. He could feel her hot, pulsing body pressing down him, swollen fatly with his blood. She made a contented mewling sort of noise like that of a kitten, sucking at his throat voraciously.

He lay there, bare feet from the water, too weak to fight, his body shriveling, his thoughts growing dark until there were no thoughts left.

$\downarrow$

It was nearly a week before they found Forest again. This time, during an intensive search for Booth. The best guess was that he had been injured badly in the crash of the rover and had wandered off in a stupor never to be see again.

But finding Forest was a real boon, because they had thought she was lost for good. True, she had a broken hip and she was in shock from her horrendous ordeal, but she was alive and would mend.

Though she was uncommunicative, when they loaded her on a gurney for the trip back to Outpost #7, she grinned happily … and hungrily.

DEATH CAMP

Date unknown

They took Howie away about three hours ago. He began to scream, and it was one of the most awful things I have ever heard. Oh, make no mistake, my unknown friend, there's plenty of screaming in this awful place, but Howie's ... well, it was special because Howie was always so tough, so taciturn. He never lost faith, his optimism about rescue never waned. *Cheer up, buck up, old shoe, stiff upper lip and all that, there's a good fellow.* He didn't really talk that way, of course, but that's the subjective impression I got from him. But when the aliens came for him, God, he fell right apart.

But enough of that.

There's so much time here to think. I keep trying to put things in some chronological order, but my mind is fuzzy. The isolation. The desperation. The horror. The hopelessness. It's all wearing me away like water dripping on a rock. Sometimes I can't entirely be sure what is real.

I should tell you my name is Dennis Page and that I was a systems tech on the starclipper *Cosmo,* a neuroplex jockey and a damn good one. At least, I always thought so.

The *Cosmo* is no more. Most of the crew are dead. There's only a handful of us left now. We have been prisoners of the Vyrmid for something like three months. *Three months.* According to Drexler, the Vyrmid are from the Achernar system, aka Alpha Eridani, a hot blue star

303

in the constellation of Eridanus. You can see it from Earth. It's roughly 139 light years away.

How does Drexler know this? Apparently, the Agency has been intercepting Vyrmid communications for years. Something no one else knew about, because to the rest of us—the uninformed and unwashed masses—the Vyrmid were a folktale, an urban legend. We were told they did not exist and were not responsible for countless missing ships and their crews in the bleak desolation of Sargassian Space. Yes, we were lied to.

According to Drexler, "If people knew the Vyrmid were out there, nobody would have ever left Earth or the colonies." So there you have it.

None of which matters now, I suppose, because we are their prisoners. And also according to Drexler, nobody will ever come for us because if they did, it would mean they would have to openly admit to the existence of the monsters that have imprisoned us.

Besides, soon as we were taken, the Vyrmid pulled our chips out, so there's no way we can be tracked to the hell that is now our home.

There are seven of us still left, including me ... well, six actually, now that Howie is gone. Brady, who's edgy and weird and likes to argue. Sales, who's afraid of everything and everyone. Corrine, who's absolutely crazy (more on that later). Pepley, who's pretty much broken and has devolved into religious mania. And Drexler, who seems to know about everything (something which makes us all more than a little suspicious). And me, of course.

Drexler, Pepley, and Sales are from the *Cosmos*. The others from various ships the Vyrmid have captured. They've got quite a collection of us by this point.

Ah, here comes our food.

Later

The one who brought our food was not a Vyrmid horror, but a kindly old lady named Mother Quigg. At least, that's how she appears to us. The Vyrmid have the ability to make themselves look like anything they want. I don't believe it's anything biological, but mental images they project into our heads. Maybe they think it'll keep their animals pacified if we don't see their true form. I think they're right.

"And how are my dears today?" she asked in the sweetest, softest voice imaginable. "Lunch today will be especially yummy. We have roast chicken and potatoes, fresh bread and buttery green beans, and a delightful cherry cobbler for dessert. Mmmm. Can't you just smell it?"

She toddled into the cage and set the food on the table (our lone piece of furniture). I knew if I concentrated, the illusion of the food would dissipate and I'd see it for the gray slop it was. But I wouldn't allow that. I wanted to see the chicken and potatoes. I wanted to smell the cherry cobbler. After you learned the fine art of self-delusion and practiced it daily, you got quite good at it.

Mother Quigg grinned at us. Saliva glistened on her swollen pink lips. "Now who's hungry?" she asked.

Date unknown

We're watched all the time like animals in a zoo. The Vyrmid know everything we do and, I often worry, everything we think. I'll keep recording on this memory micro-drive until they take it away. Though it's inserted into one of my upper lateral incisors, I'm sure they know it's there. I make my entries by whispering, but they're probably listening all the same.

I should tell you about the cage. It isn't a cage exactly, not in the way you're picturing it. It's actually a square of bile-green gleaming floor with a table in the center, hemmed in on all sides by an impenetrable blackness that's simply darker than anything you can imagine. If you try and go beyond the boundaries of our illuminated little world, you run into a wall of sorts that feels like glass and is ice-cold to the touch. Drexler believes it's some sort of energy field, despite the fact that it seems solid.

There's no way out. Not really.

When I first woke in the cage, there was another guy with us. His name was Bokeman. He had been in the cage for months, the last survivor of another starclipper. He knew a lot of things. He told us that we were basically in a huge laboratory. That there were hundreds of us held in cages and the only comparison he could give us for our situation were the old Nazi death camps of World War II. A very chilling thought.

"You will be taken out one by one and experimented upon," he told us. "Some will not come back. Those that do will wish they had not."

I should mention that he had been through the mill. The Vyrmid had taken his left arm, his right eye, and had tested various biological weapons on him. His skin was yellow and scaly like a reptile and he bore the scars of experimental surgery.

A few days afterward, they took him away.

He didn't come back.

Date unknown

More trouble, and from Brady, of course.

Mother Quigg brought our meal (we only get fed once a day)—spaghetti and meatballs—and right away, Brady started acting up. Despite fully realizing the danger he was putting us all in, he made a scene. I suppose it had been building in him for some time.

"I won't eat that slop," he announced to all.

He was in one of his rebellious moods. On a good day, he was problematic, going on about how the Vyrmid would use us as lab rats, infecting us with experimental germs, cutting and probing us, and finally dissecting us. On a bad day (like today), he was just plain trouble.

"Please," Sales begged, quivering and weak as always. "Please, just eat what they give us."

Corrine giggled because she could do little else after what the aliens did to her. If Howie had been there, he'd have talked Brady down. He was good at things like that. But without him, the rest of just sat and stared.

Drexler was the medical officer on the *Cosmos*. A kind soul, I guess, sincerely concerned about our welfare. "Brady, you need to eat. You know what will happen to all of us if you don't," he told him. "You need to think about everyone not just yourself."

"Fuck you," Brady snapped. "Fuck *all* of you!"

Mother Quigg watched the interplay with a combination of curiosity and amusement. There was no question that she was logging it. Finally, she smiled and adjusted her cat's-eye spectacles. "Now that sounds like good advice to me," she said. "I've set a fine table for you and you should enjoy my culinary delights."

Brady sneered at her, muttering things under his breath.

"Now, now," she said, lips pulling back from narrow teeth. "Be a good fellow and eat. You need to keep up your strength. Please, just one bite? For Mother Quigg? You know how I worry."

She speared a juicy, parmesan-flecked meatball from the platter and brought it to Brady's mouth. He slapped away her hand and the fork clattered to the floor, the meatball rolling away, leaving a trail of tomato sauce.

Oh Christ. The rest of us went cold. We'd all learned the hard way that you did not fuck with Mother Quigg. She could be quite disarming—a small, round woman with her hair pulled back into an iron-gray bun, her blue eyes twinkling, spectacles balanced at the end of her nose—and seemed perfectly harmless. The illusion sold itself so perfectly that you could forget that she was an alien monster from a race that delighted in medical experimentation upon their captives.

She moved quietly over to Brady. "My poor, poor boy. You're so unhappy here. I do everything to make you happy and comfortable, but, somehow, it simply isn't enough." She shook her head back and forth. "But have no worries. Mother Quigg will take you away to a place where you'll learn to appreciate your situation here."

"Fuck you," Brady said yet again, picking up the fork and throwing it at her.

She looked at me. "By thunder and Tom Walker, what a stitch he is!"

Disobedience was something Mother Quigg had very little patience with. But the enormity of his insubordination surprised even her. She actually looked unsure. And it was at that moment, that something unpleasant happened … just for a moment or two, but we all saw it: her image wavered and a gray, hulking form glistening with slime appeared, something made of wavering appendages and ropy coiling mouth parts. It was there, then gone—an absolutely repulsive alien horror.

Despite what he had glimpsed, Brady was still angry and defiant. His face was contorted into a mask of hate, a white froth of saliva at his lips. "We're not fucking animals! We're not goddamned lab rats! We're human beings! This is barbaric! This is … is … is *unethical!* You can't treat us like this! You can't—"

But that's as far as he got with his rant.

Mother Quigg was frozen there, hunched-over now, her fingers wiggling, her eyes gigantic and glassy. There was a sudden low, electronic droning and Brady cried out and hit the floor. He began to writhe and contort like a worm broiling in direct sunlight. He pissed himself, vomited out a pink foam of bile. His eyes rolled back white, a mad gibbering coming from his mouth.

"God! God! God, the cutting and the hurting and the stabbing! Stop it! Stop it!" he squealed, shuddering on the floor, an epistaxis of blood bursting from one nostril as if he was undergoing massive decompression. *"Make her stop! Stop! Stop! THE HUUUURTING! THE HUUUURTING!"*

Sales collapsed, pushing himself on his ass across the floor. "Somebody do something! Don't just let her … let her … let her…"

But nobody did anything because there was nothing we *could* do.

Brady was gasping now, shaking and sweating with fevers. Something had him. Something we could not see had hold of him and slowly, slowly, he was being dragged across the floor. He fought and swore and screamed, his fingernails trying to dig in for purchase and making a terrible scritching noise as he was pulled away toward the blackness.

"DREX! PEPLEY! OH JESUS, SOMEBODY HELP ME!" he cried in a pathetic, shrilling voice. He looked at me and my heart sank in my chest. *"DENNIS! PLEASE, DENNIS! TELL HER I DIDN'T MEAN IT! TELL HER IT WAS A JOKE!"*

It was heartbreaking, but unless we wanted to join him, we knew we had to stay out of it. He was dragged away faster, picking up speed, and then he reached the blackness. He actually stopped as he hit the invisible wall. Dark ripples rolled over its surface and then Brady was sucked through with a hollow, popping sort of sound.

Drexler was the first to find his voice. It was weary, dry, old beyond his years. "Where are you taking him?"

Mother Quigg grinned like a hungry rodent. "Yes, where exactly?" She removed her spectacles and cleaned them on her frilly apron. "Have no fear, my dears. He is going to a place where he will be fed ... oh yes, a feeding that will be most traumatic."

Date unknown

By now, of course, you realize the madhouse that the Vyrmid prison is. After the *Cosmos* was hit by some sort of unknown particle weapon and crashed onto this nameless planet, I opened my eyes in the wreckage, and Mother Quigg was there releasing me from my anti-grav harness.

"Easy, easy, dear," she told me in a voice that lulled me nearly to sleep. "Soon you'll be safe. Mother Quigg will see to that."

This is where dreams overcome reality. She got inside my head and placed a perfect fantasy in there that seemed very real, even though it was patently absurd when seen by the light of day. I was on a street that I did not know, knocking on door after door, but no one would answer. And then someone did—Mother Quigg. She smiled kindly, invited me in, commenting sympathetically on how sore my feet must be with all the walking I'd been doing, and had me sit in a comfortable chair. She gave me a tall glass of cold lemonade while we chatted. The lemonade was good, really good. I remembered it had a bitter aftertaste, but I figured it was just the lemons. Things got blurry after that.

I remember slouching in the chair.

And Mother Quigg's smiling face moving in closer and closer.

"Now you'll see," she said. "Oh yes, now you'll certainly see."

When I woke up, I was in the cage with the others.

I panicked right away, of course.

I came to fighting and crying out in absolute animal rage, wanting to kick and punch and scratch out eyes. Maybe I would have done just that but hands were holding me down, voices speaking in soothing tones. *It's okay,* I heard them say. *Really, it's okay. You just have to relax. That's it. Take it easy. We're your friends.* I did relax. My eyes blinked and blinked again. I could see a light high above me like a glowing moon. It made all the faces crowded around me look shadowy and somehow grotesque.

"Where … where the hell am I?"

"He's okay now," a man I recognized as Drexler from the *Cosmos* said. "Let him go."

The others released me, their faces pulling back. I kept trying to swallow, but my throat was too dry.

"He's thirsty," Drexler said. "Bring that water over here." There seemed to be some hesitation, so he ramped it up: *"Now."*

A woman came over with a plastic jug of water. While she held my head up, Drexler gave me a sip. It wasn't much, but it made me feel better right away. They were asking questions, but my mind was loopy and nothing they said made any sense. It was the place I was in that captured my attention. A zone of light hemmed in by blackness from all sides. It was like a soundstage in an old movie.

A cage.

Date unknown

After Brady's performance, of course, we all knew there would be repercussions. We feared what form they might take. For several hours, there was nothing. The five of us huddled in the cage, tense and uneasy. Today it was Brady—who would it be next? That's what we were all thinking, of course, at least in the front of our minds. But in the back, where the real anxieties tended to stew, we were all worrying how we would be punished for allowing him to get out of hand.

And, trust me, the Vyrmid have many ways of doing that. They don't even need to take you away to the bad place to be cut and tortured to do it. They control every square inch of the cage. They can make the floor burning hot or freezing cold. They can electrify the entire thing or just the spot you stand on. I'd seen people frozen bare feet from me, while I was perfectly comfortable. They have their ways.

Drexler, ever-observant, noticed it first. "It's getting warmer in here."

It was—I had noticed it, too, but I thought it was just my apprehension making me sweat. It wasn't. The heat was steadily rising. Every minute that passed, it became more uncomfortable.

Sales pulled at the neck of his tunic. "We'll asphyxiate. It's getting hard to breathe."

It wasn't, not just then. But within five minutes or so, I noticed it, too. A suffocating damp heat that made me think of tropical jungles and orchids blooming in hothouses. Sweat ran down my temples. My hair was greasy with it. My tunic clung to me like a wet rag. Pepley was on his knees, muttering prayers to a god who obviously despised him (judging by where he was and what the future held for him). Even old tranquil, reasonable Drexler was becoming uneasy.

Only Corrine took it in stride as she took all things in stride—dazed, mumbling, disconnected from reality.

Sales was stumbling in circles, wringing wet and gasping for air. "I can't breathe! Do you hear me? *I can't breathe!*" He directed this at me and when that got no response, he looked up, presumably at our captors. His eyes bulged, beads of perspiration running down his face. "You're killing us! You're killing all of us!"

I ran over to the invisible wall that enclosed us. It was always so cold; you couldn't hold your hands against it for more than ten seconds without getting freezer burn on your palms.

I pressed the flat of my hands against it and cried out. It wasn't cold anymore; it was burning hot like beach sand on a sweltering summer day.

There was no relief.

Drexler told us to get on the floor: the coolest place would be there. I forced Corrine down next to me. Her flesh was feverishly hot, oily with sweat.

And the heat kept rising and rising.

After that, it gets a little confused. We were all suffering from heat stroke. We lay on the floor, lost in a fugue, disoriented, our brains cooking in our skulls. The air was heavy and moist, every breath an exertion like old-time miners with black lung. I passed out. Woke. Dreamed. My body was melting into a pool of sweat, my limbs limp as well-boiled noodles.

"Enough," I heard Drexler say in a rasping voice. *"Enough."*

How many hours it went on, I don't know. But suddenly the temperature began to drop. And as it did, we all came out of it.

"Lord love a duck," I heard Mother Quigg say. "It's like an oven in here! My poor, poor dears!"

My vision focused and I saw her there, everyone's idea of a kindly, storybook grandmother in her flower print dress and string of old lady pearls. She set down a platter of cold cuts and cheeses from her little cart. Bowls of fruit and salad, pitchers of ice-cold water, ice tea, and lemonade with the requisite slices of fresh lemon.

Slowly, as the temperature normalized, we managed to drag ourselves to the table. All of us, save Pepley. Drexler had to hold him up on his lap and let him sip water gradually.

I swallowed a glass of water, too, followed by two tumblers of lemonade. The sugar in the latter spiked my system after dehydration and made my head spin. I felt better after some salad, a few slices of roast beef and ham, some cheddar cheese and several handfuls of strawberries.

I ate a lot, as did the others.

Pepley finally came around and filled himself, clasping his hands and thanking Jesus for the bounty. Something which made Mother Quigg titter unpleasantly.

Corrine, of course, had to be hand-fed as usual. She was mindless, stunned like a cow, just a big infant that had to be cared for, fed and washed, told when to sleep and when to use the toilet.

Mother Quigg watched us stuff ourselves, grinning contently as we became full and lethargic. She watched us the way you watch zoo monkeys at feeding time.

"There, there, my precious ones," she said to us. "All will be well now. You'll see. And, Mr. Sales, naughty, naughty … no coveting food. You know the rules. You do not wish to make Mother Quigg cross, do you?"

Sales dumped the cheese and meat that he had hid in his tunic back on the table. You definitely didn't want to break the rules.

Date unknown

If you saw Corrine the way she was when I first got to the cage, you wouldn't have recognized her. She was a petite, gutsy little thing with close-cropped hair the color of fire and eyes like blazing emeralds. She was athletic, tough, and undeniably pissy. Translated: she took absolutely no shit. She was the bane of both Sales and Brady, constantly riding them, giving them little to no peace as she ridiculed the former for being a whiny little mama's boy and the latter for lacking the necessary equipment to be a man in the first place.

It was quite a show.

She did not suffer fools lightly, as they say. Our job, as she saw it, was to escape and cause as much trouble as possible for our captors. Drexler and Howie both told her again and again that escape was clearly impossible because, realistically, escape to *where?* We were on an alien world deep in Sargassian space (presumably). For all we knew, the atmosphere out there was toxic to our type of lifeforms. And Sargassian space itself was a frightening dead zone where dozens and dozens of ships had disappeared along with their crews going back over a century. It had been named— appropriately—after the mythical Sargasso Sea of old Earth, a graveyard of lost vessels, sea monsters, and ghost ships. It had long been a forbidden area for starclippers and now we knew why: it was Vyrmid space.

The Vyrmid were the devils of Sargassian space, the nightmare stuff of tall tales and urban legends. Except that now, God help us, we knew it was all true.

The only reason the *Cosmo* had jumped into the Sargassian (illegally, I might add) was to search for a freighter called the *Icarus-3*, which carried enough polycrystals to power the entire starclipper fleet. The loss of them would tank the economies of a dozen worlds.

Suffice to say: we had been captured by the Devil and were now prisoners in the dirty backside of hell.

Corrine, hot-blooded and absolutely irrepressible, refused to bow down or give in.

And that brought her to Bokeman. He had survived for over a year in Vyrmid captivity. A record, he claimed, but not one he was proud of.

They had cut, slit, and punctured him. Taken biopsies and limbs, subjected him to horrible deprivations, alien parasites, and bioengineered germs. And still he lived. He knew things about the Vyrmid and the world beyond the cage that no sane mind should ever know.

It was Bokeman, you see, that told Corrine that there was indeed a way out. That there were weak areas in the field that enclosed us, and that an ambitious, clever, and fearless individual could locate them given patience and enough time.

Thus began Corrine's hunt for the legendary rabbit hole that would lead her from the cramped, desolate world we knew into a world we did not—and did not want to—know.

Howie and Drexler did everything they could to talk her out of it, but she was stubbornly fixed on the idea. Each evening at lights out she crept around the wall seeking the elusive trapdoor. I told her it wasn't a good idea because the Vyrmid watched us the way scientists watch mice in a Skinner box.

One morning, she was gone.

"She must have found the way out," Bokeman told us, as if she had only gone on a day hike.

I wanted to beat him for filling her head with dangerous ideas. I liked

314

Corrine. Maybe I more than liked her. We all got a kick out of her because she refused to give up and was more alive than any of us for that reason. She was a windy night. The sparkling Milky Way. A specimen of pure elemental force, a cosmic ray captured in a bottle. Poetic and sappy, I know, but she was the one that kept everyone going, kept the lights burning.

The cage was a miserable place without her bright eyes and mischievous smile. Bokeman, in my estimation, had taken all that away from us.

Mother Quigg brought us our food that day and she was not at all surprised that Corrine was missing. As she ladled out soup, humming under breath, she merely said, "It appears our spunky young miss has gone on a frolic, seeking high adventure. *Tsk, tsk.* One can be certain that she will not like what she finds."

Three days later, Corrine was back.

We found her near the wall one morning, naked and senseless, rocking on her haunches and hugging herself. Her head had been shaven, her cranium set with the pink weals of surgical scars. Her lovely, fiery green eyes were bleached white as if she had seen something so terrible it had leached the color from them. There were horrendous sucker marks on her belly and back as if she had been handled by a squid.

After many days, Drexler got her to speak, but it was all gibberish. Stuff about, and I quote, *"The endless black maze that leads to the room of pain."*

Further, after a time, *"They wear no masks ... no masks ... just faces that aren't faces, but the many mouths, all the many mouths,"* she sobbed in the shrill, terrified voice of a little girl. *"The glass room ... you can't feel your body in the glass room ... they cut and poke and when you scream, they scream with you...."*

That was the last time she spoke. For the past two weeks, she'd been little better than a mannequin. The old Corrine was dead.

The only ray of light in that horror was that they took that sonofabitch Bokeman away the next day. I hope they took their time with him.

Later that same day, Mother Quigg brought us a feast to celebrate Corrine's return, she said. Rare roast beef, mashed potatoes and gravy, hot buttered rolls, ice cream and sherbet.

"It's good to see the child back with us," she said, and her eyes were a bleary yellow threaded with branching red veins. There was a blank, doll-like stare to them that was perfectly repulsive and perfectly alien. "But I fear she went too far and looked too deeply, eh? Some paths must not be taken and some doors must remain shut. Oh, the poor thing. I fear that what she lost is gone forever."

Date unknown

Reinmann. Flowers. Ito. De Vries. The names roll through my brain again and again. All of them are gone now, taken away one by one for terrible things I hate to even think about, because it makes me wonder when my turn is coming. You see, every one of us knows why we're here and it's only a matter of time.

Let me tell you about Flowers. He was a med tech on the *Cosmos*. I didn't really know him very well, not until he was put in the cage with us. He was a man born without a spine or anything resembling guts. He was terrified, even more than the rest of us. And this caused him to degenerate into a simpering, chickenshit weakling, a real boot-licker who was always kissing up to the Vyrmid. Nothing was beyond him as we soon found out: he was always tattling to them about us, ratting us out, anything to ingratiate himself to them.

For doing this, like a white rat correctly running a lab maze, he was given special perks: reward biscuits. That's what the Vyrmid call them. They are white, doughy things about the size of your fist, but they become anything you want, from pizza and soda to prime rib and cherry cheesecake. They are a special treat for being a good boy. As you might guess, Flowers ate many of them.

Who's the good boy? You are! You're mama's good little boy, aren't you?

Yes, Flowers was as sickening as you can imagine.

Nobody liked him and we certainly didn't trust him. He was always listening, always looking for some little tidbit he could report to our captors. De Vries, who'd been a systems tech on the *Cosmos,* got sick of his shit one day and beat the hell out of him. It was ugly and brutal. Every bit of fear and frustration that had been pent up in De Vries came out through his fists, leaving Flowers lying there, bloody and broken. No one intervened—we encouraged it.

But there were reprisals, of course. We were starved for over a week. I refused to tell Mother Quigg who assaulted Flowers (even though she already knew; the Vyrmid studied us continually like germs on a Petri dish), so I was taken away and punished. I was stripped naked and forced to endure the shock corridor. It's a metal passage about a city block in length. The goal for the token guinea pig, that being me, is to get to the end as fast as you can. The rub here is that the floor is electrified. Squares about the size of kitchen tiles light up and you must hop onto them or you get shocked. They light up quickly and go out just as quickly, so you really have to be agile and fast. Miss one and the resultant shock is so strong you black out momentarily from the pain and wake up covered in your own vomit and foaming at the mouth. Which, of course, makes you groggy and loopy and you have a hell of a time moving fast enough to complete the circuit without a lot of pain.

When I was brought back, I had shock burns all over my body. Even sitting down was an agony.

I had one true friend in the cage. His name was Ito. Great guy. Funny, strong, supportive. We all loved him. The Vyrmid took him away and never brought him back. Though they did not let us see what they did to him (thank God), they let us listen. He screamed and cried for well over twenty-four hours. A lesson to the rest of us, you see.

And what of De Vries? He was infected with a deadly hemorrhagic virus that made his skin blister and pop open with bleeding ulcers. He lasted about three days until the virus overwhelmed his system and brought about spontaneous liquefaction of his innards. He died writhing on the floor, his organs turned to black jelly that he vomited out and expelled from his ass.

I won't even tell you about the parasite they planted in Reinmann.

But if there was any satisfaction to these horrors, it was Flowers' end. He was caught stealing food from the others and punished for it. He definitely got his just desserts, you might say. Mother Quigg took him away despite his pleading and whimpering. He came back a week later, a changed man.

You see, the Vyrmid made him into what he had always been: a crawling worm. Apparently, according to Drexler, they removed his bones, turning him essentially into an invertebrate. He slithered and inched about the cage for several days, gobbling and hissing, feeding on scraps we dropped.

When he curled up and died, nobody shed a tear. The worm had become a worm. There was poetic justice in that.

Date unknown

Brady is back. At least, something that wears his skin has returned. Let me explain. After the hothouse incident (that he caused, as you well know), we were filthy for days—festering in our own sweat and dirt, scratching at heat rashes and flaking skin … in a word, *miserable.* We asked Our Lady of Hope, Mother Quigg, if we could have our weekly shower a few days earlier. The answer was no, of course.

Like some cliched, hard-hearted Midwestern farm woman of old, she merely shook one knobby, arthritic finger at us and said, "Oh, my children! My poor misguided children of sin, my wayward lovelies … if it was only up to dear Mother Quigg, you know I would give in and let you have your way. I am but warm putty in your hands." Then, whatever warmth she had emoted (which wasn't much) faded and her heart became a cold lump of coal and her eyes huge and reptilian behind her spectacles. "But it isn't up to me, is it? Rules are rules and the powers that be will spare no rod to spoil their children. As you have sown, so shall you reap."

I tried everything from sweet-talking to begging, but it did no good.

So there we sat, itchy, stinking, and greasy, a pack of sewer rats … and that's when we heard a chilling, demented sort of voice calling out from the darkness beyond the cage. It was gibbering and mindless, an incoherent squealing punctuated by a shrill cackling that itself became a moronic babbling.

And then Brady appeared.

He stood just outside the shell (as we often called the cage), eyes blank and shiny, his trembling lips spilling drool down his chin. Like Corrine, he was bald and naked, but swollen obscenely as if he'd been pumped full of hot gas. His skin was jaundice-yellow and slimed with a clear jelly like he'd just clawed his way free of a placenta.

The sight of him was not so much surprising as shocking. My stomach rolled over, a cold chill climbing my spine.

"Dear God, what have they done to him?" Drexler said, just beside himself in a rare moment of emotion. "What in the Christ have they done to him?"

Sales, cowering behind him like a well-whipped dog, said, "What they'll do to all of us, sooner or later."

Corrine was oblivious to it, of course, as she was to all things. Even if she hadn't been blinded by the Vyrmid, it would have meant nothing to her. She slept. She ate. She emptied her bladder and bowels, but that was about it.

Pepley, right on cue, crossed himself and began to pray in a high, wailing voice.

Brady's condition offended me on some deep, intimate level. He not only disgusted me, but filled me with guilt because he was a fellow human being and there hadn't been a damn thing I could do to help him. And that made me feel sick right to my core. I loathed myself. So when Pepley started praying, I went hot inside.

"Shut up," I told him.

"The Lord shall see us through this," he told me. "We have only to ask for His guidance."

That's when I punched him in the mouth. He hit the floor, lips smeared with blood. I hadn't really thought about it; I simply reacted. Drexler pulled me away before I hit him again.

"Use your head," he warned me. "This is exactly what they want: to reduce us to squabbling, grubbing animals snapping at one another. We can't let that happen."

He was right and I knew he was right. They'd already destroyed Corrine and reduced Brady to an inhuman thing. I couldn't let them pull my strings.

Meanwhile, Brady entered the cage.

It was something I had noticed before; you could easily enter the cage from the outside, but once inside, it wouldn't let you out. Even Mother Quigg had to deactivate it with that droning noise after she brought our food. That's how the shell worked.

Making gobbling, infantile sounds, Brady stepped among us. His eyes were dirty windows looking into an empty room. He stood there making some perfectly deranged noise in his throat that sounded quizzical and confused.

"*Awwwgh? Awwwwagh?*" Then he giggled like an idiot, drool slobbering from his mouth. "*Awwwgh? En? En? Awwwgh?*"

At which point, he pissed himself.

Sales and Pepley pulled away from him. None of us smelled very good by that point, but Brady had an odor about him like warm vomit and bile. That and a sharp chemical stink as if he was a lab specimen pulled from a jar of formalin. Even his breath had a cold, pickled smell to it.

He got up close to me, sniffing around my face. I could see a network of pink scars on his gleaming head—the Vyrmid had cut into his brain, maybe removing parts of it until he was like this, a stinking animal with the mind of an infant.

Drexler tried to lead him away, but Brady snapped at him and made a low, coarse growling in his throat.

"It's okay, son," Drexler said. "It's all going to be okay now."

He finally managed to lead Brady away, who hopped about on all fours, licking Drexler's hands.

It wasn't okay. None of it was.

Date unknown

What prompted the awful events of today, I really don't know. Maybe it was my constant harping to Mother Quigg about us needing to bathe.

Regardless, after I'd finished my day's feeding—a terrible, fishy-tasting soup which I was certain was made foul on purpose—I told her we needed to clean ourselves yet again. Adding, "Clean animals are happy animals."

This time, she paid attention. She turned her back on the others, moving slowly in my direction with a rustling of her crow-black skirts (which she had taken to wearing lately as if she was in mourning). She licked her lips with a tongue that was swollen and black, and appeared hollow as a tube. I could feel her in my head and knew I was in trouble. It felt like cold fingers sorting through my memories, casting things about and making my body feel like it was filled with liquid rubber. All the while, she stared at me not with her cloudy blue eyes, but with gigantic pink crystalline eyes like those of a fly. They seemed to expand by the moment.

There was power in those eyes.

Magnetism.

And a mocking, relentless evil that made me shrivel inside.

Don't ask me what happened then. It seemed like my will, my mind, everything that I was got sucked down a spiraling black hole like water in a drain. The next thing I knew, I was in a room of black mirrored glass. The walls were not smooth, but made of black bubbles the size of softballs. I was seated at a table of blue glass or plastic. I could not move, though there seemed to be nothing holding me. My arms were flat on the table, equally paralyzed. I could feel a slight but firm pressure all over my body. The only thing I could move was my head. The ceiling above me was a funnel, gradually narrowing to a point of light that seemed at least a hundred feet above.

I saw no one else.

Then I blinked my eyes and there was a steaming cup of coffee before me. It was made of blue-speckled ceramic. Antique. Just like Mother Quigg.

I blinked my eyes again and I was looking at a grotesque nightmare across the table—how can I even describe it? It was huge and hulking, chitinous yet fleshly, purple-gray and gleaming like metal. From what might have been its chest to its segmented underbelly there were dozens and dozens of fluttering tubes. Above, there was a head of sorts jutting forward. It had those same glossy, pink compound eyes I had seen staring at me from Mother Quigg's face and a suckering black chasm of a mouth ringed by jointed, tiny insect-like legs. Coiling blue tendrils hung beneath.

"Why the look of horror, Dennis?" a buzzing, chittering sort of voice said from somewhere behind me. "You've always wanted to see us, and now you can."

As it spoke, black spines atop its head vibrated. It ground its limbs together with a rasping sound like knifes. It had six of them, three to either side of its squirming body. They were like elongated, bulbous bones that resembled interconnected mandibles with sharp, piercing hooks or teeth at their undersides. Appendages that ended in fine thrashing hooks.

The formalin stink I smelled on Brady rose from the creature in plumes of vile steam.

That's what I saw ... what I *think* I saw. An abstract horror that was many things but nothing in particular: a Vyrmid.

I screamed. I know I screamed as it leaned forward toward me. I saw that it didn't have legs, but a raft of coiling, muscular tentacles like pythons.

Then a voice said, "Drink your coffee before it gets cold."

Mother Quigg's voice.

The Vyrmid horror was gone. Mother Quigg sat across from me. But I could still smell that thing and my guts were in my throat.

"Drink your coffee." Not a suggestion—an order.

It took some time to get my mind working right again. Though it was chill in the chamber, warm sharp-smelling sweat ran from me in rivers. I was shaking and delirious. The aftereffect of absolute terror inspired by seeing a Vyrmid in the flesh ... a crawling, monstrous thing that had unhinged my mind just looking at it.

"Now, Dennis, relax. You're quivering like a chaste virgin on her wedding night." She sighed, readjusted her specs so that they were at the end of her nose like a storybook librarian. "Just sit a spell. Breathe in and breathe out. Now, child, you know that Mother Quigg would never let anything happen to a bright boy like you."

If Vyrmids were capable of being sarcastic, then that's what she was being.

"Of course, if you need a little something to calm you, Mother Quigg can certainly oblige. A little sting and you'll be loose as a goose. I have access to a wide variety of pharmaceuticals."

By then, my hand was free and I sipped my coffee. It was the best I'd ever had. But why wouldn't it be with Mother Quigg hijacking my brain and taste receptors? She could have made drainage from a septic tank taste like fresh-squeezed orange juice.

"That's it," she said. "Cozy up, my boy, and we'll have a fine little chat, you and I."

Which was the last thing I wanted, but her form drew my eye. Hypnotism? Magnetism? I think it was something as far beyond those things as a toad is above a polliwog or a bird is above an egg. I only know that I *had* to look at her. And her face, close like that, was like pale carved wood splitting with age into minute cracks and ruts. I could hear a low and steady ticking inside her like an antique watch ... or the beat of an alien heart. And every time she spoke, there was a strange clicking beneath her words like termites chewing into a dead tree.

I knew better than to stare at her directly for any length of time—the mirage of Mother Quigg was only so powerful. The last thing I wanted was to see her true appearance again.

"Oh, but there are worse things than the inhuman appearance of a Vyrmid sentinel," she promised me, a hungry slavering just behind her words. "Oh yes, most certainly, and Mother Quigg is the key. The key to serenity, peace, and fulfillment ... but also the key to nightmares beyond imagining and horrors your simple mammalian brain cannot comprehend." She clucked her tongue. "Think on that."

Oh, I was thinking on it, all right. And as I did so, an image of Corrine appeared in my head. I saw her running and crawling through a twisted maze, always looking behind her as something shapeless closed in on her. And I knew I was seeing what had happened to her. At least, the beginning of it. Whatever was after her had left the sucker marks on her. And as awful as that was, it was only the beginning of her torment. The image faded just as quickly as it had appeared and I knew it had been placed in my head. Incentive to cooperate or I would learn all about the maze and what lie beyond.

I was in a desperate situation and I knew it. I wasn't brought to the chamber for no reason. I was scared white inside, scared that my time as a lab rat was really about to begin and I would go back to the cage like Corrine or Brady.

"You said *sentinel* … is that what you are?" I asked.

"Yes, as in guardian. Mother Quigg watches over the cell you occupy which you call a cage. She is responsible for your lives and well-being. And when you must be punished, she decides in what manner. And when a specimen is required below, she makes the selection."

"Is that why you brought me here? To cut me up?"

As terrifying as the idea was, it had to be asked.

She studied me emotionlessly for a few moments. "Is that what you think, Dennis? That your torment now begins at the hands of Vyrmid vivisectionists?" She laughed at the very idea with a dry, scratching sound. "Or perhaps you believe this is an interrogation? That I wish to know the name of your ship and its mission here in the spooky depths of Sargassian Space? Or what provocation your kind will use to wage war against the Vyrmid Collective? No, no, no. Mother Quigg can extract all your dirty secrets if she wishes, peeling away layer upon layer of your mind. But if she did that, there would be very little left of Dennis."

I was shaking, just waiting. But the idea that she was telling me these things probably meant she wasn't going to do them. That was my hope.

"As long as you're cooperative, Dennis, there will be no hurting. Mother

Quigg promises you that."

At least that ruled out dissection or equally as horrible torments like the pain grid or the shock corridor. That was something.

She smiled as if she was reading my thoughts and I was pretty sure by that point that she was. "Mother Quigg will not allow such terrible things for her Dennis. Perish the thought!" She studied me the way a collector might study a beetle impaled on a pin. "Life is a matter of give and take ... is it not, my boy? One hand washing the other and all that? Yes, indeedy-do. It's important for you to remember that I am your friend. I will do things for you, but when I ask, you must do things for me. Do you understand?"

What she was really asking me was to betray the others in the cage and I knew it. I started to shake my head, but then I thought of the tortures and horrors waiting below and said, "Yes. You're my friend and I'm yours." That's exactly what I said. God help me, but it is.

"I knew you wouldn't let me down, Dennis. I just knew it." Her grin was huge and wolflike. "We have special plans for you, very special plans."

What happened then, you might ask. Well, I was given a treat like a good dog: pepperoni pizza and a pitcher of ice-cold Coke. I ate every bite and drank every drop. I hated myself, but it didn't slow me down any. They also allowed me a nice hot shower and a new set of clothes. I knew what it was all about—they were grooming me for betrayal.

Date unknown

Night chills and day sweats. That's life in the cage. We are routinely infected with everything from low-grade flus to devastating stomach viruses, nameless germs that cause headaches and temporary paralysis and even manic episodes of dementia. Our situation is ugly and desperate. Among our number we've had nervous breakdowns, rampant paranoia, delusional disorders and even a couple suicides.

And it's understandable with what we're put through. Human beings are free-living, independent creatures by nature, we're not meant to live in cages as guinea pigs or white mice.

The experiments go on and on. I've watched friends die from designer viruses and genetically engineered bacteria and infective fungi. From deadly microbes that mimic botulism, cholera, and even bubonic plague. We've been exposed to chemical weapons, blister agents, nanobacteria, and spores that make metallic hairs grow from our bodies and flesh-eating pathogens that can strip a body to bones in a matter of days.

Our minds have been crippled or completely destroyed by psychotropic drugs, our bodies wasted by running horrible learning mazes, and our spirits deadened by bionetics trials. Men have been castrated. Women have had their reproductive organs removed. People have been vivisected, tapped for blood and bone marrow, cerebrospinal fluid and lymphatic tissue. We undergo constant biopsies and grafts. We've been turned into monsters and hopping things. And there's always specialized horrors like the pain grid which mimic the most agonizing tortures, everything from being burned alive, skinned, and pierced by thousands of needles to being slowly crushed or cut to pieces. People have screamed so incessantly on the grid that the Vyrmid have removed their vocal cords.

But what's the point? You may well ask, but I don't have any good answers. I think the Vyrmid are gauging our survivability as a race, how tough and determined we are. I think they're frightened of us, how we're constantly expanding deeper into space because of the new star drives. They're xenophobic to the extreme, I believe, and fear us entering Vyrmid space on a mission of conquest. That's why they take us and experiment on us, to determine our resilience and to create biological and chemical weapons that can incapacitate us.

These are only guesses, of course. The truth may be that they're a scientific, unsympathetic race who view other lifeforms as lab animals. And maybe they're just sadistic monsters.

But I tend to think there's a purpose in it all. Maybe I have to tell myself that.

Living in the cage where the hours are like days and the days like weeks with nothing to break it up but sleep and our daily meal, breaks down something in the human psyche. It's like being in a vise that's slowly tightened, squeezing the life and spirit out of you, because any day can be the day when you are taken away for experimentation or dissection.

Once, I got bold and asked Mother Quigg what the point of it all was and she just tittered and said, "Our aims are not for you to know." In other words, the livestock does not have to understand the farmer that owns them any more than lab rats need to know why they're experimented on.

"But surely," I said, "there has to be an end game to all this. It can't go on forever."

"Can't it?"

After that, I never questioned her about it. The very idea of this going on year after year was enough to make me scream my sanity away.

Date unknown

Things happened last night that I hate to even tell you about. It went down just after lights out. In the cage, there is a set routine and the lights go out at the same time every night, always prefaced by the voice of Mother Quigg floating out of the darkness, *"Now it is time for sleep, my darlings and ducklings. Cozy up with your blankets and say nighty-night. For today is done and tomorrow is another one."* Again, you had to assume that the Vyrmid were being sarcastic. And what underscored it was that they always played Brahm's "Lullaby" immediately afterward. That sounds harmless enough, but in the desperation and horror of the cage, it was positively obscene.

A few hours after lights out, Corrine began to scream. It was a piercing wail that went right through you like a fire whistle. In the darkness, it was hard to say what was really going on. It was so black in there you literally could not see your hand in front of your face. The screaming went on and then something peculiar happened—a beam of light revealed what was going on.

Brady was trying to rape Corrine.

And, obviously, given the light, the Vyrmid wanted us to see it.

He had her pinned down, grunting and slavering, one hand around her throat while the other tore at her tunic. One of her breasts was already exposed and he didn't plan on stopping there. Her face was twisted up with manic terror and Brady was just a dumb, violent animal.

We converged on him, Sales and Pepley and I, tearing him away from her. He fought and snarled and spit. We could barely get control of him as Drexler squatted there with Corrine, soothing her like a child coming out of a bad dream. Brady hissed and tore at us, punching and kicking. We beat him down and kicked him into submission. And then Pepley had a knife in his hand. I don't know where he got it, but it was in his hand. Amid the shouting and screeching, Pepley stabbed him in the chest, slashed his face, then buried the blade in his throat.

Brady hit the floor, making a sort of squealing noise as he bled out, blood spurting from his torn neck. He should have died pretty quickly, but that's not what happened at all. In the focused beam of light, he was like an actor on a stage. He writhed and contorted and the sound of it was rubbery and rasping like someone was pulling off a wet rubber glove ... and the reason for that became quickly apparent: he was splitting open like an overcooked hot dog, bursting at the seams, his skin sloughing off in torn sheets. Gore poured out of him in red, seeping rivers, flooding over the floor, and his anatomy came out with it, like pus squeezed from an infected wound—a sea of rippling, coiling scarlet worms like strings of red licorice, finely-segmented, gushing from his remains in a maggoty expulsion of worms and meat and trembling bones. They blew out of him like spaghetti.

And still he moved.

Like a pulped red tomato, his juice sprayed everywhere, hundreds of worms spilling from him, undulating in his septic slime, converging, massing, intertwining until he looked like a living volcano spewing worm lava.

Everyone shouted, screamed, and more than one of us vomited. It was unbelievable. Easily the most sickening thing I had ever witnessed. And just as soon as it started, it ended. His broken husk no longer moved. The worms went still. There was nothing but a hissing, popping sound coming from inside him and this, too, passed. The only thing that remained was a horrendous, nauseating stink of blood, contaminated discharge, and a gassy, noxious smell.

And then the light went out and we were in the dark with his corpse and the things that infested him. It was hard to imagine a more terrible situation. We gathered together at the far end of the cage, as far as we could get from Brady. Huddled, holding onto one another, shaking, we waited for what came next. It was deathly silent in there and I imagined I heard slithering sounds more than once.

Corrine's finger brushed against the back of my hand, and I nearly screamed. I kept expecting the worms to slide into my shoes or up my pantlegs in the darkness. I thought I saw a reflection of luminous green eyes once, and I thought what remained of Brady had sat up.

That's how we spent the night: in utter terror.

Date unknown

It's been three days since Brady's death. We have not been fed nor given water. We're in a bad state. Corrine cries out whenever Drexler stops holding her. Sales is no longer speaking. Pepley prays under his breath almost continually. I just wonder how he got that knife. My guess is the Vyrmid put it in his hand so that he would do exactly what he did. I wonder now if every action in the cage isn't planned out by them as part of some experiment and whether we even have freewill by this point or are just puppets they manipulate.

Drexler is certain that the entire episode was carefully engineered. Maybe it was. Pepley, in his madness, believes that the Vyrmid wanted Brady (or the thing he had become) to impregnate Corrine. Which, of course, is blatantly ridiculous because we all know that Corrine's ovaries were removed by the aliens.

I don't know what to believe anymore.

The day after Brady's death, the Vyrmid left his corpse there along with the horrors that had been living in him. Probably to further break us down. This morning, it was gone. There wasn't even a stain on the floor to mark its position.

Mother Quigg visited us today for the first time since it happened. She entered the cage and stood there, looking at us, obviously displeased. "My poor misguided children, what have you gotten yourself into now? Mother Quigg leaves you alone and what do you do? My land! Violence? Murder? *Tsk, tsk.*" She shook her head, but there was an amused little smirk on her lips. "Yes, you've certainly gotten your tit in the wringer this time. There's only one way to make this right and I think my precious dears know what it is. So why don't we get to it and quit wasting time?"

We all looked at each other because, honestly, we didn't have a clue.

Mother Quigg sighed, looking impatient. "Well, back in my day, when a chance was given, we took it. The sooner you turn the murderer over to me, the sooner you can eat and bathe and drink all the ice-cold water you could wish for."

So that was it. We had to turn Pepley over to her. That was the point of this little experiment: to destroy any unity we had, to make us betray one of our own.

"This is ridiculous," Drexler said. "We know you watch us all the time. You know who the guilty party is. There's no doubt of that. That entire episode was arranged for our benefit ... so why play these games? If you want to punish the guilty party, then do so, dammit."

You could almost see Pepley shriveling into himself. What he had done was kill a monster, not a human being, and none of us thought less of him because of it. Poor Pepley didn't know what to do. He waited there, shaking, his eyes beady and shifting like a white rat waiting for the scalpel, his lower lip trembling. The pathetic thing was, he had been *compelled* to kill Brady; it had not been his idea. But now he would have to suffer for it.

Mother Quigg was shaking her head. "It is not my place to identify the guilty party, it is *yours*, you cocksure fool. The transgressor must be offered up by the hand of the community. Nothing less will be acceptable."

But none of us would.

We stood strong to protect our own, regardless of the consequences which we all knew would be dire. Mother Quigg seemed amused by this because she knew that, sooner or later, we'd give him up. We'd have to. But in the meantime, the Vyrmid could use this as an opportunity to test our resolve.

So it begins.

Date unknown

Six days now without food. We're so hungry. All our fingernails are chewed to nubs. We've even tried eating our tunics—at least, Sales has. But they're made of some tough, synthetic metallic material, and you cannot cut them and certainly not bite them.

The hunger pangs have been replaced by hunger pains. Though, to most people, they're the same thing, trust me they're not. It was discomfort mostly on the second and third day, a rumbling and gnawing sensation in my belly. By the fourth day, it became agony. The pangs became much sharper, much deeper, if that makes any sense. It was like a sharp-bladed shovel digging and digging into my stomach until I thought I would pass out. Yesterday, they became full-blown contractions that doubled me over and made me cry out.

Still, something in me will not give in.

Drexler stands strong as only Drexler can. He's hungry and hollow-cheeked. There are deep-set brown circles under his eyes. His teeth chatter like mine and he shakes uncontrollably, but he won't give in either.

Mother Quigg no longer visits us. I don't think she will until we give up Pepley. But how much longer can this unity, this defiance of the Vyrmid last? They have us at their mercy and we know it.

Sales is pretty much out of his mind. I know he would give up Pepley without hesitation if Mother Quigg would only come to us. The Vyrmid know this, too, I think. But they don't want just one of us to rat him out; they want *all* of us to do it as a community. To out him and persecute him.

We're starving because of him. He's the weak link in our little society, so he's our scapegoat, the cause of our suffering, so we must hand him over.

It's coming. I know it's coming.

Date unknown

We have water. The Vyrmid know we cannot survive long without it, so we're given enough to keep us going. Not like before in cold metal pitchers, but from a constant drip that falls from the darkness overhead. If you sit under it for five or ten minutes, you get enough to quench your thirst. We take turns. The downside is that it drips continually and the sound of that is maddening. The floor is wet with it and so are we. We're cold and damp, shivering and miserable.

And starving.

Oh yes, we're starving.

Date unknown

Food. It's an alien word now. I can no longer conceptualize what it once meant now that we're on our seventh day of starvation. Is it seven? I think it is.

Sales went wild yesterday night, screaming at the top of his lungs about Pepley. That he was the one. That they must come and take him and give us food. *"TAKE HIM! TAKE HIM! PUNISH HIM!"* he shrieked. *"PUNISH THE GUILTY! OH PLEASE DEAR GOD PUNISH THE GUILTY!"* His energy level was astounding. The rest us can barely sit up. We can no longer stand. I'm constantly dizzy and the pains in my stomach have become a low, steady throbbing. It takes everything I have to think coherently. There is much I wanted to tell you, but I don't remember what it was. Can't seem to think.

I lie on the wet floor all the time now, doubled up. It's all I can do. Pepley ... is that his name? Pepley? I'm confused and when you know you're confused, you're really confused. He, that guy I was talking about, the religious nut. He's paranoid and does not know why he's here or who we are. Sales talks about killing him for making us suffer. But with what? And where will he get the energy?

The cage seems to be growing darker every day.

Date unknown

Scraps of food were dropped into the cage last night—bones with a bit of meat on them. Even those little morsels gave us a bit of strength.

Date unknown

Food. I only think of food. Don't know how many days since the scraps. My heads pounds. My heart races. My fingers feel oddly numb. I'm cold and wet and can't seem to remember anything. Why doesn't that idiot stop praying? God, the noise, the noise … it's like a drum in my head. Are you hungry? What can I get you? Fresh crisp salads with Thousand Island dressing and Porterhouse steaks and cherry pie and fresh bread and pizza and pasta chocolate oh I'd love some chocolate and hot soup and hot chocolate hot turkey sandwich mashed potatoes baked ham! Ha! I'd eat a rat a worm a spider I'd relish it relish it

Can't can't think

Funny can't remember my name

Water drips and drips

Date unknown

Last night, a voice: *"Dennis, are you my friend?"* It kept repeating and repeating, in and out of my fugue state where there was no distinction between dreams and reality. It was the voice of Mother Quigg, soft and calming, just as sweet as apple pie. As insane as it sounds, something inside me trusted that voice. It wanted to please that voice.

"Yes," I said. "I am your friend."

"That's good. That's so very good to hear. Friendship is an important thing," she told me and, despite my hunger and my depleted state, I felt a sort of serenity because I knew she would make things right.

"I'm so hungry."

She made a cooing sound. "Of course you are, my dear. And Mother Quigg wants to take that awful hunger away from you. It's important for you to remember that I am your friend. I will do things for you, but when I ask, you must do things for me. Do you understand?"

I knew I had heard that before, but at the time with my head spinning around and around, I couldn't place it. "I'll do anything," I said.

"That's my good boy. Now tell me who killed Brady."

"But ... you know."

"Yes, but I want to hear you say it. It's important that you trust me."

"The others ... they ..."

"There's only you and I."

And then I heard my voice say, "Pepley. It was Pepley."

The words came out of my mouth before I could pull them back. I had just betrayed the community, but I couldn't stop myself. There was something liberating about that and I instantly felt better or was *made* to feel better."

"Thank you, Dennis, thank you for trusting me. Now I will help you."

Without being told, I reached out my hand and a juicy slab of meat was given to me. It was so hot it burned my fingers. But the slight pain was wonderful. The meat was well-seasoned and its aroma was intoxicating. I brought it to my mouth and chewed on it, gulping it down, tearing at it like an animal—a juicy, charbroiled steak. So tender. So succulent. It was the most amazing thing I've ever tasted. And then, in the midst of my secret delight, a light came on. It was the same sort of spotlight that illuminated Brady trying to rape Corrine ... except that I was the star now.

Drexler and Sales began crying out and Pepley was sobbing. Corrine slept on. I had betrayed Pepley and then betrayed the community by taking food as payment for being a rat and not sharing. I was doubly damned. It was amazing how easily Mother Quigg manipulated me and then, exposed me to the others for what I was.

But I was an animal. I could not think straight. As Sales and Drexler

334

lunged at me, I snarled at them and crawled away, coveting my steak. *It wasn't theirs! It was mine! All mine!* These are the thoughts that ran through my mind. The meat belonged to me and I was ready to fight for it, kill for it, anything to protect what was mine and mine alone. We went at it like starving beasts (which we were): fighting and clawing and hitting each other with undreamed of reserves of strength. But they overwhelmed me and beat me down and then, they fought over the meat, spitting and tearing at one another.

Date unknown

I'm better now. Oh, so much better. Remade, refitted, a brand-new man. After Drexler and Sales beat me down, I don't remember much, just a terrible feeling of self-loathing as I lay on the floor, bruised and bleeding. I was a traitor and I knew it. I guess that's why I barely fought back—I deserved every punch and kick. You, my unknown friend, have probably dismissed me as a coward, a sniveling weakling—and how right you are. I only hope that you're never starved like I was and forced to choose between food and friends. You don't think right. You don't feel right. You have utterly no sense of balance. Things like right and wrong, ethics and morals become abstract concepts in the need to fill your belly. That's all I'm going to say.

When I woke from all that, it was many days later. It could have been weeks later. I'm not sure of anything. I opened my eyes, and I was in the chamber of black glass with Mother Quigg. She kept smiling, but she would not speak.

"What happened?" I asked. "What's going on?"

I was only aware of a dull throbbing in my head, a sort of latent headache. It reminded me of when I cracked my head as a kid. I had the same kind of headache for days.

Mother Quigg sat across the table from me, her eyes huge and glassy behind her spectacles. I didn't dare stare at her for any length of time, because when I did, she began to change into the repulsive Vyrmid horror that she really was behind the kind-old-lady illusion. Her image would waver like a heat mirage and I'd see immense crystalline eyes watching me, shining and pink. What was in them was not hate nor love, just a cold neutrality the way you might look at an insect that intrigued you for a moment or two before you stepped on it.

"Dennis," she finally said, "eat your breakfast before it gets cold."

I blinked my eyes and there was a breakfast platter before me: scrambled eggs and bacon, hash browns and French toast. I wasn't particularly hungry, yet I was compelled to eat. The smell of warm maple syrup was overwhelming. The eggs were perfectly light and fluffy, the hash browns crispy and the bacon smokey-flavored. The French toast was heavenly with melted butter and sweet, luscious syrup. I washed it all down with ice-cold orange juice.

"There," said Mother Quigg and I could see black spines growing up from the steel-gray bun of her hair, vibrating madly. "Things are always easier on a full belly."

"Tell me what happened," I said, though what I really wanted to ask was what's going to happen *now?* Was I being groomed for dissection? Would I be infected with something? Parasitized by some alien horror?

Mother Quigg chuckled and for a moment I was looking into the black, glistening chasm of her mouth: the chitinous appendages that surrounded it wiggling, the blue tendrils beneath coiling like thick worms. Then it was all gone.

"You know what happened, Dennis. You cooperated and have been rewarded."

But there was more to it than that and I knew it. My head kept throbbing and when I reached up to touch it, I laid fingers on my cool, bald skull. *We have special plans for you, very special plans.* I remembered her saying that and I heard it now, echoing in my head.

"What have you done to me?" I said, beginning to panic. "Oh, good God, what have you done to my head?"

"Relax, my boy. Relax." She patted my arm with something like a blue-green crab claw. As I watched, trembling, it became a multi-jointed skeletal limb ending in sharp hooks that wiggled like fingers. "We've put something in your head. It's nothing terrible. Just a tiny device that will help you communicate with us."

I was shaking. "I don't want it! Please, I don't want it!"

"You prefer the alternative?"

I think at that moment, the device was activated because I saw a huge chamber of what appeared to be glass and I could hear men and women screaming in agony to the accompaniment of droning, shrill Vyrmid voices that rose and fell with volume, grinding my thoughts like powdered glass. It was then that I saw Bokeman. He wasn't dead as I thought, but I'm sure he wished that he was.

Oh, what they had done to him. The filthy, evil monsters. Poor, poor Bokeman. Sure, I still hated him for filling Corrine's head with false hope that ultimately led to her undoing. But even Bokeman deserved better than this—they had him pegged, spreadeagled and naked, to a board of sorts, a matrix of something like blue-gray metal that quivered from time to time like gelatin. His mouth was frozen in a scream and his eyes were bulging from their sockets. I could just imagine the unbelievable agony he had endured. His skin was transparent like glass and each anatomical system beneath—digestive, nervous, lymphatic, endocrine etc.—were dyed a different color: blazing red, electric blue, neon yellow, fiery orange. They were all brightly lit from within, practically glowing.

And the perfectly obscene thing was that they appeared to be functioning. His heart was beating, his lungs breathing, his circulatory system transporting blood. Then I saw his eyes look in my direction with stark terror and his mouth began to form words ...

Then I was back in the chamber with Mother Quigg. She looked at me and laughed with a scratching, strident sound that I could feel along my bones. And as she did so, the fluttering tubes from her chest to underbelly fluttered like sea grass in a tidal current.

I saw other things there besides Bokeman, but I don't even dare say what they were. Mother Quigg studied me from behind her glasses.

"I think we understand each other now, Dennis. We can communicate with you anytime we want and you can do the same. You'll find you have other gifts as well, but I'll let you discover what they are."

Then I blacked out and when I woke up, I was back in the cage.

Date unknown

The last two days have been trying. The others are keeping their distance from me. They no longer trust me and with my head shaved bald, they figure I'm no longer human anyway. Oh, they speak to me, but only in brief, clipped sentences and always with that suspicious look in their eyes that tells me I am not to be trusted. I am the enemy in their midst. Part of it, of course, is my concealing the food from them, but that's only part.

Corrine stares at me with her glazed, stoned-out eyes like she's just coming out of heavy sedation. Pepley begins praying madly whenever I approach him. Sales becomes very nervous in my presence. Only Drexler has made any real attempt to talk to me.

"Where have you been, Dennis?"

"I was interrogated by Mother Quigg … then, I just don't know. I'm not sure what they did to me." I was lying my ass off and I think he knew it, being annoyingly perceptive. "Don't you think you guys can forgive me already? I was starving. I lost control."

"Of course. It could have happened to anyone."

But that's all he said. I'm not just the enemy. I'm a turncoat, a Judas, a traitor. So be it.

Now and again, I hear a low, distant buzzing in my head.

Date unknown

Howie's back. I never actually thought we'd see him again. Well, let me rephrase that: I was *hoping* we'd never see him again. I liked Howie. I liked the man he was. I respected him. We had a lot of good talks together. He was always the guy in the cage who had a cool head and an easy way about him. When people lost control—broken by fear and anxiety and dread—

he was the guy who could talk them down, make them see the light, as it were.

I was sitting in my corner of the cage, Drexler and Sales keeping an eye on me and Pepley petting Corrine with one hand like a favorite puppy and crossing himself with the other whenever he dared make eye contact with me. That was the scene. Then Howie walked in out of the darkness that surrounds us. Unlike Brady, he didn't make a sound and the reason for that became instantly obvious: he no longer had a mouth. He was shaved bald and I could see the scars on his head.

"They've been cutting into his brain," Sales said, as if that needed saying at all.

I don't know what they did to his head and there was no way we could find out because he no longer had a mouth. In fact, he didn't really have a face as such—skin had grown over his eyes and mouth and there were just two little breathing holes where his face had been. He just stood there, reaching out like a blind man with his hands, stumbling this way and then that.

We managed to lead him away and sit him down ... something which was not very easy in that he flinched and fought anytime you touched him. The only sound he made was an awful, hollow breathing noise like a kid blowing through a straw.

It was horrible.

Drexler did everything he could to calm him down, but he still continued to quiver and shake with weird spasms. He tried to communicate with him, but it was pointless: he didn't even have ears.

"I hope you're happy," Sales said to me. "Look what your masters have done to him."

My initial reaction, of course, was to pop him in the mouth, but even as I thought that, I heard that odd buzzing in the back of my head and a voice that was mine yet not mine at all, said, *and we can do much, much worse.* Then it was gone.

Sales gave me more shit, but I ignored him. Arguing was pointless. I felt as bad as anyone. Drexler kept trying to figure out a way to slit open Howie's mouth, but we had nothing sharp. I felt along his smooth, pink face, but I couldn't find anything like a depression where a mouth would be. Same for his eyes.

"But ... but how's he going to eat?" Sales asked and that was the very thing there was no answer for.

Date unknown

We have a new pastime—watching Howie starve to death. It's a slow and ugly process, but there's nothing we can do about it. Believe me, I tried. I knew I'd get punished, but I kept after Mother Quigg again and again until she got sick of me and said, *"Day after day, you play the same tired tune on your well-worn harp, Dennis. It's grown tedious with repetition."* I told her if she could just open his mouth again so he could eat. That's all I wanted. I asked, I pleaded, then, feeling bold, I demanded.

I was taken from the cage.

I won't pretend I didn't scream and cry, because I did. I'd never known such terror before. I was taken to the black chamber once again. And again, I was held in place by a force that I could neither see nor feel. My arms were flat on the blue glass table, as were my hands, fingers spread.

Mother Quigg was there, watching me. "Now tell me what troubles you, Dennis. You have me worried."

Beads of sweat were rolling down my face. I could taste their saltiness on my lips. My guts were rolling in my belly. It felt like I was going to throw up any minute.

"We just want Howie to be able to eat," I said. "What good does it do to starve him?"

Her tittering laughter became a scratching sound inside my head that made me want to scream. It echoed and echoed, cutting through my gray matter like glass shards.

Finally, she sighed. "Now let's not be a stupid little boy, Dennis. You know darn well what the point is."

And I did. Even if I didn't, she placed the information in my mind so I could mull it over: starving him was part of the experiment. He was just a lab rat and she didn't care about him. What she cared about was *us,* our reaction to his starvation. That was essentially what the experiment was about.

"But why? What do you hope to gain by his death?"

That tittering again. "We want to know how much the community is willing to sacrifice to save him. A window, you might say, into extreme human behavior." Her image blurred momentarily and I saw her for the alien horror she was. "How about you, Dennis? What are you willing to sacrifice to save him?"

I shook my head; I didn't know how to answer that. Was she wondering if I'd give my life for him? Was that it?

I noticed then that there was something in her hand. It was about the size of a pen. "Are you willing to sacrifice a digit for him?"

She passed the object over my hand and my left pinky finger was severed at the knuckle. I screamed at the agony. I'd told myself again and again that when my time came, I wouldn't scream. I wouldn't give those monsters the satisfaction of it. But the pain had other ideas. I screamed my head off. There was no blood, just the stink of burning flesh from the cauterization of my finger stump.

She brought the object in again and I shook and whimpered and begged her not to hurt me again.

"Will you sacrifice two?"

She took my left ring finger, but this time it was not a quick severing, but a slow and agonizing separation. I shrieked and she hummed as the scalpel (I don't know what else to call it) gradually cut my finger off. When it was done, I sat there, immobilized, sweat running down my face, filling my eyes and dripping off my chin. And I could hear my own whimpering voice pleading with her to stop.

"Would you sacrifice your entire arm?" she asked. "What about that, Dennis? Can you? Will you?"

But I wasn't willing to do that. No, weakling that I was, I begged her to stop cutting, to stop hurting me. I begged her forgiveness for disrupting the experiment, promising her I'd keep my mouth shut, that I would never interfere again. Believe me, if it had been possible, I would have dropped to my knees before her and kissed her feet to get back into her good graces.

"Very well, Dennis. You are a survivor and we like survivors."

With that, I was back in the cage.

Date unknown

Operant conditioning. Are you familiar with the term? It comes from behavioral science. It's what they do with white mice in a maze, a series of rewards for the proper behavior and punishments for the wrong behavior. It's considered to be a learning tool. You make the right choices or suffer the consequences. I'm sure by this point that you see the comparison with the cage.

But let me illustrate it for you: food. It's the only thing we have to look forward to in the cage, and like good little white mice we invariably do what the Vyrmid want, or it'll be taken away from us. Food is the stimuli and proper behavior is rewarded with it.

Apparently, our behavior was not acceptable to our keepers, so they took away our good meals (or our illusion of the same) and replaced them with very simple fare: bread and water. The typical medieval punishment diet. Mother Quigg assured us that everything we needed to survive was in the nutrient bread. It was soft, kind of spongy in fact, and completely flavorless, but I suppose even this illusion was better than the gray slop it actually was.

Now here's the rub: though there are five of us in the cage (Howie doesn't count in this instance), only four pieces of bread were offered. Mother Quigg said we needed to choose who would not eat (and I knew better than to question her or the experiment it surely was).

"Make the proper choice, children," she told us. "Much depends on it."

Drexler, being the martyr he was, volunteered to go without. He told us that we should follow his example, each day a different person going without. I wanted to laugh. Did he really think he was going to outwit our keepers so easily?

I wasn't sure exactly what the point of this little exercise was, but I assumed in my naiveté that it was to see if we would sacrifice for the good of all. With that in mind, I let Drexler have half my bread. He ate it with no ill effects. I began to eat mine and my mouth filled with a foul, rotten taste that made me spit it out—it was decayed and writhing with maggots.

As I gagged and tried to keep my stomach down, Mother Quigg appeared outside the cage. "Oh, Dennis, now you've made a mess of things again." She sighed. "You leave me with no other choice—you must come with me now."

Drexler stood in front of me. "He was doing the right thing for the benefit of the community."

"I'm afraid he must be punished. Step forward, Dennis."

I tried to fight against the compulsion to go to her, but it was hopeless. Drexler tried to hold onto me, but I was pulled from his grasp. I hit the floor, trying to crawl away from her, but like Brady, I was drawn across it and sucked through the invisible wall. I remember crying out and fighting, but not much more … save Mother Quigg's huge pink crystalline eyes watching me, like a collector with an interesting butterfly in his net.

Date unknown

I'll recount for you now what happened. I was sure in the back of my mind that I would be cut open, subjected to horrible surgeries or infected with some terrible pathogenic disease strain, but that's not what happened at all. I remember the darkness closing in from all sides and then later (hours? days?), I opened my eyes in freezing cold water. I was drowning in it, sinking down to the bottom of a black tank.

That's how I woke up: in utter panic.

Above me, I could see a light, a persistent sort of glow. I swam up toward it. That's when I realized I wasn't alone—four or five other people broke the surface with me, thrashing madly in the water. We were in a cylinder-like chamber in ice-cold water. In the back of my mind, I knew I had very little time before I became hypothermic. There was a lighted passage above, a foot above the waterline, and I went for it. It wasn't big enough to stand in, more of a crawlway than anything.

I leaped and grabbed hold of the lip and pulled myself in. That's when I realized that the floor of the passage was moving like an escalator. It dumped me back in the water and the others were grabbing me, tearing at me, trying to use me to pull themselves up. I fought free of them, leaped up again and pulled myself into the passage. But this time, soon as I was in there, I scrambled forward on my hands and knees like a monkey. The passage canted upward, so I had to climb and climb as fast as I could so it wouldn't carry me back into the pool.

The others were crying out, but there was just no way I could help them. I heard a few others follow my lead. I kept going and going, but there was no time to rest and think things out.

The passage opened up until I was able to stand in it. I saw a door, but there was no way to open it. Three globular red bulbs protruded from the wall. When I touched them, they lit up. It was a puzzle of sorts: I had to figure out the pattern of the lights to open the door. No easy bit when you're on a treadmill and you have to keep walking so you're not carried backward.

Naked and freezing, I tried to sort it out. I lit the bulbs in sequence—1-2-3. No good. I tried 3-2-1, 1-3-2, 2-3-1, and finally hit it it with 3-1-2. The door opened and I got through. It closed immediately. The others would have to figure out the pattern themselves, I guessed.

The passage before me twisted and turned, gradually narrowing until I was on my hands and knees again. The roof brushed my back, the walls pressing against my shoulders. I could hear others behind me, scrambling ever forward. We were in one of the awful mazes I'd heard about. I knew I had to fight forward as fast I could because they were timed. I kept going, refusing to give into claustrophobia. I found an oval opening that led into complete blackness and fell into it.

Behind me, another person, a woman, was coming through the passage. But just as she got to the opening, it constricted and trapped her. I made a mad dash to help her, but it was no good. The passage squeezed down on her and I heard her bones shatter from the immense pressure bearing down on her. As I reached out for her, she was crushed like a bug under a boot, gore and viscera erupting from her mouth. A wet spray of blood was ejected into my face.

It was horrible, yes, but the warmth of her blood felt good because I was so desperately cold. She had tried to follow me, but that's not how it worked. Only one person could enter the passage at a time.

In the blackness, I stumbled about, searching for a wall. After a time, I found one and followed it, feeling around for a door but not finding one. That's when I saw a light. It came from high overhead, descending. It was a spiral staircase that glowed blue as if it was made of neon. I grabbed hold of it and climbed. About twenty feet up, I saw another guy below me grabbing onto it.

It began to rotate. Slowly at first, but then faster and faster until it was spinning like a centrifuge. I had to hold on, keep moving upward as it spun, trying to throw me. It was like being on some crazy carnival ride. The faster it went, the harder it was to hold on. My head was whirling, my guts coming up the back of my throat. I finally reached the top and I was sucked up a funnel and deposited on a metal rectangle. I looked down and I saw that other guy. He was trying to fight his way up, but he was barely holding on.

Move, you idiot! I thought at him. *You have to move! You have to keep going or ... or ...*

Then I saw why: a blade shot up from below like that of a guillotine. He had time to scream before it split him in half, his remains dropping away into the darkness.

The rectangle I was on went up and up. I clung to it, shivering and nauseous. I smelled terrible odors like rotting flesh, bile and gangrenous wounds, nose-reaming chemicals, and a bitter sweetness that made me gag.

My eyes burned and my lungs ached. Tears ran from my eyes and my guts were filled with a shivering yellow repulsion. There was a stink of warm vomit that I realized was my own.

I was finally deposited in a gigantic, cylindrical chamber made of some black, sparkling matrix. I was in a laboratory of cruel-looking abstract machinery, huge lenses, and spirals of transparent tubing. Some pale blue gas was sprayed in my face and I lost control of my body. I collapsed on the rectangle and it instantly secured me like metal filings to a magnet. I was on my back, legs and arms spread. A fan of glowing fibers descended on me, then pierced me. I couldn't even scream from the pain; my mouth and tongue were completely numb.

Things get a little blurry at that point, but I saw the Vyrmid around me, perfectly repulsive in their natural form. They studied me with their compound eyes but did not approach me. Things crawled around them, and I saw that they were skinned human carcasses, but alive, horribly alive. I saw a flat sheet of gray material that looked soft as a toadstool. Human heads projected from it like trophies in a hunter's den. I thought they were specimens, pickled things, but then I saw their eyes blinking and mouths moving as they attempted to call out to me. The heads of Reinmann and Ito were there.

I was drenched in a warm, globby jelly that smelled like rancid pig fat but burned like lye. Needles were jabbed into my stomach, a metal hose shoved down my throat. I remember spiking episodes of pain, my head filled with distorted (and scary) imagery from my childhood, but not much else. I was in and out of consciousness.

Then I was completely awake.

I was able to move my head and look around, and dear God, what I saw. From the concave floors to the spiraling apexes high overhead there were unusual helix-shaped structures of some gauzy, membranous material that might have been mineral or might have been tissue. They were pale green in color and looked like nothing if not some gigantic representations of the DNA helix itself. Oblong pods grew from them and branched out into great netted clusters like cocoons, which broke apart into elaborate networks of white strands and filaments like some insane, complex spiderweb. Up there, millions of those threads ran in every direction like some insane circuitry.

It was like looking up the chimney of an ancient, abandoned house festooned with intricate cobwebbing. That's what it reminded me of.

The webs themselves looked very much like living tissue. Morbid, maybe, but very much alive. As I stared up there, they actually pulsed, tiny eddies of yellow and green light occasionally running along the intricate threading.

I realized then that they looked like nervous tissue, neurons branching out into dendrites and axons and synapses....

An amazing, disturbing plexus of nervous tissue and caught in it, like flies in the webs of spiders, were human beings. Not rotting, drained things, but living men, women, and even children. They were suspended high above, those threads and fibers growing right through them. From their heads came forests of fine filaments that connected to the main strands themselves.

There were dozens and dozens up there, people snatched from Sargassian space and brought here to be plugged into the network. I could sense, possibly with the implant in my head, their raw mental energies and psychic discharges. They were very high above, but they seemed to be in some type of coma. Now and again a hand would twitch or a leg would jerk, but that was about it.

It was horrible.

Offensive.

Obscene.

But a perfect example of organic technology at its purest form. Human batteries hooked to an incredibly complex network of living nervous tissue. No, I didn't know that to be true, yet I was certain of it. The light reflecting off the crystalline helixes and sparkling webs made my head ache deep inside.

It was insane, but some sort of sleeping, suppressed psionic sense within me was activated, and I was looking down on myself through the eyes of those strung above. I had a tactile sensation of the webs that connected them. I could explore the anatomies of all those minds.

Then I was back in my own head, staring up at the galvanic webwork high above and the human subjects entwined in it. My mind travelled each single thread at light speed, racing down synaptic networks, invading brains and sucking energy and knowing every joy and terror and abstract memory of the subjects themselves. I could hear the multitude of dormant, dreaming minds sobbing and begging and praying for death as they were slowly drained of life force and memory, individual identity and awareness of self.

I should have felt pity, but I felt none—I looked on them as the Vyrmid must have looked on them, as livestock to be exploited, a simple technology to be harnessed. I understood completely that the minds plugged into that great psychic battery were but a utility, part of an ongoing experiment and I felt no more compassion for them than a farmer does for the udders that supply him with milk or the soil that brings forth his crops.

Then it all simply switched off, and I was myself again, fixed to that metal rectangle, my belly, my head, my limbs exploding with agony. I thrashed and screamed, and through the haze of agony and madness, I heard Mother Quigg whisper in my ear, *"Don't raise such a fuss, Dennis. It's all at an end now ... until next time."*

Date unknown

I don't know how long I've been away. Is it weeks? Months? A long, long time. But I'm back in the cage again. Everything has changed. I don't even know where to begin. Most of my information comes from Pepley. When he's not praying or delusional in some fucked-up religious fugue, he's fairly rational, even though the Vyrmid experimented on him while I was gone: he no longer has a left eye, just a sutured mass of scar tissue where it once sat. Other than the metallic synthetic skin grafted to his belly and chest, he's relatively unscathed.

Howie died while I was away. Corrine is still here. There are fresh scars on her bald head. Pepley said they took her away for three days. She's still hopelessly mad, but she's vicious and aggressive now. They turned her into a feral thing that claws and snaps at anyone that gets too near. I don't dare approach her. Her eyes are like those of a rabid dog, and like one, she growls and shrieks and foams at the mouth.

Drexler and Sales. Apparently, they made a big stink about our treatment to Mother Quigg and were taken away. They returned a few weeks later (Pepley claims), much changed. Do you know what parabiosis is? It's the surgical joining of two organisms to create a single physiological entity. Long ago, before animal experimentation was outlawed, researchers used to do it to dogs and cats, mice and rats, to study aging, blood chemistry, neurology, and endocrinology etc. A disgusting, barbaric practice by modern standards, but all the rage back in the experimental biology circles of the twentieth century.

With that, I think you can guess what happened to Sales and Drexler: they were fused into a single life form. Their minds are completely gone and they stumble as one about the cage like Siamese twins of yore, drooling and hissing.

The Vyrmid are nothing if not sadistic in their experimentation.

We have new arrivals, too. Pepley calls them *Squealers*. I suppose that's apt in that they do squeal and screech quite a bit. Some of them are just harmlessly crazy, broken by the nightmare of the cage, like Helen and Father Mike. Others like Grubber, Stan the Man, and Billy McBee are disfigured from cuttings—lacking limbs, bald skulls crudely sutured, mouths opening and closing like sucking holes of torment. Then there's Whistling Bob who can't speak because the Vyrmid cut out his voice box so he wouldn't scream when they injected him with various parasitic brain flukes (which are gradually, painfully, devouring his brain stem).

Did I tell you about Herman? Oh, this one's good. If you're not sick to your stomach by this point, this should really revolt you. Herman is a gigantic, hulking monstrosity, easily over seven feet, a real monster ... in more ways than one. You see, the Vyrmid with their boundless surgical creativity have grafted heads onto him. There's one on his chest, another sprouting from his belly, and a third on his left shoulder.

They're alive, very alive.

They have no vocal cords, thank God, or they'd be screaming nonstop. The heads are all completely insane—their eyes roll and stare, their mouths drool, they gnash their teeth and grimace … whoever they were, they are no longer. If that isn't bad enough, Herman's left hand is missing and has been replaced with the head of a child, a girl. His own eyes are missing, the lids sutured shut, but he sees through the child head. He holds it up and its eyes guide him back and forth from one end of the cage to the other. He marches about like that all day long.

One thing you never want to do is meet the girl-head's eyes. They are yellow pits of madness in her puckered gray face, absolutely deranged, the pupils horribly dilated like those of an owl. If she catches you looking, her mouth grins and her jaws chomp and she licks her lips while profusely salivating. Believe me, you don't want her to take an interest in you.

This is the reality of the cage at the moment.

God, I thought it was bad before, but I had no idea. I know there are other cages out there, and I wonder if some of them are even worse. Every night, I have nightmares about them and the distorted horrors that crawl in them.

I think my mind is going. My thoughts are jumbled and I hallucinate a lot. I try to remain strong, but I often wake in the night, sobbing in my sleep. If my mind's not gone, there can't be much left of it. The only thing that gives me any comfort is a fantasy where a fleet of Agency warships and viper drones arrive and exterminate the Vyrmid and free us. It won't happen, but it's all I have to cling to. If only the drive in my tooth can survive me and reach the Agency.

But I know better.

I hate the fucking Vyrmid the way Jews in concentration camps must have hated the Nazis in World War II. I want to kill every one of them slowly and painfully.

Goddamn monsters.

Goddamn fucking monsters.

Date unknown

No food for six days. I'm not sure why; we haven't done anything. But we're not being fed and we can't even ask Mother Quigg because she never comes to see us. She told me once that I could use the implant in my head to contact her and I've been trying, trying, trying until the tears run from eyes, but no good.

Things are desperate.

Some of the squealers in the cage, the strong and lunatic ones like Grubber and Herman, are eying up the weaker ones and I don't like what that could lead to. Is this another experiment? Another survival test?

Date unknown

Mother Quigg came in today, but she brought no food. Even the wild ones stopped screeching and growling at each other. Herman stopped pacing. It was like feeding time at the zoo.

"We need to eat," I told her. "This can't go on."

Mother Quigg tittered at me and I wanted to beat her face in. She put her eyes on me and I could feel the smoldering hatred she felt for my kind.

"Is that what would make you happy, Dennis? Truly content and happy?"

I felt I was falling into a trap, but my mouth spoke before I could stop it. "Yes."

Mother Quigg shrugged. "Why then, you'll have food. This is your cage, Dennis. You are master and commander here. If you desire it, you shall have it."

More head games, more manipulation.

The squealers were all excited, jumping and shrilling, screaming out and clawing at one another. It was like being in a monkey cage at feeding time. The shrieking was so loud it was unbearable.

Mother Quigg held up her hand and there was a high-pitched droning that was painful to hear, but it shut them all up. Those that had eyes, looked in my direction.

"If you wish to eat, you must be cooperative like Dennis. He is now the overseer of this containment unit. You will do as he says. If you wish something, you may obtain it only through him. He is better than you. If you wish to survive, you must act like a survivor like Dennis. Let him be your role model, my children."

That was it: I lost it. Breaking point. I'd suffered absolute horrors for months and I generally kept my mouth shut, but something in me couldn't take any more. It exploded inside me and I lunged at Mother Quigg. That's the last I remember before everything went black.

Date unknown

It has been days since I've been strong enough to make an entry. I'm a lab rat now, a guinea pig, a little white mouse. Yes, a rhesus monkey that exists only to be experimented on. I asked for trouble and now I've gotten it.

About all I can tell you is that I woke up on a table in the lab with all those weird machines around me, hoses and clear tubing coiling around me, that hideous web of comatose people high above.

Mother Quigg was there. "Well, this is a fine fix you've gotten yourself into, Dennis. Back in my day, this is what we called getting your tit caught in the wringer. Silly, stupid little boy."

Then I was left alone. It didn't take me long to realize that they had taken my left leg. I screamed when I realized it. I ranted and raved, my voice echoing through the cavernous lab, but I was politely ignored by the Vyrmid (who bustle about, disguised as scientists and technicians in white lab coats).

They think this will break me and turn me into a good little pet, a submissive and docile little mouse. But it won't. I hate them more than ever know. I'm not sure how I'm going to do it, but I'm going to revenge myself for this. I'll make those fuckers pay. They'll have to take more than my leg to make me snap.

What's a leg anyway? Just a conjoined piece of meat and I've gotten very good at crawling around the lab, studying it, planning out their destruction. My stump barely even hurts now.

Date unknown

I'm already frustrating them. Ha! It is they who will break, not me. Never me. They want me to eat, but I refuse. I'm on a hunger strike, and I dare them to force me. Oh, how hard they try! They've offered me their stinking gray slop (it looks like vomit, like steaming warm vomit) and disguised it as roast beef and cheeseburgers and chocolate cake and steak and even as barbecued ribs from a little place I knew in St. Louis that had the best BBQ on planet Earth.

Well, I won't eat it!

Fuck you! Fuck you! Fuck you!

I'm getting weaker and am enjoying it. I will never be under their heel. Let me die, just let me die so this ends. God, please let it end already.

Mother Quigg came to me again about an hour ago. "Dennis, this will not do. You must eat. I cannot protect you if you continue to be so contrary." Then she leaned in, whispering like she was sharing a state secret with me. "Tomorrow will not be a good day, my child. You will be taken before the Imperator and you will find him a cold, cruel individual. He is not kind like me. Please cooperate or I cannot guarantee your safety or sanity."

I told her I would cooperate if I could go back to the cage. That's the only concession I was willing to give, but she said that wasn't possible at this juncture.

I told her to go fuck herself.

Date unknown

Mother Quigg was right: the Imperator does not screw around. He does not even bother cloaking himself as a human being. Although I managed to stand strong, it wasn't easy, because he's the most hideous, repulsive thing I've ever seen. Mother Quigg's true appearance is unpleasant, too, but the Imperator is even worse.

And at this point, you'll have to excuse me for using personal pronouns relating to gender (in a mammalian sense) because I don't believe there are genders to the Vyrmid. The Imperator is certainly not a he, but an *it*. Believe me, nothing can prepare you for the sight of that abomination. The Imperator is a living nightmare, a stark alien horror that literally made me sick to my stomach with terror and repugnance.

He's a clicking, whirring, slithering, abstract biological machine that seems to continually inflate and deflate like a breathing lung, even though he does not seem to be made of tissue as we understand the word, but bone fused to bone. Like Mother Quigg, he sits on a cluster of thick, coiling, steel-gray tentacles whose sides are set with pulsating suckers and end in appendages rather like wriggling centipedes … if the many legs were replaced by bony hooks.

He is much larger than Mother Quigg and must be of a different subspecies. His body is a skeletal mass of rungs and mounds and bony architecture with a huge mouth of white fangs set in the middle with a smaller side-to-side opening mouth above it. They may not even be mouths. I don't know. He has four arm-like limbs that look like the connected, hinged jawbones of predators in a series, their undersides set with white threshing hooks and ending in fine wormy feelers that must be capable of the finest manipulation.

And he has a head … sort of … an oblong sphere, an ellipsoid, made of interconnecting tendrils of blue-gray flesh. There are two large, red-orange compound eyes and two smaller ones sitting beneath them, a collection of squirming hoses where a mouth should be. His face seems to be bifurcated down the center, the hemispheres held together by suture-like tendrils woven together. Whenever he speaks, they flash different colors like the chromatophores of a jellyfish.

That is the Imperator.

"You belong to us," he said. *"You are our animal and we are your masters. You must cooperate or be punished. You are part of a study in human survivability and must not damage yourself. This cannot be tolerated."*

The voice didn't come from the monster itself, but from above and behind me: a warbling, discordant noise that gradually modulated itself into a scraping sort of voice.

"I want to go back to the cage."

"Your desires are of no importance to the study."

If I hadn't been so scared, I might have told him to go to hell (even though we were already there), but I could feel him in my mind, picking away my memories with a cold invasion like icy fingers in my head, exposing childhood traumas and fears.

"Do you understand the words I have said?"

"Yes."

That was it. The entire conversation, what there was of it, lasted maybe five minutes with plenty of drawn-out silences in-between. If I don't cooperate, they're going take me apart and I know it.

Date unknown

It's been three days now since I came out of it. The trauma and agony blanked most of it out, but believe me when I say the Imperator does not fuck around. Apparently, I wasn't subservient enough for him, because they fixed me to a table and took my other leg. Only this time, there was no anesthetic—they sliced through my leg with a rod of light like a laser that cauterizes the stump as it goes. They did it slowly, slowly and the pain was beyond anything I've ever known. I passed out, came to sweating and screaming only to pass out again.

My name is Stumpy now.

I drag myself around the lab. There's nothing else to do. Since the Vyrmid don't have the humane decency to end my life, the only thing I have left is to be a pain in their ass. Which, I might add, I am at every level.

Make no mistake, I'm punished constantly for disobedience, but I am teaching them something about human resilience. We do not bow down before monsters. The time will come when we will exterminate them.

There's no hope now. None.

Date unknown

I still refuse to eat. They don't even bother dressing up the gray vomit as tasty food any longer. Now it's just slop. Today, as punishment, they put a tray of rotting, maggoty meat before me. I laughed at them. I laughed with everything I had. Funny thing was, once I started laughing, I couldn't seem to stop.

Date unknown

The Vyrmid let me wander at will. I'm simply an amusing lab animal to them. In my exploration, I found a new place in the laboratory labyrinth, a secret place, I think. Let me describe it to you. It's still my absurd hope that somehow, someway, the drive in my tooth will survive me and be discovered by other humans one day. The idea is ridiculous, but it's the only thing that keeps me going.

The new place.

My God.

There are great transparent tanks in which human subjects drift in cloudy serum. Some of them are apparently still alive. I could see them moving. One of them—a man—pressed his face against the glass (or whatever the material is) and leered at me, scratching his fingers against the tank. There were smaller tanks around him with body parts and organs and what might have even been human fetuses … or something like them.

To the Vyrmid, that place is a lab, to me a biomedical sideshow.

I saw machines or things like machines, helixes of hoses and spidery protrusions like fiber-optic lines. Great lenses and what might have been screens. Collections of plastic blades jutting from dangling triple-cylinders overhead. Rectangular blocks set with knobs and coils and bumps that had human-shaped recesses set into them. It was an absolute menagerie.

I also found Pepley.

Oh Christ, oh God, what they did to him. I can barely even tell you.

He's been meticulously dissected, rendered to his basal anatomy and this with great skill and technique. His eyes can see. His ears can hear. His tongue can lick and his skin can rise up in gooseflesh, but no longer as part of the same integrated unit, because he's been taken apart and displayed like an anatomical specimen.

A living anatomical specimen.

His nervous system has been removed in its entirety. Same for his vascular system and lymphatic system, circulatory system and endocrine system … in fact, *all* of his systems. Each are attached to sheets of flat black matrix like biomechanical circuit boards. And each are still connected to one another via a spiderwebbing of ultrafine synaptic wiring, even though they're each now many feet apart.

His eyes are still attached to his brain and he looks around, horrified and disillusioned at what they've done to him. His heart still beats and his blood still pumps. When he cries, tears spill from his ducts across the room. When he clenches his fist, his muscles work, still attached to his skeleton on a table some distance away. His skin has been pasted-up opposite him and I saw his eyeless face, the look of dread and torture on his features. And when he screamed, the muscled skeleton opened its jaws and the lips opposite parted, but the scream came from somewhere behind him.

Yes, this was they did to him.

But not just him. There were others, mostly in pieces. I saw two headless bodies across the room wired into some machine. Both men. The one on the left had its legs crossed, and the one on the right was snapping its fingers as if to some catchy tune only it could hear. There was the torso of a woman, armless and legless and headless, strapped to a clear table not far away and she appeared to be pregnant. Worse, it looked like she was ready to deliver. Arms were attached to a black matrix wall beyond, the hands of which were still moving. One of them kept flipping me the bird.

Dozens of eyes with attached optic nerves stared at me from a glossy gray board nearby.

And the heads. Did I mention the heads?

I saw eight of them. They had been removed and wired to a sheet of something like acrylic plastic that was hooked to a variety of hoses and pumps and tubing. They were alive. All of them had the tops of their skulls removed so the brains were visible. And one of those heads belonged to Bokeman.

While the others whispered and hummed nonsensical little tunes, Bokeman recited nursery rhymes: *"Three blind mice! Three blind mice! See how they run! See how they run! They all ran after the farmer's wife! Who cut off their tails with a carving knife! Did you ever see such a silly sight as three blind mice?"*

He was as stark raving mad as a living decapitated head could be.

"Shut up! Just shut up!" Pepley screamed at him, his muscled skeleton on the table thrashing with rage, jaws opening and closing, his face off to the left sneering, lips parting to form the words … which, again, came from somewhere above him.

"Ha, ha, ha, ha!" Bokeman tittered. "What's the matter, Peppo my boy? You no like music? Sweet, wonderful music? Ha, ha, ha!"

"Shut the fuck up!"

But Bokeman wouldn't. *"MARY HAD A LITTLE LAMB, LITTLE LAMB, LITTLE LAMB! IT'S FLEECE WAS WHITE AS SNOWWWWWWW!"*

Several of the hands found each other and clapped. The headless bodies stomped their feet. Limbs swayed and moved; muscles flexed. Things in tanks bobbed up and down and stuck their tongues out at me.

A madhouse.

A fucking madhouse.

I got out of there before I went insane, too.

Date unknown
I'm in trouble trouble trouble.

Trouble like I never saw before.

I know it. Mother Quigg tells me I wasn't supposed to visit the secret part of the lab, not until it was time for me to go there. It is a forbidden place and the Imperator is very angry with me. There will be pain involved, she says.

So I wait for the Imperator, my legless husk fixed to a rectangle of black glass once again. He's going to take my arms. I know he's going to take my arms. But that won't stop me! Oh no! It will fucking not! Even if I'm just a crawling sack, I'll keep whispering my observations about this torture chamber. They can't stop me. As long as I have my voice I'll never, ever shut up.

He's here now.

The sight of him makes me sick to my stomach. What are the Vyrmid supposed to be? Insects? Reptiles? Slithering invertebrates? Why are they so many things but nothing in particular?

The Imperator is reaching for me and I'm still talking and I will until I scream because oh yes oh yes oh fucking yes I will scream because he'll make sure I feel every second of it

What's that?

What? What?

No, no no … oh dear Christ you can't do that! You can't take that from me! Mother Quigg! Mother Quigg! God, help me help me oh sweet God help me

oh please

no

don't take that

you can't take that

not my

not my tongue

ABOUT THE AUTHOR

TIM CURRAN is the author of *Skin Medicine*, *Hive*, *Dead Sea*, *Resurrection*, *Blooding Night*, *Dead Sea Chronicles*, and *Horror of the Blood Devils*. His short stories have been collected in *Alien Horrors* and *Horrors of War*. His novellas include *The Underdwelling*, *The Corpse King*, *The Brain Leeches*, and *The Sunken City*. His fiction has been translated into German, Japanese, Russian, Spanish, and Italian.

ABOUT THE ARTIST

Steeped in the enthralling fantasy and science-fiction illustrations of the 1960s, '70s, and '80s, artist and illustrator **K.L. Turner** brings a bit of old-school painterly style to today's methods. With more than 30 years of experience in the arts, he expertly brings an expressionistic style into his illustrations to create compelling works which captivate and draw the viewer in. His works are found in media and galleries around the world, and celebrated in pop culture. A versatile creative type, Turner is also accomplished in the mediums of photography, sculpture, and the fine arts. Choosing to live and work on the beautiful front range of the Colorado Rocky Mountains where he was born and raised, he continues to derive inspiration from nature as well as cultural influences both at home and in his travels.